Veiled Memories

Angela O'Malley

VEILED MEMORIES

Disclaimer: \ This is a work of fiction., characters, businesses, places, events and incidents are either the products of the author's imagination or used in a fictitious manner. Any resemblance to actual persons, living or dead, or actual events is purely coincidental.

Ewelme Brook Publishing – BOX 300 Thame OX9 OFP

ISBN: 978-1-9194692-1-8

DEDICATION

To those who have lost a loved one and feel their absence.

VEILED MEMORIES

Table of Contents

Part One

Part Two

ACKNOWLEDGMENTS

My gratitude extends to all my family everywhere; through every challenge and joy, your strength, and comfort in good and troubled times has always mattered to me. I want to thank my siblings, their children and grandchildren and their partners for their unwavering support, their encouragement stays a constant foundation.

To my friends and colleagues, thank-you for your companionship and ongoing support throughout my journey.

I am deeply grateful for my husband's unwavering support. His constant encouragement motivated me to persevere. Whenever I faced obstacles, his belief in me gave me the strength to keep moving forward. To every member of our blended family, each of you is unique, each contributing kindness, resilience and humour.

My three daughters inspire me daily, and I am proud of the remarkable Women they have become. Thank-you to my granddaughter for her invaluable help, and to my grandson for his enthusiasm and curiosity. I cherish every moment spent with them. And I must mention my dogs; In remembrance of Boycie who patiently stayed by my side waiting for me to finish my early morning writing, and it is now Bud who sits alongside. It is my family's reassuring presence and steadfast faith in my abilities that empowered me to reach my goals and cross the finish line.

Finally, I remember those we have lost. To my dear cousin who holds a special place in my heart. My mum's strength gave me courage, my dad's storytelling ignited my imagination, my stepfather's dependability, and my grandparents, aunts, and uncles filled my childhood with warmth and laughter. Whenever I write, I hear their stories echoing in my mind, and my mum's resilience reminds me to persevere through challenges. Their love and wisdom are woven into every story. Their memories continue to inspire my work and guide me every day.

VEILED MEMORIES

PROLOGUE

July 1964 – Harrow on the Hill

Sipping an iced lemonade, Mandy swallowed hard, aware of the lump in her throat and the heaviness in her chest. She fixated on the glass she was drinking from, avoiding eye contact with people sitting at nearby bench tables. Only if she were here to enjoy an after-work drink in the long awaited, early evening sunshine.

Mandy had arrived just after opening time, as he suggested. She glanced towards the entrance every time she heard footsteps on the gravel or the gate open.

A young couple struggled to manoeuvre a pram with an oversized sunshade and two young boys through the narrow side entrance. The husband went into the bar, leaving the woman to settle the children at a nearby table.

The boys charged around, receiving disapproving looks from those who were moments ago, enjoying the peaceful setting. A toddler strapped to a pram seat cried, expressing a desire to get down. Mandy recognised the whimpering of a noticeably young baby from within the pram. The exhausted mother warned the boys for the third time in as many minutes that they would not get crisps and a drink if they didn't come and sit down.

This young family did little to support Mandy's argument for the joys of family life. It was better that he hadn't shown.

Since having her pregnancy confirmed, she had romanticised about their future. They talked about moving away and starting afresh in a new town. He started these discussions, so she's had no qualms about sharing her news.

Mandy still felt wounded by his reaction. At first, there was surprise (or shock) in his expression, but it was his cool indifference that stung. This dejection transformed into anger.

Thoughts spun as she walked. She considered every argument and violent encounter she had experienced, realising how delusional she had been to imagine an alternative life away from the toxic environment she was living in.

Wandering aimlessly since late afternoon, Mandy had reached a decision to go alone. She had not worked everything out yet, but it would happen soon. However, before she left, she intended to cause some commotion. She envisioned the scenario clearly in her mind and felt elation despite the pending consternation.

She had to ensure her departure was sensational, to make up for her disappointment at being denied the satisfaction of seeing him squirm and plead with her not to tell. Mandy glanced at her watch—it was Six-thirty. She had left Madeline with the babysitter long enough.

He promised he would break away from work to continue their conversation, away from home and away from their daughter's ears. Well, he had his chance. Enough is enough!

Fighting back tears of frustration, she left the glass she had been drinking from on the table and exited the pub garden through the side gate. She followed the cobbled paving until she reached the alleyway that led to the south side of the hill.

Mandy halted, sensing foreboding. In contrast to the day's weather, the alleyway felt cool, shaded by trees and brambles weaving through wire fences on either side of her. She pulled her cardigan around her shoulders and looked behind before continuing into the narrow walkway—slowly at first, then steadily quickening her pace, feeling a sense of uneasiness. She turned to look behind, walking the path in anticipation of someone appearing.

The breeze caught a branch, rustling it, causing Mandy's stomach to lurch. Electricity bolted through her veins, and the hairs on her arms and the back of her neck pricked. Was that a person crouching ahead? Mandy stopped and squinted, trying to make out the silhouette. With relief, she realised it was sensory deception—a shadow created by a large shrub.

She quickened her pace as much as her heels allowed. Despite the brightness of a midsummer evening, this isolated cut-through—with its twists and turns—diminished the natural light leading to the exit. Mandy jumped and turned towards the sound of rustling from within the hedge. 'Why so jumpy? Almost there—keep going!'

It's not surprising. Pregnancy hormones and upset have contributed to her heightened anxiety. Slowing down a little more, a few more strides toward the sunlight.

She felt welcome relief upon reaching the open space. The sun was still high in the sky, and its rays ignited Mandy's soul. In contrast to the other side of the hill, with its cut green lawns, the coarse meadow grass on this side was long, dry, and scorched corn yellow. Because of the lack of a path, few people used this cut-through from the village at the top of the incline to the town below.

The oppression she felt within the restrictive space of the alley had lifted, and she recognised a return of the determination and strength she used to own. Though an obvious cliché, she believed, 'Today is the first day of the rest of her life.'

A blow followed this thought—a crack to her head, then another that sent her to the ground.

Disorientated, Mandy tried to stand but only managed a crawl. A warm, sticky substance blurred her vision. A sudden pain made her neck crick. She was hauled backwards by her hair. Her only hope of rescue from any passerby was to prevent herself from being taken from this open space. Mandy screamed, grabbing at the long, dry grass entwined with stingers. In a last attempt, she dug her nails into the ground.

Unsuccessful in her resistance, she was being dragged along by someone with enormous strength to an area of brambles and stinging nettles—a clearing behind a hedgerow. Mandy felt the force of a large being weighing her down, preventing her from moving, and a familiar voice talking to her all the while.

In this moment, she was aware of his intention, paralysed by fear of what was about to happen next. She tried another scream, but a large, gloved hand covered her mouth, stifling any sound. Held face down, Mandy could not breathe, lacking the strength to struggle.

She felt a cold; thin strap being placed around her neck. There was no give as he tightened the strap, as if relishing extinguishing her life.

VEILED MEMORIES

PART ONE

CHAPTER ONE

Present Day- Fading Memories

A suspended glow of orange from streetlamps line the footpath that leads to the top of the hill, then darkness engulfs the woods that skirt St. Mary's Church. Its spire raised black against an inky sky, with a red light glowing at its tip.

I watch as I exhale vapour. My breathing is rapid against the chilly air, and I feel light-headed.

During the time spent here, I have pieced together my memories through mental visions, like a jigsaw puzzle. However, as I grasp at significant details, they fade away, like in a dream.

Thoughts of my mother—she would be furious if she knew I was here. I promised both her and George that I would stop searching a long time ago. But they weren't aware of all the facts, and I was always too cowardly to tell them.

I am the keeper of secrets, but I should reveal what I know to those close to me before it is too late. The fear of permanently losing what is locked inside overwhelms me, as the abyss swallows all words, people, memories and my brain shrivels like a prune.

The letter! Now where is it? I reach for my... Maggie, think! I often mislay words, or names for things, and each time it takes a little longer to find them. The worst of it is I cannot forget this forgetfulness is happening.

It's not here! Panic sets in as I realise, 'I must have left my... in the...'

A burning sensation rises from the pit of my stomach, burning my throat. I struggle to understand jumbled thoughts, hoping to recall what I read in the letter, but it is near impossible.

I have tucked it underneath the bench. That's it, my handbag! I find the word I am looking for.

Searching on my hands and knees, but it isn't here. My knees feel stiff and damp from the moisture on the ground. Most people remark on my fitness and how good I look for my age, so why do I feel so weak today? Panic intensifies as I cannot rise to my feet.

CHAPTER TWO

Present Day - Cycle to Work

Winter was finally over, and as the mornings began to brighten earlier, Kate felt genuinely pleased—she had missed the gentle glow that made the start of the day feel hopeful once more. Just a week ago, it had still been dark at this hour, and she realised how much she cherished the return of light. The clocks go forward next week, marking spring.

If the weather report from last night is to be correct; it will be a lovely day. Mornings such as this one make her grateful that she switched to cycling instead of taking the bus to work.

The cycle route to the hospital is along a purpose-built lane next to a busy road out of town. While the immediate area is typical of a London suburb, the landscape changes significantly as Kate reaches the streets at the foot of the hill.

This part of town unchanged throughout the years. On her way to the hospital, Kate passes double-fronted Victorian houses, followed by the early 19th century red brick college buildings, the rear entrance and small car park of the train station, a street of 1930s semi-detached houses across from the nursery's wrought-iron gates, and greenhouses next to open fields and farmland. A van, a bus and some cars drive past. In an hour, expect heavy traffic crawling along on both sides, as vehicles head away from the city or towards the capital. Because of the light frost, the road, and pavement sparkled under the streetlamps. Kate alights at the usual place, on the service road where taxis drop off and pick up for the station. She wheels her bike across the road at the traffic lights and walks it towards where the cycle path continues from the base of the hill. Cycling is new to Kate, and she needs to become more confident before trying this complicated stretch with too many junctions.

In a leafy part of town, the hill is an ascending green space where people enjoy lying on the grass during their lunch breaks or eating sandwiches on fine days. The hill is desolate at this time of day. From the pavement, a path winds up towards St. Mary's Church, a hidden landmark with only its spire visible above the trees.

The council has placed random benches so people can sit and enjoy the green space. Office buildings obscure the view of the ever-changing town centre. Alongside recently built modern high-rises, there are 1970s and 1980s blocks donned in scaffolding to update their exteriors for this millennium.

As usual, a handful of pedestrians head briskly towards the back entrance of the station. Kate notices a figure by the bench at the lower part of the hill: an older woman wearing a dark coat and hat. She was low to the ground and appeared to be searching.

Instinctively, she pushes her bike up the grass verge towards her and stops a couple of feet away.

"Are you okay?" she whispered, trying not to startle her.

The older lady was having difficulty rising to her feet. Kate leaned her bike against a rubbish bin and offered her arm as leverage. Snow-white hair was showing beneath a brown fur hat that sat a little skew-whiff. Her face is pale, and her lips are tinged blue.

With support, she steadies herself as she stands. The coat and hat look clean and expensive. 'So, she is not a rough sleeper,' thought Kate.

"I've lost my... The letter, I must find the letter!" she replied, getting agitated.

Kate quickly evaluates her mood. Having received many a clump from confused or delirious patients, she is aware a person's behaviour can be unpredictable. Even those usually placid may become aggressive when in a state of confusion.

"Why don't you sit down on the bench, and I will help you look?" Kate suggested gently, relieved when the older lady agreed. Noticing that she didn't have a handbag, Kate sat beside her, offering reassurance.

"Don't worry, I'm sure you will find it," Kate said, trying to provide comfort. The older lady clasped Kate's hand with her own. Her fingers are blue and bony, with prominent veins visible beneath thinning skin. They felt ice-cold to the touch.

"What is your name? Is there someone I can call?" Kate asked, hoping to gather enough information to contact the authorities if needed. The woman revealed her name as Maggie Randall but could not provide her address. Becoming agitated as she struggled to remember.

Kate redirected the conversation to the present, focusing on their surroundings. "What a beautiful red sky! Look at how the sun is rising. I love this time of year with all the pink blossoms on the trees, don't you?" Maggie's glassy eyes followed the line of trees next to the path. She quickly calmed down.

Once Kate was satisfied Maggie was calm and comfortable, she stepped away to call the emergency services; she provided them with as much information as she could. She promptly returned to the bench. Kate noticed that Maggie's cheeks were flushed, and her eyes were red-rimmed. She had a fever. Kate took a clean tissue from her pocket and handed it to Maggie.

"Have you seen my mother?" Maggie asked, sounding childlike.

"Maggie, are you feeling cold? Would you like my coat?" Kate said, focusing on the present situation.

"I'm feeling shivery," Maggie replied.

Kate removed her coat and wrapped it around Maggie's shoulders, providing an extra layer of warmth. She also draped her scarf like a shawl over Maggie's hat.

"Help will arrive soon, and then you can go home. This will help keep you warm until then," Kate assured her. Maggie smiled, although the smile did not reach her eyes.

"What about you?" she asked.

"I'm okay! I'm wearing a jacket," Kate said, stroking the sleeve of her NHS-issue fleece.

"That's so kind of you," Maggie said, pausing before she announced, "I'm the one to blame for all this, you know!"

"It won't be long now, and you will be home safe and sound," Kate said, trying to distract her from distressing thoughts. "I can never forgive myself for what I put my parents through,"

“Everyone puts their parents through something or another, I’m sure you were no worse than anyone else,” Kate replied, hoping to lighten the conversation.

Maggie dismissed the remark, determined to reminisce, but Kate was concerned that delving into these memories could upset her further.

“My family are shopkeepers...” Maggie informed, and sensing that this reminiscing was having a calming effect, Kate allowed Maggie to continue.

CHAPTER THREE

June 1964 – Fragments of Yesterday

It is a wet Tuesday afternoon in June. The inside of our shop is dreary, with its dark board flooring, dark stained service counter, and shelves. The walls have discoloured over the years to a mustard yellow.

All month long, we have been dealing with awful weather, non-stop rain! I switch on the ceiling light, bored out of my mind. All there is to do is refill the shelves, mop, and sweep. At least when I'm at the Poly, I mix with people of my age. It would kill me if I had to work here for the rest of my life!

Fridays and Saturdays are our busiest days, with regulars shopping for the weekend or coming in to pay their grocery tabs. I'm told the large supermarket that opened in town has not dented our takings so far, but then they don't provide credit. Dad allows credit to our locals to prevent them from shopping in town, although he doesn't allow them to run past payday.

"It's for their own sake!" he reminded us.

Despite his attempt to provide credit responsibly, the cycle of debt continues. No sooner do our neighbours receive their housekeeping and pay off last week's tab, a new one begins.

Locally, people know us as the 'Back Shop' because of our location—a double-fronted property within streets of Victorian terraces that perimeter the principal town. Our shop is one of two on our street. Hall's Newsagents is on the corner, and like us, Mr and Mrs Hall live-in accommodation 'outback.'

Most days are similar, with a steady flow of customers during the morning, but then it's quiet after lunch, with the odd customer running errands or kids running in for larder items after school. Time drags, especially on rainy days.

The bell rings as the shop door opens. It's Jim bringing this week's delivery.

"Good afternoon Bill," he said, addressing my dad. Holding the door wide, a young man I haven't seen before follows him, steering a trolley packed high with cardboard boxes.

"Alright Jim, good to see you my man," Dad greets our regular delivery driver as if he were an old friend, shaking his hand.

"How's life treating you? Been busy?" Jim asked, nodding a greeting in my direction.

"Not bad. You know how it is." Dad takes the delivery slip that Jim is holding and compares the load stacked on the trolley with what's listed.

"Take that lot through to the store, son," Dad said, turning his attention to Trolley Lad and then back to me.

"Stack them as they are, and we'll sort later. C'mon, Jim, come through the back. I'll put the kettle on... Maggie, mop the floor afterwards. There's a good girl. We don't want anyone slipping."

While holding open the counter, I make sure not to get in his way. I feel self-conscious. A ponytail held my hair, and I wore an unflattering polyester button-up apron.

Dad hooks back the coloured plastic door curtains hanging from the doorframe. Jim signals his mate to a large walk-in cupboard behind the shop wall, which we refer to as 'the store,' and a whistling Jim follows Dad along the dark passage that leads to our living quarters out back.

Jim's delivery mate is wearing grubby grey work overalls. His near-black hair slicked-back, except for a quiff that softly flops forward onto his forehead. Our eyes meet briefly, and he has the most piercing blue eyes with long dark lashes, lashes for which I would die.

My stomach flips, but he continues about his business without another glance. I try to work out how old he is — early twenties, perhaps?

I grab the mop and bucket and awkwardly wipe up the wet. After a couple of minutes, he returns, pushing the empty trolley, leaving a trail of more wetness. I mop up after him.

When he gets to the door, he turns and looks disapprovingly at the floor and then at me.

"Give it here!" he makes a gesture for me to hand him the mop. He swiftly mops from behind the counter, moving backward toward the door. Handing the mop back to me as he reaches the threshold, he takes a cigarette from behind his ear and pops it into his mouth.

"Tell Jim I'll be waiting in the cab," he said, with an unlit cigarette dangling from his lip. He closes the shop door behind him. I watch him while standing back from the window; he strolls towards the van.

For the next few Tuesday afternoons, Jim goes out the back for a cuppa with Dad while 'The Trolley Lad,' as I now refer to him, drops our goods and then goes to wait in the van.

Our delivery of stock arrives in the afternoon, so at lunchtime, I back comb my mousy fair hair for a French pleat and turn up the collars on the blouse, so they stick out from under the awful apron. Although my hair colour is not right, I aim for a 'Tippi Hedren' style. I bought hair bleach, but mum would not let me use it.

Standing on tiptoe is necessary for me to use the mirror suspended on a chain above the fireplace. I applied one of my new pastel lipsticks and a little mascara, bought at Woolworths with my wages.

Aware Dad is watching me; I spit on the mascara brush to moisten the mascara block, and I see him grimace.

"Why do you put that muck on your face?" he frowned over the rim of his glasses as he continued to watch me.

"Leave her be," Mum chuckles as she clears away our dinner plates. Dad pulls another disconcerting expression and settles back to read his paper.

"If she stands in front of that fire for much longer, she is going to end up with corned beef legs," he added.

Despite my efforts, I may as well be invisible to 'Trolley Lad'... The odd grunt of acknowledgment is about as much as I can hope for. Although I am certain my father does not help this situation, 'the look' from over his glasses, the serious unspoken warning as Dad's eyes flick between Trolley Lad and me. It is so embarrassing!

My parents are overprotective! I am seventeen, but Dad behaves as if I were ten. To be fair to my parents, I have not had a terrible childhood. Being an only child, I have not gone without, especially my clothes, thanks to Mum.

Most evenings, Mum and I sift through magazines looking for ideas for outfits. Mum has a photographic memory; she can watch a film at the pictures and then recreate what the lead is wearing. Mum draws her own patterns or sends off for similar and visits the Thursday market to buy material. She often spends evenings replicating our favourite designs, highlighting her skill as a seamstress.

On Wednesdays, we close early, so it has become customary during this summer for Mum and me to spend the afternoons together while Dad visits the Conservative club.

First, I help hang our washing in the backyard, then listen to the radio or quietly read. Sometimes Mum pins while I model her latest creation. On fine days, we go for a walk up the hill and take a picnic and our books with us, stopping on the way to gossip with our neighbours.

Dad detests gossip. If Mum and I appear too friendly with customers, he objects.

“Don’t get involved in other people’s business!” he often reminded us, or...

“Maggie, when you ask a customer how they are, don’t seem overly eager.” Mum just raises her eyebrows at this comment.

“I’m only being polite! What should I ask them?” I asked him, puzzled.

“The only thing you should be interested in is what they want to buy!” he answered impatiently.

My mother claims this habit began during rationing, influenced by my grandfather and the necessity to stay distant from customers, preventing them from asking for more than their share. He is courteous but speaks formally, referring to people as Sir or Madam, or using Mr or Mrs if he knows them.

1964 - Half-day closing

It's Wednesday. Mum complains of a headache, so I encourage her to take a nap. I pack my bag with a cheese sandwich, a slice of Victoria sponge baked this morning, and my book. I roll up the picnic blanket to carry under my arm and head out alone.

With no interruptions, I reach the hill and begin climbing the steep path, occasionally glancing back at the view of our town — a sea of red and grey roof tiles. I lay my blanket down on the neatly manicured grass, kick off my sling-backs, and sit down to eat my lunch and read my book. I check the time; it's one-thirty, and considering the warmth of the afternoon, there are very few people about.

After about an hour, I gather up the blanket and continue uphill, through the short alley that leads to St Mary's graveyard from the north side of the hill. I stop to make out names on the gravestones, twisted with time, dating back centuries.

Feeling hot from the walk, I enter the large wooden doors of the church, welcoming the coolness as a sanctuary. I sit on a wooden pew at the back of the church, embracing the coolness and admiring the stone interior of St Mary's. We can see its spire for miles, and I contemplate how complacent we are towards its beauty and stature. It's like another world up here on the hill, with its grand houses and the public school.

I realise I am not alone in the church. Whispers echo from behind a pillar near the altar. I lean so I can see past the pillar; a couple are sitting close together on one of the front pews. It sounds like the male voice is becoming agitated, although I can't make out what is being said. Harsh whispers are enough for me to feel like an intruder. I stand to exit, unable to avoid the clip-clopping of my shoes on the stone floor. Outside, I walk to the back of the church, avoiding stepping on the inset gravestones. St Mary's Church graveyard soothes, though an eeriness pervades.

From the shade of a tree, I notice them leave the church. He gripped her arm. They are in their mid-to late twenties. He is wearing a dark suit, and she has brunette hair styled into a bob, wearing a print petticoat dress and a pink cardigan. With my back against the exterior church wall, I watch the couple.

Her back is to me, but I can see his face twisted with anger as he leans into her talking in her ear. I cannot hear what is being said, but his mouth contorts with every word. Her body bends to one side as if in pain, and he continues to squeeze.

I gasp and place a hand over my mouth. He releases her arm pushing her away from him, she stumbles on the uneven ground. She attempts to walk away but he forcefully grabs her by her arm again she lets out a whimper rather than the screech I would expect. His face is so close to hers that I am rooted to the spot. This is more than just a "lovers' tiff."

I back up to the rear of the church, using the gravestones and tombs to duck in between, and dash through the wooden arch that leads me to the streets next to the Infamous School. I walk down the cobbled path that meets the tarmac road and pavement back down the hill to town. Trees overarch, their shadows dancing beneath my feet, and the pavement narrows the further down the hill I go. I am jumpy, disturbed by what I saw.

At the junction at the bottom of the hill, I turn left and then hesitate. It could be embarrassing, especially if they had seen me leave the church, if the couple walks my original route, as I could easily meet them. I abruptly change direction when I physically bump into somebody.

"I'm so sorry!" My cheeks blaze. It's 'Trolley Lad!'

We awkwardly sidestep each other, and now he shows recognition.

"Hello!" he said, his eyes brightening. My heart flutters: he seems genuinely pleased to see me!

"They let you out then?" he teases.

"Yes, sometimes," I coyly reply.

"Are you heading home? If you are, do you mind if I walk with you?" he asked, to my excitement!

"Yeah, sure," I say casually.

We chat freely as we stroll the long way home. He introduces himself as Matthew and explains that his brother is a promoter, fixing gigs at pubs and clubs. He has invited Matthew to become a junior partner. Some names of the popular bands Matthew claim to have met have left me impressed. As I listen intently, Matthew explains he doesn't aspire to be a "driver's mate" forever.

"So, I shall work with my brother evenings and weekends and with Jim until the end of this summer."

With enthusiasm, he informs me that the British music scene is thriving.

"New bands are constantly emerging; we want to work in the United States eventually." Matthew speaks with a determination that I admire.

We continued to walk, and I told him about my secretarial course. A mix of nervousness and hope coloured my words. I feel a flutter of excitement as I described my dream of working in a bustling office. The thought of having my own desk and being part of large enterprise giving me a proper sense of purpose.

As we reach Hill's Sweet Shop on the corner of my street, the scent drifts through the open door, a sugary aroma of sherbet and toffee. The colourful jars of sweets gleam in the window, catching the afternoon sun and inviting us to linger for just a moment longer.

"The new Beatles film is playing this week. Would you like to see it?"

"Sure, I would love to... when?" I realise I sound too eager.

"Tomorrow? It's just... I must work most weekends," he added.

We agreed on a time, and he is to meet me at home. I provided him with directions to our back door from the alley on the next street.

"It's a date! See you tomorrow at seven o'clock!" Matthew said.

While I strolled away, turning to wave as I reach the curb, I struggle to hold my excitement. I wanted to skip the short distance home, which I did once I was certain that Matthew has turned the corner, and out of sight.

“Hello, love! Had an enjoyable afternoon?” Mum called from the kitchen.

“The best,” I replied, heading for our stairs, not thinking to ask how her headache is.

I take the stairs two at a time and crash onto my bed, and by the sound, breaking a spring as I do.

Falling asleep took forever, and I had no appetite for breakfast the next morning. I slumped in a dining chair, hair in rollers, and wearing a quilted dressing gown.

“You had better get a move on if you are going to be ready for opening time,” grumbled Dad.

Mum served breakfast, appearing worried.

“We don’t want you going up that hill alone anymore. Well, at least not until the police catch this person!” Mum placed the brown teapot onto its coaster, waving towards Dad.

“I just can’t believe I was fast asleep, while you were up there all on your own yesterday... it makes my blood run cold!” My mums’ words sound to me like rambling. “Who would have thought such an awful thing would happen around here? What’s the world coming to? They think she was murdered!” Mum shakes her head as she speaks with a furrowed brow and takes her seat at the table.

Her words interrupt good thoughts. Since I woke up this morning, my date, and the dilemma of what to wear has preoccupied me. My gaze follows Mum's flailing arm to where she is pointing—the headlines on the front page of the newspaper Dad is reading:

'Harrowing Discovery on the Hill.'
"The body of a young woman discovered dead in open space, very near to the 300-acre grounds of the public school attended by former prime ministers."

VEILED MEMORIES

CHAPTER FOUR

Present Day- The Long Night

Maggie's family experienced a worrying night after discovering that Maggie was missing from her Hampstead home. Lucy whispered to the committee secretary seated to her right.

"Louise, please can you chair the rest of the meeting; I have a family crisis, I must leave."

Lucy placed her mobile in her handbag and scooped her paperwork from the table in front of her. Rosalind, the treasurer, stopped reading her budget forecast.

"Is everything okay Lucy?" she enquired.

"It's my mother," Lucy sighed, not elaborating.

Lucy placed the papers in her briefcase, swung her handbag over her shoulder; while keeping hold of the car key, she dashed towards the exit.

"Sorry, everyone, I must leave. It's an emergency. Email me the minutes or anything else to action," she said, exiting the church hall.

Lucy started the engine, and it didn't take long for the interior of the vehicle to warm up. Connecting her mobile to the Range Rover's Bluetooth, she used the controls on the steering column to return her brother's call.

"Sorry I missed your call. Luckily, I saw your text. Is there any news?" she asked him.

"Not yet, I've looked in all the obvious places!" Lucy heard the worry in Billy's voice.

"I can't imagine where she is, she was expecting me! We were going to get a takeaway," he explained.

"Mum seemed fine this afternoon, and she never mentioned she was planning to go out," Lucy replied, realising that her mother had not mentioned Billy was visiting either.

"Should we call the police?"

"You haven't done that yet? Why not?" Lucy did not wait for her brother's response. "Call them now, tell them she has onset dementia!"

Lucy tweaked the car's heater, increasing its output to clear the condensation obscuring the windscreen.

"I'm on my way!"

The police asked many questions: when had they last seen their mother? Was she vulnerable? They also asked about places and people that they thought she might have gone to. Besides the immediate family, who were all present, they could not think of anyone.

A passing neighbour offered some useful information. When she saw the police presence. She saw Maggie getting into the rear seat of a black Mercedes at about eight-thirty! They did not think anything of it as it shared the make and colour of Lucy's son.

Following a conversation with Nicholas, they confirmed the vehicle was not his. The neighbour said that Maggie was wearing a winter coat, and hat, and carrying a handbag.

"She was dressed then, and she didn't leave the house in her pyjamas," earning a confused look from his older sister, so he explained.

"It's not uncommon to hear about older people who go out and forget to get dressed, right?"

Lucy disregarded Billy's observation with a tut: "I can't imagine where she was headed; wouldn't she have spoken about it?"

They responded with more questions about Maggie's health: Was she mobile? Did they have concerns about her mental health? Lucy informed the officers that their mother's mobility is good.

"She is very active, but recent tests suggest she has a degenerative brain disease and has been diagnosed with vascular dementia."

An older uniformed police officer, Sergeant Wright, listened while a younger officer scribbled notes.

Lucy found it difficult to explain because the changes in her mum's behaviour had been subtle. They first noticed something was not right after their father's funeral. Their mother became more anxious, confused, and distracted mid-conversation. The family discussed this as a symptom of her grief, but felt Maggie should go for a general health check. A routine referral for tests confirmed the GP's suspicion: onset dementia. The doctor couldn't say how quickly her health would decline. Maggie didn't take the diagnosis seriously, and Lucy also had doubts. Although in recent months concerning behaviours have surfaced. Maggie was forgetful, so she became frustrated when unable to perform regular tasks, and noticeably less engaged during their conversations.

Before leaving, the police provided some assurance, starting from their experience, their mother would be found safe and well.

"Either of you want another cuppa?" said Ray, stretching and yawning, adding a phoney London accent to the word 'cuppa.'

"Yes please," answer Lucy and Billy in unison.

Ray, Lucy's husband of nearing forty years, was on his way home from work when he received the distressed call from his wife. As he was driving close by the heath, he parked up, took the torch from the boot, and walked the path through the open space, hoping to spot Maggie. She often took this walk.

The chilly night blazed with stars. The deserted area had only a jogger and a few dog walkers. Once he confirmed Maggie was not on her usual route that leads to the rear entrance of her property, he went back to his vehicle and drove the short distance to her home.

"Your mother can still take care of herself; they will find her!" he said, pecking Lucy on the cheek before going to make more tea.

Ray was pragmatic in his approach to Maggie's diagnosis and led the planning whatever the future held for her, making sure she took part in all discussions. Maggie agreed to Lucy and Billy having a joint power of attorney with the authority to decide on her behalf for medical, financial, and care provision, should the need arise.

Standing in front of the French doors, Lucy peered beyond her reflection into the darkness. The lawn and foliage sparkled under the moonlight, showing that the outside temperature had dropped significantly. For a moment, she watched the leaves on the willow dance in the wind, obscured by the artificial light behind her. She diligently tried to focus on that area.

"Where shall I put this?" Ray held out a mug.

"Oh... um... here will do," This ordinary gesture had startled Lucy. Ray furrowed his brow, worrying about his wife.

Tonight felt reminiscent of just over a year ago, when they had comforted Maggie in this very room as paramedics tended to their father upstairs after his second stroke. The outcome was terrible on that occasion.

Lucy used the tissue in her hand to wipe away tears. Feeling drained, she slumped in her mother's favourite chair, with the steaming mug of tea on the little table nearby. Pulling the oversized cushion from behind her, she cuddled it close, as if this action would manifest her mother's appearance. She closed her eyes.

Woken by the ringtone, Lucy felt disoriented. A dark tan had formed on her tea. At first, she heard it as a distant and insignificant bell, but as her senses came to, so did the recollection that this was why she was sitting in her mother's chair only feet away from the house phone! They had expected this call all night!

"Mrs Langford, this is Sergeant Wright."

"Have you found her?"

Billy was standing in the doorway, mouthing something. Lucy turned away so she could focus, and while she was sure the police officer said a lot more, Lucy distinctly heard the words,

"She is safe!"

VEILED MEMORIES

CHAPTER FIVE

Present Day – The Meeting

Although muddled, Maggie remained focused, pausing for thought, tears streaking her cheeks.

"The first date with my Matthew, did not go as expected, you know, because of Mandy's murder," she said.

Kate smiled in acknowledgment but did not speak; traffic noise masked the genteel birdsong they had heard earlier. Maggie appeared oblivious to the two police officers who had approached them several minutes ago. Kate had provided them with an outline of the situation, and they were standing a few feet away. Onc is speaking on his radio. Kate sees an ambulance and a car pull up against the kerb, causing havoc amidst the rush hour traffic.

Two paramedics and a woman were walking towards them. Kate did not react but continued to allow Maggie to hold her hand.

Maggie noticed the paramedics' presence, and while Kate aimed to reassure her, Maggie appeared frightened. An attractive woman, appearing to be in her fifties, rushed forward. Maggie flinched as she hugged her.

Kate was aware of how heartbreaking dementia could be, especially when a person struggled to recognise their loved ones.

"I can't thank-you enough. Has she been here all night?" Kate believed the woman was addressing her, although her primary focus was with Maggie.

"I am not sure, but she was cold when I found her, and I think she has a fever," Kate explained.

A female paramedic crouched at Maggie's level.

"Mrs Randall, my name is Denise. I am a paramedic, and we are going to take you to the hospital to get you checked over,"

The early morning sun had risen, and although delivering warmth, Maggie's hands were still cold to the touch.

Kate gently removed Maggie's tightened grasp and moved away from the bench to allow room for the paramedics. Maggie's daughter joined her.

"We have been so worried!" She introduced herself as Lucinda Langford. Kate responded, remembering to use her readopted birth name.

"Kate Davis, I'm a nurse at the hospital. I spotted your mother on my way to work; she is very confused and..." The daughter appeared astonished; she looked at Kate with a perturbed expression. Sensing Mrs Langford had more pressing concerns, Kate grew uncomfortable and stopped speaking.

Denise wrapped a foil sheet around Maggie's shoulders. The two police officers stood a short distance away, and Maggie soon disappeared out of sight and into the back of the ambulance, with Mrs Langford following.

The police officers took a brief statement, informing Kate they might be in touch. Once the ambulance drove away, she continued her way to work. Arriving late, Kate moved on with her shift, although her thoughts kept returning to Maggie. She wondered how she was. The woman on the hill also intrigued her. Who was she?

"I will Google when I get home!" she thought.

At lunchtime, Kate returned to the hospital ward from the canteen. The ward manager was walking towards her with a yellow Post-it note stuck to her hand.

"Kate, I have a message for you," she said, holding out the note.

Kate took the Post-it note. A telephone number and a name she recognised.

"A message from HR... someone you assisted this morning has asked you to call them?" The ward manager appeared puzzled, so Kate explained the events from earlier.

"Such a shame! HR said they were keen to talk to you."

"I will make the call when I get home."

Kate arrived home at a few minutes to eight, having already eaten. After taking a hot bath, she put on her pyjamas. Following four consecutive twelve-hour shifts, she felt exhausted.

Before sitting in front of the television, she poured herself a glass of Pinot Grigio. With the Post-it note in mind, she reached for her bag and mobile. It was nine o'clock; was it too late to call now? She recognised the dialling code as a central London landline.

"Hello," answered a male with an American accent.

"Hello, can I speak with Mrs Langford, please?"

May I ask who is calling?

"My name is Kate Davis... uh... I found her mother," Kate struggled with this introduction.

"Oh... the guardian angel," replied the jovial American.

"I will fetch my wife; she is eager to thank-you."

Kate hears a clunk and waits for Mrs Langford to come to the phone, listening to the silence for a minute.

“Hello, Kate, thank-you for calling,” Mrs Langford’s voice is bright.

“Sorry for calling so late. I have only just got home... How is your mother?” asked Kate using an empathetic tone.

“The hospital has advised her to stay with them for a while,” Mrs Langford explained.

“They are treating her infection with intravenous antibiotics, and she is dehydrated.” She confided.

“They said the infection is affecting her cognitive abilities. We must meet with a hospital social worker prior to her discharge to discuss care arrangements,” she explained. Mrs Langford hesitated, her voice trembling. “I’m worried about how she’ll manage once she’s home.”

“Yes, an assessment prior to discharge is quite usual,” Kate said. “Did you find your mother’s handbag? She was looking for it,” Kate asked.

“She left it in the back of a taxi. The driver found it and returned it this morning. I gave him a piece of my mind. Fancy leaving an old woman in the middle of nowhere!” And then added,

“I hope you didn’t mind my contacting your personnel department. I requested your contact details, but they refused, something to do with data protection?”

“Hospital policy,” Kate replied.

“Would you consider meeting with me?” There is a pause.

“I would appreciate your advice.”

"What about?" Kate asked, surprised by the request.

Mrs Langford explained Maggie's recent dementia diagnosis.

"My mother is in fine fettle most of the time. However, it is time to consider care options for the long-term," she said.

"Speak with the hospital social worker. They are in a better place to offer advice for health care planning."

"The hospital has suggested this, but I would appreciate your advice about questions to ask, that sort of thing... please?" said Mrs Langford, emphasising the word "please."

Kate hesitated. This may also be against hospital policy. Maggie, though not her patient, and they met outside the hospital.

"I am off for the next three days," Kate said.

"Thank-you, thank-you," Mrs Langford answered, sounding relieved.

"We are off to our Oxfordshire home this weekend, but how about tomorrow lunchtime?"

CHAPTER SIX

Present Day – The Proposal

Kate agreed to meet Lucy Langford as suggested in Hampstead. She checked the best underground route before leaving home. They met at an Italian bistro at twelve-thirty. The walk from the station was further than Kate imagined. She walked fast so as not to be late and was out of breath by the time she reached her destination. A green canopy hung over the outdoor eating area, with circular stainless-steel tables and chairs.

Taking a minute to compose herself and catch her breath before entering the glass-fronted restaurant. She recognised Mrs Langford, seated at a table for two in the area by the window.

"From where the woman is sitting, she would have seen Kate charging the last stretch, red-faced and huffing and puffing." Kate cringed at the thought.

The server, Kate guessed, a student, met her and escorted her to where Mrs Langford occupied her seat. Kate noticed the black coffee in front of Lucinda on the table, so she ordered a cappuccino before taking a seat opposite.

Mrs Langford smiled. She styled her brunette hair and wore an olive suit that flattered her, emphasising her curves within her petite frame. She loosely tied a silk scarf, splattered with a bold colour that matched, at her neck. She applied her make-up to a professional standard, choosing shades that complemented her fair skin.

Kate felt dressed down in her casual padded coat with a faux fur collar (now hung on the back of her chair), jeans, sweater and boots. She tied her hair in a ponytail, and applied a little foundation, lip gloss and a touch of mascara before grabbing the scuffed 'old faithful' handbag used for every occasion, holding her principal possessions: purse, keys, mobile phone, while doubling as a rubbish bin for receipts, train tickets and old sweet wrappers.

Inferiority intensified when Kate noticed Lucy sweep her gaze up and down before fixing eye contact. "How was the journey? I hope it didn't take you too long?" "It was fine, thank-you," Kate replied. "I am not eating, but don't let that stop you. There is a wonderful selection!" Mrs Langford handed Kate the menu, and so as not to appear rude, Kate pretended to read it.

"I will stick to coffee. I had a large breakfast," Kate lied, and placed the laminated menu back on its wooden holder. She had struggled with eating full-size meals since the breakup, picking at food, and eating just enough to fuel up. She still had difficulty swallowing past the persistent lump in her throat.

Kate admired the setting. The décor is bohemian, with a half-melted candle placed in a green wine bottle splattered with candle wax sitting on the oak table between them. Some may think with its water ring markings, the table has seen better days. But it fit the overall 'distressed' style of Angelo's: bare floorboards, lofty ceilings, and chandeliers created from wine glasses.

The warmth of the heritage green paint on the walls created an intimate cosiness. Without it, the result would have been just shabby, without the chic. Kate wondered if Lucinda Langford had chosen her outfit to coordinate with the décor.

The server had delivered Kate's coffee, and Mrs Langford was talking, repeating what she had already said during the telephone conversation the previous evening. "The medical team have advised them that with the right care, my mother should be able to stay at home in surroundings that are familiar to her." Lucinda added.

"They believed that our father's death, and an underlying infection has accelerated her condition."

"Yes... your mother mentioned Matthew?" Kate said. From Mrs Langford's expression, she regretted this. It seemed like someone had just struck her for a moment, but then she answered without showing powerful emotion.

"Matthew was my biological father. He died when we were young. I am surprised my mother mentioned him!"

"I am so sorry! She was reminiscing while we were waiting. I presumed..."

"It was our stepfather, George, who died last year. We always referred to him as our father," Mrs Langford sighed. 'What a year! Mum's diagnosis had caught us all by surprise... and such an intelligent woman!'

Having worked on senior wards, Kate thought she would like a pound for every time she heard a family member reiterate a loved one's intelligence. Dementia was not a disease of prejudice; it could affect any of them.

"Are you married, Kate?" Lucinda asked. Taken by surprise, Kate answered by summarising her current situation in one sentence: She had divorced, they didn't have children, so it was an uncomplicated split. They sold their flat the previous year, and shared the equity, and was currently renting a bedsit.

Kate questioned why she labelled her situation 'currently,' since she doubted, she could buy again amid soaring property prices... unless of course she won the lottery!

"I am going to cut straight to the point," said Mrs Langford, appearing eager.

"We are considering hiring a full-time nurse to live in. My brother and I have busy lives, and we agree it's for the best that our mother be cared for by a professional in her own home."

"That is a good solution, if your mother agrees," Kate acknowledged, sipping her coffee to avoid dripping.

"We can offer excellent benefits: a live-in position, a very generous salary, and two days off a week plus statutory holiday. What do you think?" she asked.

Kate responded that she thought those terms were very fair to someone with the right experience and qualifications.

"Please call me Lucy... My brother and I have discussed it and we would like to offer you the position, would you consider? Of course we will manage alternative cover from an agency to ensure that mother is taken care of on your days off and during holidays."

"Me?" Kate spluttered her coffee, placing the dripping mug back on its saucer and mopping the table with a paper napkin.

"Mrs. Langford... I mean Lucy, I am grateful for the offer, but..." Being put on the spot, Kate could not think of a good enough reason to decline.

"Of course, I realise it's something you must think carefully about" Lucy said. "Take a couple of days."

"Thank you, but..." Kate said,

"Please, will you consider this? Our mum needs companionship, and we worry about her living alone in her big house," Lucy Langford spoke sincerely, her tone losing its formality.

Kate replied, "Thank you for the offer, and I will consider it."

"Excellent! We will feel so much happier knowing that a qualified nurse is on hand to provide adequate care if mum's health deteriorates. We can discuss formalities like contracts, references, criminal record checks, and whatever else is necessary... if you accept of course. In the meantime, if you have time after you finish your coffee, would you like me to show where you will be living? It's close to here!"

'There is no harm in looking!' thought Kate.

"I would like that," she said.

Searching For What Was Lost

I sit hunched in the cracked plastic chair, the relentless tick of the clock thrumming in my skull. The air is stale, thick with anticipation and the bitter edge of disinfectants. A child's laughter floats in from the corridor; a ghost of another life, reminding me of everything lost. The receptionist spoke her name. I startle, standing at attention, caught between hope and disbelief. The conversation at the desk draws my ear—"A woman had been in last week, also asking after her". My heart convulses. I step forward, voice strained. "Who was it? Do you have a name?" I ask.

The two women behind the counter exchange a glance, silent communication passing between them before one speaks up. "I already informed you that you need to submit a written request to the head of the department." Her response was measured and rehearsed. The other receptionist studies the computer screen, brow furrowed. "What we can tell you is a close relative made the enquiry. But I can see no record of you being listed as a contact name, sorry." Her voice is apologetic but firm.

I try again, desperation sharpening my tone, but the answer is unmoving. "What we can do is take your details and ask the person who is listed to contact you," the first woman offers. "They said they'll be returning later this week, but as I told them—if the person in question doesn't wish to be contacted, we'll log the enquiry until such time that they do, if ever."

The words land heavily. I cannot speak—years of grief and longing twist inside me, memories of my family I thought had perished surging up. Why did they let me believe she was dead, buried beneath the weight of my father's violence?

I leave with the email address scribbled on a slip of paper, an ache blooming in my chest. What else did they keep from me?

Outside, the world feels unchanged, but everything within me is shifting. It will take patience, and time I have plenty of both. I am prepared to do whatever it takes to find out where she is, even if it means returning daily and watching for the so-called relation to come back.

CHAPTER SEVEN

Breakfast on the Lawn

"You know nothing about this girl!" Raymond placed his knife and fork down with precision on his plate as he finished the last mouthful of his scrambled eggs and bacon.

"She's not a girl; she is about the same age as our Nick, or perhaps a year or two older, a qualified nurse, and we have applied for all background checks."

"I wish you had spoken to me about this first... before offering her the position."

"It's a provisional offer until we hear from the agencies!"

Lucy stopped eating her granola and pushed the bowl away.

"Mother seems to like her."

"For goodness' sake, Lucy, how can you be certain of that? She had only met her once and was confused and wandering. Your mother couldn't even remember her own name!"

"So, what would you suggest?"

"Residential. she will have twenty-four-hour care, seven days a week.

Lucy watched a flock of around twenty starlings gather on their manicured lawn, pecking away before taking off across the Oxfordshire countryside and beyond the woods that reached as far as the eye could see.

She wondered how birds cared for their old. Did they have to think about placing the frail into an old bird sanctuary or having a nominated carer bird look after them for the rest of their lives? Or did they just live and then die?

She imagined them sitting around having a family bird meeting, discussing what they were going to do with poor old mum or dad? Nature took care of wildlife. Why was everything so complex for us humans?

Lucy retorted, “Billy agrees with me. It would kill her not to come and go as she pleases, not able to go for walks or do some gardening.” Lucy was aware of her clipped tone.

She added, trying not to rant, “I believe, its being alone twenty-four hours a day that’s contributed to her becoming so unwell.”

“Your mother has dementia. Her condition will worsen. Isn’t it better for her to live in residential? There, she’ll get the care she needs and companionship.”

“Onset dementia!” Lucy corrected under her breath.

“I know my mother, and she would be miserable sitting in the dayroom of an old people’s home, with only other old people for company.” Lucy barked.

Ray refrained from reminding Lucy that Maggie was old. They sat with only the light clink of cup on saucer and birdsong to break the silence while Ray considered what words to make Lucy see sense.

“There’s no argument here: staying at home is best if it’s possible. But your mother’s condition is worsening. The hospital won’t discharge her until we have proper care arranged. What if a live-in nurse isn’t enough in a few months? Wouldn’t it be wiser to start thinking about long-term care options now?”

Lucy accepted some of what Ray said as true, but she still believed she knew best and decided to change the subject.

"I forgot to mention Nick telephoned this morning while you were in the shower. He is coming for Sunday lunch," she said, beginning to clear the table.

Their son Nicholas is a Detective Seargent in the Serious Crimes Unit for the Thames Valley Police and lives a short distance from their Oxfordshire retreat.

"It will be good to see him and have a catch up. Are you planning to cook lunch, or shall I book a table at The White Bear?" Ray asked, relieved at the change of topic but hoping his observation would hang with his wife.

VEILED MEMORIES

CHAPTER EIGHT

Moving Day

Kate unpacked the last of the boxes and hung her clothes in the built-in closet. The attic apartment was of an adequate size, a perk of her new job, with lots of alcoves, nooks, and crannies; a mix of cupboards built into the eaves filled with boxes belonging to the family, and modern wardrobes and drawers fitted to the wall opposite a double bed for Kate to use.

The bedroom had lights in its angled ceilings, and only natural light from skylights over the wardrobe and drawers. A small open arch led into a much brighter living area with a two-seater sofa, opposite a table sized for two, next to French doors that led to an outside balcony. The kitchenette was minimal and included a sink with mixer taps and drainer, a laminate work surface, a microwave, toaster and a kettle against the only full-sized wall with a door leading into the modern fitted ensuite bathroom.

It all happened quickly; once Kate had weighed up the pros and cons of leaving her job, bedsit, and the familiarity of her hometown. Despite her initial reaction, once she had viewed the house and her living arrangements the decision to accept the position was taken almost immediately.

Since completing her training, she had worked at the same hospital. Her "nursing family" was an extensive friends' list on Facebook. Steve and Carol were the closest to natural parents a child in foster care could hope for. They provided her with a stable home for most of her teens and supported her decision to become a nurse. They even applied to adopt her, but the adoption agency denied their application because they were in their sixties.

Carol died of a heart attack two years into Kate's nursing training, and Steve's health had deteriorated soon after. He died eighteen months later; Kate was just twenty-two. Despite not adopting Kate, Carol and Steve had considered her their daughter, leaving a modest sum for her in their will with a footnote saying how proud they were, suggesting she continue to work hard, and they hoped their gift would help her fulfil her hopes and dreams.

Kate's mobile rang. She saw her friend Claire's name appear on the screen. "Are you all settled in?" Claire asked. "Nearly finished, unpacking the last few bits." She put her mobile on loudspeaker so she could talk while placing the folded jumpers and sweatshirts pile onto the shelves in the wardrobe.

Kate and Claire clicked from day one, chatting over coffee during their induction training. Their accommodation was in the same block, and they soon became close friends.

Claire's support was invaluable to Kate after Steve and Carol died, and without Claire's friendship, she was sure she would not have coped as well during this past year.

"How are you feeling?" Claire asked.

"Excited!" Kate replied.

"Put your foot down from the off, set out your boundaries; otherwise, some will have you working twenty-four seven," Claire said, not hiding her concern.

"The family is delightful, and I have my own living space."

"Lovely," Claire responded.

"There is a small Juliet balcony, it overlooks the heath. It used to house the family's au-pair."

"But what if you don't like your job? You will have nowhere to live!"

"As you keep repeating," Kate said, trying not to sound impatient.

Claire was the most organised in their friend group and always thought things through. Sometimes a little too outspoken, but this was the reason Kate loved her. You knew exactly where you were with Claire.

"You worry too much!" Kate laughed and explained the terms of her employment contract again.

"We have agreed on a two-month notice period. This means if it doesn't work out, the family can use the time to make alternative arrangements for Maggie's care, and I have time to find alternative accommodation, I was going to keep my studio on for a few months, but to be honest it would be a waste of rent money,"

"Sorry, Kate. I am not being a pessimist. I worry about you, especially after what you have been through lately."

Kate explained that, although she appreciated Claire's concern, she hadn't decided lightly.

"Speaking of worry... you have received more post sent to my address from your old flat. There are more letters from the same solicitor. What do you want me to do? The same as before?"

"Yep, return to sender. I have paid enough already for Neil's debts."

"Don't you think you should ring them?" asked Claire.

"No! I'm not calling them to be told it's my duty to pay off debts on behalf of my husband. Our divorce is final now, so he can clean up his own mess from now on."

"This is me pressing the restart button." Kate jested, "I'm breaking free from the cocoon, and looking forward to becoming a butterfly," she heard Claire hum.

"If it doesn't work out, well, I can flutter off somewhere else, even abroad!"

"Okay, I get it! And I really do hope it works out for you! Anyway... when will I see you? Soon, I hope?"

"Give me a couple of weeks, and I will have withdrawals for one of your amazing Sunday roasts," Kate said.

They met their prospective spouses at a New Year's Eve party, although the men did not know each other. Claire's husband Steven is a police officer, and Neil is a paramedic. They went on a few double dates, but it was plain Steven and Neil would not become friends, they had little in common.

Kate and Neil married a year later, and Claire and Steven a year after them, although that was where the similarities ceased because each of their marriages turned out quite different.

"Hold you to it!" Claire said.

"See you in a couple of weeks... hey, Lacey, come here, blow Auntie Katie a big kiss... say bye-bye!" Kate hears Claire's two-year-old daughter in the background, followed by her sweet little voice coaxed by Claire.

"Bye-bye, love you!"

"See you soon sweetheart. Big hugs... love you too!" Kate said smiling.

CHAPTER NINE

The Memory Board

Kate handed Maggie the translucent plastic container holding her morning medication and watched her swallow her pills. She made a record using the form, the quiet rustle of paper as she slipped the document back into its plastic folder. The morning sun was low in the sky and shone through the French doors, causing Maggie to squint as the crispness of the air drifted in, carrying with it the faint scent of cut grass. Kate pulled the heavy drapes halfway to block out the light.

"How were you feeling today?" she asked.

"Bored!" replied Maggie.

"You will finish your antibiotics by Friday, and you are getting a little better every day. If you'd like, we can walk around the garden later if the weather is nice."

"Lovely. I shall look forward to getting out into the fresh air. Are you settling in, Kate? Are you comfortable all the way up there?" Maggie pointed towards the ceiling.

"Oh yes, it's lovely, thank-you. The views are amazing," Kate replied.

"I am pleased. I appreciate your being here. It was quite by chance that we met like we did. Not that I can remember too much. I believe I gave everyone quite a fright wandering off like that," said Maggie.

Kate smiled and cleared away Maggie's breakfast tray.

"What day is it?"

"It's Tuesday, May 21st," said Kate.

"I find it difficult remembering the days. Do you think it's because of my condition?" Maggie asked, and Kate saw the fear in her eyes.

"It's because you have been unwell. You are still weak and have not been outdoors since you came out of the hospital," Kate said.

"The doctors are happy with how you are progressing. You are doing well! ... and remembering the days of the week is easy to resolve!"

Kate, seeing Maggie settled, strolled towards the High Street. She visited a stationery store to buy a wipeable whiteboard and a black felt pen. She then crossed the street to the coffee shop to buy a takeaway coffee and strolled home, feeling a little guilty. This did not feel like work!

The warm sun and coffee made Kate's day feel very pleasant. A new chapter unfolded, and she revelled in her newfound independence.

She felt excited like she had never experienced before, not even when she got married. Probably because nothing really changed after their wedding. They lived separately to save for a deposit for a flat. Kate stayed in hospital accommodation where the rent included bills, while Neil had made the choice to continue renting a room in a flat shared in town.

This had been fine until Claire moved to Milton Keynes. Steven's promotion had prompted Claire to apply for a job at a nearby hospital. As a newlywed, Kate had felt lonely. If she wasn't working, she would sit alone in her room after her so-called husband had repeatedly disappointed her.

Neil had offloaded stress by catching up with his mates down the pub, and since this was usually a last-minute plan, they had rarely invited her. Kate had been lonely and had desperately missed Claire. She had seldom gone out because they were skint! They needed to add a significant amount to their savings if they were going to raise a deposit large enough to afford a mortgage.

Kate had managed their savings, putting away as much as she could afford each month, while Neil contributed little, coming up with a new excuse each month. “If only I had recognised the red flags then,” Kate thought. At first, Kate had been drawn to Neil’s laid-back and easy-going attitude. She appreciated how little seemed to faze him and how nothing, apart from his work, was treated with much seriousness. However, as time passed, these very traits became more difficult to accept. Neil often behaved as if he were still single, coming and going whenever he pleased and rarely considering Kate’s feelings or their relationship in his daily choices. She threw her empty coffee cup into a recycle bin and sauntered home, enjoying the fresh air.

Using her key to open the wide green front door with its inset stained glass, Kate entered the house. She heard a male voice and then laughter. She knocked on the door before entering.

“Hello, Kate. Come on in and meet my grandson, Nicholas,” Maggie said.

A tall, fair-haired man of about Kate’s age stood up to greet her.

“Gran has been telling me all about you. It’s nice to meet you,” he said, smiling warmly.

He then held out his hand. Kate dropped the large plastic carrier bag at her feet and wiped her hand on her jeans.

"Nice to meet you at last. Maggie spoke of you too," she said.
"What do you have there?" asked Maggie, nodding towards the large carrier.
Kate removed the whiteboard from the bag and raised it.
I figured it would be helpful to put this up where you can see it.
"That's a great idea!" Nicholas said, well-spoken and self-assured. "I'll do that for you while I'm here."

'Maggie'

I'm usually in this room. I love looking out of the French doors at the garden, "so how about putting it up there?" Maggie points to the wall opposite her chair.
Having these young people here feels like a tonic, and I feel so much better this afternoon. Nicholas shows he is making the right decision in choosing a career that does not involve manual labour. Watching him erect the memory board, as Kate calls it, is comical. First, the screw is too far in the wall, so the board will not hang. On his second attempt, the screw loses its thread. Eventually, he disappears into the shed, returning with a handful of nails and a hammer.
"Which one?" he said, holding up one three-inch nail and another more appropriately sized.
Once the board is in place, Kate uses a marker to write today's date.
"It will be my first job of the day to write the date and any reminders," she said, placing the lid back on the marker and putting it behind a photograph on the sideboard.

At lunchtime, Nicholas fetches a garden chair for me to sit on and places it in a shady spot by the willow tree. Between them, they move the garden table and chairs nearby so we can have lunch together. The sun is hot for the time of the year, and the sky is pale blue, with a few thin streaks of cloud. I must have dropped off because I awoke to hear the clanking of tea plates. Nicholas is carrying a tray with a teapot and teacups, while Kate follows behind with a tray of sandwiches and a lemon drizzle loaf cake.

I nibble on a triangular ham sandwich and sip my tea. Days like this are reminiscent of days when I was a child, Sunday afternoons spent with my grandparents, and I say as much.

Nicholas and Kate listen as I describe memories from my childhood. I played alone while the grown-ups ate sandwiches, drank tea, and discussed the events of the war.

"Must be a family tradition because my childhood memories are much the same. I had to amuse myself too," said Nicholas, cutting himself another large slice of cake.

"I used to pretend the pagoda at the bottom of your garden was my fort."

"How lovely that you had such a big garden to play in," I remarked to Nicholas. "Ours was just the paved back yard behind our shop, so it never quite felt the same."

Reflecting for a moment, I added, "It's a shame you were my only grandchild." The thought made me pause, considering the shape of our family and how things had turned out.

"Thanks, gran!" Nicholas chuckled, and spat out cake crumbs, and I laughed.

"You know what I mean. I always thought Billy would settle down and have children one day, but it wasn't to be."

"Never say never! There's still time; Some of the old rock stars are still having kids," Nicholas said.

While I would have liked more grandchildren, Nicholas has grown-up to be a grandson to be proud of. Not only is he handsome and intelligent, but he is also caring and kind. I turn my attention to Kate.

"Do you have brothers and sisters, Kate?"

"No, I have no siblings, being a foster child." She said.

"Oh, I am sorry!" I replied.

Nicholas stops smiling and fumbles to top up our cups with the remnants of tea that has stewed in the pot.

"When I was young, I moved between foster homes, then to an amazing couple who dedicated their lives to fostering children. Over thirty during the time I lived with them!"

"That must have been tough!" In my remark, I feel a deep empathy towards this girl.

"I don't know any difference, and my foster parents were lovely! "So, my life as a foster child, from my experience, isn't as bad as it's sometimes portrayed in the media," Kate was very matter of fact.

"I enjoyed a happy childhood, despite the circumstances, and they encouraged me to do well at school. And because of their kindness, I wanted to help people too, which is why I became a nurse."

"Do you keep in touch with them?"

"Unfortunately, they died!"

"Oh, I am sorry! What about your natural parents?"

"Gran, Kate may not want to speak about this anymore," Nicholas is fidgeting uncomfortably in his seat.

"No, it's fine, honest! My mum and dad died when I was about two years old. I don't remember them, and I'm not sure exactly how or why it happened," Kate said.

"Social Services could provide me with more information. Although I have not felt the need so far." Kate appears thoughtful for a moment. "I think it's for the best that I don't look too hard into my past. I'm worried about what I'll find." Kate's answer is lighthearted, and she is even mocking herself.

Nicholas shifts the subject.

"Are you okay, gran? Are you feeling cold?"

"No, I am feeling fine, thanks to you and Kate." I smiled at Kate, causing her to blush.

"Good! And you are not tempted to go wandering off again?" Nick teases.

"No, I am not, cheeky!"

I have spent most of my life trying to erase from my memory the horror! The worst thing that a person could imagine happened to me! But the information within a letter I received recently fills me with hope!

I lost my family as I knew it on 'that day' many years ago, and nothing has ever been the same. The only way I coped, for the sake of Lucy and Billy, was to suppress painful memories and escape the familiarity of the town where I grew up.

When they informed me about my condition and explained that my brain is diseased, and this will eventually affect my thought process and memory, strangely, my biggest fear is that I will forget memories I have tried to suppress for years! I feel fine today, but that's not the case every day, and I worry good days will become less frequent as time goes by.

Dementia has forced me to face my demons and to discover what happened to him. Regrets abound. I am frustrated because now I feel I must find out, but I feel too frail to do it alone. Time is short; I must enlist my grandson's help to do what I should have done long ago.

'Kate'

Kate retired to bed at around half past ten, weary from the day's events. Yet as she lay awake, her mind replayed the conversation with Maggie, recalling every detail. Sleep eluded her; thoughts raced and swirled long past midnight, refusing to settle.

She couldn't help but reflect on the bond between Nicholas and his grandmother — so close, so full of unspoken understanding. Kate felt a pang of sadness for Maggie, sensing the unresolved grief that lingered in her voice and the almost desperate hope that flickered in her eyes. The weight of Maggie's request pressed upon her, leaving Kate torn between empathy and confusion, uncertain how she might help.

Maggie's hands quivered as she spoke, her words slow and deliberate, a mixture of vulnerability and resolve. 'It was an accident,' Maggie began, her voice barely above a whisper. “Matthew, he was your biological grandfather, he died in Ireland. It happened so many years ago... in the early 1970s. They never found his body, but he was presumed dead.”

Kate and Nicholas exchanged glances, recognising the significance in Maggie’s tone. After a pause, Maggie continued, her fingers tightening around the edge of her chair. ‘I tried to forget,’ she admitted softly, her eyes distant with memory, but now I need to know There were things left unfinished, questions unanswered. Did any unidentified bodies turn up in the months after?’

She glanced at Nicholas with quiet determination. “I’ve erased so many details from my memory over the years. But I can’t go on like this. Will you help me, Nicholas? With all your resources, as a detective, surely you can find something.”

Kate watched Maggie, moved by the courage it took to break the silence of her sorrow. In the dim light, she saw a woman wrestling with the past—hope and regret entwined—finally daring to seek the truth.

Nick explained to Maggie that reopening old cases presented significant challenges. He told her that, in most instances, such matters were handled by specialised teams, and even for those teams, the task was complicated by the fact that police stations had either archived or misplaced paper files when they closed down. Despite these obstacles, Nick assured Maggie that he would do his best to uncover whatever information he could.

Initially, Kate suspected that Nick was merely humouring his grandmother, offering reassurance without any real intention of following through. However, as the conversation progressed, it became clear to her that Nick was genuinely committed to helping Maggie, and his promise was made in earnest.

Maggie worried that the truth about the past would be lost if she didn't act, mentioning her worsening health. She claimed to have a letter challenging the official story of the disappearance but hesitated to share it, keeping its contents unknown. Throughout the conversation, Maggie remained lucid and genuinely troubled by these unresolved matters.

As evening approached, Maggie asked us to go with her to her room. I thought she would show us the letter, but she seemed to forget about it once she was there. After she settled, we sat in the kitchen and discussed the matter briefly over a cup of tea before Nick left for home.

Kate fidgeted in bed for a while longer, trying to get comfortable.

"For goodness' sake, Miss Marple, get some sleep!" Kate said, while plumping up her pillows and turning on her side to try again.

"I will pick up these thoughts again in the morning," as eventually her eyelids weighed heavy, and she closed them.

VEILED MEMORIES

CHAPTER TEN

Unravelling Threads

Nicholas left the work meeting at about six-thirty. Deciding against driving back to his flat in Oxford, he went to his parents. He had planned to work from home tomorrow but had his laptop with him, so he could work from his parents' house. Besides, it would be interesting to find out how much his mum knew about her father's accident.

"What must Kate be thinking? Probably wondering what type of family, she is working for!" he pondered while sitting in the rush hour traffic. "And do I really have the time to investigate an age-old case on behalf of my grandmother?"

"Good timing, gran," he said aloud. He was planning to announce his engagement to Elaine to coincide with a job relocation to London! He had yet to introduce Elaine to the family, but he was certain they would love her as much as he did. She was intelligent, independent, and beautiful.

Elaine lived in a tiny one-bedroom flat in Finchley. She was a criminal barrister employed by the Crown Prosecution Service. They had met when she was a guest speaker at a police conference a couple of years ago.

Nick often stayed overnight at his parents' house when in London on weekdays. Elaine worried she would disturb him often working into the early hours. They planned to start house hunting as soon as they found the time, with a property with office space as a priority.

Nicholas pulled into the driveway of his parents' mews, locked the car, and rang the doorbell. After several minutes and tries of the doorbell, his dad answered in a fluster, red-faced, with a damp T-shirt and sweat beads on his forehead.

"Nicky Boy... we weren't expecting you," he said, taking a handkerchief out of his jogging pants pocket and wiping his face.

"Hi dad, what have you been up to?" he said, smiling teasingly.

"I didn't hear the doorbell; I was on the treadmill."

Nick followed his father into the kitchen and watched him run the cold tap for a few seconds before filling a glass and gulping it down.

"Is mum not around?" he said, looking about, expecting Lucy to appear.

"No, she is at one of her mectings," Ray replied.

"Is it okay if I stay for the night? I've been in a meeting for most of the day, and I am shattered."

"Thought I might work from here tomorrow if that's okay? I've got quite a lot of paperwork to clear before I return to the station." Nick leaned across the kitchen island and started leafing through the Evening Standard that was lying there.

"Fine by me, but not sure how much peace you'll get. Your mother may be here tomorrow. I'll leave you the key to my study; you can lock yourself in?"

"Thanks Dad," they laughed knowingly.

Nicholas enjoyed the time spent alone with his father. Lucy commandeered his attention when she was here. His dad was Irish

American and had inherited the Irish sense of humour, born of great darkness with an appreciation for irony.

“How’s work?” Ray asked his son.

“Run ragged, I’m working on a complex case.”

“Haven’t you solved it yet?” Ray mocked.

“Unfortunately, no. Our prime suspect has done a runner!”

“Ah, the case in the news?” Ray asked.

“That’s the one!”

“And what about the other thing... have you heard any more?” Ray whispered this as if worried someone might hear him.

“I thought you said mum was out!” Nick laughed.

“Can never be too careful. She approaches like a thief in the night!” Ray chuckled.

“I assume you’re talking about my transfer to the ‘Metropolitan,’ That’s why I am in London this week. I’ve been told the second stage of the interview is simply a formality to meet with superiors, so the position is in the bag.”

“Well done son! And I still haven’t mentioned it to your mum, as you asked.”

Ray filled the kettle, and they chatted casually about the weather, the traffic chaos in London, and recent elections. They sipped their coffee.

“Did you drive up this morning?” Ray enquired.

"No, I came to London yesterday. I was going to prepare for today's meeting, but I called in on gran and ended up spending most of the day with her."

"So, you met Kate?"

"Yes, she seems okay."

"What do you know about mum's real dad? His name was Matthew," Nick asked unexpectedly. Ray initially appeared startled but then answered casually.

"Not a lot. Why?"

"According to gran, he died while on a trip to Ireland, but nobody ever found his body. She wants me to find out more about what happened and dig out the old reports!"

"This is something else not to mention to your mother Nick, she is worried about your gran's mental health and how quickly her condition is deteriorating... in truth, we both are."

"Don't worry, I am taking what gran said with a pinch of salt, but I can't help feeling intrigued. It all sounds a bit cloak and dagger."

"And I think you have enough to do in your day job!" Ray takes the mugs, places them in the dishwasher and opens the fridge.

"Have you eaten? Lasagne?"

Nick welcomed the offer of food, responding, "Yes, that sounds great!" He then shifted the conversation back to the topic of his grandmother's beliefs. "From what gran said; she believes Matthew is alive, although she didn't actually say that." Nick found his grandmother's behaviour puzzling, questioning the timing and motivation behind her interest. “Don’t you think it’s odd she would want to rake this up now?” he asked, deliberately sidestepping his father’s earlier comment. Nick’s words conveyed both his uncertainty about his gran’s perspective and his curiosity about why she might want to revisit painful memories at this point in time.

“He’d better have died, or you’d better take your handcuffs with you next time you visit her. She married your granddad!” Ray responded, and belly laughed. It was infectious.

“Seriously, Dad, if you don’t think it’s a good idea to ask Mum about it, tell me what you know?”

“Your gran gets confused, and with her condition, she may have difficulty accepting little Matthew died!” Ray said, becoming sombre.

“I’m confused. Who is ‘little Matthew’? I was under the impression she was talking about her first husband! Nick stood tall, waiting to hear the details.

“From what I’m told, little Matthew is your uncle. They were both killed. Your biological grandfather and your mother’s brother were in a car accident, although whether it was an ‘accident,’ is debatable! The car ended up at the bottom of a cliff. “

“Gran did not mention a son!” exclaimed Nick.

“Suicide?” he asked.

“Who knows? I am only reading between the lines, but from what your mother has told me, her little brother died when she was just seven. He was a year younger. Maggie was so grief-stricken she spent weeks in a Psychiatric hospital. A grieving grandmother and neighbours took care of your mother and her toddler brother, Billy."

"This tragic event must have affected the entire family," Nick remarked. Ray shifted slightly and nodded in agreement with Nick's statement.

"Events still traumatise your mother. Maggie disappeared for a few days looking for them, then returned home to receive the news they were dead. She was so distraught; she could not remember or more accurately, would not say where she had been," Ray said, looking solemn and slowly shaking his head as he spoke.

"Your mother mentioned that during her childhood, your gran often became silent and deeply depressed. While she was in the hospital, her father also passed away."

"That's awful! Do you think Matthew killed himself and the child? And if so, why?" asked Nick.

"I don't know! Although I suspect so. It is easier for the family to have accepted it as an accident rather than face discovering the truth."

"Your mother doesn't speak about it, far too painful! And I have never heard her refer to Matthew as her father. I believe she has tried to eradicate his existence from her memory. So, heed my warning Nick, please tread carefully!"

"When did gran meet grandad? Because I've seen photos of mum with granddad, and she couldn't have been much older than seven."

Nick listened intently as Ray continued, providing more insight into the family's past. "Granddad was Maggie's psychiatrist," Ray explained, careful to choose his words. "Even back then it would have been considered crossing professional boundaries, but the rules about doctor-patient relationships were not as strict as they are today." He paused, recalling the details as best as he could. "Your mother once said George, recognising the situation, arranged for a referral to another doctor. But their blossoming relationship was a new chapter for everyone… and they went on to be a happy couple, you know the rest!"

"God, this is tragic! I can't believe I didn't know any of this," Nick felt saddened by the information his dad had shared.

The Bridge Between Us

The early summer rain falls in relentless sheets, soaking me as I trail her through the city's pulsing streets. Each step feels burdensome—resentment and longing churn within me. I watch her closely, noticing the guarded tension in her posture. I hope this stranger will give me the answers I deserve. I don't understand why, but after days of waiting, I knew she was who I was waiting for; the moment she entered the local authority office. I had followed behind, smiling politely at the security guard by the door. Feigning purpose, I had browsed the noticeboard and flipped through leaflets, staying close enough to overhear her conversation at the desk. My heart had leapt when they spoke her name. She checks her phone and hurries on, sensing me, or only responding to the intensity of my eagerness not to lose her. I realise this may be my only chance to find out where she lives and lead me to what I am desperately looking for. A line of doubt cuts through my resolve—does my longing for answers truly outweigh my fear of the truth. I wonder, feeling increasingly betrayed, is this woman aware of me or is she too just another casualty of a family warped by secrets? When she disappears behind the door of a mews house, I know with certainty: she will lead me to her for sure. Left outside, clutching the address, I shiver—not only from the rain, but from the uncertainty of who I am and who I have become. I will return after fetching enough belongings to settle locally and be prepared for the long game.

CHAPTER ELEVEN

July 1964 - A Town in Mourning

I was conscious of the extra police and reporters hanging near the town, but it was not at the forefront of my mind.

We were busy that Thursday. The murder was all anyone could talk about. Mum hung around, ignoring Dad's disapproval, to discuss with our customers the what's and wherefores.

Most of the people who showed up that day claimed they either knew the murdered woman or knew someone who did. Someone mentioned that she was a young mother in her twenties. My thoughts went to the couple I saw in St Mary's Church, but I didn't mention them.

When I said I was going out, my mother and father were not happy, especially when I said it was a date, with a murderer on the loose. Once I pleaded and shed a few tears, they relented but told me I must be home right after the film finishes at 10 o'clock.

As soon as five in the afternoon hit, I charged upstairs. It was the moment to get ready!

"Maggie, come here and have your tea," Mum called from downstairs.

"I don't want any," I shouted down.

"You will go nowhere, unless you come down these stairs and eat," she replied.

I scoffed down boiled eggs and soldiers and swigged back a cup of tea, then went upstairs to finish getting ready.

Wearing a lemon floral petticoat dress and a lemon knitted cardigan, I back-combed my hair and pinned it into a French roll. I sat patiently, waiting for the knock on our back door. My white handbag sat in my lap.

I realised that he had stood me up at eight-thirty. Aware of the look between my parents, who were listening to a play on the wireless, I stomped upstairs, undressed, and got into my nightdress. Even though it's a warm night, I snuggled into my quilted dressing gown.

My mum knocked on my bedroom door and entered, passing me a cup of Ovaltine. We didn't exchange words, but she gave me a knowing wink and a sympathetic smile before closing my bedroom door behind her, leaving me in my sorrow. I didn't cry, although I felt like it.

1964–The following week

Today is Tuesday, and Matthew will arrive with our delivery shortly. My stomach is lurching at the thought, but after some deliberation, I have decided I will not disappear out back. I will continue as normal but completely ignore him!

I jump every time the bell on the door rings. The delivery was late. Jim arrived close to three o'clock.

"Sorry I'm late, Bill. I'm all alone today. I have been flat out!"

"Where's that lad of yours? Is he ill?" Dad asked, glancing my way. But I continue to stack the shelves, pretending that I am not paying any attention to the whereabouts of the Rat.

"Now there's a story, Bill! Put the kettle on, and I will tell you all about it," Jim said. Dad and Jim have been out back for an hour. I'm itching to find out what they are talking about. Perhaps Matthew is ill? He may have a terrible bout of flu, unable to get out of bed. Although it would have had to come on quickly, or what if he has had an accident?

Jim eventually comes through to the shop.

"Thanks for the tea and biscuits, Bill. I must get a move on now if I am going to get all my deliveries done," he chuckled, pulling the empty trolley behind him.

"See you next week," Dad opens the door so he can manoeuvre the trolley out.

Once he had gone, I asked him what they had been talking about for so long. Dad doesn't reply; he gets on with cleaning the meat slice.

Later, we were settling down to listen to the news when Dad finally revealed his earlier conversation with Jim.

"The lad that works with Jim, young Matthew, his brother's wife, was who was murdered!"

'Maggie - present day'

Where am I? My bedroom looks different, and I want my mum. There is a knock on the bedroom door, and I feel a wave of confusion sweep over me. That's not my mum! I am bewildered by the unfamiliar surroundings and the absence of my mother.

As I try to make sense of where I am, I notice a young man standing quietly in the corner of my room. He appeared suddenly from behind the drapes, and he is smiling at me. My heart races with uncertainty, and I call out, "I can't find my mother! ... where is she? Please help me find her," hoping for reassurance in this strange moment.

Suddenly, the scene shifts. "Morning, Maggie. It's me, Kate. How are you feeling this morning?" The nurse enters the room, breaking my confusion. I look around, but the young man is gone, leaving me unsettled and questioning what is real.

"I was dreaming." Embarrassed, I mumble something else, and Kate smiles, helping me sit up.

"Take your time. There's no rush. Once you feel awake, I will help you get up so you can dress and go downstairs for your breakfast!" Kate said gently, her voice reassuring and calm.

Still feeling exhausted, I looked up at her and asked, "Is it okay if I stay in bed for a while? I am feeling quite tired today."

"Of course! I will fetch breakfast to you," Kate replied. She moved around the room, plumping my pillows and straightening my bedclothes to make me more comfortable.

My dreams had left me feeling utterly drained. They were so vivid—almost as if I were reliving moments from my past. The emotions of being reunited with mum and dad had lingered, stirring something deep inside me. Yet, as I tried to hold on to those memories, the details slipped away, leaving only a faint echo of what I had just experienced.

CHAPTER TWELVE

The Stalker

Kate wanted Maggie's GP to examine her at home. Maggie had spent the last couple of days in her bed and lost her appetite, even with encouragement. She seemed depressed, which may be another symptom of dementia. The receptionist said the doctor would visit after the morning surgery.

Lucy called Kate to say they were travelling to their Oxfordshire home for the weekend.

"Do you need us to turn around and come home?" Lucy asked, sounding concerned.

"I don't think that is necessary," Kate replied, hoped to ease her worry. "Your mother appears out of sorts, but I don't believe it to be serious. although a doctor should see her."

"Thank you Kate, call me after the doctor has been and let me know what he said. We can come home if we need to. I will ask Billy to pop in sometime over the weekend, too."

Kate didn't think Maggie was sleeping very well at night. She had been calling out in her sleep again and then needing to sleep during the day. She was asleep the last time Kate checked.

Kate was sat in the 'snug' a small sitting room near the kitchen. In one of two high-backed armchairs near the log burner in the fireplace, she was reading. Due to the significant temperature drop with the changing weather, Kate lit it for warmth.

The house felt chilly because of its many floors, lofty ceilings, old windows, and lengthy, draughty hallways. Even though it wasn't needed to turn the central heating on, a convector heater was put in Maggie's bedroom to warm it up.

Kate closed the French doors that led to a small glass orangery to make it feel less draughty. Even her little attic annexe was cold this morning as she came out of the shower.

Ria, a polish woman in her mid-forties, came in to clean for three hours each weekday morning. Kate heard her put away the vacuum in the hall cupboard. Ria appeared in the doorway, wearing a grey raincoat and tying a grey polka-dot scarf over her curly blond hair.

"I'm off home now. I've finished mopping the hallway, I'll use the back door to leave. I have a key, so I'll lock it on the way out."

"Thank you, Ria," Kate, said warmly.

"Say goodbye to Mrs Randall. I hope she feels better soon. Have a good weekend. I'll see you on Monday."

Heavy rain hammered the glass panes of the orangery, and a rumble of thunder echoed. Kate placed her book on the coffee table. It appeared dark outside, unusual for the time of day, especially since it was supposed to be summer.

Allowing enough time for floors to dry; Kate decided to check on Maggie again. Along the short passage that led to the main entrance hall. She headed towards the staircase, feeling uneasy but uncertain why.

"Awful weather!" she spoke aloud.

Kate sensed someone behind her, obstructing what little natural light there was. Kate noticed the silhouette through the obscure glass and suddenly realised, It's the doctor!

'Why hasn't he used the doorbell?' she wondered, checking her watch. It was only eleven thirty, earlier than she was expecting his arrival.

Determined to greet him, Kate made her way towards the main entrance. However, before she could reach the door, the figure turned and began walking towards the side gate instead.

Kate opened the door after struggling with the sliding bolts, top and bottom. Despite the side gate swinging in the wind off its latch, Kate couldn't see anyone in the side alley.

She faced the heavy rain as the wind drove it into her face as she walked the front path. Leaning on the closed front gate, despite the wet, she tried to see up and down the street by peering past the tall hedge. There were a few people with umbrellas up or wearing hoods, but they all appeared to know where they were going, and she didn't note anyone of significance.

Kate thought Ria might have come back and remembering the bolts. went to the kitchen door instead. Kate made her way through the house, the kitchen with its big oak table, and through to the scullery to see if the door at the back was secure. Kate found it locked.

A paved alley ran from the side gate, alongside the house with access from the door from the scullery with its half-opaque glass The silhouette of anyone would be visible. Past the orangery and around the lawn, to where it meets a rough brick pathway. This path lined with rose bushes, leading to an original wrought iron gate opening to the heath.

Kate climbed the two flights of stairs, two at a time, and reached her loft apartment, where the heath gate was visible from her window. It was closed this morning. But from here, she saw it was open.

She saw someone in a green hooded parka near the hedge. They were facing away from her. The person on the doorstep unsettled Kate, but she didn't know why. Besides, the person could have been dropping off flyers. However, their stance reminded her of an eighties horror film character. Kate's eyes remained fixed on the person near the heath gate. Suddenly startled by their movement.

With a call and an inviting gesture, a golden dog appeared; as they continued walking, it became plain that it was simply a person out with their dog.

CHAPTER THIRTEEN

When Darkness Knocks

Dr Lewis showed up soon after lunch. Maggie barely touched her breakfast, or the ham sandwich Kate made for her lunch. This was explained to the GP by Kate. He decided constipation was the cause of Maggie's grogginess after the examination.

"This medicine should last you two days, but I'll write a prescription for more." The doctor said speaking to Maggie but handing a small box of sachets to Kate.

"It might take a couple of days to get better, eat plenty of fibre this weekend."

Kate told Lucy what the GP said, and then she called Claire. She got invited to Sunday lunch but won't be able to go.

"This is what I was worried about! It's only been a few weeks, and you are already feeling obliged to cancel your days off!" Claire's tone suggested irritation.

"Push back my day off!" Kate replied, trying to sound cheerful.

"Can you make this Wednesday so I can plan the agency staff's schedule?" Kate proposed that they go for lunch before seeing a film.

The doorbell rang as she loaded the dishwasher while the soup, she made stewed. Kate turned down the burner and went to answer the door. It was Nicholas.

"I'm sorry to bother you, my mum called me to say gran was sick, and if I was passing..." he said while removing his damp raincoat and placing it on a hall stand hook.

"Maggie will be delighted to see you." Nick followed Kate upstairs, and Maggie looked much perkier.

"I have a vegetable soup on the hob for your supper. I will leave you to catch up with your grandson while I go to check on it," she said, leaving them to chat.

Kate returned to the kitchen and stirred the soup. Even though it was only just after five o'clock, there was a need for the ceiling lights. She searched for a blender and found a hand blender at the back of a larder cupboard. It appeared untouched for a long time, so she brought it to the sink and ran the tip under hot water.

She gazed out the window, admiring the rear garden. She wasn't mistaken; someone was there, next to the willow, and they were watching her. They were cloaked in a dark, hooded coat, with a black scarf hiding their face. She froze where she stood and let out a gasp. Despite Kate clearly seeing them, they stayed put. Based on their appearance and build, she knew it was a man.

After a tense, silent moment, they fled quickly down the garden path towards the house. Kate, her heart pounding, rushed into the kitchen just in time to catch a glimpse of a shadowy figure moving past the back door. Panic rising, she dashed from the kitchen, sprinting down the hallway towards the front door, on this occasion, the entrance was not bolted. She looked frantically outside, but whoever had been there had already vanished. Both the back gate and the front gates stood wide open, swinging and creaking in the wind.

CHAPTER FOURTEEN

In the Grip of Shadows

Nick finds Maggie looking better than expected; she has colour in her face and a sparkle in her eyes.

"Glad to see you looking better gran," he said, leaning over to kiss her on the cheek.

"I am fine. I'm not sure why everyone is making such a fuss. Although I wish I could shake off this tiredness."

"What did the doctor say?"

"He suggested I take it easy today, and if I feel up to it... to get moving tomorrow, as staying in bed could be the cause of my problem."

They chat about various things for a while, then gran looks serious.

"I hope you haven't made a specific journey to London just to see me?" she said.

Nick hasn't talked about his interview, nor will he bring up the potential transfer. He thought about telling them the other reason he needed to spend the night in London, but he'd see how his grandmother was doing first. Following the weekend, he will be unable to investigate Matthew's case again.

Kate opened the door with her leg as she wrestled with a tray. Nick hurried to help. she looked worried.

Nick set the tray with soup and bread down for Maggie on the table with the white cloth.

"Thank you!" Kate said, grateful for his help.

"That soup looks delicious," Nick said, offering Kate a smile. But he realised Kate was deep in thought.

"There is plenty if you would like a bowl," she offered.

"I will take you up on that offer! Shall I join you in the kitchen when I finish here?"

Maggie leapt out of bed, taking them by surprise.

"Take it easy," Kate chuckled, helping her into a dressing gown and sitting her down to eat at the table.

After making the bed, Kate got a jug of fresh drinking water and put it on the bedside table. Her departure from the room allowed Maggie to eat her supper at her own pace. Kate came back to retrieve the tray, and Nick went downstairs behind her.

Nick considered if Kate was just weary, or if the old house was the source of her troubles. How will she get by living here through the winter? The interior design is unchanged from his childhood, with furniture that matches its Victorian era.

He remembers the feeling he experienced as a young boy when his parents expected him to use the toilet going alone. He slowly ascended the twisting stairs, his heart racing with each footfall. By comparison, his home was brightly lit and contemporary. An eight-year-old's imagination conjured countless dark corners where snakes, monsters, and the Hulk could lurk. He climbed the stairs, hand over hand on the twisting, dark wood banisters, each slow step filled with a sense of suspense about what he'd find at the top. While there was no-one at the top of the stairs, that wasn't the most unpleasant aspect of the 'toilet trip' He thought the staircase on the first-floor landing, shrouded in shadows, led to an unknown place.

He ran down the stairs, trying to escape what he believed was chasing him, after relieving himself as quickly as he could. He'd only start to slow down when he got to the lounge door, secretly hoping his family hadn't seen how terrified he was. Nick finds this memory amusing, and he chuckles.

Nick and Kate made small talk as she dished up the soup.

"Are you alright?" Nick asked, expressing genuine concern.

Kate placed the bowls on the table, fetched cutlery from the drawer, and sat down opposite Nick. Her blue eyes are wide, and she hesitated before answering.

"There was someone hanging about near the house," she whispered.

"What do you mean, hanging about?" Nick asked, sounding surprised. Kate explained the two incidents from earlier in the day.

"Would you recognise them again? Do you think it was the same person both times?" Nick asked.

"I cannot be certain. The person in the garden had their face covered, and I didn't see enough of the person on the doorstep."

"A mask?"

"No, not a mask. A scarf pulled up under their eyes. They were also wearing a hood, obviously hiding their features." Neither of them had touched their soup yet.

"Why on earth didn't you fetch me?" Nick asked, appearing puzzled.

"I'm sorry. I was a bit shaken," Kate replied, embarrassed.

"It gave me the creeps seeing someone watching me and not knowing for sure how long they had been there?" She shuddered.

"I wasn't sure whether to mention it. I did not wish to appear neurotic." She feels her face redden.

"You were right to mention it. It could be someone casing the house," Nick said,

"Or maybe I'm blowing this out of proportion, and they simply entered unintentionally?" Kate added with a lighter tone.

"You're right," Nick said, his tone changing, "I'm programmed to expect the worst. It's my inner police officer." He still believes someone entered the property via the heath. He's always thought this house and its garden as not secure enough.

"I was planning to ask a favour. I have a meeting in London tomorrow would you mind if I stayed in one of the spare rooms tonight."

"I usually stay at home... mum and Dad's, but I forgot to ask them to leave me a key," Nick explained.

"Of course, Ria has made up the guest rooms; choose whichever one you like."

Kate is relieved that someone else is staying in the house tonight and feels her mood lift as they eat their soup.

After finishing, Kate inspected the bed in Lucy's former room and Nick retrieved his bag from his car. He sits in the driver's seat to call Elaine to explain the situation, as his original plan was to stay at her flat.

"Are you sure you don't mind? I don't feel happy leaving two women alone in the house now I know someone is hanging about," Nick explained.

"Of course I don't mind; although it sounds as if something needs to be done about security in that house, and sharpish," Elaine said.

"I will secure the heath gate temporarily in the morning; it shouldn't be accessible." Nick agreed.

Elaine sighed, "It's a shame I haven't seen you this week."

"I promise that I will make amends tomorrow evening. We will eat out... wherever you like!"

"Sounds lovely!" Elaine replied.

Nick went to Maggie's room to let her know that he planned to stay the night; and then joined Kate. Nick's entrance caused Kate to stop reading and close her book.

"Do you mind if I join you?"

"Please do," she gestured towards the other armchair.

Kate and Nick settled in together, both taking comfort in the quiet presence of the other. Their conversation flowed easily, filled with lighthearted small talk that brought a sense of calm to the room. Throughout the evening, Kate remained attentive, rising at intervals to check on Maggie, ensuring that she was comfortable and well cared for before returning to rejoin Nick. Their easy companionship created a warm and relaxed atmosphere as the evening drew on.

"Maggie was asleep. I had to wake her to take her medication," Kate informed him.

"What do you make of what gran asked of us the last time I was here?" Nick asked.

After a moment's reflection, Kate spoke thoughtfully. "It is important to recognise that various illnesses, such as fever or even something as common as a bladder infection, can have a profound impact on the mental state of older people. These conditions may lead to delirium, causing confusion and distorted senses of reality."

Nick, considering her words, asked, "So you think if Maggie watches a film, reads a book, or even experiences something in a dream, she could end up confusing those events with her own reality?"

Kate nodded in agreement. "Yes, exactly! When listening to Maggie's accounts or stories from her past, it is worth considering that while some elements may be true, others could be fabrications influenced by her altered state of mind."

Nick acknowledged her point, prompting Kate to elaborate further. "Careful consideration and sensitivity are needed to distinguish between genuine memories and those that may have been unintentionally invented."

Nick hesitated briefly before confiding, "Suppose I told you I've been looking into Matthew's death?"

The mention of Matthew caught Kate's attention, and her demeanour changed; her interest was clearly piqued. Nick continued, "I've learned that Matthew went to Ireland with his son to avoid the police, and according to reports, both died in a car accident."

"His son... also Maggie's?"

Nick explained his father's revelation and his findings in the old reports.

I am meeting with a retired investigator tomorrow afternoon to discuss a cold case from 1964. The Amanda O'Donnell murder.

Kate's curiosity was unmistakable; she leaned in, eager to uncover more. "O'Donnell—could she be related to the family?" she wondered aloud. The name Mandy surfaced in her memory, recalling that Maggie had mentioned a murder involving someone named Mandy during their first meeting. Despite her intentions, Kate had never actually checked online to verify the details, but now she listened intently, hoping Nick might provide the answers she sought.

Nick nodded. "Yes, that's correct. Amanda was my great aunt by marriage –my biological grandfather's sister-in-law."

Nick continued, sharing his recent findings about Matthew's family. He had uncovered that Matthew had a brother named Sidney. During his younger years, Sidney earned a reputation for being somewhat of a troublemaker—often finding himself at odds with the police and involved in various scrapes. However, as time passed, Sidney managed to turn his life around. He eventually set up a business that, at least outwardly, appeared to be legitimate and above board. This transformation from his tumultuous youth to a seemingly respectable businessman intrigued Nick and added another layer to the family's complex history.

"Sidney was interviewed, but there was no evidence that he killed his wife. Although, when looking through the archives, I came across some witness statements, and my grandfather's name appeared more than once. So, I am hoping the detective I'm meeting tomorrow may be able to shed some light."

Nick hesitated, then added, "I wanted to ask Gran about it before I talk to him tomorrow, but I've changed my mind because she's not feeling well."

Kate considered this and suggested, "How about your uncle Billy?"

Present Day

I watch her through the kitchen window, concealed in the darkness. Her features blur behind the lamplight, but her movements strike me with a piercing ache. She moves just as my mother once did. Hope flares inside me. She is alive. They all lied to me. Rage simmers beneath my awe. The emotions twist within me, making each breath a struggle. I balance the overwhelming urge to reveal myself with the paralysing fear of the truth's destructive potential. Night after night, I return to watch her. I search her gestures, longing for a sign that she remembers me. But the barriers divide us. Doubt gnaws at me. Would she ever welcome me if she knew? Earlier in the day, I found the courage to knock on the front door. I rehearsed what I might say. Then, I saw her silhouette approaching. Panic overtook me; my bravery faltered. I darted away, escaping towards the heath.

Now back again, watching from the shadows, my anger rises. Resentment builds within me—not just at her unknowing rejection, but at the sense of invisibility that defines me. I adjust my scarf, tucking it beneath the hood of my navy parka. My knuckles turn white as I grip the fabric, desperate for stability. With the shift, Kathryn sees me. For a moment, I stand my ground, brazen and breathless. Excitement courses through me; at last, my presence has stirred something in her. Even from a distance, I sense the fear in her eyes. It is not the response I longed for, but it is a response. I matter, if only as a shadow at the edge of her world.

CHAPTER FIFTEEN

Unmasking the Threat

Billy was relieved to find a parking space outside his mum's house. He pulled up behind what he recognised as Nick's Mercedes. He searched the glove compartment for a permit and tutted as he scratched off the date and time, making sure he had displayed it well within the windscreen. Billy has lost count of the parking tickets he has received, and he doesn't shake off the frustration easily.

Gone are the days when there were only three or four houses with cars along this road. They were among the few residents who owned a car back then. Kids could play on the street,

Billy received a call from Nick late last night; he couldn't speak over the phone but reassured him that his mum was fine. Curiosity piqued; wondering what it is that must be discussed face to face. he entered the house using his key. He made his way along the hallway to the back reception room,

Billy watched from the doorway. His mother, Nick, and the nurse were sitting together, chatting, and laughing. It took a few moments for them to notice him. His mother's face brightened; she rose from her seat to welcome him. Billy felt guilty for not visiting her for a few weeks; Lucy had, as usual, taken charge. His older sister has consistently been the responsible and reliable figure in their lives. As children their mother often needed her space.

Displaying a maturity unusual for her age, Lucy would say, "mummy is sad today."

Billy collected stamps with passion before he became a teenager. They would spend hours at the kitchen table, meticulously measuring each stamp's perforations with a gauge and then carefully putting them in the stamp album. Their father, George, brought home bundles of envelopes from the hospital where he worked, secured with rubber bands, and they would look for valuable stamps.

George Randall, the man they called Dad, was a strong and emotionally upright person. He was practical and a pioneer in mental well-being. Psychiatrists mostly used drugs such as Librium and Ativan or electric shock therapy. However, even back then George understood the value of a healthy lifestyle, diet, exercise, and meditation for mental well-being.

George always encouraged their mum to exercise, and Billy remembers her spending hours walking over the heath or gardening. George had hired a live-in au pair when Billy and Lucy were children so that their mother could focus on her own well-being.

Billy doesn't remember his mother as an overly emotional person or someone who cried often. They were aware she was having a 'sad day' when she became introverted and lost in thought His childhood wasn't a happy one, overshadowed by his mother's underlying depression. As they reached adulthood, her health improved, and she became more engaged as a parent.

After their father's death, their mother became introverted once again. Lucy was especially worried, and the family was in shock when they received a dementia diagnosis.

Billy wasn't surprised. He believed his mother had forgotten more than she cared to remember throughout her life.

As an auditor for finance, he is often on the road. His colleagues are aware of his mother's situation, usually they try to assign him to London clients. But he has been working in Leicester for the past month.

"What's this all about?" Billy followed Nick up the path to the gate at the end of the garden. He noticed him carrying a bicycle lock.

"Somebody has been hanging around, watching the house, so I'm going to reinforce the security at the heath gate. I'll use this for now," Nick held it up.

"It can only be temporary. We should plan to increase security and fit CCTV."

"That's fine! "Billy slightly perplexed, aware this could have been discussed over the phone. "I'll get some quotes."

"There's something else." Nick's tone became serious. Billy senses the gravity of the conversation to come.

"Uncle Billy, this may be a sensitive subject, and I don't wish to worry you," Nick starts cautiously.

"I'm worried now!" Billy said light-heartedly, not one for long-winded drama.

"I was here a few weeks back. Gran asked for my help in a professional capacity to find out more about how your father died." Nick winced in anticipation of Billy's reaction.

"George?"

"No, not George. Matthew, and Matthew junior, she's received a letter, and believes it's from your brother, which explains why she went to the hill."

Billy stays silent for a few moments, processing the information.

"Matthew! my father? we mustn't mention him," he utters, unable to hide his sarcasm.

If Nick noticed the edge in Billy's voice, he doesn't react but continues to inform Billy of what he knows so far. They sit on the seat under the pagoda as it's the only dry spot in the garden.

"I've always wanted to know more about my father and brother, but the subject was never discussed," Billy said, bitterness entering his voice. "If I tried to talk about it, it was shut down. It seems odd that Mum wants to discuss this now!"

Sensing Billy's frustration, Nick decided it best to listen without comment.

"Whenever I dared to ask questions, my dad — or I should say George — would hush me, and your grandmother believed it to be her own private grief. They never once considered our loss and the gaping hole it left in our lives. I have so many unanswered questions."

"Did she speak about my brother?" Billy enquired suddenly overcome with sadness.

"I didn't know about your brother until Dad told me," Nick replied with sympathy.

"Does your mother know about this?" Billy believed Lucy wanted to erase any memory of before that day.

"No, Dad told me not to mention it. Kate suggested I speak with you," Nick responded.

"Kate is aware of this too?" Billy asked, surprised.

Nick explained he was conducting his own investigation and was meeting with a former detective later that afternoon.

"Can I come along?" Billy asked, surprising Nick.

"Sure! I mean, of course," Nick agreed.

"Before we go anywhere, a little chat with mum is called for." Said Billy, standing, then strolling towards the house. Nick purposely follows slowly behind.

'Maggie'

Out in the garden, Billy and Nick are securing the heath gate. Kate is tidying while I listen to the news on the radio.

The men enter the room together shortly after the news bulletin finishes. They both wear serious expressions. Kate moves towards the door as if to leave the room, but they ask her to stay. Billy speaks first.

"I need to discuss something with you," he said. I don't answer, but I feel like I know what this is about.

“Do you have concerns or information you’d like to share about my father, Matthew, and brother?” Billy asks, his voice filled with concern. I do not respond.

I have always protected Billy. Because I thought he was too young to understand, we avoided the subject as he grew older. His expression revealed my betrayal. This upsets me.

Leaving my chair, I retrieve my handbag from the table. I remove a letter from it and pass it to Billy to read. Reading the letter takes him a minute or two before he gives it to Nick.

Having read the letter in full, they look at me, bewildered. Billy examines both the letter and envelope.

“No return address? What the...”

“The postmark is dated February, from Ireland!” Nick added, his brow furrowed.

CHAPTER SIXTEEN

August 1964 – The First Date

A few weeks have passed since someone found the body of a woman on the Hill, and they have not caught the assailant.

The newspapers report they have named her as Mandy O'Donnell, a twenty-four-year-old and the wife of Sidney O'Donnell. It is also revealed that she was expecting her second child.

I am walking home through the town centre on a late Saturday afternoon. I spot Matthew on the other side of the road. I increase my pace, hoping that he does not spot me, but it's too late. He breaks into a jog as he darts between the traffic and heads towards me.

"I'm sorry; I was going to come by to see you, but there has been a lot going on," he said, catching his breath.

"Do you fancy a frothy coffee?" he asked. We head down a side road to the cafe, which is still open, just! Stan, the cafe owner, is wiping down the tables and putting up the chairs.

I sit down at a table with its wooden chairs still in place, while Matthew goes to the counter and orders two cups of frothy coffee.

"I'm sorry to hear about what happened to your sister-in-law," I said awkwardly.

"Thanks," Matthew replied, then silence. I begin to think this was not a good idea. But then Matthew speaks again.

"It's been awful. There have been press hanging around for weeks!"

I am not pushing for information, but it seems like he needs to talk about the tragedy that engulfs his family.

Matthew explains that his brother is distraught, and his parents are just about coping. He reveals they are beside themselves with worry for his niece.

“Sidney has Maddie to think about, she’s only two years old,” Matthew said.

He reveals that his parents have taken the child to visit family in Ireland for a couple of weeks, so Sidney can deal with the situation here.

“Do they have any idea who did it?” I asked genuinely concerned.

“No, but the police are continuing to question my brother instead of getting out there to find whoever did murder her,” Matthew said, his voice filled with bitterness.

“Why are the police questioning your brother?”

“They always question the husband, although Sidney has a watertight alibi,” Matthew pauses, as if considering whether to provide the detail.

“Mandy was four months pregnant!”

“That’s awful!” I exclaimed, though I had already read this detail in the newspaper.

“Thanks for listening!” he said sincerely, his dazzling blue eyes framed by dark lashes looking deep into mine.

“Just so you know, I really like you. I didn’t want you to think I let you down purposely.”

"I understand. It must be a distressing time for your whole family." Of course, I didn't reveal how furious I was with him for letting me down. Although this was short-lived once I found out what happened. But I was disappointed Matthew had not been into the shop or tried to make contact before now.

"How do you fancy a day in London tomorrow?" He suggests, "I must get out of this town for a time. "This invitation was quite unexpected.

"I would love to," I beam.

They meet at the station the following morning. Church bells fill the air, ringing from many churches around town. We talk during the forty-minute train journey, getting off at Baker Street.

We walk for hours, visiting the gates at Buckingham Palace, through St. James's Park, down by the river to Westminster, and back to Regent's Park, where we eat the packed lunch that I have prepared.

While on my picnic rug in the sunshine, a squirrel took a piece of bread from Matthew's hand. We laugh, and he leans in to kiss me.

For an hour or two, he acts as if he hasn't another care in the world.

We arrive back at the station in our town at about five o'clock. As we come down the stairs at the main entrance, we overhear a middle-aged couple speaking.

"I knew it was him!" the woman said confidently.

"It's usually the husband. I don't know why they bother looking elsewhere," the man replied.

"Sidney O'Donnell deserves everything that's coming to him!"

Matthew suddenly disengages from the conversation we are having. He stops the couple and speaks abruptly.
"Excuse me, what did you say? Who are you to make judgement?" Matthew is defensive, and I blush with embarrassment.
At first, the man is taken aback, but then he quickly responds.
"I know you! You are his brother, I have seen you going in and out of the house. Sidney and is wife, they are our neighbours. Didn't you know? the police came and arrested Sidney earlier today. They say he murdered his wife!"

CHAPTER SEVENTEEN

Meeting The Detective

Billy and Nick walked into the lobby of the boutique hotel where they had planned to meet Stanley Chaplin. As they went to the bar, Nick realised he had never met Stanley before. Despite the bar's lively atmosphere, he noticed a man who he thought might be Stanley sitting in an armchair in the back of the dimly lit space.

Burnt orange and deep brown decor adorn the windowless bar, creating an ambiance that obscures the distinction between day and night.

During their journey to the hotel, Billy and Nick had discussed the contents of the letter, deciding not to bring it up with Stanley just yet. Observing Stanley, Nick noted he is a stout man, although his age is difficult to gauge, likely in his eighties. Nick noticed a slight unsteadiness as Stanley stood to greet them, but overall, he was in good health for his age.

His uncle took charge, and Nick listened as he described their link to Matthew and Margaret O'Donnell. Billy also updated Stanley on Maggie's current health condition.

"She's revisiting certain periods of her life," Billy shares.

"Old age — it's a terrible thing," Stanley sighed, added with a chuckle, "Although preferred to the alternative!"

Nick then described the information he gathered from police archives and expressed his desire for clarification. He mentioned finding a statement written by Stanley at the time of Mandy O'Donnell's murder.

"Can you tell us why Matthew was being questioned?" Nick enquired.

"We arrested Sidney O'Donnell in connection with his wife's murder. It became known that he may have been abusive during their marriage," Stanley revealed.

"And Matthew?" Nick presses.

"He provided his brother with an alibi," Stanley explained.

"Why didn't you bring charges?" Billy asked.

"Nothing concrete to go on, only circumstantial evidence. It was a tragic case. Mandy O'Donnell was four months pregnant and the mother of a two-year-old daughter. It has haunted me for years that we were unsuccessful in solving that case," Stanley recalled, shaking his head in frustration.

"How did she die?" Billy asked, shock clear in his expression.

Stanley reveals, "Someone strangled her whilst she walked home," and he added they found her body in an open space on The Hill.

"When did this happen?" Billy probes further.

"August 1964," Stanley responded.

"Wait!" Billy appears perplexed. "I was born in 1970, and my father died in 1972. I cannot see the connection between Mandy's murder years before and the reason my father disappeared with my brother."

"Is there a connection?" Nick ponders aloud.

Stanley hesitates, seeming uneasy about what he is about to tell them.

"Sidney was bad news! He thought of himself as a bit of a 'gangster,' involved in various shady activities, and Matthew was his henchman," Stanley explained. "Many people claimed Sidney abused his wife, but of course, nobody testified. Sidney supplied us with the names of witnesses who could confirm his location from the morning he left home until Mandy's body was discovered late in the evening. We were certain he was the culprit but lacked concrete evidence."

"It wasn't until January 1972 that we received a call from a witness claiming to have evidence implicating the brothers in serious criminal activity. Unfortunately, someone beat one witness before we questioned him," Stanley continued.

"I received another call on the day before your father's disappearance. It was from your mother, and she told me she knew who killed Mandy and why," Nick and Billy listened intently as DI Chaplin revealed as much as he could recall from memory about the arrest of Sidney O'Donnell.

CHAPTER EIGHTEEN

1964 – Prime Suspect

The witness walks up and down the lineup. She does not hesitate as she passes Sidney. After a few minutes, she informed us, "Sorry! I do not recognise anyone here!"

Robert shows the witness a photograph of Mandy, and the witness is sure it is the same woman she saw at the station on the 15th of August. She claims she saw her with a man! I can't help but wonder if she is mistaken about Mandy's identity because I showed her the same photo that was released to the press.

I feel our only hope of charging Sidney O'Donnell for the murder of his wife is to get a confession.

"Right, come on Bob, let's question him again. If we get nowhere this time, we are going to have to let him go!"

Robert and Sidney are sitting in the interview room. Sidney is sulking like a child. I walk in and sit opposite him. I'm going to try another tactic.

"Right, Sidney, what have we got here?" I pause while I sift through papers, allowing him to think I am going to produce suggestive evidence during this interview.

"Your wife was pregnant?"

"So you say," he said.

"She hadn't told you she was pregnant?"

"I told your mate here, no! I did not know she was pregnant, and I don't know what this has got to do with anything."

"Does your wife often go to the pub on her own?" Sidney looks surprised.

"Pub? No, not on a weeknight!"

"We have witnesses who say they saw Mandy at The King's Head pub early evening on the day she died."

Sidney's expression does not hide the cogs turning, but I can't tell if he is questioning why his wife was at a pub or if he is thinking about how he will talk himself out of a connection with her whereabouts that afternoon. I am now going to go for the jugular!

"Why do you think your wife did not tell you about the pregnancy? Is this possibly due to uncertainty on your paternity of the child?" I enquired in a measured and objective manner.

It worked. I am relying on his arrogance to trigger a reaction. His neck is bright red, and he is frowning.

"What the fuck!"

I've got a reaction to work on!

"You say you were with either your brother or your parents the entire day... between the hours of eleven o'clock in the morning and eight-thirty in the evening on the 15th of August 1964," I flick through more paperwork while Robert is busy scribbling.

"You were with your brother this whole time?"

"Yes, as I told him," Sidney points towards Robert.

"My brother Matthew can confirm I'm telling the truth, and the others I told you about?"

"We believe your wife was murdered on the evening of Wednesday, August 15th, 1964. She left the pub at 6:30, so we believe she was attacked soon after. Who do you suppose the man is that Mandy was with in the park and at the station at two o'clock on the same day?"

"What fucking man?" Sidney appears furious.

"Mandy wasn't with another man! She wouldn't" he said.

"So why do you think Mandy organised a babysitter? Where was she going?" I asked.

"No idea," he snapped.

"Your wife didn't tell you much, did she Sidney? Why is that?"

Sidney leans back in his chair. I can see I have touched a nerve, but he is staring me out. Robert takes a cigarette out of a packet and makes a point of lighting it, taking a deep breath in as he drags on it before blowing out a bellow of smoke in Sidney's direction.

This action has agitated Sidney. He fidgets in his chair.

"Either charge me or let me go and then get your arses out there and find the asshole who did murder my Mrs."

"One more thing."

"We have received information that your relationship with your wife was pretty volatile."

"Pretty what?" Sidney appears confused.

"Volatile, you know... lots of arguments that you hit her?" I continued without breaking away from his stare. Sidney's face is bright red.

"I know what it means, I am not an idiot!" Sidney becomes calm suddenly losing the hot headiness he displayed only moments before. "Well, they are fucking lying. Prove it!"

Other than a couple of growls as we continued to poke the bear, Sidney did not budge and did not give us enough to bring a charge.

"And the conversation with Maggie O'Donnell never happened; priority shifted with events."

CHAPTER NINETEEN

1964 – The Bridge Hotel

I have the afternoon free. I tell my mum and dad that I am meeting friends and then going to see a film. It feels easier than telling them the truth, that I am going to meet Matthew.

Especially since we agreed to meet at the pub. He asked if I minded going with him to meet his brother and suggested it as a good place to decide over a drink what we wanted to do for the rest of the evening. There's no doubt my parents would never agree to that.

Since I have never been to a pub before, I dress up, trying to make myself look older. I wear a two-piece grey suit and pin my hair up.

I meet Matthew at the door of the department store in town at six o'clock. We walk towards the Bridge Hotel. We talk while we walk, and Matthew informs me the police have released Sidney because he is innocent.

"The police kept him in custody for a couple of days when they could have been out there looking for whoever did this," he said.

"That's awful! But at least the police are now satisfied that your brother has nothing to do with his wife's murder," I said, but with genuine concern.

The evening feels autumnal, and I shiver as we walk. Matthew places his arm around my shoulder. He holds open the swing door, and the pub smells of stale beer, and cigarette smoke hangs in the air. I feel like choking.

"Sit down here, what would you like to drink?"

"Gin and tonic, please." It's the first drink that comes to mind.

Matthew chats with a couple of men at the bar and laughs with them before bringing over the drinks.

"Are you okay?" he asked.

I realise I must look like a rabbit caught in headlights, as this is so out of my comfort zone.

"Yes, thanks," I sip my gin and tonic, and it takes all my effort not to spit it out.

"I hope you don't mind starting our evening in here?" Matthew asked. "Sidney is meeting us here for a quick drink, and we just need to go over a few things."

"Of course, that's fine," I said, taking another sip of my drink. It's growing on me!

"I have finished working with Jim a bit earlier than I had planned, but my brother needs me with all that's going on, so I am going to step up to give him some time off to sort stuff."

"That's so thoughtful of you. Your brother must be grateful for your help!"

"He needs as much help as we can offer right now. My mum and dad will be back from Ireland later tonight. They heard about Sidney's arrest and booked the ferry home."

A man in his mid-twenties swaggers towards us. He is wearing a grey suit, his dark hair is slicked back, and he is holding a half-drunk pint with a cigarette hanging out of his mouth.

My heart is pounding. I recognise him as the man in the churchyard! Sidney acknowledges me by nodding before taking a seat at our table.

"Hello mate, I was wondering where you had got to," Matthew said affectionately slapping his brother on the back.

"I was round in the public bar," Sidney replied. His eyes are a distinctive blue, but more icy, not warm like Matthew's, which makes him appear cold.

Matthew and Sidney talk about work, and Sidney presents a note pad turned to a page listing pubs, clubs, and opens a leather-bound diary. After arranging them on the table, they discuss potential fill dates and locations.

"These may need convincing." Sidney points to named venues that have red ink next to them.

I feel uneasy, a sense of homesickness, which is weird, as the pub is only a mile away from home. I cannot erase the memory of seeing this man, Matthew's brother, grabbing what must have been his wife's arm in St Mary's churchyard only hours before she died.

The vision sketched in my mind is all I can see: his sadistic facial expression as he shoved her. Being physically shaken and rooted to the spot by his violent action, I am certain I am not mistaken, it was definitely him!

Sidney looks towards the bar where a woman enters from the door to the right of the bar. She has her back to us and is working the counter that runs along the back wall. Sidney appears distracted, and Matthew follows Sidney's gaze towards her direction. If I am not mistaken, I notice a 'look' between him and his brother. Sidney swigs the remnants of his pint and nods to our glasses.

"What are you drinking?" Sidney's gaze and steely blue eyes shattered my soul upon our first eye contact.

Matthew answers for me. I am not sure if it's because I have hesitated for too long or because it's the gentlemanly thing to do, not being familiar with pub etiquette.

"I'm sorry Mags, we won't be too much longer. We'll catch a film once we're finished here," Matthew said.

"Yes, okay," I said, only half-listening.

My eyes follow Sidney to the bar; the woman turns to serve him. I have seen her before! Although I only glimpsed her face, I recognise the way she wears her hair; It's the woman who was with Sidney in the graveyard! I hear myself gasp.

"Are you alright?" asked Matthew, his brow furrowed in concern as he studied my face, clearly perplexed by my sudden reaction.

"Yes, I... I just remembered something I meant to do today," I replied, hastily swallowing my drink to mask my unease. Matthew seemed to accept my explanation without question and diverted his attention back to the scattered papers before him.

My curiosity, however, was aroused by the ongoing exchange between Sidney and the woman behind the bar. They appeared to be engaged in a serious conversation, with Sidney maintaining a calm and collected manner. In contrast, the woman's body language betrayed her agitation; she shook her head repeatedly, visibly distressed by whatever was being discussed. Despite her unease, Sidney pressed on, his expression unchanging.

Eventually, with their conversation ending and the drinks now arranged on a tray, Sidney turned away and made his way back to our table. The woman lingered for a moment, her gaze fixed on Sidney, before she hurriedly disappeared through a door at the back of the bar.

Without a word, Sidney placed the tray in the centre of the table.

"Thanks, Bruv. Is everything okay?" Matthew asked, with similar concern he had shown me moments ago.

"Yeah... everything is just 'tickety-boo!" Sidney said with an air of sarcasm.

CHAPTER TWENTY

Deepening Divide

It was late afternoon, and Maggie would soon retire to her room. Kate checked on her. Maggie appeared lost in a daydream, gazing at the garden from her comfortable 'day chair' in the lounge. Kate approached and asked if she could join her.

"Of course, sit down. I was just thinking about my mum and dad," Maggie smiled.

"You know, you don't fully appreciate your parents until they are gone! You think they will always be here. When you are young, time is slow... and then you get old, and you can't keep up with the pace!" Maggie reflected.

"Yes, I can imagine," Kate replied, empathising with Maggie's sentiments.

"That was insensitive of me. I'm sorry," Maggie apologised.

"Don't apologise, you only miss something you've had. But I understand. I still miss my foster parents," Kate reassured her, lending an attentive ear as Maggie reminisced.

"When I was young, I often reflected on how deceitful I was. I never lost a wink of sleep. I lied to my parents for an entire year. They believed I was going out with friends from college or going to an art class or even to the library. I always made sure I was home on time because my mum and dad were paranoid about the murderer at large! Rumours spread about Sidney O'Donnell getting away with murder, so I didn't dare tell them I was courting his brother! Although eventually I had to tell them, and worse, that we planned to marry, I was pregnant!"

Curious, Kate interjected, "What year was this?"

"I married twice! Matthew and I married in 1965, and ten years later I married George. My first marriage was for love, the second was practical reasons. I must admit the second marriage was far happier, I often wonder if I had done things differently... listened to my parents. I could have avoided so much heartache!" Maggie reflected on her own experiences, chuckling, "But you can't put an old head on young shoulders."

Maggie's words made Kate consider her own marriage. In retrospect, she did not heed the many warning signs. Perhaps youth and naivety were to blame.

After eighteen months of living separately, Kate and Neil saved enough money for a deposit and bought a flat together. Kate had hoped that this milestone would mark a turning point, However, reality proved to be quite different from her expectations.

Neil's immaturity and lack of interest in creating a stable home life placed significant strain on his relationship with Kate. While Kate yearned for a future built on shared domestic goals and the possibility of starting a family, Neil's repeated reluctance left her feeling uncertain and insecure about what lay ahead for them as a couple. Instead of embracing their partnership, Neil often seemed to long for the independence and freedom of his single days. This yearning was clear in his frequent nights out with friends and his disregard for the financial limits they had agreed upon, further fuelling Kate's disappointment and sense of isolation.

The difficulties in their marriage extended beyond Neil's irresponsibility. A growing atmosphere of mutual distrust led to frequent arguments and periods of separation. As tensions mounted, Neil's engagement with their marriage diminished, especially as Kate's emotional needs became more pronounced. The widening emotional gap between them ultimately proved insurmountable, and their marriage ended in divorce.

Kate was thankful for Claire and her husband's constant support during this tough time. They offered her someone to talk to, comfort during her most vulnerable moments, and a safe place to stay when she decided to leave home. Kate valued their patience and understanding, as they never judged her emotional turmoil or pressured her to talk if she didn't feel like it, but instead provided her with the compassion she needed.

As Maggie kept exploring her memories, sharing more about her early married life with the mysterious Matthew, Kate understood Maggie seemed happy in revisiting those moments.

CHAPTER TWENTY-ONE

September 1967 - Growing Family

We never discussed Mandy's murder or the fact that the case is still unsolved! My heart goes out to their little girl. They didn't charge Sidney, but I have my doubts about his innocence.

I dislike Sidney and do my best to avoid him wherever possible. I also have concerns about the influence Sidney has over my husband!

Our joy was complete when our beautiful daughter arrived in August of 'sixty-six, just after England's World cup win. The suggestions for names became ridiculous; Goldie being one!

I rejected names referencing a football trophy or players! But I said yes to naming our first child after both of our mothers, so it's Lucinda, after Matthew's mother, and Violet after mine!

Lucy was just four months old when I discovered I was pregnant again. My mum debunked the myth about breastfeeding preventing pregnancy, which alerted me to the possibility of a new pregnancy so soon after my daughter's birth.

Our son, Matthew junior, was born in mid-July, so I now have two children under fourteen months old!

When Matthew agreed to Dad's suggestion of getting regular work, it pleased me, although Sidney is pressuring him to stay working in the pubs and clubs. Matthew has struggled to support both day and night jobs, and several employers have fired him for being late.

Matthew is determined to achieve his dream of fame and fortune. He refuses to abandon his brother, even though regular wage packets are not forthcoming because of ongoing company expenses and the need for the brothers to reinvest for the business to grow.

"The Army would have sorted him out!" I hear Dad grumble to my mother when he thinks I'm not listening.

Dad is insistent that Matthew earn a wage and take work suitable for a 'family man.' Matthew cannot resume as driver's mate for Jim, as Frankie, a friendly young man, replaces him. So, he called in a favour with a friend at a local warehouse. Matthew is working there, and I am aware he has only taken the job to keep Dad happy!

It must be difficult for Matthew to live with my parents. I so wish we could afford a place of our own! He feels like he's under scrutiny and criticism; it's as if we are living in a goldfish bowl.

My dad has insisted that we make-up a single bed in the storeroom behind the shop, which now doubles as Matthew's bedroom! Dad claimed Matthew disrupts the house by coming home too late.

Early morning finds me in Dad's chair, bottle-feeding the baby. Lucy is in her highchair, and mum is feeding her porridge.

Dad is eating a full fry-up, and a full plate of the same is sitting getting cold.

Matthew brushes through the plastic vertical blinds hanging from the door, bleary-eyed and partially dressed. I know he came in at around three o'clock this morning because I heard him while I was giving baby Matthew a night feed.

Dad glances at Matthew, who is sitting opposite him, and I recognise his anger; his face is red, and his eyes are flashing, although he said nothing!

Dad makes a point of looking at his watch and then the wall clock, as if comparing timepieces. It is eight o'clock; Matthew should already have left if he is to reach work by eight-thirty.

I get up from where I am seated and place the baby over my shoulder, patting his back.

"Do you need the bathroom? I am going to get the children dressed," I say to Matthew.

"Just finishing my breakfast, you go ahead, sweetheart," he replied, oblivious to Dad's anger or my mum fussing about to keep the peace.

"Do you want me to bring Lucy upstairs?" said mum, undoing the harness. I look at both men, and I feel uneasy leaving them alone.

"Yes, please!" I feel exhausted, and the day has only just begun.

Both children have gone down for a nap, and I am washed and dressed. Mum is in the kitchen doing the dishes, and Dad has gone through to the shop. I take a clean tea towel from the drawer in the sideboard and begin to dry.

"Where's Matthew?" I ask.

Mum, with a weary sigh, emphasises Matthew's tardiness as she hangs wet tea towels over the clothes-horse. "He washed in this sink and has gone off to work. Late!" Her frustration is tangible, and she wastes no time in putting away the dried breakfast crockery, her movements brisk and purposeful.

She continues, her words sharp with concern, “Your father has put his neck out by recommending Matthew, and it’s a slap in his face when Matthew does not get there on time!” The clatter of dishes punctuates her point, underscoring the tension lingering in the air.

Feeling the familiar irritation at my parents’ constant criticisms of my husband, I try to defuse the situation. “I know, I know, I’ll have a word with him!” I respond, though the frustration simmers beneath my calm reply.

“Matthew should try a little harder; we are only thinking of you. You should have a place of your own by now.” Mum stops what she is doing and turns to speak to me.

“It’s as if Matthew is just playing at being a husband and father...” I don’t allow mum to finish. I sling the tea towel I am holding down on the drainer and stomp upstairs.

This evening, Matthew has not come straight home from work, not even to change for his night work. This is unheard of!

I pace for a while with baby Matthew in his most comfortable position over my shoulder. Once I settle the children, I decide to go to bed since I feel worn out.

I am disturbed by the noise from downstairs. Glancing at the alarm clock beside my bed, I see it is near midnight, and I have been asleep for a few hours.

I go to the top of the stairs and can just make out an argument between Matthew and my dad! I creep downstairs. The door is ajar, and I can see my dad through the gap with his hands in his pockets, standing in front of the fire, which is now just embers of glowing ash.

Matthew is sitting on a kitchen chair with his back to me, leaning forward, using his knees for support. Even from this angle, I notice he is drunk.

"You bring trouble to my door, and I will skin you alive. Did you hear me?" My dad's face is bright red, and the veins in his neck are prominent.

"You're a hypocrite, Bill. Don't pretend you've been doing me a favour. You've never liked me. If I were to leave Maggie, it would suit you and Violet to have your little girl back to yourselves," Matthew slurs as he speaks.

"She is so socially awkward. It's pathetic and embarrassing!"

"Instead of running around town with your brother, playing at being a 'gangster,' it would suit us if you did a decent day's work to earn enough money to take care of my daughter and your children." Dad is furious. He continued to spit out his words.

"I know many people in this town! Never underestimate me or treat me like an idiot! I've been told what you and your brother are up to!" My dad's tone changes, losing its hot-headedness. His tone becomes more calculated.

"Do us all a favour. Why don't you leave tonight? I will take care of your family. You are a waste of space. Go on, walk out that door and don't look back. I will pay you too." The venom shocked me.

"Money talks with you, and you needn't threaten me to get it."

I swing open the door. I am facing my dad, and the fury is bubbling within until, like a volcano, I explode.

"Well, Dad... I will do you the favour because in the morning, I will pack up my family, leave, and I promise you; I will never look back!"

Matthew staggers to his feet and turns to face me.

"Hello, sweetheart," he slurs. I cannot respond. Turning away, I return to my bed.

Matthew has apologised this morning and has gone to sort 'stuff.' I am busy packing up our belongings. We agreed to stay at Matthew's parents' house. It will only be for a couple of weeks! My mum is sobbing as she helps me gather our things.

"Please don't do this, Maggie," she pleads.

I do not reply. I am still furious with my dad. He didn't speak to me before disappearing into the shop, and I haven't seen him since.

It is lunchtime by the time we have all our belongings. The pram with the babies sat end to end on the kerbside, waiting for a van to come and collect us.

I see my dad through the glass look my way before turning the 'closed for lunch' sign and then turning his back without a second glance.

A black Bedford van pulls around the corner. Matthew is in the passenger seat, and Sidney is driving. And like a sledgehammer, it hits me. Regardless of the temporality, we will be sharing a house with Sidney.

CHAPTER TWENTY-TWO

The Roses

Living in this beautiful house, Kate listened to Maggie's memoirs, and it was a struggle to picture Maggie as once homeless with two small children.

Kate sometimes wondered if Neil had agreed to have children, whether their relationship would have been different.

On his days off, it was the norm for Neil to go out with friends and not come home. The suspicion grew that he was being unfaithful. Kate was accused of being self-centred when she voiced her grievances. He needed 'down time!'

Then the bombshell: Claire announced she was pregnant, and Kate felt a twinge of envy. Life seemed to work out fine for Claire and Steven, while Kate was longing for the 'family life' she had never experienced. Feeling broody, she approached the subject with Neil.

"Isn't it lovely news about the baby?" she mentioned.

"Yea, when's the sprog due?" he asked, hope was lifted by this show of interest.

"In the new year," A grunt of sorts came from Neil as he lay on the sofa watching television.

"Wouldn't it be nice for us to have a baby?" she said.

"Fuck-off... I don't want kids; I can barely look after myself!"

"Not now! We have only just got our own home. I mean, in a year or two?"

"You must be joking... if you want kids, you married the wrong man!" This conversation led to an awful argument, and the more Kate became upset, the more Neil dug in.

She was stunned. Had they never spoken about this? In three years, had they never talked about whether they wanted children? It dawned on her... they hadn't!

The following February, Claire, and Steven welcomed a baby girl into their family. They named her Lacey, and she was every bit as beautiful as her parents had hoped. The arrival of Lacey marked a new chapter for Claire and Steven, cementing the happiness that Kate had so often admired in their relationship.

In contrast, the conversation about having children marked the beginning of a turning point in Kate and Neil's relationship. That discussion, fraught with misunderstanding and emotion, became the first stage in the gradual breakdown between them. Despite this, Kate was able to reflect and recognise that her time with Neil was not all bad. It only felt so when she was caught up in the intensity of her feelings.

With the benefit of hindsight, Kate could even acknowledge that Neil might one day become a good husband—just not now, and perhaps not until he had had the opportunity to gain experience and mature. At least Neil was aware of his own shortcomings, a trait that Kate now appreciated. In contrast, she recognised that she herself had been unable to see their marriage for what it truly was: a disaster, made easier to blame on Neil alone.

Kate understood that both she and Neil had been too young to give their marriage a real chance, each pulling in different directions rather than working together. This realisation brought her a sense of relief. She found herself able to let go of the disappointments of the past and begin to look forward to her own future, feeling renewed hope and possibility for what lay ahead.

Kate must admit to feeling bored and a little lonely during the past few weeks. She went to the theatre with Claire, which was nice, but since then has not gone out socially. It hadn't previously occurred to her that working as a personal nurse could be isolating. Maggie's family is aware of this as well. They have all been supportive, visiting regularly, and considerate of her well-being.

Maggie has her strength back and said she prefers to go for walks alone on the heath. Kate felt uneasy about her going at first, so she talked through her concerns with Lucy during one of her visits.

"Mother has always taken long walks on the heath, sometimes for hours at a time. It's the reason we decided against residential care," Lucy explained over a cup of coffee.

"We will respect your judgement!" Lucy added before suggesting "Perhaps you can assess how she is from day-to-day?"

Kate pondered for a few minutes.

"There are easy-to-use mobile phones on the market, especially designed for older people. We can programme my number into the memory."

"That's a good idea!" Lucy agreed.

"Maggie can call me if needed, and if she is out any longer than an agreed period, I will go looking!" Kate added.

Maggie is a stickler for routine. She walks for one hour every morning before lunch and works in the garden most afternoons. The weather has been kind too, sunny but not too hot.

They usually eat a meal together at lunchtime and have tea late afternoon. Maggie prefers a light supper at six-thirty in her bedroom, where she then settles in for the evening.

Not only has Maggie got to grips with her mobile, but Kate has also added an emoji sticker to the button she must press if she wants to call her. She has also taught her how to use an iPad, and she has downloaded Maggie's favourite music and audiobooks. Maggie does not enjoy watching television these days.

Nicholas has not visited for a couple of weeks, although he calls Kate's mobile to check on his gran. Kate gave him Maggie's mobile number, but he still rings hers, saying he doesn't want to disturb Maggie if she is resting. Nick explained he was terribly busy at work as they had caught up with a suspect in a case he was working on, but he would try to visit his gran soon.

It's an overcast afternoon. Maggie will be in from the garden shortly; Kate goes to the kitchen to set the tea tray.

Maggie enjoys formal afternoon tea using a Royal Doulton tea set, with biscuits and cake. Kate knows she is enjoying sweet food more. Tastes change, and food becomes bland for some people with dementia. So, while it is good that Maggie eats food she enjoys, Kate also watches her sugar intake. She has assessed negative for diabetes so far, and she wants to keep it that way.

Just as Kate finishes preparing tea, she hears the back door open. She hears Maggie washing her hands at the sink in the scullery.

"That's good timing," Kate calls out. She can hear Maggie mumbling to herself. She walks over to the scullery door.

"Who are you? What are you doing here?" Maggie said.

"Maggie, it's only me, Kate! I am preparing tea, and we have your favourite ... lemon cake!"

Kate allows Maggie a minute or two to decipher the situation before suggested they go through to the back room so she can admire her afternoon's work from her favourite armchair by the French doors.

She moves the trolley near to Maggie within easy reach and pours tea for both. She cuts a small slice of lemon cake and places it on one of the delicate china tea plates next to her.

"We should let it cool for a bit," Kate said.

Maggie is looking out at the garden. She appears less agitated than she was a few moments ago.

"Is Matthew going to join us?" she asked.

"It's only us for tea today," Kate replied casually. To tell someone their reality is false may cause extreme distress.

"I thought he was staying over, has he gone home?" asked Maggie, looking surprised.

"We had a lovely chat, so much to catch up with after all these years!" Maggie exclaimed, her eyes sparkling with delight.

"Yes, Maggie, it's only us for tea."

Kate aimed to steer Maggie away from talking about Matthew. She was concerned that recent events were having an adverse effect on her. Reminiscence could be therapeutic for some people with dementia, but it could also stir up disturbing memories, and Kate suspected this was happening to Maggie.

"Did you manage to 'dead head' all the roses, like you wanted to?" Kate asked, intending to bring Maggie back to the present.

"Yes, and I pulled plenty of weeds from the beds," Maggie replied.

"Sorry about before," she added after a few minutes.

"Of course, I know who you are; it's just... I didn't recognise you; my eyesight is getting worse!" Maggie appeared concerned, and Kate listened attentively.

"It's as if I am looking through a pair of... you know, what do the birdwatchers use over on the heath?" Maggie tried to describe her visual impairment.

"Binoculars?" Kate offered.

"Yes, of course, binoculars. But from the wrong end!" Maggie sounded exasperated.

"Would you like me to make an optician appointment for you this week?" Kate asked.

"I think that's an excellent idea. My glasses may need changing. I can only see when something or someone is right in front of me these days," Maggie agreed, sounding more positive and more like her usual self.

"Matthew had to point out all the roses that needed dead heading," she said.

Kate felt a pang of concern. She hoped Maggie hadn't developed another infection.

"I couldn't reach all the climbers around the pagoda, so Matthew reached them for me too. He is a good boy!" Maggie's thoughts seemed to wander again, a common occurrence with vascular dementia.

Kate hoped that Nicholas and Billy would uncover the identity of the person who sent the cruel letter. Targeting an old lady was despicable, and she had heard too many stories about older people being swindled out of their savings. Con artists went to great lengths to gather information and gain their victims' trust.

Also, Maggie's mention of her brother-in-law and his murdered wife troubled Kate. She wondered if it held any significance to why Maggie had been reliving the past so much lately. She made a mental note to mention it to Nick. Memories of Sidney had made her feel uncomfortable, and she didn't seem to trust him.

As evening approached, Maggie retired to her bedroom for a rest. Kate took a walk around the garden. The beautiful place was meticulously landscaped.

A wide patio ran along the back of the house, leading two steps down into the garden. Stepping stones adorned the lawn, guiding to the many flower beds. Hydrangeas, shrubs, bushes and hedges lined the fences. The willow tree stood proudly in the centre of a large lawn. A neatly laid path circled the grass areas and beyond this, more stepping stones led to stone raised beds, a pond and another patio area with stone seating beneath a large pagoda. Wisteria hung gracefully, and roses climbed up each side.

Kate had not ventured this far into the garden before. She sat on the stone bench, feeling the chill seep through her uniform. She watched as the large orange and black goldfish surfaced to eat, while a swarm of gnats danced above the water. It was peaceful, and she understood why Maggie enjoyed spending time down here.

Although Kate recognised that Maggie's condition caused delusions, something she had said earlier continued to bother her. She inspected the roses that grew up the sides of the pagoda.

The roses had reached the full height of the pagoda, seven feet tall. Kate noticed Maggie had recently dead-headed the plants at a lower level. She lifted her gaze above her head and stumbled backward as if struck by an electrical current. Beyond her reach, neatly cut stems greeted her.

Perplexed, Kate looked around, uncertain of what she was searching for. Her eyes scanned the ground, and then she spotted a shoe or trainer print in the soil of one of the rose beds.

Maggie had a gardener named John, a middle-aged man who visited regularly to tend to the lawns and conduct any heavy work. In recent weeks, John spent only a few hours each week working in the garden, cutting the grass, and trimming back hedges. Maggie preferred to potter by herself. Just last week, John had complained about cutting the grass too often or too low because of the dry weather. He had also mentioned treating the lawns and hoping for significant rainfall before his next visit. Kate was certain John hadn't been there today.

She returned to the house and glanced at the memory board, a communal tool they all used. Ria and John would add the dates of their next visits. Every day, Maggie would enquire about the date Ria and John had added to the notice board and ask about the day's events. Kate attributed it to her failing eyesight.

Today's board reads:

Today is Tuesday, August 6th August 2024

Lucy to visit on Thursday 8th August, (early evening)

John (garden) - next visit Friday 9th August, 8 am

GP appointment - Wednesday 14th August 14th, 10:20 am

Collection for church summer fete - Saturday 10th August (wine)

Waitrose delivery - Friday 9th August 9th, 10-11am slot.

Ria - next visit Wednesday, August 7th, 9 am

Kate's hunch was correct. John was not due until later in the week. She went upstairs to Maggie's bedroom, where Maggie was dozing in her armchair. Not wanting to startle her, Kate moved swiftly toward the table. Maggie opened her eyes.

"Did you enjoy your supper?" Kate asked as she collected Maggie's plate.

"Very nice, thank-you," Maggie replied.

"Maggie... who helped you in the garden today?" Kate enquired casually.

Maggie appeared puzzled.

"Why, John, of course! Do you know he's been our gardener since he was a lad?" Maggie responded. Without wanting to add to Maggie's confusion, Kate said,

"That's it, John!" pressing no further.

CHAPTER TWENTY-THREE

Safeguarding

Nicholas entered the kitchen, placing a white carrier bag holding his Chinese takeaway onto the counter. He slipped off his jacket, tossed it over a chair, and retrieved a plate, knife, fork and spoon from the drawer before settling onto a stool. Famished, he began opening the foil containers, but just as he was about to eat, his mobile phone rang, interrupting his meal.

Grumbling about the late hour and his empty stomach, Nicholas fetched the phone from his jacket pocket. He was surprised to see Kate calling when he glanced at the screen.

"Hi Kate, everything okay?" Nicholas answered.

Kate apologised for disturbing him so late, prompting Nicholas to ask after his grandmother. "Good to hear from you, is gran okay?" he enquired.

"That's why I'm calling. I am worried about her," Kate replied, her tone steady and purposeful. She began to outline her concerns about recent events, choosing her words with care and deliberation. Nicholas at once sensed the professionalism in Kate's approach, recognising that she was intentionally reinforcing her role as Maggie's carer. By speaking in this manner, Kate was clearly setting boundaries and ensuring her concerns were taken seriously, not just as a family friend but as someone responsible for Maggie's well-being.

"That's a worry. Have you spoken with my mum or Billy? They will need to know my gran's condition is deteriorating," Nicholas suggested, trying not to sound as though he was passing the responsibility.

"That's just it. Maggie's physical health is currently quite good, but she's been choosing to spend more time by herself. I have found evidence that makes me think she was not alone while gardening today." Kate went on to detail the events of the afternoon, she added, "My concern is that whoever sent that letter may have contacted Maggie. I have an obligation to report any concerns I have about her welfare as a potential safeguarding concern."

"I appreciate your position, and I'm pleased that you brought it to my attention," Nicholas assured her. He explained that they were taking the situation seriously, but tracing the posting location of the letter in Ireland had proved impossible. The investigation had led them to family members who might know more about the events leading up to his grandfather's accident and the immediate aftermath.

"Billy and I have scheduled a trip to Ireland at the beginning of September to see if we can find out more," Nicholas explained. "We are also hoping to find the source of the letter."

"I'm sure you're doing everything you can," Kate replied.

"We had hoped we could travel to Ireland sooner, but I am changing jobs and need to tie up a few loose ends," Nicholas admitted.

Kate reassured him. "I hope you don't think I'm fussing. It's just that when I worked for the NHS, we had clear policies. I feel a bit like a duck out of water with all that's going on!"

Nicholas looked to provide further reassurance. "We have booked the installation of CCTV, although it could take another couple of weeks. The new alarm system, too."

Kate remained unconvinced that these measures would keep Maggie safe when she was outside the house. "Maggie values her 'alone time' and spends so much time in the garden or out walking on her own. I believe it will upset her if I don't allow her this space."

"Is it possible to keep a diary and record anything gran reveals that may cause concern?" Nicholas suggested.

Kate explained that she kept daily records and had already documented her concerns in her notes.

Although uncomfortable asking, Nicholas asked that Kate not reveal to Lucy or Maggie the reason for his and Billy's trip to Ireland. "I don't want to upset them unnecessarily, and our trip may come to nothing," he admitted.

CHAPTER TWENTY-FOUR

September 1969 – The Night Visitor

It had been two years since we had left the shop, and we are still living in Matthew's parents' house. Matthew and I sleep downstairs in the front room, while Sidney, when he is around, occupies Matthew's old room. The three children share what used to be Sidney's bedroom. Sidney has chosen not to return to the house where he lived with Mandy. He felt overwhelmed with the dual responsibility of work and taking care of Maddie, so he has moved back home, where his mother can help take care of Maddie. The police determined Sidney was not involved in his wife's death.

Yet, it bothers me that the O'Donnell family behaves like Mandy never lived. It also troubles young Maddie, who is looking for love and affection, but her father seems emotionally distant. You can tell Maddie is upset by her behaviour. I try to include her, so she comes with us to the park and sits with Lucy and Matthew on my lap when we read. I try, but Maddie has frequent tantrums, and I carefully watch her with our kids.

One day, I discovered Maddie being spiteful to Matthew junior. I heard him scream in pain and rushed from the kitchen to find Maddie pinching his leg as he sat on the floor. She pinched harder as he cried louder. On another occasion, I had to intervene, as Maddie and Lucy scratched and pulled each other's hair. Although Lucy is four years younger than Maddie, she puts up a good fight in retaliation, Maddie is older and should know better! I expressed my concerns to Matthew, but his reaction disappointed me.

"She's just a kid, all kids fight! But you wouldn't know that being an only child," Matthew dismissed my concerns, and it is frustrating me.

"Matthew, Maddie is seven years old and crying out for attention! She has lost her mummy, and Sidney doesn't give her the affection she needs! She's angry and hurting!" I was furious with Matthew's dismissive attitude towards the child.

"She is too young to remember her mum," he said.

"Perhaps! But she's old enough now to know she's being shuffled around, ignored by Sidney! And your mum and dad are just as bad! They treat Maddie like a pet!" I exclaimed, unable to hold my frustration.

"What do you mean by that?" Matthew grew angry.

"Well, really! The only time they acknowledge Maddie is when they tell her to sit!" Matthew's defensive reaction resembled his brother's; his bright blue eyes turned black. But I couldn't stop myself; I continued my rant.

"And as for Sidney, he doesn't care about his own daughter! He is more interested in staying out all night with the 'barmaid' while he expects me to dress, feed, and take care of her," I vented, unable to keep the frustration from my voice.

I could empathise with Maddie's feelings, because, in many ways, I felt like a grown-up version of her. The O'Donnell family is so closed-off and insular that there seems to be no space for anyone from the outside. I find myself longing for the warmth and comfort of my own home with my mum and dad. Matthew has tried to reassure me every day for the past two years that our situation here is only temporary, that we wouldn't be living with his parents much longer—yet here we still are, with no end in sight.

"What bothers me is... none of you even mentions Mandy, and I wonder why?" I accused, my voice trembling with the weight of my emotions.

"You better watch what you say!" Matthew turns on his heel, slams the lounge and front door behind him, and he is gone. Leaving me to spend the evening with his parents, our two children, and Maddie.

I cannot concentrate for pondering on earlier events. The thought of packing my things and going home right there and then tempted me, but it has been two years, and Dad and I are still not speaking. Tears well in my eyes. I am aware of Matthew Junior clinging to my leg, anxiety showing in his wide eyes; I tousle his curly blonde hair. I reach down to lift him. His worried expression changes to a cheeky smile, and he hugs me around the neck, stroking my face and peering deep into my soul with big blue eyes. It feels as if we are one, my son and me.

Maggie - Present Day

I awoke from my dream, tears streaking my cheeks familiar sensation that always follows these moments. The image and scent of my little boy remain vivid, almost as if he were physically present beside me.

Lucy, even as a child, displayed confidence and independence, while Matthew was her opposite: shy and sensitive. The memory of his worried face, seeking comfort and security from me even when I was only a short distance away, is painful. It is heartbreaking to imagine the fear he must have felt on that dreadful day.

Lucy would often shrug off my attempts at affection, preferring her independence, but little Matthew cherished our cuddles. I wonder how he coped, knowing that I hadn't searched for him. Guilt is difficult to bear. Consumed by my own grief, I abandoned him when he was still so young.

Matthew senior held firm expectations for his son, hoping he would be boisterous and lively, but it was Lucy who enjoyed rough and tumble play. Had Matthew senior realised the depth of his daughter's admiration for him, perhaps he would have acknowledged her love. Looking back, he was no better father than his brother, not meeting his responsibilities to the children.

I place the blame with Jack and Lucy, Matthew's parents. They divided their attention between two places—here and Ireland. Sidney and Matthew were the youngest among four siblings. I only knew of their older, married sisters and their families, though I never met them since they lived on Ireland's west coast. The O'Donnell's skimmed over them, treating their sons as if they could do no wrong, while everyone else, including the grandchildren, seemed insignificant.

This parenting technique fostered a sense of entitlement and boastfulness.

Now, I sense I am being offered a second chance, even if only in fleeting moments. I appreciate being near him, even if his image is a little blurred.

A floorboard creaks outside my bedroom door. "Hello Kate, is that you?" I call out into the darkness. Reaching for my mobile, I see the time is 5:15. I hope she's all right—perhaps she believes I am still asleep.

I put on my dressing gown and slippers and walk down the hallway. It's dark, and I hear something moving below. I turn on the light, but the stairway stays dim. Feeling uneasy, I carefully go downstairs.

"Hello Kate, is that you?" I repeated, thinking she may not have heard me before. As I reach the halfway point, I lose my footing and, grabbing for the banister, my balance slips away.

CHAPTER TWENTY-FIVE

The Fall

Kate arrived downstairs early. She did not hear Maggie shouting until she reached the first-floor landing. She ran down to where Maggie lay in a heap at the bottom of the stairs. Maggie was in agony and let out a painful groan. Kate reassured her, told her to keep still, and hurried back up the stairs to fetch her mobile.

Within twenty minutes, the ambulance arrived, and the paramedics informed Kate that they would take Maggie to 'The Royal Free'. Before getting dressed, Kate contacted Lucy. She locked the house and hurried to the hospital. The casualty department was busy, and Kate discovered they had placed Maggie in a side room with several cubicles separated by purple curtains. Recognising Maggie's voice as she called for 'help' Kate joined her behind the curtain, and Maggie seemed very disorientated.

The young junior doctor informed Kate that Maggie was waiting to be taken for x-rays. In the meantime, they had given her powerful painkillers that should take effect soon. The doctor then disappeared out of the cubicle, and Kate could hear him speaking with another patient.

Behind the curtain, Kate noticed through the gap at the bottom, a pair of black lace-up patent shoes shuffling. She pulled the curtain aside to see Lucy hovering, ready to speak with someone.

"Lucy, we are in here," Kate said.

"Oh Kate, how is she?" Lucy rushed to her mother's side.

"We are waiting for an x-ray on her hip," Kate explained, detailing how she had discovered Maggie slumped at the bottom of the stairs.

"Was she conscious?" asked Lucy, stroking Maggie's head as she slept.

"I'm not sure if she became unconscious, but she was calling out when I found her. The doctors have prescribed painkillers, and she has only just dropped off," Kate said.

The porter arrived to wheel the bed down for X-rays, and Lucy and Kate followed them down the corridor.

They waited for about an hour before someone came to explain the results. A senior registrar from orthopaedics explained Maggie had fractured her hip, and they believed surgery was necessary. They informed Lucy and Kate that they would take Maggie to a ward, make her comfortable, and that she would go for surgery the next morning.

"How did this happen?" Lucy cried, and Kate felt awful.

"I did not hear her get up," Kate said.

"I don't blame you. We were not to know the stairs would be a problem, and she is usually so mobile!" Lucy was considerate of the guilt Kate was feeling, and she seemed sincere enough.

After settling Maggie on the ward, they left the hospital. Lucy returned to the house to collect Maggie's nightclothes and a wash-bag.

"Do you want me to come with you?" Kate asked Lucy.

“No, don’t worry,” Lucy felt it must have been quite a shock for Kate finding her mother.

“You catch up on some rest, and I will call you later and let you know how she is.”

CHAPTER TWENTY-SIX

Maddie's Ghost

The lamp attached to the headboard in the side room where Maggie was placed after her hip operation emitted a soft glow, which created a comforting atmosphere. Lucy had been sitting with her mother since she had returned to the ward. The effects of the anaesthetic were causing Maggie to call out in her sleep, repeating names like 'Rita' and 'Maddie.' Lucy remembered Rita, but the mention of Maddie made her stomach lurch. Maddie was her cousin, and her memories of Maddie from childhood were of a spiteful bully who would often bite and scratch her. Lucy had learned to fight back, especially when Maddie hurt her younger brothers.

The last time Lucy had seen Maddie was in 1989, when she turned up on her doorstep. Maddie had traced her through the telephone book, after discovering Lucy's married name.

She should have felt sorry for Maddie, but she was ashamed to admit that she didn't. Maddie stood on her doorstep, looking dishevelled.

"Hello, can I help you?" Lucy said, pretending at first not to know who she was, but at once recognising Maddie's piercing blue eyes.

"Hello Lucy, it's me!"

She smiled as she gripped the buggy handles, with a child inside whose gender was unclear due to denim dungarees and a colourful orange-and-blue T-shirt. The child had white-blond hair with tight curls and appeared to have just finished eating a packet of savoury 'corn puffs' based on the orange around their mouth and on their hands.

Lucy invited them inside but explained she had a doctor's appointment.

"I'm hoping that you or your mum can help me out." Maddie insisted she would not ask unless she was desperate.

"I'm not sure how we can be of help," Lucy replied in a cool tone.

Maddie explained that they had not sorted out her social security payments, and she requested a loan until she received an expected payment the following week.

Lucy went to her purse and took out two twenty-pound notes and a ten, which was all she had, and handed it to Maddie.

"I don't need that much," Maddie said.

"Keep it!" Lucy insisted.

"Thank you. I'll pay you back next week," Maddie said.

"No! I don't want to be paid back, and anyway, we're quite busy preparing for my baby's arrival, so it's best you don't call again!"

Maddie seemed deflated.

"Yes, of course. Thank you, Lucy. It's wonderful to see you. I was very confused when I returned from Ireland," Maddie's expression showed genuine sadness.

Lucy didn't comment. Maddie explained they placed her in a care facility not long after her return to England.

"When granddad died, grandma moved to Ireland, and after what happened to my dad, she couldn't. or wouldn't take me with her," Maddie revealed.

Lucy felt sympathetic toward her situation, but she didn't see herself as responsible. After all, Maddie was their cousin. They had problems of their own back then, and Lucy believed Maddie was revelling in being a victim. But they were victims too, and they had to brush themselves down and get on with it.

"Is there a possibility of reconciliation for you and your husband?" Lucy asked.

Maddic looked stunned by the question and remained silent for a moment or two, keeping eye contact. Lucy looked away, twiddling her fingers and thumbs while studying her hands.

"In the situation I find myself in, I have considered going back to him many times," Maddie replied.

"He is wealthy and well-respected. But he is cruel behind closed doors, and because others see a different persona, this makes him even more dangerous. That's what stops me from going home."

"In what way is dangerous? Did he hit you?" Lucy asked, appalled.

"Sometimes, but it's psychological, like a dripping tap," Maddie explained, leaving Lucy struggling to understand what she meant. It felt dramatic to her.

"At the start of our relationship, I confused his obsessive behaviour with his caring for me. Over time, he didn't allow me to go out alone, restricted my finances, and accused me of having affairs. It became difficult when I became pregnant, and he doesn't believe our child is his."

"And is it his?" Lucy asked.

"Of course!"

Lucy's question offended Maddie, but whether because of hormones, naivety, or just being unkind, Lucy felt little empathy for her cousin's situation. She wanted Maddie to go away.

"He's successful... done well in his profession," Maddie went on, her tone a mixture of resignation and irony. "He owns his own business—a communications company that's growing all the time. He employs hundreds of people." She paused for a moment, letting the weight of her words settle between them. "To everyone else, I appear to be a privileged woman, someone in a two-point children marriage who has everything she could possibly want!"

Maddie watched Lucy's facial expression closely, noticing her cousin seemed miffed. "You look surprised Lucy," she remarked, her brow furrowing with a hint of frustration. Lucy felt her cheeks flush, but she offered no reply and saw no reason to justify her reaction.

"I'm not only worried about my safety, but I'm also concerned about the safety of my child. He's jealous," Maddie continued.

"Where did you meet your husband?" Lucy enquired, a little intrigued.

"He was my boss," Maddie replied. Lucy pulled a face as if to say; well, what do you expect?

"I've been reading in new mother magazines that husbands can feel a little left out when a child is born. Women should act to reassure them since the relationship came first," Lucy said, as if an authoritative for the topic.

"Parents owe it to their children to try harder in their marriage. Children need two parents. It's too easy to leave a marriage," Lucy scoffed.

Maddie looked hurt by Lucy's remark and prepared to leave. Maddie's description of her life felt alien to Lucy.

"Thank you for your help, Lucy," Maddie said, handing her a piece of notepaper.

"Would you mind passing my number to your mother? I'm only allowed to give it to close relatives in case of an emergency. I've written a password that she needs to say if she calls. Please don't share it with anyone else," she added, pushing the sleeping child's pushchair out of the door.

Lucy crumpled up the lined notepaper with Maddie's contact details and threw it in the bin. She didn't want Maddie's problems to disrupt their lives. She never told her mother about Maddie's visit.

As Lucy was about to embark on an exciting journey, her parents eagerly expected the imminent arrival of their grandchild. She didn't want to risk anything that could cause her mother to become unwell again. However, in the months after her son was born, Lucy realised she should have been more compassionate toward her cousin. Where was the female camaraderie? Lucy saw her younger self and realised she had only thought of herself. After all, Maddie's entire family abandoned her when she was just a child.

Now they were in a side ward, and Lucy watched as her mother's eyes flickered beneath her closed eyelids. The doctors increased her medication to help her relax after her surgery. Maggie had been waking up startled and confused about her whereabouts, but now she seemed at peace in her dreams.

CHAPTER TWENTY-SEVEN

December 1969 – Rita

Matthew and I feel like ships passing in the night, and my exhaustion grows as Christmas approaches. Maddie is in my care by unspoken arrangement since Jack and Lucy are in Ireland to celebrate with their daughters.

Last night, the woman from the Bridge Hotel arrived at our house, her emotions spilling over as she screamed and shouted outside. I watched from behind the net curtains in our makeshift bedroom at the front of the house. Sidney, barefoot and dressed only in a vest and trousers, went out to confront her, urging her to be quiet because the children were sleeping. Her anger unchecked, accused Sidney of betrayal and threatened to reveal all to anyone who would listen.

Sidney, exposed to the cold, tried to lead her gently towards the house. Though she resisted at first, she allowed him to comfort her as she sobbed. Meanwhile, Matthew stirred beside me, the orange glow of the streetlamps casting shadows through the curtains onto our makeshift bed—just a collection of sofa cushions. He rubbed his eyes, confused by the commotion.

"What are you doing? Come back to bed!" Matthew asked, still half asleep. I whispered back, "It's the barmaid; she's here!" But he seemed unconcerned.

I listened as their argument moved from the street into the hallway. Sidney dismissed the barmaid's accusations as madness. From what

I could gather, she was accusing Sidney of having an affair, and I found the nerve of the accusation astonishing.

After listening behind the door briefly, I returned to bed and wrapped my jacket for warmth. Matthew had pulled the sheet to his side, leaving me uncomfortable, so I snuggled up to his back and tried to sleep.

Sidney and Matthew left early the next morning. Sidney had not left his bedroom door open leaving me unsure whether the woman was still in the house. Since I had not heard her leave, I assumed she was. I prepared breakfast for the children—porridge—and dressed them in their hats, coats, and scarves for the cold walk to Maddie's school. She only had a few days until the Christmas holidays. Jack and Lucy had asked Maggie to bake cupcakes for Maddie's end-of-term party. Matthew sat in the pram wrapped in a blanket, Lucy perched at the end, and Maddie held onto the handlebar. At school, I watched Maddie line up with her class until her teacher led them inside, then returned home. Matthew Junior was sleeping, and I parked the pram in the hallway. Lucy wandered off to the back room.

"Hello, pet," said the woman, stood there in her short purple dress and white PVC boots, her brunette hair messy and a red mark under mascara-smudged eyes.

She introduced herself as Rita. "You must be Maggie, its nice to meet you finally!" I offered a limp handshake. "There's tea in the pot," she added and returned to her seat at the dining table and resuming her newspaper.

The thought of tea made me feel nauseous. Rita noticed my pallor. "Are you okay? You've gone several shades of green," she said, seeming genuinely concerned. I asked her to watch Lucy before rushing outside to vomit.

When I returned, Rita was sitting on the floor, showing Lucy the doll. She asked if I felt better. I groaned, and she suggested I lie down. Despite the temptation, I refused, got water, and then sat with her. Rita moved opposite me, and we had a polite conversation about the children and Christmas plans. I realised I enjoyed her company.

Rita lamented her appearance, explaining that all her belongings were still at the pub. I asked if something had happened, noting her distress the night before. Rita revealed she had been sacked after losing her temper behind the bar and admitted attacking the landlord's daughter. The situation was messy.

Rita had confronted the young woman after hearing rumours of her involvement with Sidney. The daughter confessed to an ongoing affair with him, which devastated Rita. "She's only eighteen!" Rita exclaimed, angry and disgusted. Sidney denied everything, but Rita's tears flowed as she recounted how much she had given to the pub over the past ten years.

Lucy, sensing the tension, handed Rita her doll to comfort her, and together we laughed at the child's innocence. I offered Rita clean clothes and showed her the bathroom. With her make-up removed and wearing my clothes, she looked younger, her freckles visible and the red mark on her cheek now revealed as bruising.

Curious about the mark on her face, I asked her about it. Rita replied, “I believe the little cat hit me back,” relieving me of my suspicion that Sidney was responsible. Rita sensed my concern and confronted it.

“You’re wondering why I haven’t run for the hills after finding out about Sidney and the landlord’s daughter?” she asked. I nod. Rita replied, “He treats me well enough most of the time. If it’s handed to them on a plate, most blokes will take a bite! I’ve seen how she flirts with the punters.”

When I asked how long she’d known Sidney, Rita hesitated, saying a few years. I suspected she was being evasive, recalling seeing her years ago during my first pub date with Matthew.

“I’ve seen you before,” I said. Rita looked surprised, and I explained she had served us. Rita laughed, joking about her role in my ‘love story, but I pressed further, mentioning another occasion and my memory of seeing her hurt at St Mary’s Church on the day Sidney’s wife died.

Rita remembered the day Mandy died, acknowledging its significance but denied being with Sidney and I must be mistaken. “That was an awful tragedy, but lucky for him Sidney was with Matthew all day!” This surprised me, as I knew it was not true. My surprise not hidden I asked, “Are you saying Matthew is Sidney’s alibi?” She affirmed as if standing before a judge and jury, “Yes, and witnesses can corroborate!” This revelation left me confused and frustrated. The strength of my conviction seemed to catch Rita off guard.

"You're lying to protect Sidney, I know who I saw!" I accused, struggling to believe that Matthew would also agree to conceal the truth about something so serious. My questions tumbled one after another, not giving Rita the chance to respond. "Matthew could go to prison. Why would their parents agree to this?"

Rita's face grew tense with worry as she urged, "Maggie, you must let this go!" Her concern only fuelled my suspicions. "Are you covering for Sidney for something he did?" I pressed.

She shook her head. "No! but you are right, I was with Sidney on the day his wife died... all afternoon and evening. He did not murder his wife!" she insisted.

"Then why would he lie to the police about who he was with if he didn't do it? He has nothing to worry about!" I countered.

Rita sighed, her voice softening. "It's more complicated than that." She explained that on the day Mandy was murdered, she asked Sidney to meet her in St Mary's churchyard to end their relationship. "I soon realised Sidney would never leave his wife and child," Rita then recalled the churchyard incident, describing how Sidney became angry. Fleeing from him, Rita tripped, catching her heel and falling onto the gravel. The impact resulted in bruising and a cut on her head, along with visible grazing on her face and arm. She paused, reflecting on the moment, and then pointed to a small scar on her forehead as evidence.

"Sidney regretted his actions and persuaded me to come here," Rita continued. "His mum suggested that I go to hospital because the cut on my face was deep, but I refused. She cleaned the wound instead." Rita's voice softened as she explained the aftermath.

Sidney told his parents she was a stranger whom he had helped after a nasty fall in the street. "They didn't ask questions; they were kind," she said. "I suspect they realised there was more to the story, but they didn't press for details."

I am stunned by this revelation, struggling to reconcile Lucinda and Jack's protective nature with the idea that they would allow Sidney to involve Matthew. "That does not explain why Matthew is Sidney's alibi instead of you or his parents, if what you say is true," she pointed out.

Rita explained that she and Sidney had agreed she should make her way back to the pub. When she arrived, she told the landlord she had fallen. Due to the grazing on her face, the landlord accepted her explanation without question, and as far as Rita was concerned, that was the truth.

"The next day, Sidney called me from a call box to report that someone had found his wife dead. He sounded shocked. The police questioned Sidney and everyone who had been with him the previous day. Sidney was insistent that I stay out of it; he said my involvement could create complications."

Rita paused, her hands twisting in her lap as she avoided my gaze. I watched her, thinking she looked guilt ridden.

"Matthew testified they were together all day, and his parents were there to witness it," Rita continued.

I frowned. "Of course, he didn't want the police to question you if you had cuts and bruises!"

Rita looked anxious, her eyes darting to the floor as she fidgeted with her sleeve. "Maggie, you mustn't tell anyone what I've told you! They could get into big trouble! I am telling the truth; I was with Sidney from one-thirty in the afternoon until I arrived home at eight-thirty. None of this matters because Sidney did not murder Mandy!"

CHAPTER TWENTY-EIGHT

Confronting the Fear

A soft glow bathed the house, with the main hall, landing, and lobby lights left on. Kate sat in her usual cosy chair by the log burner in the snug, feeling on edge; the house feels cold and empty with Maggie being in the hospital. Persistent rain marked the bank holiday weekend. On Sunday, Kate attended Claire's annual barbecue, where Steven insisted on cooking under a gazebo. Claire had rearranged the outdoor furniture in the conservatory to accommodate the guests. Claire offered Kate to stay with them for a few days, she was concerned about her being alone in the large house. However, Kate, not wanting to impose, and feeling quite at home in Maggie's house, declined. At the barbecue, James, Steve's brother, entertained the gathering with his anecdotes while the children ran around enjoying the desserts laid out on the kitchen table.

After bidding farewell and heading home by train, Kate arrived to find the house shrouded in darkness, save for the orange glow of the pavement. As she walked along the tiled path, she noticed what resembled the shadow of a person in one of the ground-floor windows. Feeling uneasy, Kate entered the house, leaving the main entrance wide open just in case. With her heart racing, she fumbled to find the light switch and was relieved when the room illuminated. The intruder turned out to be nothing more than a standard lamp in the bay window of the front reception room.

Kate secured the main door and prepared for bed. The evenings were getting shorter as autumn seemed to approach, even though it was still August. The persistent rain had made the evenings dark and dreary. Kate appreciated the grandeur of the house during the day but admitted that the shadows and emptiness made her nervous at night. She had been used to living in a modest flat before. Maggie was recovering nicely; doctors praised her physical fitness and lean body for her remarkable recovery. Maggie's family often phoned Kate, knowing she might feel lonely.

Kate had visited Maggie the day after her operation, and she was initially sitting up and looking well. Other family members were also there. Morphine managed her pain. Maggie soon became sleepy, causing her to share muddled dreams and distant memories. Sensing Lucy's discomfort, Kate kept the conversation light and the visit short to give the family space. Trying to refocus her thoughts, Kate returned to her book. She planned to read a bit more and then make herself a sandwich. The dire weather had kept her indoors, and she hadn't left the house since returning from Claire's barbecue. Planning to go shopping the next day after visiting Maggie. She read by lamplight, struggling to see the print. Glancing at the clock, she realised it was almost eight o'clock, and darkness had settled in the orangery.

Deciding to turn on the lamps, Kate walked to the sideboard near the glass doors. But as she switched on the lamp, she saw a silhouette through the glass—a man in a dark hooded coat with a scarf wrapped around his face. Frozen in fear, she wondered if she had secured the French doors. Her eyes darted to the handle, and she noticed the key was in the lock. The man stood motionless in the darkness, staring at Kate. He then turned casually and walked through the open side door, which led to the side alley and past the scullery door. Trembling and struggling to breathe, Kate grabbed her mobile phone and dialled the emergency services. She requested the police, struggling to articulate her emergency.

The operator tried to assess the situation, asking if Kate was in immediate danger and if she could remove herself from the situation. Overwhelmed, Kate described the detail; the operator assured her that help was on the way. Recommending that she stay put, keep her phone nearby, and lock all doors from the inside, the operator's words offered little comfort. Kate realised she needed to leave the room and check all the doors. She cautiously checked the French doors, relieved to find them locked. Kate moved through the lobby to the kitchen, switched on the lights, and made sure that she locked the back door as well. As she returned to the main hall, she noticed the front door was ajar.

A Presence in The Crowd

I sit in a coffee shop across the street; my eyes fixed on the entrance of the station. My coffee, untouched and growing cold, is forgotten. Kate has been absent the entire day, and I hadn't seen her leave. I slept through the morning, the exhaustion from the previous night's commotion in Hampstead overwhelming me. The area had been lively with bank holiday revellers; their singing and laughter lingering long after midnight. Oversleeping was the price I paid for staying in the central part of town., leaving me with a familiar sense of frustration mingled with anxiety. Now, I am forced to predict Kate's movements, determined not to miss another opportunity. A memory intrudes—just weeks earlier, I had found myself concealed behind a shrub, watching Kate as she tended to the garden of the large Victorian house. Sunlight danced through the willow leaves, illuminating her features. She looked startled, and her resemblance to her mother was so striking that it stole the breath from my lungs. That moment—the surprise in her eyes, the uncanny echo of a woman lost to me, the only woman I remember as mother—planted the seed of my obsession. Every encounter since has been a search for that same connection, as if understanding Kate might finally reveal the truth behind my fractured family.

I have befriended the old woman; I am another thread in the tangled web. I visit her often; she recognises me, though she mistakes me for her own son. My mind, adrift in time, loops over memories. Our first meeting had been unexpected; I was trespassing in her garden when she surprised me, walking sprightly behind me. She found me among the hydrangeas, confused but kind, her thoughts drifting to a son who had left long ago. I allowed her the fiction; it gave me access to her stories, whispered fragments about Kate and the person I ache to understand, if she is real at all. Earlier, the old woman had mentioned that Kate was visiting a friend by train. I cling to this detail, desperate, convinced that she will return the same way. As dusk falls, I stand in the cold doorway of a shop, the rain relentless and unyielding. The downpour soaks through my coat, chilling me to the bone. They say it has been a good summer; I'm unable to endorse this, for each surveillance has been accompanied by a downpour. Each drop intensifies my nerves, prickling my skin and quickening my heartbeat. I wonder why Kate moves through life untouched by the storms that batter me.

My grandparents once warned me: Kate's mother had bewitched my father, leading him down a path he might not have chosen alone. Now, I fear that Kate holds a similar power over me. The idea gnaws at me, my obsession twisting into resentment. Is it an inherited spell, or merely the echo of a longing passed through generations? As night deepens, I wrap my scarf tighter, trying to hold off the shivers. When Kate finally appears at the station entrance, my patience is rewarded; my instincts have been correct. I follow her through the gloom, keeping just enough distance for doubt and dread to linger. The rain dulls the streetlights, blurring my vision and cloaking me in anonymity. Each step is silent and measured, anxiety thrumming beneath the surface. Kate unlocks the door to her house, and I slip in behind her. The walls close around us, the air thick with riddles. Her keys, tossed carelessly onto the oak hall stand, seem almost an invitation boundary crossed, a line I cannot uncross. I hesitate, the hush amplified by the sound of rain on glass, each uncertain heartbeat echoing in the silence. Inside, my obsession sharpens; I am closer to her now, yet no nearer to peace.

CHAPTER TWENTY-NINE

Missing Keys

Billy parked his car behind Nick's Mercedes outside the house and turned off the engine. The time was just after ten. Nick had called him after finishing his telephone conversation with Kate. A police car was also parked a short distance up the road.

They entered the house using Billy's key and called out. Kate and a male police officer were coming down the staircase. Kate apologised. "I am so sorry to have called you so late, but I was afraid the intruder might still be in the house,"

During her call, Kate had explained to Nick that the intruder had used her keys. The set she believed to be in her handbag were missing! She was apologetic, she hadn't noticed they were gone because she had been using the set hanging on the hook in the kitchen since returning from her visiting friends.

"After the search, they found the house empty," the police officer confirmed. "Upstairs looked undisturbed," Billy noted their meticulousness. The officer dismissed Billy's gratitude with a shrug. "My colleague is checking out the back." They suggested they change the locks that night, and when they got a chance, update the security. "Have you considered an alarm system?" the police officer asked. Billy replied defensively, "We've scheduled an emergency locksmith for tonight, and we're already requesting quotes for a new CCTV and alarm system."

Kate's worried expression encouraged Nick to take the lead in any further discussion. They headed towards the kitchen, where another police officer was checking the windows.

"They expected the property to be empty, and seeing you probably scared them off," said the second officer.

"It's lucky you spotted him before he entered the house. Coming face to face with him made him flee." By her expression, Kate didn't seem reassured.

"Most thieves are opportunists. You may have dropped your keys outside; they found them and returned when they thought the property was empty or you left the door open by mistake? Who knows!" advised the first police officer.

"But he was watching me from the orangery? He could have been in the house without me knowing because the front door was open!" Kate pointed out.

The two officers exchanged glances, and Nick noticed their shrugs. Their deduction did not convince him either, especially considering there had been an intruder on two earlier occasions that they knew about.

The first officer remarked, "We have finished here! There is no evidence of anything being taken. Of course, if you discover anything missing, you should contact the local police station, and they will provide you with an incident number."

"Thank you, I will see you out," Nick said, and the two officers followed him to the front entrance.

"Kate has seen someone lurking in the garden on a couple of occasions."

"A coincidence, you live on a cut-through from the heath to town," said the second officer before adding, "An opportunist taking a shortcut. As my colleague had suggested, enhance the security for peace of mind."

Nick had ushered the police officers out, reflecting on the fact that he was supposed to be staying in Finchley with Elaine, how can he leave Kate alone in this house after tonight's events? They had intended to share the news of their engagement this week, but Maggie's accident had led Nick and Elaine to postpone both the announcement and informing his family about his upcoming work transfer and his relocation. He reasoned that such news could wait until after his trip to Ireland.

Meanwhile, Billy had poured two generous glasses of wine. As Nick entered the kitchen, he watched Billy and quipped, "Do you carry that stuff around with you? I take it I'm driving you home?" Billy smiled as he studied the label of the red wine bottle he was holding. "What's this? I found it in the larder, leftovers from Christmas! About your other question, the locksmith has just called, and he will not be here for another couple of hours. Billy said, "Anyhow, Kate looks like she needs a drink!" Billy handed the glass to Kate. "Get yourself a glass Nick. You won't want to be driving back to Oxfordshire tonight!"

Nick did not correct him or explain that he has been staying local. Although this prompted Nick to call Elaine. A flash of annoyance appeared in her eyes when Kate had called his mobile, surprising him, and if he wasn't mistaken, a hint of jealousy. "Hi, my darling, I thought I would call and update you on how things were here."

Nick explained that they are waiting with Kate until the locksmiths arrived to secure the doors and because it could take several hours; he will stay over so as not to disturb her. Elaines earlier reaction must have been his imagination, as her response now was one of clear understanding.

"My god Nick, you can't leave Kate alone, I bet she's terrified!"

After finishing his call, Nick returned to the kitchen, fetched a glass from the Welsh dresser. He joined Kate at the table. Billy poured wine into Nick's empty glass as he sat down. Kate listened to Billy's travel stories through bustling Asian cities, and the kitchen filled with laughter. The aroma of wine mingled with their shared amusement, creating a warm and convivial atmosphere.

Billy's eyes sparkled with mischief as he recounted, "There I was at monkey island; abandoned by a taxi driver to whom I'd paid my last bit of cash. All I had left on me was a few baht." He chuckled, shaking his head, his voice ringing with incredulity. The kitchen lights glinted off the wine glasses as Kate leaned in, her cheeks flushed from laughter and the late hour.

"So, I flagged down a tuk-tuk, and we were about to set off when, out of nowhere, a monkey jumped up onto the seat beside me," Billy continued, his hands miming the monkey's sudden appearance.

"Oh, no! What did you do?" Kate asked, her laughter bubbling over, eyes wide with delight as she pictured the scene.

Billy grinned, glancing between Kate and Nick. "I sat still like a statue, absolutely petrified. Those animals can be vicious! The monkey just sat there, staring me down, it was intimidating." He gave a theatrical shiver, making Kate laugh even harder, while Nick grinned, shaking his head at his uncle's misadventures.

Without missing a beat, Billy added, "But the driver didn't bat an eyelid. The monkey rode with us for a couple of miles, then at the traffic lights, it hopped out and dashed off; as if nothing had happened!"

The laughter lingered, echoing off the kitchen tiles and softening the earlier tension in the room. Their amusement subsided, and the evening settled into a calm, drowsy hush. Just as the last giggles faded, the faint rumble of a van pulling up outside signalled the locksmith's arrival, the sound cutting through the quiet comfort of the kitchen.

The locksmith worked; his tools chimed in the hallway. Changing the lock on the front door was straightforward, but he explained that ordering new mortise locks for the orangery and scullery doors would take a little longer because of their age. The faint scent of metal and oil mingled with the aroma of wine as he secured the doors with Yale locks, also fitting a sturdy security chain to the back door.

"Once we replace the original locks, you can keep the Yale locks for extra security, or if you'd rather, I can make good the doors and restore them to how they were," the locksmith explained as he packed away his tools. Billy nodded, walking the locksmith to the front door and exchanging quiet words before returning to the softly lit kitchen.

"It's one-thirty, Kate. You look shattered. I know I am," Billy said, stretching as he returned to the kitchen.

"Yes, I'm going to turn in," Kate said, standing.

"Both bedrooms are made up, and there are plenty of towels in the airing cupboard. Good night."

"Good night, sleep well," replied Nick.

The sun is shining through the window; it's ray's stream across Nick's face, and he stirs. He hadn't pulled the curtain the night before! He rubs his eyes and looks at his watch; it is ten minutes to seven.

The house was silent; the only sound was the soft creak of floorboards beneath Nick's feet. He fetched a towel from the airing cupboard, its familiar warmth comforting as he padded towards the shower. Under the spray, Nick lingered a moment, letting the water chase away the residue of a restless night. He dressed in the same jeans and T-shirt as yesterday, feeling the weight of their staleness—evidence of how unsettled he still was. Billy's room next door was quiet. Nick paused outside, listening for any sign of movement, but heard nothing. He took a steady breath and made his way downstairs, craving the solace of a hot cup of coffee.

In the kitchen, he found Billy already up and about, dressed, reading the newspaper, and with the breakfast table laid as if it were the most ordinary of mornings. The scene brought a flicker of normality, though Kate's absence hung in the air like a misplaced note.

"Morning, nephew, sleep well?" Billy sounded bright; his cheerfulness was almost infectious.

"Morning, uncle, like a log!" Nick replied, matching his mocking tone. He poured himself coffee, grateful to find a fresh pot waiting.

"Freshly baked croissants if you want one," Billy said, nodding towards the plate in the centre of the table.

"Wow, you have been busy!" Nick remarked, helping himself as he settled.

"I didn't bake them, although happy to take the credit. I fetched them from the bakers when I went to get a newspaper. There are some fresh breads and a pot of artisan jam, too," Billy chuckled, a touch of pride in his voice.

Nick smiled, the simple breakfast easing his tension. "What time did you get up? I didn't hear you!" he asked, curiosity piqued.

"About half five. I crept down so as not to disturb anyone," Billy replied, folding the paper. Nick glanced at the clock, noting how much time had passed without sight of Kate. The morning stretched before them, the hush of the house deepening, feeling, waiting for something to happen.

With their plates cleared and still no sign of Kate, Billy broke the contemplative silence, his expression turning thoughtful. "Do you think this intruder has anything to do with the letter Mother received?" He asked, searching Nick's face for a clue.

Nick hesitated, the question hitting a nerve. He felt the familiar tug of indecision, torn between protecting his gran from escalating worry and the persistent dread that something more sinister might be unfolding. He shifted in his seat; the silence stretching between them as he weighed his words.

"I don't know," Nick sighed, his voice betraying his uncertainty. "I don't know what to think." He looked away, debating whether to share Kate's concerns, her anxiety from the other night still fresh in his mind. Was it right to raise the alarm when so much seemed uncertain? Yet, he couldn't escape the gnawing sense that ignoring it might be worse.

He took a deep breath. "Billy, perhaps there's something you should know..." He paused, gathering his thoughts. "Kate is concerned that someone is masquerading as gran's son and may have already contacted her. In fact, she called me to say she was anxious that an unidentified person might have spent several hours in the garden with gran one day last week."

Billy's demeanour shifted, his humour evaporating, replaced by a stern intensity. "And the reason you decided not to share this information?" he asked, his tone sharper and eyes fixed on Nick.

Nick felt a flush rise on his cheeks. "If I'm to be honest, because Kate couldn't be certain, and with gran being so confused of late, it's difficult to decipher fact from her memories." He rubbed his hands together as if warming them. "I didn't want to alarm anyone..." His words trailed off, the conflict clear in his voice.

Billy's expression softened, empathy flickering through his concern. "I know what you mean. But we need to be realistic. There's someone, a relative, or maybe not, who's focused on mum for reasons that could be dangerous." Billy spoke, the weight of the situation settling between them.

Nick nodded, sharing the significance of that possibility. "I wish we had a copy of that letter," he admitted.

Billy seemed to decide, standing abruptly. "It could be upstairs in mum's room?" Purpose returning to his voice as he led the way.

"The letter is either upstairs among her things or with her at the hospital. Let's look!"

Billy and Nick enter Maggie's bedroom. The room smells of lavender water and perfume. The bed seemed orderly.

Personal items cluttered the bedside chest and table. Billy approached a built-in closet displaying shelves laden with handbags and hat boxes.

Billy wandered over to the cupboard, a fond grin on his face. "This takes me back," he said, his voice tinged with nostalgia. "We used to raid this cupboard when I was a child. I'd clamber onto the bottom shelf and pass down the hat boxes to your mum—she always treated it as our secret prop cupboard." Billy's eyes sparkled at the memory. "Your mum relished sorting out our costumes and 'make-up' for our little 'shows'," he chuckled.

Nick chipped in, a smile forming as he pictured it. "I can just imagine mum bossing you around, already in charge of the entire production."

Billy laughed, opening the cupboard with ease. “Oh, she was relentless! We’d entertain ourselves for hours while mum was busy elsewhere—where the au pair disappeared to, I do not know.” He began pulling handbags from the shelves and laying them across the bed.” We’d spend entire afternoons rehearsing, and just as we nailed our song and dance routines, it was always time for tea—never enough time for an audience.”

Nick raised an eyebrow, grinning. “Did she ever let you have the lead role?”

Billy’s eyes twinkled as he rolled them. “Absolutely not! Your mum always cast herself as the main character, leaving me with the second-rate parts. I still remember one time—I argued until I was blue in the face that as a boy, I ought to be Oliver! She wouldn’t budge.”

They both laughed, and then Billy said, “Aha, look here! I’ve found it.” He brandishes a black handbag and dramatically pulls the letter from it. Nick at once recognises the crumpled envelope.

Billy lays the two pages out on the bed, pulling out his phone and snapping a picture of each. Meanwhile, Nick picks up the first page and reads the typed letter aloud, his voice steady.

Dear Mrs Randall (Margaret)

My adoptive parents raised me near Boston in the United States.

The reason I write is my own memories contradict what my parents were told about my adoption; that I was orphaned and being cared for by an aunt. The agency arranged the adoption, and my aunt and uncle allowed it.

One of my earliest memories is, I was living in England. I believe in London. From what I remember, there was an older sister and a baby boy. I can also remember being taken on a holiday to Ireland and being left with family members. Although I cannot remember much more, and what I do recall is a haze.

I am in Ireland to learn about my early life. The aunt and uncle who allowed my adoption are now deceased. I have traced more relatives. Another aunt, who suggested I contact you; she gave me your last known address. She seems certain that you are my biological mother.

It would be wonderful if you could fill in the gaps. A veil shrouds my memories, and so many unanswered questions. It would great if you would meet me. I am in London next month because of my work.

My adoption confuses me, but my life is happy. I have a wonderful family of my own. My wife is Canadian, so we live in Ontario. My adoptive parents are the kindest of people, and my childhood was happy.

It will be a flying visit to London, staying one night between meetings before flying back to Canada.

Would you agree to meet with me? I was thinking of the town that my aunt believes I was born in. At the hill behind the station? I will be there on Wednesday 22nd March, at 10:15.

If you do not show, I will understand. I have enclosed my business card with my contact details and look forward to hearing from you.

Yours sincerely,

Matthew Lott

Nick handed the letter to Billy, who read it once more with furrowed brows before folding the pages. He rummaged through his mother's handbag, muttering, "His business card must have dropped in here somewhere."

After a moment, Billy shook his head. "No, it's not in here," he said, disappointment flickering across his face as he returned the letter to its envelope.

Nick frowned. "Why didn't he just come here?"

"Perhaps he didn't want to make things awkward for Mum," Billy offered.

Nick sighed, frustration tightening his voice. "If only gran had shown someone the letter before going off to meet a stranger! Although I am suspicious, why be so vague about the details of the meeting?"

"To be fair; mum has lost concept of day or night".

Nick studied his uncle's features for guidance. "So, what do you think, genuine or a con artist?"

Billy hesitated, letting out a heavy sigh. "I don't know; you're the detective. I'm just a mere accountant."

Nick shook his head. "To me, it just does not add up. Excuse the pun! What sort of family would arrange a child's adoption and then make his mother believe he died?"

Billy's expression darkened with distaste. "The sort of family who were happy to receive financial compensation, perhaps?"

He paused; the weight of the conversation settled over him. Billy's hands trembled as he placed the handbags back on the shelf, his voice above a whisper. "My head is saying be cautious, but my heart is hoping my brother is alive. We must try to find out. The information gives us something to go on, at least when we are in Ireland next week."

He lingered in the closet, lost in thought, as a piercing scream shattered the silence from the attic above.

CHAPTER THIRTY

The Attic

Startled by the scream, Nick and Billy rush out of Maggie's bedroom and quickly ascend the stairs to the attic apartment where Kate lives. They find Kate standing near the entrance, pale, and trembling.

"What happened? Are you okay?" Nick asked, concerned.

"I... I saw someone outside, staring in through the balcony window!" Kate stammers, her voice filled with fear. Nick's heart races as he scans the area outside thc attic. He notices the Juliet balcony, a small outdoor space with ornate railings and a picturesque view of the Heath. He sees no-one now.

"Are you sure?" Billy asked, trying to remain calm.

"Yes, I'm positive! He was looking right at me, his eyes locked on mine," Kate replied, her voice still shaky.

Nick and Billy exchange concerned glances before deciding to investigate further. They carefully step onto the Juliette balcony, scanning the surroundings for any signs of the mysterious man. The cool breeze brushes against their faces as they peer into the sunlight, still low in the sky.

"He's gone now, but I swear I saw him," Kate insisted, her eyes still wide with fear.

Nick makes a mental note to enhance the security measures near the Juliette balcony too, to prevent any potential intruders. They step back inside the attic and follow Kate through the arch into the bedroom. That's when Nick notices a small cupboard tucked away in the corner. "What's in this cupboard?" Nick asked, gesturing towards it.

Kate looks at the cupboard and then back at Nick. "Oh, that's where Maggie keeps some of her memorabilia. Old letters, photographs and other mementos."

"Do you mind if I look?" he asked.

"Sure, nothing belongs to me in there."

Intrigued, Nick opens the cupboard, revealing a treasure trove of memories. Stacks of letters were bound by faded ribbons, photographs documented precious moments, and trinkets represented sentimental value. He unwraps the shawl from around the old shoebox and carries it through to the sitting area.

As he sifts through the contents, he finds the child, Matthew's birth certificate, a black-and-white photograph of a small boy sitting on the bonnet of a Rover and an envelope addressed to Maggie, postmarked from Ireland years ago.

Nick carefully unfolds the letter, its edges fragile with age. The words inside bear the weight of deep emotion. Jack, the author, expresses profound regret and sorrow over Maggie's loss, his voice resonating with genuine anguish. He apologises for having become too unwell to fulfil the promises he once made to her, a burden that seems to haunt him even now.

Jack emphasises his remorse, admitting that the last time they met, he was unable to carry out Maggie's wishes. In his message, he implores her to take what she knows to her grave, suggesting that the truth would benefit nobody. His tone is both apologetic and protective, as though he wishes to spare Maggie—and perhaps others—from unnecessary pain.

The content of this letter hints at deeper stories concealed within Maggie's collection of memorabilia.

"Look at this," Nick said, showing the letter to Billy. "Seems like Maggie had a close connection to this man. "I wonder how he connected to Matthew." Nick said.

Billy takes the letter and reads it with furrowed brows. "This is significant." I wonder if she remembers him, and why has she hidden this letter up here with Matthew Junior's birth certificate and photo?

Before they can ponder further, Kate gasps, drawing their attention to an unused alcove at the back of the attic. They turn to find a cupboard slightly ajar in the bedroom, as if someone had hastily closed it.

"That was closed; what if someone has been hiding in there, all night!" She shudders.

They edged towards the cupboard, each creak echoing through the attic's heavy hush. Nick's hand hovered over the handle for a heartbeat, his palm clammy, before he drew a breath and pulled the door open. The cramped interior yielded nothing but sagging hangers and piles of forgotten trinkets. A musty scent clung to the air, redolent of moth-eaten coats and hidden yesterdays.

"No one here now," Nick said, his voice tinged with confusion as he surveyed the disordered space. Despite the apparent emptiness, it was clear that someone had been in the eve cupboard recently. Evidence of this presence lay scattered about—a half-drunk bottle of cola and an empty crisp packet, hastily discarded.

After searching the confined space, Nick stretched to ease his cramped limbs, casting a wary glance in Billy's direction. You could feel the tension; he was uneasy about their intentions. The safety of his family pressed relentlessly on his mind; every unfamiliar sound or shift in the darkness sent a jolt of anxiety through him, igniting his nerves.

Billy's gaze drifted over to the skylight, its frame rattling faintly in the draught. "Look," he whispered, pointing, "that windows is open. Whoever you saw must have come through there. In or out—easy enough if you know your way around rooftops."

Nick swallowed, his voice tighter now. "We can't take any chances. Let's secure this window and add it to our list. No more gaps. We must think of everything."

As they left Kate's attic flat, the oppressive silence lingered, every footfall on the stairs resounding like a warning. Downstairs, Billy and Nick exchanged a look of wordless agreement, a silent pact to do whatever it took to protect those they loved. The house, once a place of warmth, now felt like a stage set for dangers crouching just out of sight.

"We need to call the police," Billy said, his tone firm. "This—none of its right. We'd best tell them everything. The bloke outside, the cupboard, all of it."

Nick nodded, already reaching for his phone, his thumb trembling as he dialled. While they waited, the tension ratcheted higher—the floorboards seeming to amplify each creak, the old house settling around their fears. Every shadow seemed longer, every gust at the window sharper. The discovery of Maggie's letter and the sight of the man lurking outside haunted them, questions multiplying with every passing minute. All they could do now was hope that the trip to Ireland would finally unravel the truth behind these relentless uncertainties.

.

CHAPTER THIRTY-ONE

1972 –Doctor Randall

The woman who helps me walk has just left. I dislike her. She said I must try to move more, but it hurts too much. I do not understand what caused the pain! I am in the hospital. They say I had a nervous breakdown. I don't like it here. I want to go home, and I miss my mum and my children.

A nurse is taking my temperature.

"How are you feeling today, Maggie?" she asked. She has an Irish accent. She sounds like Matthew's mother, and for a moment, I am reminded of the strained dinners spent with his family, a mix of homesickness and resentment simmering beneath polite words.

"In pain, it hurts," I replied.

"You are doing ever so well, but I will fetch you some more painkillers before lunch," she said.

"Am I going to see Dr Randall today?" I asked.

"Dr Randall? No, Mr Jenkins," she replied, "he is your consultant."

"Is your daughter coming to see you today?" she continued.

"Who? No! I do not want my little girl to visit me here. It will scare her!" I exclaimed, surprised by even the suggestion!

"Your daughter is all grown-up. She visits you every day! Would you like to try the carton of drinks she brought for you?" The nurse is moving items from the locker onto the table tray at the side of the bed.

I feel angry. This nurse does not know what she is talking about! She does not know me. I don't know who brought me those drinks in, but it wasn't my little Lucy. She is with my mother.

"I want to see Dr Randall," I insisted.

I remembered another moment with Dr Randall—a day recently when I found comfort in his presence. Dr Randall is a kind man. I understand him; he will listen if I need to talk, or we simply sit together, gazing out of the aluminium-framed window to the beautiful hospital grounds. The trees are full of leaves. Once, when I told Dr Randall how I loved to walk, he walked with me through the grounds, and we sat for a while on a bench by the beautiful rose garden, the blooms vibrant and alive. He held my hand whilst I read the letter from my mother informing me of the death of my father. The news shattered me, and Dr Randall gave me his shoulder to cry on. Oh, Daddy, how I miss you, those wasted years apart weighing heavily on my heart. I regret not reaching out to him sooner, wishing I could have offered him the love he always gave me when I needed it most. My father did not recover from the assault, and part of me will always carry the guilt of that lost time.

Although Dr Randall is putting in maximum effort to encourage me to talk, I am struggling to find the words stuck in my throat. Patiently, he waits for me to respond to his questioning. Thoughts swim around my head. He said it is damaging to hold in my feelings. I feel I can trust him; Dr Randall wants me to show emotion because he keeps asking me about how I felt when I held my children for the first time and to remember how that joy felt. To be honest, I cannot remember! There were mixed emotions throughout my pregnancies. When I gave birth to Lucy and Matthew, the strained relationship between my parents and the husband I loved distracted me. When I found out I was expecting Billy, I was anxious because we were living with Matthew's parents, and we desperately needed a home of our own. But even during all the worry, I recall the first time I kissed each of my babies, the overwhelming rush of love that pierced through my exhaustion. I wish I could hold on to that feeling now, allowing it to carry me through these uncertain days.

May 1970 - Maggie

I am heavily pregnant with my third child, and finally, we have a place of our own.

It was not long after Christmas when I informed Matthew that I was expecting. He appeared indifferent to our news. Whether it was his attitude towards my pregnancy, my hormones, or because I could not tolerate living under the same roof as his parents and his brother any longer, I made my position clear. Either he does something about getting us housed, or I am going to leave.

"We really need a place of our own. We do not even have our own bedroom," I cried.

"Stop whining, you should be grateful. My family have been good to you!" Matthew responded.

I decided I would not argue this point, feeling as I do; I could not trust where it might lead.

"Sidney has provided us with a living by making me an equal partner in his business, and I am earning good money because of it. You and the kids don't go without," he said.

"So where are we going to put another baby? It's already a tight fit," I asked.

"Just think, if we had a place of our own, Maddie could go back in the boxroom, and Rita and Sidney could have a proper bedroom instead of sharing a single bed," I watch Matthew as he considers this. Matthew has a soft spot for little Maddie. He feels sorry for her not having a mummy. Although I wish he would be more sensitive when little Lucy is around, I have caught the green-eyed monster a few times recently.

"Okay, don't go on! I know someone who works at the council. I'll go down and see him tomorrow," he agreed.

A few days later, a council officer sat at Matthew's parents' table. She was asking questions and taking notes about our living arrangements while Matthew's mum, Lucinda, sat frostily and only answered when spoken to.

"Well, Mr and Mrs O'Donnell, overcrowding is certainly a problem here. I will pass your case to my superiors, and you will receive a letter in the post with a decision within a week."

As good as her word, the letter arrived the following week, and Matthew collected keys from the council to a three-bedroom terraced house a few streets away from my parents.

Our Victorian semi-detached house has three bedrooms, a sitting room at the front and a dining room at the back, and through the kitchen to a lavatory, within a porch outside the back door. It is the ideal home for our family.

Being so near to my parents, my mum pops in daily and brings groceries. I rarely mention my dad as I still have not seen or spoken to him since I left home.

I pack away the groceries Mum has brought today and place them neatly in the larder.

“How much do I owe you?” I ask curtly.

“Maggie, stop this!” Mum said, looking hurt.

“I’ve told you before, I don’t want your money.”

“I’m sorry,” Softening my tone, I say, “I’m tired.”

“How is Dad?” I ask gently.

“He is not good!” she said.

“Is he ill?”

“Heartbroken!” she said grimly. I scoff.

“You are both stubborn as each other! He misses you so much!”

“Come and see him. Do it for my sake. I miss you!” A tear drops onto mum’s cheek.

“Okay, come here,” I said as I hug her. Even with the bump in the way, I hug tight. If only she knew how much I have longed for this moment, but she must understand I cannot go against the will of my husband.

CHAPTER THIRTY-TWO

The Dinner Party

Kate broke the silence, her voice low. "Maybe I should move out while Maggie's in the hospital. It's not fair to you, and I'm afraid."

"Where would you go?" Nick asked, concern flickering across his face.

"We can stay here with you until the weekend. But you know we are going to Ireland as planned next week," he said.

Kate's words are tumbling out in a rush. Her emotion caught her off guard. "I'm so sorry," her cheeks flushed and her hands trembled. She tried to steady her breath, embarrassed by the sudden display of vulnerability. Billy reached out to comfort her, hesitating for a moment before resting his arm around her shoulders.

"No, Kate, you have nothing to apologise for. I'm sorry," Billy said softly, his sincerity clear in his tone. "You've been through a terrible time. This is your job, and as your employers, we have a duty to keep you safe. We'll do whatever we can to..." His determination faltered, realising that for now, they'd done all they could.

Billy's gentle nature and ability to understand others filled Kate's heart. Nick tore a piece of kitchen towel from the roll and handed it to her, a small, awkward gesture that felt like a lifeline.

"I'll ask my friend in Milton Keynes if I can stay there for a bit," Kate said, dabbing her nose. But as she spoke, a surge of anger rose to the surface. "But to be honest, if I leave, it's like they've won." Kate wrestled with the urge to flee for her own safety and the stubborn desire to stand her ground, unwilling to let fear dictate her life. "I want to know who's behind this—who could do something like this to an old woman and her family?" she said, her upset morphing into defiance.

"I understand how you feel, but I would be too worried if you stayed in this house alone," Billy said, expressing his concern.

Nick expressed his conviction that the incidents were linked to the letter writer, certain that their Irish journey would reveal more. Billy nodded in agreement.

"We know some guy is claiming to be Maggie's son, my brother. No contact number or address? It's unusual for someone not to include their address. And someone is doing their utmost to scare you half to death. We need to make every effort to sort this out and find out what is going on!" Billy said.

"I have an idea," Nick said, breaking the silence.

"Kate, come to Ireland with us. I will ask Elaine, my fiancée, to join us, too. She isn't working next week, and I'm sure she'll be happy for a break. You deserve to know why you are being targeted," Nick proposed.

"Fiancée? You kept that quiet!" Billy appeared surprised. Nick shifted uncomfortably.

"We were going to announce our engagement this week, invite everyone out for dinner. But with gran's accident; and until we know for certain that she is going to be okay, we delayed the announcement for a few weeks," Nick explained.

"And have your parents met Elaine? Your mother hasn't said," Billy enquired, curious about Nick's relationship.

"No, not yet. It's not a whirlwind. We have been together for a couple of years, but the opportunity has not arisen for everyone to meet her yet," Nick clarified.

"Not even at Christmas or on birthdays?" Billy asked.

"Elaine is a barrister, and I am a detective. We wanted to wait to see if it worked out first."

"Very sensible, and congratulations son. I'm happy for you," Billy shook Nick's hand enthusiastically.

"What about your mum? When are we going to tell her?" Billy asked, pressing the question. Nick pretended to ignore it.

"What do you think, do you want to come with us?" Nick asked, turning to Kate.

"I would love to come to Ireland if it's okay with both of you. I would rather come along than stay here wondering," Kate replied.

"That's settled, Kate—pack your bags, you're coming to Ireland," Billy said. "But first, Nick, let's invite your partner for dinner so we can meet her. I'll cook tonight," he added enthusiastically.

From that moment, Kate felt like she was being babysat, not left alone in the house for a minute. Billy left to pick up some clothes from home and said he would shop for ingredients on his way back. Nick spent most of the day making telephone calls and communicating with his police colleagues. When Billy returned, Nick went to fetch Elaine from her flat.

Billy prepared seafood pasta with lobster, prawns, mussels, and squid in a creamy white wine sauce, served on a bed of fresh pasta. He also made homemade garlic bread and a Mediterranean salad, pairing the meal with a crisp Chardonnay. The group hit it off. Billy found conversation with Elaine fascinating and was interested in her work. The evening was relaxed and full of laughter. Elaine appeared excited about the forthcoming trip to Ireland, showing them pictures on her phone of a luxury four-bedroom whitewashed holiday cottage overlooking the bay. She had chosen a cottage on the outskirts of a town on the west coast of Ireland.

“I thought it would be nice to overlook the sea, so it resembles a proper holiday. Kate, what do you think?” Elaine asked, pushing her phone towards Kate.

“The cottage looks so pretty,” Kate responded, feeling a little overwhelmed by Elaine’s genuine friendliness.

“This afternoon, I confirmed the booking after Nick explained what was going on.”

“Hey, let’s set up a social media group, so I can share these photos. Also, it’ll be handy for sharing flight details,” Elaine suggested, her tone practical and enthusiastic.

The companions each took out their phones, following Elaine’s instruction. For a moment, the lively conversation quietened as everyone focused on their screens, tapping away to create the group.

Within minutes, a new chat was formed, ready for photos, updates, and all the information they would need for their trip.

"We have also cancelled the rooms that were booked at the bed-and-breakfast in town, and I have arranged the hire of a jeep to pick up from the airport to make sure that we can fit all of our luggage in," Elaine added.

She reminded Kate of a girl she knew in primary school, Celina Williams. Everyone loved Celina. With a warm and bubbly personality, along with her talent in various areas, unsurprising when she became the school prefect. Kate learned from social media that Celina became a high-flyer in adulthood too.

PART TWO

CHAPTER ONE

Arrival in Ireland

"Is this your bag?" Billy asked Kate, his hand hovering over a medium-sized grey case on the conveyor.

"I think so!" she replied, although Billy had already taken the case off and was examining the label.

"Yep, that's yours," he said, placing her case by her feet.

Nick was walking towards them, pushing a trolley.

"Elaine has gone to the Car Hire office. I said we would meet her there," he said.

The drive to the cottage took just over three hours. Nick was driving, and as they approached their destination, the road narrowed and wound its way away from the cliff-side main road. They climbed yet another hill, with the sea behind them. The land on either side appeared grey and barren, with only the occasional tree. The road narrowed, ascended, and then dipped again, with non-agricultural moorland surrounding them. Rock formations made up the landscape. Ahead, white open field gates led to a gravel drive, and a white cottage with a dark grey slate roof came into sight.

The gravel crunched beneath the tyres as the vehicle approached the cottage. Nick had plenty of choices for where to park on the sweeping gravel drive in front of the isolated property that would be their home for the next week. A lawn lay next to and behind the property, with its boundary marked by the structure of an ancient stone wall.

Nicholas's mobile started ringing again. Billy picked it up from the compartment between them and looked at the screen.

"It's your mum again!" he said. Nicholas took the phone and answered it.

"Sorry, I was driving."

"No, there is nothing going on! Yes, I know, yep... yep... we have sorted it! Yes, there was an intruder at the house, which is why Kate is with us! Yep... yep... Billy has arranged everything... No, not the trip! The security at grans. CCTV is being fitted while we are away. We will tune in on our phones."

Nick listened as his mother continued to rant. He glanced at Billy and raised his eyebrows.

"Okay, put him on... Hi, Dad! Yes, we have just arrived! No, I didn't want to upset her, that was not my intention! Of course, she was happy to come along..." Nicholas turned towards Kate, who was sharing the back seat with Elaine, and gave an awkward smile.

CHAPTER TWO

Game of Cards

Lucy's hands shook as she set down her mug, unable to quiet the storm of anger and confusion swirling inside her. Her family, once her bedrock, now felt like a house built on shifting sand. Nicholas, her only son, had flown to Ireland with her brother and Kate, the young woman who had only recently become a prominent presence in their lives. Lucy had always assumed her relationship with Nicholas was close, but lately, she sensed a growing distance. As for Billy, she'd trusted him implicitly, but now she wondered if she'd been naïve.

"What on earth are Nicholas and Billy thinking?" Lucy burst out, her voice trembling. "Billy rang me last night, barely giving any details, and told me they're off to Ireland this morning. Kate's going with them! Why am I always the last to know?" Ray, her husband, munched his cheese sandwich in silence, he hoped by keeping quiet would shield him from the brunt of her fury.

"And it seems," she continued, her voice growing hoarse, "that someone who may or may not be my dead brother, is tormenting Kate! And I only find all this out now." She felt a chill when she mentioned her brother. That the man she had long mourned might be alive was shocking and unsettling. The wounds of his disappearance had never healed.

Ray looked up, concern etched on his face. “Lucy, perhaps they didn’t want to worry you. You know how you get when—” He hesitated, searching for the right words. “I mean, maybe they thought they were protecting you.”

She shook her head, struggling to process the betrayal. “If Kate was scared to stay in the house alone, she could have stayed here with us,” Why didn’t anyone think I had the right to be included in that decision?

“None of this was in my plan when convincing Kate to come and work for us.” The word ‘plan’ slipped out. Ray frowned. He leaned forward. His tone was gentle but insistent. “What do you mean by plan, Luce? What plan?” Lucy’s cheeks flushed. She hadn’t meant to reveal so much. “It’s nothing,” she said, brushing him off.

Ray pressed on. He put down his sandwich and took her hand. “Lucy, there’s no need to plan or schedule everything. You don’t have to take charge for everyone all the time. Our family can sort out their own lives. I am here. I am just as confused as you are. I believed Nicholas would tell us he is getting engaged... But he is our son. I respect his decision to announce such big news in his own time.”

Lucy’s anger softened. She felt isolated. She felt sidelined in her own family’s life. Her roles of mother and wife felt uncertain. She worried she had pushed them away. Did they no longer trust her guidance? Nick called her in a hurry after everyone made the decisions. She hadn’t even met Elaine! Ray squeezed her hand. He tried to reassure her.

"Let's not jump to conclusions. We'll talk to Nicholas. Maybe there's more to it. You know how he is, sometimes he keeps things close to his chest." His words highlighted how disconnected Lucy felt.

She swallowed hard, gathering herself. The visit to her mother's hospital bedside would provide no respite; the family she has worked so hard to build is as fractured as the family she'd grown-up in, and her mum is always central to any instability. In finding Kate and bringing her into the fold Lucy believed she had begun smooth over the gaps, but there is such a long way to go, Lucy is determined to fix the past even if she has had to face the ghosts of her past to do it.

"Hello, mum, you're looking well today," Lucy said, approaching her and pecking her cheek.

"Hello, Rita, it's so lovely to see you," Maggie said, beaming.

"I'm not Rita... I'm Lucy!" Lucy snapped, feeling impatient. her impatience quickly turned into guilt as Maggie's beaming smile quickly disappeared.

"Of course, you are Lucy. I know that! It's just I have a lot of time to think in here. I was thinking about Rita. I wonder what became of her?" Maggie said.

"Didn't you keep in touch?" Lucy asked softly.

"No, I think she felt guilty because of what happened."

"Why, mum? Why would Rita feel guilty?" Lucy enquired, remembering her mother's friend.

William was nine months old, and with three children under the age of five and a nine-year-old niece to care for, life was tough for a time!

Until Rita and I became friends, that is. We were so close; she was wonderful with the children, especially Maddie. Providing the stability she needed, life was fun.

Sidney and Rita became an official 'couple,' and she moved into the O'Donnell house properly once we moved out of Matthew's parents' home.

1970 was a marvellous year, when summer days went on and on. Rita helped with the children, which was much appreciated, especially having a newborn baby. We spent so much time together, with Rita planning days out and family picnics, which meant we spent even more time with our partners.

Sidney and Rita came to our house regularly, where summer pop hits blared from the radiogram as the children played in our garden. We typically settled Maddie to bed with our children, while we adults spent the evenings socialising over a fondue and drinks. Matthew and I spent more time together than we had in our entire marriage, and even Sidney was settling down; he was behaving like a proper father to Maddie.

Rita was a generous and kind person and would give half of her last away, but also feisty, which became clear during our evening card games, especially when we entered discussions about women's rights! I refrained from commenting when our men made derogatory remarks about women, but she would react angrily, answering back and expressing her thoughts on the matter.

The last time I saw Rita was between Christmas 1970 and the New Year. Rita was quizzing me about why I had given up secretarial training once I got married.

"Lots of women work when they have kids; pick up where you left off," she said to me encouragingly.

"Maggie doesn't have to work," answered Matthew, hearing a defensive edge to his tone.

"I am not saying she needs to work, but she might want to?" replied Rita.

"Hey, you two, I am still here," I said, trying to remain jovial but feeling the atmosphere change.

"Anyway, Maggie has never had a proper job!" Matthew responded.

"How old are you now, Maggie?" Rita asked, ignoring Matthew's comments.

"Nearly twenty-four, although I feel as if I am fifty-four." I laughed.

"You are still a baby! Plenty of time for a career," she said triumphantly, leaning back in her chair.

"Maggie doesn't want to work, and I don't want my kids to become 'latchkey,' and you're happy, aren't you?" Matthew appeared agitated.

"Women can do both these days. Take me. I work and still look after Maddie," Rita said, taking another sip of her gin and tonic.

"Yes, but she's not yours," said Sidney coldly, studying his hand of cards. Rita appeared hurt by his observation.

"If she were yours, things would be quite different, for one, I would not allow you to work in a club. I just wouldn't have it!" he said.

Rita tried to diffuse the tension with a lighthearted laugh, "You can't tell me where I can work." Her tone suggested she was trying to keep the situation amicable, but there was an underlying firmness in her words.

Sidney, however, did not respond in kind. His expression became unreadable, a familiar mask that made it difficult to gauge his true feelings. He replied coldly, "Don't you believe it! All it would take is a few words from me, and you would never work in another club or pub." His statement hung in the air, a stark reminder of the authority he felt he held over Rita's employment prospects.

"I hope you're joking?" She said, glaring at him.

I tried to change the subject as I noticed the change in Rita's expression and felt the tension between them, but Rita was not letting Sidney's remark go.

"I am not your property, Sidney O'Donnell, whatever you may think. You cannot control my life!" Rita exclaimed.

"Rita... you are a common barmaid. You are not a professional, and it does not take brains to pull a pint!" he scoffed.

"And also, you would not have got the job at the club in the first place if it weren't for me," Sidney spoke in a monotone.

"Sidney O'Donnell, you speak rubbish. I work through my merit. I practically run that place, and Frank was pleased to take me on as Bar Manager," argued Rita.

Initially, Sidney laughed, and then suddenly, shockingly even, he leaned towards Rita threateningly. She sat next to him at the table, and his face was only an inch away from hers. My blood ran cold as it felt like déjà vu.

"Frank took you on at my request, promoted you on my say so, the hours you work, are under my order and he will also sack if I tell him to... never forget it!" Sidney sneered as he spoke.

I looked to Matthew to do something, but he did not respond to Sidney's unacceptable behaviour or even appear to notice.

"You work where you work because it suits me, for now!" Sidney said, turning his attention back to his hand of cards.

I saw the flash in Rita's eyes at first fear and then anger. She left the table, grabbed her coat, and slammed out of the front door. Grey-faced, Sidney followed without a thought to his child asleep upstairs.

During the week that followed, I did not hear from Rita, which was unusual. According to Matthew, whom I quizzed, he hadn't seen her at the club. Despite trying to telephone the house many times, I received no answer. Matthew's parents are in Ireland again.

New Year's Eve came and went, and Matthew had returned to work. I spent the evenings alone and the days caring for the children, although I allowed Maddie to stay up with me to see in the New Year. The constant fear of abandonment in that child's eyes tugged at my heart.

A genuine concern was that from that evening onwards, Maddie remained in my care, persistently asking when Rita or her father would come to collect her. I found myself at a loss for words, uncertain of how best to respond to her worried questions. In an attempt to reassure her, I told Maddie that Rita was feeling unwell, though I could not be certain if she believed me. Despite the uncertainty, I did my best to provide her with comfort. Thankfully, Maddie had my own children for company, which helped to distract her from her worries. She blended in with them so seamlessly that she was more like a sibling than a guest.

Maddie was supposed to return to school after the Christmas holidays, but I noticed that Matthew was not taking the situation as seriously as he ought to. Feeling responsible for Maddie's well-being, I decided to address the matter with him directly.

"Matthew, Maddie needs to be in school," I insisted, hoping he would understand the importance of her education and routine.

However, Matthew's response was dismissive. "Mum and Dad will be home soon. Maddie can go home then. I will not pressure Sidney. He has enough on his plate right now. Maggie, stop going on!" With that, he left the house, ending the conversation abruptly and leaving me feeling frustrated and worried about Maddie's welfare.

Several days later, one morning, I discovered an envelope on my doormat. It had been hand-delivered, and as I opened it, I realised it was a letter from Rita.

Dear Maggie,

I am terribly sorry that I did not come to see you in person as I consider you a dear friend. But after leaving yours last week, Sidney and I had a row to end all rows, and I would rather not go into detail or for you to see me as I am now.

But I am writing to let you know I have gone back home to Newcastle, to be near my family. Once things settle down, I will send my address so you can write, but now, I cannot risk Sidney finding out where I am. (I didn't tell him I was leaving).

It saddens me to leave Maddie behind, and I wish it were possible to take her with me. I am sorry that I could not even say goodbye, but as you may realise, the situation is impossible. I really love her to bits, and my heart is breaking, although it makes me feel a little better knowing you will always be there for her.

Besides not being able to put up with Sidney's behaviour or mood swings anymore, I have discovered other things, and it is enough to make me want to distance myself from him as much as I can. And if I were you, I would consider doing the same.

Look after yourself and all those little ones.

Take care,

Rita x

I never revealed to Matthew that Rita had written to me, not even when he told me she had left. Sidney's version is that he had tired of Rita's argumentative ways, that she was mentally unstable, and that he had sent her packing. Although I had already decided about whom to believe.

Echoes of Belonging

I drifted like a ghost through the hallways, fury, and grief mingling, searching for solace in the cramped attic cupboard. The small space offered a sense of retreat, its walls shielding me from the world's harshness while simultaneously magnifying my loneliness. Each scratch etched into the wood, and every muffled footstep from below served as painful reminders of nights lost to abandonment. The question that plagues me—why did they leave me so utterly alone? echoes in the stillness.

Raised by my spinster aunt, I endured a childhood of punishment and emotional captivity. An overwhelming sense of guilt shaped her actions: she was the daughter who survived, while her sister—my own mother—had died so that I might live. My grandparents, bitter and twisted by their own grief, bore deep resentment towards me. Their daughter, my mother, had sacrificed her life, refusing treatment during pregnancy, and the cost of that decision shadowed every corner of my upbringing. I have no memory of her—I was only a baby when she died—but sometimes, a fleeting recollection surfaces: the gentle way Kate's mother tucked me in at night, a moment of warmth amid my aunt's cold discipline. Yet, to keep the fragile security of childhood intact and appease my grandparents, I was forced to suppress any memory of Kathryn's mother, instead venerating the memory of a stranger I never knew.

I listen to this family as they talk, the truth swirling just beyond my grasp. The daughter is aware of Kate's identity; I have overheard her in conversation with an official. But I am uncertain; does she know about me?

How do I fit into this web of deception and with the whispered references to Ireland? The urge to confront them, to unravel the mysteries that bind their pasts together, burns inside me. Yet, fear keeps me silent, rooted in place as secrets continue to pass me by. When new locks are fitted, forcing me out, I am left with no choice but to escape across the low rooftops and over the gate to the heath, the wound of betrayal raw and unresolved. Despite the night closing in around me, desperate hope for answers compels me onwards, driving me through darkness in search of the truth that continues to elude me. I have heard enough to know that this family is built on lies.

It's too late to confront her now, or is it? Listening from under the window last night, as the group excitedly discussed a trip to Ireland, I am at a crossroads. Do I go back home and allow them the triumph and allow these months to disappear into the past, or shall I follow to Ireland? I have come this far undetected within the shadows causing just enough commotion to stay present in their thoughts without revealing myself directly. My heart pounded as I weighed my choices; each burdened with consequences I could not yet predict. The suspense pressed in, my longing for answers warring with my fear of their implications—and with each passing moment, the urgency of my decision intensified, making escape seem impossible.

CHAPTER THREE

Hospital Visitor

Lucy sat quietly, listening to her mother recount the story of how Maddie had come to live with their family for such an extended period. As Maggie spoke, Lucy felt a familiar pang of childhood jealousy rise within her. Although she was the eldest by birth, it had always seemed to Lucy that her mother regarded Maddie as the elder sibling, giving her a position Lucy felt should have been hers. Maggie continued to reminisce, sharing memories and details about events from Lucy's early years—stories that Lucy either could not recall or had never known about at all. With each recollection, Lucy wrestled with a sense of exclusion, realising just how much her own childhood felt obscured or overshadowed by Maddie's presence in their family.

"Lucy, let me tell you about when Rita's letter arrived."

Lucy, feeling uneasy with the memory and wanting to avoid the conversation because of what she knew replied, "You have already told me about it!" hoping to discourage Maggie from continuing. But Maggie, determined to share her feelings from that time, pressed on. Maggie described how its contents stirred unexpected emotions, leaving her feeling uneasy for days afterwards.

"I tried to question your father, with gentle and subtle questions, hoping he might offer some clue or shed light on what he knew, but he insisted that he knew little about why Rita's departure was so abrupt. His answers were always vague, and I was no closer to understanding what had truly happened—especially since Rita had endured so much of your uncle Sidney's difficult ways over the years, so I was left in the dark," Maggie's expression was grave as she recounted this time.

Maggie's voice softened with regret as she continued, "I thought that, for once, since her mother died in such horrific circumstances, little Maddie would finally have the love and stability she so desperately needed in Rita." She paused, her eyes clouded by memories and what-ifs. "But it wasn't to be!" Maggie's words hung in the air. "I wish I knew what became of the child," she admitted, her tone a mixture of sorrow and unresolved concern for Maddie's fate.

Lucy felt guilty when her mum talked about Rita and Maddie. She should have delivered Maddie's message. Yet, it's too late to feel regret now! Lucy's attempts to make amends have just made things more difficult. Her mother looks exhausted.

"Mum, I'm going to head off. I will come back tomorrow. Is there anything you need brought up?" Lucy replaced the blue plastic chair provided for visitors against the wall where she found it.

"I would love another bar of that chocolate,"

"What chocolate is that?" Lucy asked.

"The bar Matty brought me."

"Who?" Lucy follows Maggie's gaze towards the locker on the other side of her bed to the red chocolate wrapper of a half-eaten bar of dark chocolate.

"Mum, who gave you this chocolate?" She insisted, rushing to it and holding it up.

"I have told you; it was little Matthew!" Maggie said, obviously irritated by Lucy's tone.

"Matthew is dead! Who has been here, who gave you this chocolate?" Lucy's voice raised.

"Is everything ok in here?" asked a nurse with an Irish accent, entering the ward.

"I need a word!" Lucy insisted, rushing into the corridor and beckoning the nurse to follow.

"Mrs. Langford, please lower your voice with your mother or we may have to ask you to leave. If you need help coping, I can—" the nurse started, her tone firm but calm.

"You don't understand. She could be in danger," Lucy replied, struggling to catch her breath as anxiety tightened her chest.

"How can we find out who has visited?" Lucy pressed, her urgency clear.

"Come with me to the family room. We can speak in private," the nurse responded gently, offering Lucy a measure of privacy and understanding.

Lucy followed obediently, allowing herself to be led through the ward. Once alone in a small consultation room, the nurse introduced herself as Andrea. With the door closed behind them, Lucy explained in detail what was troubling her, her concern for her mother's safety was clear in every word.

"I returned to work today. I have been working since 7:30 this morning, and as far as I am aware, you are the only person who has visited Maggie today," Andrea explained calmly.

"My colleague has been caring for your mother recently. She's on break but may be back on the ward now. Please wait here while I check."

Andrea has left Lucy seated on a blue PVC chair while she has gone to fetch her colleague.

After a few minutes, Andrea returns with another nurse whom I recognise. She introduced herself as Sangita.

"Your mother has had several visitors, a young woman, but she comes regularly, and I have seen her here with you," said the nurse.

"That will be Kate!" Lucy interrupts.

"You cared for my mum when she came out of surgery. My husband, brother, and son were visiting too. Except for my family, I am concerned about any other male visitors, someone during the last few days?"

"Yes, I remember your family!" recalled the nurse.

"It was the day before yesterday, The young woman Kate had just left, and soon after, a man arrived. Your mother introduced him to me as her son. Maggie also informed me they had recently reacquainted."

"What did he look like? How old is he?" Lucy persisted.

Sangita paused, considering Lucy's question. "I'm not entirely sure about his age or appearance," she admitted. "He kept his anorak and hood on the entire time he was here. Now that I think about it, that struck me as rather odd, especially since the ward is always quite warm at this time of year. It was only a brief visit, so I didn't get a proper look at him."

"Was he young, old, middle-aged?" asked Lucy, feeling frustrated that Sangita was not offering more information.

Sangita responded to Lucy's enquiries with an apologetic tone, admitting, "I couldn't say. I'm sorry, to be honest I paid little attention; we were busy!" adding to Lucy's annoyance and concern.

Lucy explained to the nurses that the person Sangita had described might not be a family member.

"My mother is extremely vulnerable." Lucy insisted on an immediate telephone call should this man visit her again.

Andrea responded by making it clear that simply contacting Lucy by telephone would not be an adequate resolution to the situation. Instead, Andrea explained that, given the recent events, the issue must be formally reported as a safeguarding concern. Lucy hesitated at this suggestion, expressing her uncertainty about whether such a step was necessary.

Lucy explained to the nurses that the situation was particularly complicated due to the possibility that the unknown visitor might be her missing brother, who had long been presumed dead. This revelation added a layer of confusion and uncertainty to the matter, Lucy emphasised how crucial it was to first verify and confirm the true identity of the man.

Andrea clarified the hospital's procedures, saying that the social worker would speak directly with Maggie, she explained, "It is our responsibility to ensure her well-being." Andrea further noted that, following this first assessment, a decision would be made about whether the matter should be escalated to the wider safeguarding team for further investigation.

After concluding their conversation, Lucy made her way back to the ward to say goodbye to Maggie, who appeared visibly unhappy.

"I am off now," Lucy said, stroking Maggie's head.

"Okay, love," tears well in Maggie's eyes.

"Hey, come on, don't get upset. I will be back tomorrow." Lucy swallowed down the lump that has risen in her throat.

"I want my mum and dad," Maggie said, a single teardrop falling from her eye.

Lucy's heart wants to break. In this moment, she realises she is losing her mum. "I know, don't worry. I am here. Why don't I fetch the nurse to help you back into bed? You are tired; you need a good sleep," she replied. Lucy called for the nurse, who helped Maggie into bed.

"Do you feel better now?" Maggie's eyes were closing, but she started to speak again...

"If only I had known then what I know now. Precious years wasted. Do you know I didn't speak to Nanny and Grandad for years?" she said.

"I was too pig-headed to understand they were trying to help."

"Shh, maybe you should try sleeping," although Maggie didn't stop. Maggie's voice shook as she admitted, "I've never had to be self-sufficient." She paused, the weight of her admission settling in the quiet room. Having relied on others for years, she was now bothered by a feeling of dependency.

Maggie's words were deeply vulnerable, revealing a pattern that had defined her life. As a child, she relied heavily on her parents to make choices and maintain stability. Later, Matthew and George were her main support, giving her protection. Now, with Lucy by her side, Maggie realised that her reliance had simply shifted from one person to another, never allowing her the opportunity to stand alone.

Lucy offered a gentle suggestion, her voice softening, "Perhaps Daddy was trying to protect you too?"

Maggie knew George acted out of care and concern. Though he tried his best, his insecurities hindered Maggie's exploration of her past. She viewed herself as an experiment in George's life, and he wanted to protect her and keep her anchored. Yet, his desire to keep her grounded caused Maggie to give up looking for her son, which she now saw with sorrow and regret.

Reflecting on her past, Maggie considered the pattern that had shaped her adult life. She realised that she had often mistaken financial stability for genuine emotional support. This confusion had guided many of her choices, and now, looking back, she felt the weight of the consequences. The pursuit of security had come at a significant emotional cost, leaving her with regrets and a deeper understanding of what she truly needed.

CHAPTER FOUR

June 1971 – Building Bridges

In contrast with last summer, I spend less time with Matthew than ever before. The business expands, and I am still unsure what he does exactly, but I know it has something to do with finding musicians and singers and providing entertainment for pubs and clubs, which is why he is out until the early hours most nights. Although cash seems to be abundant, Matthew arranges the delivery of modern furniture, choosing everything himself. We stand back, admiring our new sitting room. It looks like a picture from a magazine. As Matthew explains, he is in a far better position to choose than I am since he knows what is stylish and fashionable. "It looks so lovely. I love it!" I squeal with delight. "The Trolley lad's done alright then?" he replied, beaming from ear to ear.

Matthew provides well for us, and I take care of our home and family. He sometimes leaves little gifts on our kitchen table, like cosmetics or perfumes from department stores 'uptown.' Although if I am to be honest, this is little compensation for my loneliness. I feel guilty because I know he is doing his best, and I am aware I am being ungrateful.

Maddie practically lives with us now. She changed schools, so I can take her during the week, and then she spends most weekends with Matthew's parents. The conversation about her going into care has arisen on more than one occasion, so I do whatever I can to avoid that happening. Matthew is very generous. He shops for all our clothes, although most of my new clothes hang in my wardrobe unworn, as what he buys me is not always suitable for day-to-day wear, and it's not like I go anywhere! Every Friday morning, without fail, Matthew leaves my housekeeping money of fifteen pounds on the kitchen table. Matthew is an excellent provider! Dad and I are speaking again; I get our groceries from our shop. I haven't mentioned this to Matthew; I don't think he would like it. Matthew would prefer me to shop at the new supermarket in town, but I find it difficult with all the children in tow. I am also saving money, taking my mum's advice. Every week, I deposit any surplus housekeeping (which can amount to five pounds) into a post office account, Matthew does not know about this account, my father acted as guarantor! At mums' suggestion; it will be a nice surprise for him one day. I need to make payments to the milkman, the newspapers and the rental on our television. In addition, I must pay for Lucy and Maddie's school dinners, and I distribute the remaining amount to food shopping. When the shop is shut during lunchtime, mum helps me with my groceries while Dad eats his dinner. We then join him for a cup of tea afterwards.

"Put your money away," Mum insisted, as I try to pay for goods.

"Take the money; Matthew wouldn't like it... and we are okay for money." I say with pride.

"Stop being so bloody awkward! this has nothing whatsoever to do with Matthew; you are still our daughter! Save the housekeeping money you don't use, put it in your post office account The tide can turn at any time!" With this arrangement, my savings are increasing significantly too.

One day, I will take mum 'up town' and treat her to lunch in a posh hotel. We will go shopping at Selfridges or somewhere and try on loads of clothes in the changing rooms, getting the assistant to bring me assorted sizes. I do not have any friends now that Rita has left, and my neighbours do not speak to me. Although I am aware of their whispers and nods in my direction. "Ignore them. They're jealous. Most haven't got two bob to rub together," Matthew replied; it is a rare occasion he is home at teatime. "I heard Lillian next door call me a stuck-up cow," I say. "So, what?" Matthew said dismissively. "Lillian hasn't got a good word to say about anyone. Anyway, the way things are going with the business, we won't be living here for much longer." "What do you mean?" I am surprised. I love our little house, and I thought Matthew did too. "We will soon be able to buy our own house, and it won't be around here." A new delivery of furniture arrives, including a G Plan dining suite, sideboard and radiogram, which replace the previously used second-hand items in our front room.

I am excited to show off our modern furniture to my parents, so I invited them for Sunday tea. The relationship between Matthew and dad is still strained, but with some nagging from mum, dad reluctantly agreed to attend. My mum tries to overcompensate for dad's lack of enthusiasm. "Oh, Bill, look at this. Isn't it lovely? And I love your orange curtains," mum said, running her hand over the teak of the radiogram. Dad just frowns: he won't even remove his coat and cap, and grunts at Matthew's attempt to make conversation. I prepare a ham and egg salad and open a tin of new potatoes. I even bake a Victoria sponge, all laid out using my best set of 'china' on a white linen tablecloth to protect my shiny new table.

Little Lucy and Matthew function as intermediaries between the two men, running between them and showing off their crayoning. "Maggie, watch those kids with their crayons on this new furniture!" barks Matthew. "Doing much?" Dad asked him. Matthew looked surprised and shifts in his seat, "Yes busy! You?" "Busy enough to keep the wolf from the door," Dad replied coldly. My mum and I look at each other. I cannot stop smiling because the two most important people in my life are actually talking to each other! which is a step in the right direction.

CHAPTER FIVE

Ireland – The Cottage

The owners of the cottage had thoughtfully provided an 'information manual' holding details of pubs in the local vicinity. As the women busied themselves with unpacking and freshening up after their journey, Billy, and Nick took on the task of determining the walking distance to the nearest pub and made a reservation for their evening meal.

The group found themselves staying about five miles outside the lively town of Clifden, a place set on the Owenglin River as it flows into the Atlantic Ocean. Clifden is renowned for its bustling selection of shops, hotels and restaurants. Its unique location, nestled between a dramatic mountain range and the sweeping Atlantic, gives Clifden Bay its reputation as one of the largest and most notable seaside towns in Connemara.

While reflecting on their surroundings, Nick remembered a previous visit to Clifden with Ray. On that occasion, they had spent a couple of nights in a local hotel, their trip motivated by a desire to trace the roots of Nick's father, which stretched back through several generations in the area. Now, however, Nick found himself pondering the possibility that his mother's connection to this corner of Ireland might be more recent, prompting a new perspective on their family history.

After browsing through the information manual, the group learned that the closest pub was approximately a twenty-minute walk from their cottage. The pub was located on the main road leading toward town, offering views of the untamed Atlantic Ocean, where the water was a constant swirl of white foam and grey. Despite its proximity, the pub still felt quite remote, surrounded by wild landscape. When Nick and Billy asked to reserve a table for four, Nick couldn't help but notice the bartender's amusement at their request. In such a rural setting, it seemed the idea of booking a table in advance was a rare occurrence, perhaps even unnecessary, but they wanted to be certain of having a place for their evening meal.

The men made their way back to the cottage along a steep coastal road. The journey uphill, compounded by a strong wind, left them feeling battered and made the return trip far more challenging and time-consuming than expected.

Upon their return, Elaine was found curled up on the sofa, watching an episode of 'Friends' on television. Dressed casually in jeans and a sloppy sweatshirt, her red hair tied in a ponytail, she looked beautiful to Nick. He was used to seeing her in more formal attire, and in that moment, he felt quietly pleased with himself for suggesting this getaway. He realised how little leisure time they managed to spend together and appreciated the rare opportunity simply to relax.

"The internet connection is useless, the TV keeps buffering and if you want to make a phone call, go out and stand on the drive," she said. Nick recognised the amusement in her tone.

“What? No internet, I don’t believe it!” he said at once, taking his phone from his pocket.

“I’m sure the advertisement said there would be a good internet connection. Accessing my email is important. I emailed myself the addresses of family members questioned in relation to Matthew’s accident. If only I had printed the scanned information before we left,” Nick is moving from one side of the room to the other while holding his phone in the air and scrutinising the signal bars.

“Is everything okay?” asked Kate as she entered the room from behind a latch door in the lounge where wooden stairs lead up to the first floor.

“Expect to see cold sweats, and withdrawal symptoms soon. I have just told Nick about the terrible internet and mobile phone reception,” Elaine chuckled.

Kate and Elaine are laughing whilst Nick looks on sulkily.

“Well, I’ll leave you to sort this out. I’m going to get changed out of these damp clothes,” smiled Billy, bending to fit through the latch door from where Kate had appeared.

“I can try to retrieve my emails from my mobile phone.” Nick grabs a notepad and pen from a desk, then goes outside to stand in the driveway. He watches as the signal bars increase and as quickly decrease depending on where he stands.

“This is impossible! “He vocalises his thoughts.

While checking for any new emails, he synchronises his phone. He is also awaiting an email from the local police. Most people who gave statements back in the seventies have either died or moved home.

It has proved complicated. Nick's role in the police did not grant him information access. Nick has been clear about his reasons for accessing certain files but still needed make a formal request for information from the Irish police.

A chilly wind whipped around the cottage, causing the pages in Nick's shorthand pad to flutter uncontrollably. Frustrated and on the verge of giving up, Nick decided he would wait until they made their way to the pub before attempting again. Just as he resigned himself to this plan, his phone rang unexpectedly. It was Lucy.

Nick hesitated before answering, his mind immediately jumping to the worst—perhaps his gran's health had deteriorated further. Bracing himself, he answered with a wary, "Hello."

"Hi mum," he replied, uncertainty in his voice as he anticipated another telling-off. To his surprise, Lucy instead spoke of a mysterious visitor who had appeared at the hospital ward. Her tone was urgent as she asked Nick to do everything possible to discover whether little Matthew had died in the same accident that claimed her father's life and then return home as quickly as possible.

Nick did his best to reassure his mother. "Of course, Mum, we will try to find out whatever we can," he promised, his voice steady despite his growing concern. Recognising the potential threat, he urged her to ask the hospital staff to vet anyone who was visiting gran, emphasising that the mysterious visitor could pose a danger. Lucy agreed to his suggestion, responding, “Okay, I will do.”

The situation left Nick feeling unsettled and increasingly wary. The sinister undertones of recent events only strengthened his instinct to shield his family. As he moved restlessly around the cottage, he struggled to maintain their conversation, the poor phone reception causing his mother’s voice to fade in and out. The wind howled relentlessly outside, compounding his frustration and making it even more challenging to communicate.

Then, Lucy’s tone shifted, filled with regret. “Nick, another thing, I should have been honest with you all, and especially with Kate. Look after her... we are her only family,” she said, her words hanging heavily between them.

“Of course, we will look after her. She is safer here with us than at home right now, by the sounds of it,” Nick assured his mother, determination sounding in his voice.

He paused, growing concern. “But what do you mean you should have been honest?” Nick pressed, his curiosity and worry intensifying.

Lucy’s response was hesitant; her words tinged with emotion. “I will explain properly when you get home, but Kate is family, although she doesn’t know it!” The upset in Lucy’s voice was unmistakable.

“Family? What are you talking about?” Nick’s confusion deepened, unable to make sense of his mother’s revelation.

Lucy pleaded with him, “Please don’t mention to Kate what I have told you. I owe it to her to explain in person.” Nick noticed the vulnerability in her voice—he had never heard his mother sound so unsure of herself. The conversation left him feeling unsettled and insecure.

“You can’t leave it like this, because you haven’t actually told me anything!”

“I’ll explain everything when you get home. Just look after her. What I must tell her will come as a shock.”

Suddenly, the line went dead. Nick tried to call his mother back, but there was no signal. Exasperated, he muttered, “This blasted signal!” before heading back inside.

Back in the cottage, Kate, and Elaine were waiting for him. Kate asked, “Any luck?” but Nick, distracted by the conversation with his mother, struggled to respond.

Elaine’s irritation was clear as she prompted him, “Nicholas, Kate just asked you a question!”

At that moment, Billy joined them in the lounge. Nick, still distracted, said, “I’m waiting to hear from the local police; it could take a while, so let’s make the most of our free time.”

CHAPTER SIX

The Tenacious Aunt

Nick and Elaine had made the most of the past few days in the company of Billy and Kate. Together, they wandered for miles along the sweeping, sandy beaches, the salty Atlantic breeze leaving its mark in their hair. They hiked up to the old castle, their footsteps echoing under ever-changing skies, and found comfort in hearty meals at local pubs, where Irish coffees warmed their hands and spirits.

The evenings were filled with laughter and music; the lively melodies of fiddles and bodhráns mingled effortlessly with their own voices, all basking in the inviting glow of crackling stone hearths. Despite this warmth and conviviality, each person recognised the importance of solitude. Billy and Kate, sensitive to the mood, instinctively knew when to give Nick and Elaine space. Elaine cherished these quiet moments with Nick, appreciating the gentle understanding shown by their companions. In these rare pockets of privacy, Nick found room to reflect and gather the strength he needed for what lay ahead.

Yet, beneath the lighthearted atmosphere, a sense of anticipation lingered. Especially for Billy, who was aware that they were preparing to meet someone who was connected to the tragedy that had changed the direction of his life. The shadow of Matthew senior's accident, seldom discussed, subtly tinged the edges of their holiday, a gentle but persistent reminder of their purpose for coming.

So far, the trip had felt much like a holiday—so relaxing that they hardly missed having internet access.

Whenever Nick managed to find a signal for his iPad, he seized the opportunity to download information from his emails. He had been anxiously awaiting key details related to the accident that had claimed Matthew senior's life. At last, the awaited information arrived in his inbox, prompting Nick to make a crucial telephone call. With everything in place, he and Billy prepared to set out to visit an individual who had provided a statement about the tragic incident. This meeting was a significant step in their search for answers and closure.

"How are you feeling?" Nick asked as Billy settled into the passenger seat of their rented jeep.

"Numb really, if I am to be honest," Billy replied. "I was only a baby when all this happened. I remember having a brother, but I don't actually remember him, if that makes sense. Still, the gap he left has been noticeable my entire life."

Nick glanced at the scribbled notes in his A4 notepad, a frown of concentration creasing his brow. "Okay, so remind me—who is who in the family tree?" he asked, turning to Billy for clarification.

Billy leaned in, scanning the hurried handwriting. "From what I found out from my mum," he began, "my grandparents were John and Lucinda O'Donnell. They had four, possibly five children. There's Aileen, Joan, and I believe there's another sister named Mary. I'm not sure how reliable mum's memory is about that last one."

He paused, then continued, "What I do know for certain is that all the girls—Aileen, Joan and Mary—were older than my father, Matthew, and his older brother, Sidney. The girls were already married by the time my grandparents moved to England, so they stayed behind in Ireland."

"We're visiting Aileen today, the middle sister," Billy concluded, using his index finger to show her name on the scribbled notes as they prepared themselves for the meeting ahead.

Nick and Billy arrived at the address using directions provided by the woman Nick had spoken to over the phone the previous day. Nick parked their vehicle on the road, just outside a yellow-washed bungalow, and together they approached the white picket gate. A small, well-kept lawn bordered the path leading up to the opaque front door.

When they knocked, a woman around his own age greeted them. Nick made the introduction: "Hello, this is William O'Donnell, and I am Detective Sergeant Nicholas Langford!" seeing the concerned look on the woman's face, he questioned whether formal introduction was necessary.

Nick quickly clarified, "There is no need to worry, we are not here on official business?" he said, regretting the mention of his rank. He explained they were there on a personal matter and their connection to Aileen O'Shea, who was expecting them.

The woman called over her shoulder, “Grandma, visitors claiming to be your...” Nick interjected, “Nephews!” The younger woman appeared confused by this.

A forthright voice responded from the hallway, instructing, “Let them in girl.” An older woman, whom the men deduced must be in her late eighties, appeared and ushered them through the narrow hall into a bright, immaculate room. Patio doors at the back revealed a small garden and impressive sea views beyond.

The younger woman said, “I’ll stay for a bit, grandma,” and entered the room. Aileen, sprightly for her age and wearing an apron, held a yellow duster and a can of polish. She acknowledged Billy with, “Oh, so you are Matthew’s lad,” and regarded Nick with visible scepticism, as if to say, ‘Not sure about you!’

Aileen remarked, “You are the spit of your father! I had a feeling you might turn up one day. Although I would have thought your mother would have been here long before now. But then she never set foot on Irish soil!” The men sensed a hint of bitterness in her words.

Aileen pointed to the seating an unspoken instruction to the men, both obeyed, taking seats on a green velour sofa. “Colleen, put the kettle on and make some tea,” revealing an authoritative presence. Aileen’s steely blue eyes and mostly dark hair with just a few grey streaks made her appear mentally sharp despite her age. She nodded towards the direction of the door, “My granddaughter! your distant cousin I suppose!, anyhow...not sure how I can help you?” and noted that she was as much in the dark as anyone about the tragic death of her brother.

Recognising Aileen's commanding presence, Billy gathered his resolve and addressed her directly, "Mrs O'Shea, or can we call you Aunty Aileen? We are only here to discover what happened!" His tone was firm but respectful, looking to bridge the familial gap.

He continued, "As Nick explained in his call to you yesterday, we have many unanswered questions about the death of my father and older brother." At this, Aileen's stern expression softened slightly, showing a willingness to engage.

Billy pressed on. "We need to learn more about the circumstances that led them to be in Ireland."

Nick, referring to the document on his tablet, added, "In your statement to the Police, you said that you were expecting your brother, Matthew and his family; it was a planned holiday to join your parents who were staying with you."

Aileen nodded in confirmation. Nick then queried, "But they didn't arrive?"

"No, Matthew cancelled just a few days beforehand. My parents were so disappointed..." Aileen replied, her voice tinged with reminiscence. She then added, almost as an afterthought, "Did I say little Maddie was also staying?"

Nick, unfamiliar with the name, asked for clarification. "Maddie?"

"My niece, Sidney's young one. My parents brought her over most school holidays," Aileen explained, her words revealing a fondness for the family tradition.

"Were you informed about my father taking my brother without my mother's consent, either when it happened or sometime after?"

"That is utter nonsense! We received a message; it was the morning before the accident from Matthew saying circumstances had changed, and he was on his way to the farm,"

"The Farm?" Nick asked.

"Yes, my home for over forty years! I moved to this little bungalow a few years back; when my John died, and my son took over, although he's sold off most of our land now for development. The Americans enjoy a holiday home here!"

Nick aimed to steer the conversation back on track. "Apologies for all the questions, it's just... we would like to establish the reason Matthew was in Ireland when he died?"

"It was a planned holiday of course... to join my parents; Jack and Lucinda," Aileen said, sounding impatient.

The two men glanced at each other, with eyebrows raised on hearing the name Jack.

"I thought my grandfather's name was John?" Said Billy

"Yes, you thought right, but everyone called him Jack," clarified Aileen. "Your mother should know that!"

"Do you know what made Matthew change his mind, or why he brought only my brother and left us in London?" Billy pressed, his curiosity laced with frustration.

Aileen gave a sharp sigh. "Well, I can't claim to read minds! But they couldn't find their arse with two hands, that lot!" There was a hint of irritation in her tone, as memories of family indecision surfaced.

At that moment, Colleen entered, carefully balancing a tea tray brimming with cups and a steaming pot. She set it on the coffee table, trying to suppress her amusement at her grandmothers sharp wit, and then took a seat opposite Aileen.

Nick, sensing the levity, felt a surge of annoyance. They were here to investigate the tragic death of a child, Billy, sharing his concern, turned back to Aileen, his face earnest.

"Aunt Aileen, may I call you that?" he asked, his voice steady and respectful. "We're trying to understand my father's intentions. According to what we've been told, he took my older brother—without my mother's agreement—a six-year-old boy, taken from his family. We want to know if the child met his end at the bottom of a cliff, and his body swept out into the Atlantic, or if, as is recently suggested someone might have sold him off like a parcel of land to a wealthy American."

Colleen looked down, visibly embarrassed by the gravity of the allegations. Aileen's piercing blue eyes flashed with resolve. It was clear that the conversation was about to reach a critical turning point.

"I told the police everything I knew back then," snapped Aileen.

"Okay, what about more recently? Have you had any visitors asking questions about my mother?"

"Gran, what about the man that came by not long after Christmas? I really think you should help these people!" Colleen was talking sternly to her grandmother.

"Ok, but keep in mind this was a distressing time for our family, especially my parents. My sister, and I were having to help them through their grief as events unravelled... and anything else was just hearsay and rumour."

CHAPTER SEVEN

The Assessment

I am not in so much pain now; the physiotherapy is working; I hope I can go home soon.

A woman dressed in casual clothes is walking towards me. 'No, I don't want a radio request!'

"Hello, my name is Maria Williams. I am the hospital social worker. I am here to assess how you are and see if there is anything we need to arrange for when you are ready to go home."

"Hello dear," I answered politely.

"I first need to ask you a few questions. Some may seem odd but just answer the first thing that comes to mind."

"That's fine," I said, although I have a burning in the pit of my stomach.

"May I know your full name?"

"Margaret Rose O'Donnell," I said.

"And what is today's date?"

I am scrambling to think about what the date is. I need the memory board...

"That's okay, don't worry. Can you tell me what year it is?"

"1972. No, it's not, it's 2024."

"And the month?"

"July, I mean August" am I right? This woman isn't giving anything away; she is just scribbling away on her form.

She continues to ask stupid questions like...do I know the name of our King, and asks me what year the war ended, and to count backwards from one hundred! I've never been good at sums, even at the best of times!

"Now I am going to ask some questions about your home," she said. "What type of home do you have? For instance, do you have to go upstairs to go to bed?"

"Yes," I replied.

"When you are ready to go home, who will live in your house with you?" She asked,

"My nurse, and my son said he may come and live with me when I get out of hospital."

"What are their names?" Maria asked.

I have a blank moment... I cannot remember the lovely girl who has been caring for me at home. She brought me the memory board! What is her name? I know this!

"It's ok Margaret, don't worry, we can come back to that question! Can you remember the names of your children?

"Why of course, Lucy, Matthew and William!" I said triumphantly.

"Which of your sons said he may come to live with you?"

I look up to see Lucy walking into the ward.

"Here is one of my children now!" I said as she approaches.

Lucy beams a smile. She turns to the social worker and holds out her hand.

"I am so sorry I am later than agreed. The traffic is awful!"

"Don't worry, we have started without you. Your mother is about to tell me all about your brother, the one she thinks may move in once she gets home!"

I am pleased Lucy is here. I don't feel so worried about all those test questions now!

"Matty wrote to me, and now he's coming to see me," I said.

Lucy is looking worried. The problem is my head is throbbing. I feel dizzy, and I am feeling worried too because I cannot remember?

"Did Matthew tell you he was your son?" asked Maria.

"No, Matthew and I are married," I said.

"My husband is Matthew, and 'Little Matthew' is our son; the eldest often shared their first name with their father back then."

"Do you know, your father stays out way too late for a family man. He thinks he can get around me, but I know what he's up to," I am feeling angry.

"Mum forget that this lady; Maria... she is not asking about your marriage to Matthew." Lucy said gently, "She wants to know if you have received any visitors other than us while you have been in hospital." Lucy spoke in a measured and clear manner.

"I don't know what you are talking about?"

"Why are you both staring at me?" They don't understand how I feel.

"I am at home every night on my own with four children to look after. The only people I ever see nowadays are my mum and dad; nobody else visits!"

CHAPTER EIGHT

November. 1971 - Gratitude

You would think I would be used to Matthew coming home in the early hours, reeking of whiskey and perfume, but it never gets any easier to accept. Each time, the pain is fresh—no matter how many times it happens. Apparently, it is perfectly normal for me to look after our children, care for Maddie, and keep the house spotless, while he comes and goes as he pleases, with no concern about how it affects me.

One night, I finally confronted him, unable to keep my frustration inside any longer. I asked where he had been, but he just treated me as if I was foolish, acting as though my suspicions were baseless. Night after night, he returned with the unmistakable scent of perfume clinging to his clothes, not even bothering to hide it anymore. Desperate for a change, I pleaded,

"Please, can I come out with you?" I reminded him that my mother had offered to babysit any time we needed. I wanted him to realise how hard it was for me to look after four children every week. "Your brother should do his share. Maddie is with us more often than she is at home," I pointed out, emphasising the imbalance in responsibilities.

But yet again Matthew brushed off my concerns. "Give it a rest, Mags. We must entertain to bring in business. You would be bored," he said dismissively, as if my exhaustion and isolation were trivial.

His lack of understanding made me feel undervalued. "And what difference does one more child make? You are always on at her," Unable to hide my irritation. "How can you say that?" I retorted

"Maggie, you've become a nag," he accused, unwilling to see how much his words and attitude were hurting me.

"What did you call me?... I am just fed up with being on my own!" I cried out, the loneliness overwhelmed me.

"Do you have to drink so much? And your clothes stink of perfume," I said tearfully.

Matthew brushed off my concerns with irritation, saying, "Now you're imagining things. You don't go without—look around! There are plenty of women who would love to be in your shoes." His words were sharp, making it clear he was annoyed by my questioning.

As I stood at the stove stirring the pot of gravy, I felt tears prickling in my eyes. The weight of his dismissal settled over me. Matthew walked behind me and wrapped his arms around my body. The gesture didn't feel warm or comforting; instead, it felt more like a restraint, holding me in place rather than offering support.

He leaned in and whispered, "You should consider yourself a lucky woman because it's you I come home to. And anyway, I have a pleasant surprise for you in the new year... we are all going on holiday!" The words, though intended as reassurance, did little to soothe my hurt.

CHAPTER NINE

The Photographs

Whilst the men are visiting a traced relative. Kate had a lazy morning—it was already lunchtime, and she hadn't even dressed yet. It had been a whirlwind since they had arrived, but she found it enjoyable.

"Come on, lazybones, get dressed. Let's go grab a pub lunch," Elaine said as she stood in the kitchen doorway.

"Shouldn't we wait for Nick and Billy?" Kate asked, feeling uncertain.

"No, they could take ages. We'll call them from the pub, and they can join us there," Elaine replied, dismissing the idea of waiting.

Kate dressed in a pair of jeans and a jumper, tied her hair up, and grabbed her coat. She didn't bother with make-up, as it seemed unlikely, they would meet anyone.

Elaine and Kate walked along the lane that led to the nearest pub. The sun cast a hazy glow, causing the peaks to vary in colour depending on where the light caught them.

The wind was troublesome again, leaving Kate feeling breathless as they walked and talked. She never expected to meet someone with whom she had an immediate bond, not since Claire.

Elaine and Kate quickly became friends. Elaine's approachable personality and humour helped Kate move past her first feelings of inferiority about Elaine's high-powered career, making it easy for

Kate to relax. As they laughed together and shared stories, Kate felt truly accepted, allowing them to bond deeply.

Nick held a special place in Kate's heart. He was a lovely guy, and spending time with him and Elaine made her realise how compatible and in love they were. Nick adored Elaine.

No matter what the future held, Kate knew she had made lifelong friends on this trip. Setting aside the reason they were there; she was glad she had accepted their invitation. It was unusual for her to take risks and try new things, but she had been doing that a lot. Billy was also a fantastic companion, a sweet man who had ensured Kate felt comfortable from the start.

Elaine and Kate arrived at the pub, windswept and finding it empty. Elaine went to the bar and ordered two large glasses of red wine. They settled in seats by the stone inglenook fireplace, where a fire roared in the hearth.

Their phones dinged simultaneously with incoming messages. Both sat in silence, gazing at the screens of their phones.

Claire had sent a text, hoping Kate was having a fun time and asking her to call when she could. Another text from the bank warned Kate that she was about to go into overdraft. She made a mental note to transfer some money from her savings while she was there.

The next notification Kate opened sent a chill down her spine.

Elaine noticed the sudden change in Kate's expression and immediately asked, "What's wrong?" The concern was evident in her voice as she tried to read Kate's face for any hint of what might have caused such distress.

Without saying a word, Kate began swiping through a series of photos she had just received on her phone. Her hands trembled slightly as she handed the device to Elaine. Elaine's eyes widened as she looked at the images, a gasp of disbelief escaping her lips. Before she could fully process what she was seeing, Elaine's own phone buzzed, signalling a new message. Glancing down, she realised she had also received similar photos, deepening the sense of shock and unease between them.

CHAPTER TEN

The Holiday

Billy sat across from Aileen, struggling with an unshakable sense of disconnect. He desperately hoped she might hold the answers he looked for about the day that had haunted his childhood for so long—a day he could not remember himself, no matter how hard he tried.

Aileen prepared to share her account, falling into the gentle rhythm of a storyteller. It was almost as if she might have said, "Are you all sitting comfortably? Then I'll begin." Although these words were left unspoken, the intent hung in the air.

She began, "The two boys were young when they first left for England, so my parents brought them back to visit regularly, up until the point they were old enough to stay at home on their own." Nick and Billy glanced at each other, silently urging Aileen to move the story forward, hoping her recollections would soon touch upon the matters that weighed most heavily on their minds.

Then, the conversation turned abruptly. Aileen admitted, "I can't remember exactly how we found out, as the shock was overwhelming, but someone murdered Sidney's wife."

Aileen recounted how her parents brought Maddie, a sweet child of about two years old, over to give Sidney some much-needed space. However, the arrangement was short-lived, as the family returned home once Sidney became a suspect in the ongoing murder investigation.

Nick's curiosity was immediate, and he asked directly, "Did any of the family suspect Sidney murdered his wife?" Aileen turned to him and, with a firm tone, replied, "No, we did not!"

In the years that followed, visits continued. Sometimes Maddie accompanied the family on these trips, while at other times she remained at home with Margaret, Matthews young wife. Aileen then addressed Billy, explaining that her own mother often voiced worries about Margaret's well-being, especially while the family lived with them. She noticed that Margaret became increasingly frail, lost weight, and bore dark rings under her eyes—obvious signs that she was struggling to manage the demands of motherhood.

Aileen observed, "Not all women are natural-born mothers." She paused, thoughtful, before adding that Margaret had declined repeated invitations to join them on their trips to Ireland, which would have given her a much-needed break. The family began to think of her as 'mollycoddled' and a little spoiled. Moreover, Matthew confided in them that he found it difficult to cope with Margaret's frequent mood swings.

Billy and Nick suppressed how protective they felt for Maggie,

Billy leaned forward, his curiosity evident. "Did you meet my mother in person?" he asked.

Aileen shook her head, a hint of frustration in her voice. "No, in all those years, we never met her or any of the children. With our own brood to care for, and the responsibilities of running the farm, it simply wasn't practical to travel to England. Matthew often said he'd try to get some time off work and bring the family over, but each time, the visit was postponed until 'next time'."

She paused to recall the moment. "In early 1972, Matthew said the family would visit for February half-term and rent a nearby cottage. We prepared, and my parents arrived early with Maddie."

Billy asked, "Why did Matthew change his mind?"

Aileen replied, "Maggie and the baby—you—were ill, and Sidney and Matthew were busy with work. We were all disappointed."

Billy continued, "Then how did Matthew and my brother end up in Ireland?"

Aileen's eyes filled with tears. "Matthew left a message at the pub since we had no phone. He was coming to Ireland, so we got ready for your visit. But he didn't arrive, and after several attempts to call, the local garda came and told us the terrible news—Sidney had died."

CHAPTER ELEVEN

The Confession

I am back on antibiotics. Although they make me feel queasy, at least my mind feels clearer and less fuzzy. My daughter, Lucy, is visiting me today, but I can't help noticing she seems distracted.

Looking at her with concern, I ask, "Are you feeling alright?"

Lucy manages a small smile. "You are asking me?" she said, but her sad eyes betray her true feelings.

Trying to reassure her, I say gently, "Please don't worry about me."

Lucy shakes her head. "Mum, I am not worried about you... well, of course, I am, but that's not it."

"What is it then?" I ask, growing more concerned.

Lucy hesitates before finally telling me, "Billy and Nick are in Ireland."

I am surprised. "What are they doing there?" I asked.

She explains, "They have gone to see if they can find the whereabouts of the person who wrote to you, Kate has gone with them."

"They have gone to find Matthew Junior?"

"Yes, little Matthew!"

I know Matthew's not in Ireland; he is here! On his last visit, he told me he would never leave again! But I don't bother saying anything that might upset Lucy further.

Lucy's eyes well with tears.

"Lucy, what is wrong?" I reach out for her hand.

"Oh mum, I've done a terrible thing," she sobbed.

"Tell me about it. Sharing will make you feel better, and if it's that bad, I will have forgotten what you've told me by tomorrow!" I jest.

Lucy is crying and laughing as she wipes her nose with a clean tissue from my tissue box.

"Whatever you have done can't be that bad," I reassure her.

"I never told you something... it's about Maddie. She needed our help! She came to see me when I was pregnant with Nicholas," she reveals.

What Lucy shares with me next shatters my heart. Through her tears, she recounts how Maddie came to her seeking help. Instead of welcoming Maddie into her life, Lucy admits that she turned Maddie away, offering her only enough money to get by. Just weeks later, Lucy received the devastating news that Maddie's husband had taken both her life and his in a tragic act.

Lucy continues her confession, her voice trembling as she reveals another painful truth. She explains that she and George had worked together to keep essential information from me, specifically about Maddie's orphaned child. The weight of their decision is clear in her expression, and I can sense the struggle she endured carrying this burden.

Then, Lucy admits to something even more astonishing. She confesses that when she first met Kate, she immediately suspected that Kate was actually Maddie's daughter. The realisation left her unsettled, yet she chose to keep her suspicions to herself. Lucy recalls

George's reasoning for withholding information about Kate after her mother was murdered "Daddy felt that if you were to be told, it may cause you to become unwell again!".

It becomes painfully clear that George had no right to make such decisions on my behalf. Still, I am forced to confront my own role in this web of secrecy. I have been the keeper of many secrets, convincing myself that I was shielding my children from pain. But now, I understand that it is time for the truth to become known, no matter how difficult it may be.

"None of this is your fault, I should have been honest a long time ago. I thought that by keeping it to myself, I was protecting you and Billy. The truth is what I know has haunted me in my dreams and every waking hour," I confess.

Tears are now stinging my face.

"Oh, Mum, I am so sorry. I didn't want to upset you. That's why I never told you about this," Lucy said.

"Lucy, you know as well as I do, I am gradually losing my mind... sometimes good days and sometimes bad. Today I am having a good day!" I take a tissue from the box and wipe my tears.

"Listen carefully. I must tell you what happened back then as it is significant to all of you, but this time it's up to you to share the details.

CHAPTER TWELVE

February 1972–The Attack

Matthew has been away for three days. I have not seen him since Saturday lunchtime, although he telephones to say that he and Sidney are staying in Liverpool. The music scene is changing, so they need to go further afield to find suitable musicians. These days, Matthew spends more nights away in a week than he spends at home. The brothers are still scouring the country for a 'band' that will make them rich and famous.

Maddie usually stays with me but this week her grandparents have taken her to Ireland for the half-term. We were all supposed to go, but disappointingly Matthew cancelled our holiday last-minute because of work commitments. It is a dreary, bitter day, and I am visiting my parents to collect groceries. Mum refills the teapot, and I am at the table leafing through the latest copy of Woman's Weekly. Lucy is by the fireplace reading a comic. She is such a clever little girl, always reading something, and the boys are playing rough and tumble.

"How's Matthew?" mum asks as she fusses over the children. I look up from my magazine, surprised. Mum seldom asks after Matthew. "Working hard as usual," I reply, noticing she is watching me with an expression of concern. "What's up?" I snap. "We are worried!" "What now?" I say dismissively. "The police have been here," she said solemnly. "What did they want?" My mum does not answer at once. "It's about Matthew. I must warn you about something."

"Mum, stop talking in riddles. If you know something, tell me," I say, feeling uneasy but not wanting to appear too worried. "The police suspect that Matthew and Sidney's entertainment business is a front for criminal activity."

'Here we go,' I think to myself with a sigh, expressing my reluctance as I tut and rise from my seat. I walk over to the chair where I'd left my coat, slip my arms through the sleeves, and pull it tightly around me. Approaching the mirror that dangles from a chain above the fireplace, I retrieve my headscarf from my coat pocket and carefully arrange it over my hair, smoothing it into place. Then, reaching into my handbag, I find my pink lipstick and compact mirror. With practiced movements, I apply a fresh coat of lipstick and check my reflection, ensuring everything is in order before I leave.

"Gossip!" I say flippantly. "Margaret, you have three children who depend on you!" My normally placid and non-confrontational mum speaks sternly, a tone I haven't heard since I was a child.

"When was the last time you see Matthew?" she asks. "This morning," I say unconvincingly.

"Don't bother lying to me. He hasn't been home for days." My mum's tone makes the children look towards us. My mum provides them with a reassuring smile before beckoning me into the kitchen.

"The police have been watching Matthew and your house," she whispers. I am unable to hide my shock. I have noticed no-one.

"Why would the police be watching our house? How do you know this?" "There is something else." Mum hesitates, deciding whether to tell me. “Your father has been helping the police! “She mouths half the sentence, so I’m not sure if I hear correctly.

“Collaborating with the police... about what?” I cannot hide my horror.

“Your friend Rita visited us not so long ago.”

“Rita visited you. Why?”

Mum explains that Rita revealed details that suggest Sidney and Matthew are criminals, involved in serious robberies. Although Rita isn’t sure if they carried them out, she believes they function as puppeteers, keeping their own hands clean. “Rita took documentation out of the house before leaving and produced evidence from the club where she was working,” mum explains.

“Matthew is a criminal. That’s how they earn so much money, and they were even demanding money from Rita’s then-boss!” With my mouth hanging open, I strain to hear what mum is saying as she continues to speak in whispers. “They loan cash, and if people don’t pay up, well, God help the poor buggers.” mum speaks with urgency. “Your dad already knows about some of this from local business connections.” Her expression changes from disgust to pity. “They are a pair of bully boys!” Mum exclaims. “What is probably the most serious of all is that Rita said the alibi provided by the O’Donnell family to the detectives investigating the murder of Sidney’s wife is false, so they may all be covering for a murderer.”

“Why has Rita told these lies? She was my friend!” I exclaim.

"Rita is your friend! That's the reason she told us, not the police!" I am stunned. The 'two-faced cow'—after I agreed to keep quiet about Sidney, she goes behind my back and slags Matthew off to my parents, of all people! Mum has read my mind.

"Maggie, Rita hasn't told us anything that we haven't already considered. We have suspected for years that Matthew has an unhealthy hold over you."

"Your father has gone to the police with the information Rita gave us! Dad has also been told by acquaintances that Matthew and Sidney are dealing drugs!"

"Drugs! That's ridiculous. Why would Dad involve himself like this?" I am furious.

"It's because he loves you. We both do. Leave him; come and stay with us. The police have enough evidence to put both brothers in prison, Maggie. They hurt people."

"Watch the kids. I am going to ask Dad what's going on. He has had it in for Matthew since day one!" I hear myself ranting.

I march down the hallway, ready to confront my father. As I reach the plastic blinds hanging at the threshold, the bell above the shop door rings, and two men dressed in suits enter the shop.

One man stops to bolt the door and turns the closed sign. Are these the police again? Although they are not behaving like the police, their manner is threatening. I back into the hallway, watching from the darkness, my vision obscured by the hanging blinds.

"Hello Bill, we have a message from some people, you know," said the darker of the two men.

I have never seen either of them before today. They have London accents and dress in smart attire. I presume them to be in their late thirties. The fairer of the two has his back to me and is watching the door.

"Our boss has asked that we come over and have a little chat. We have a deal for you."

"Take back anything said to the 'Old Bill', and we won't kick your head in." They are not the police, then Maggie thinks.

"I don't need to guess too hard what toerags are pulling your strings. Tell them from me, I was fighting in a war when they were still in nappies," Dad replied obstinately.

"Go on, sling your hook... get lost before I call the police," Dad is pointing to the door, anger rises with each word, and he is not backing down despite the threat.

The taller of the men laughs, then stops abruptly and viciously punches my dad in the face, sending his glasses flying off his nose. Dad could not have seen that coming; he stumbles as the other man punches him in the stomach.

"How does that feel, Bill? It's your wife next," said the taller man, leaning over dad, he is clearly winded.

"Where is she? Out the back?"

Dad holds up his hand as a gesture to stop. Despite my instinct to run to his side and protect him, I chose to get Mum and the kids out of the house.

I back up slowly towards where I came from, keeping within the shadows so as not to be seen. Closing the door behind me, I enter the parlour and lean my back against it.

"What is it?" Mum's face is ashen. She reaches for the door handle, and I grab her arm to stop her.

Suddenly, a piercing cry rings out from my dad, his voice filled with agony. The sound is swiftly followed by a cacophony of crashing noise; objects being hurled and battered, the chaos unmistakable. Without hesitation, Mum and I spring into action. Working together, we swiftly gather up the children, urgency fuelling every movement. We race through the kitchen, our footsteps echoing the panic that grips us, and burst out into the yard. Navigating the familiar maze of alleys behind our home, we flee through the back gate, hearts pounding as we put as much distance as possible between ourselves and the turmoil inside. We lean against a wall. The two older children's eyes are wide, and Billy is crying.

CHAPTER THIRTEEN

The Search Party

Elaine swiped through photographs sent to her social media account. The photos captured moments of their walking, chatting, and laughing, taken just twenty minutes before as they made their way to the pub. The text came from an unknown number. Elaine stood up to survey the area while making a call, but all she got was an automated voicemail. "They are out of range or they have blocked us," she whispered, sharing her thoughts with Kate. "You try!" Kate's voice trembled as she rang the number.

"Someone had been following us along the secluded road, close enough to take these photos without our knowledge." She shuddered. Elaine, trying to offer reassurance, replied, "They probably used a pay as you go phone; Nick will be able to find out if it is from the number!" Her tone carried a hint of determination, even as the uncertainty lingered in the air.

"I'll text to inform Nick where we are." She decided wouldn't mention the photos yet, they could stay there until they arrived, Elaine suggested, keeping the unsettling discovery to themselves for now. "Don't look so worried, Kate. We are safe here! Let's have lunch and another drink. What were you having?" Elaine tried to ease the tension, suggesting they enjoy a meal and relax. By the time they finished their stew pots and crusty bread, more people had arrived at the pub, taking their seats as individuals or in couples. The barman smiled at them as he added a couple more logs to the fire, which crackled and spit.

Elaine rummages through her handbag and retrieves a packet of cigarettes and a lighter.

“I won’t be long; I’m going outside for a cigarette. But do not tell Nick I convinced him I’ve given up!” Elaine admitted guiltily.

“I allow myself the occasional indulgence, especially when I’m stressed, drinking, and after a lunch like the one we just had!” Elaine justified her habit, trying to shrug off any concerns.

Elaine placed her small holdall on the table in front of them. Meanwhile, Kate sat alone in their cosy spot by the fireplace, watching the new arrivals—mostly walkers in weather-resistant jackets, carrying sticks and backpacks.

A man in a grey suit stood at the bar, looking businesslike. With greying hair and a coffee cup in hand, he seemed out of place in this pub at lunchtime—perhaps waiting for a meeting. He held a rain-spattered trench coat. When their eyes met, Kate quickly turned her attention to the fireplace but still felt his gaze upon her.

Elaine had been outside for several minutes, and Kate grew concerned. Should she go out and look for her friend? Or was Elaine on the phone with Nick or someone from work?

Given the unsettling circumstances, with the knowledge that someone had been following them and had captured photographs without their consent, Kate’s anxiety grew. The images sent to Elaine’s social media were proof enough that their privacy had been invaded on the walk to the pub, and now, with Elaine still absent, Kate's worries intensified.

She stayed seated by the fireplace for a while, wrestling with her apprehension and glancing occasionally at the door in hope that Elaine would soon return. As the minutes dragged on, Kate tried to reassure herself that perhaps Elaine was simply taking her time. Twenty minutes had now elapsed since Elaine had stepped outside for a cigarette—surely enough time for several smokes, and work calls.

Despite her efforts to stay relaxed, Kate could no longer ignore the knot of unease twisting in her stomach. Mustering her resolve, she finally decided to venture outside and check on her friend. The moment she stepped out, she was met by a fierce wind whipping around the pub and a fine, stinging rain that forced her to squint against its bite. Each step heightened her concern, the wild weather mirroring the storm of worry inside her. Dark clouds obscure the mountains, and mist cascaded from the peaks down to the valley below, rolling toward the road. Kate searched for Elaine but found no trace of her. She went to the edge of the lane, scanning both directions, with visibility reduced to a few hundred yards. Noticing the absence of ashtrays, Kate spotted a stubbed-out cigarette on the gravel, close by the pub. Worried, she called out Elaine's name, looking toward the small car park beside the pub, surrounded by a stone wall. Beyond it lay moorland. Kate climbed the wall, continuing to call for Elaine. On this side, the terrain was wild, filled with spiky common gorse bushes and bell heather. She moved through the mist, the low-growing shrubbery impeding her progress. Her trainers felt soaked, and her jeans were sopping from the knees down. Then, she heard a sound behind her, distorted by the wind. Someone was calling out to her from behind the car park wall—it's the man from the bar. "Hey!" he beckoned. Kate made her way back towards the pub, where the rain intensified, driven by the strengthening wind. Raising his voice to be heard over the pounding wind, the man said, "You have to be careful out there. The ground is uneven, and it gets boggy in this weather.

"Have you lost your dog?" From over the wall, Kate responded,

"It's my friend! I'm worried, she came outside a while ago and hasn't returned to the bar."

The man glanced at Kate and urged, "Let's go back inside!" Noticing her lingering hesitation, he tried to reassure her, raising his voice above the wind. "Your friend might have come back in through another entrance or perhaps she's gone to the ladies'—she's probably waiting for you inside. If not, I'll help you look. The fog and mist roll in quickly this time of year, and if you're not familiar with the area, it can be dangerous!" His words were nearly lost to the roar of the wind as Kate climbed back over the wall, pointedly resisting his outstretched hand. Despite her wariness—uncertain if she could trust anyone at this moment—she followed him back toward the pub, her nerves taut as she weighed her next move. The man approached the bar and spoke with the barman, while Kate headed through an adjoining door to the ladies' room, calling out for Elaine. To her dismay, Elaine wasn't there, intensifying her worry. Returning to the bar, Kate found the man with a small group of people gathered. "We're going to search the immediate area. I suggest you stay here with Lou in case your friend returns," he advised. "No, I'm coming with you," Kate insisted, determined not to remain idle. The man looked down at her wet feet and jeans but didn't comment. Then he asked, "What's your friend's name?" "Elaine, uh, Elaine..." Kate realised she didn't know Elaine's last name. "Would she have gone back to where you're staying without you?"

"No, definitely not, I have tried her phone, but it goes directly to voicemail!," Kate replied, her mind racing with indecision. Should she contact Nick and Billy for help, or would it be wiser to begin searching for Elaine at once? Lou gestured towards the man, offering him an old-fashioned landline receiver. The sight of the corded phone startled Kate it felt oddly out of place in the modern world.

"DI Walsh, I have an officer on the line," Lou announced, handing over the receiver. The presence of DI Walsh—a Detective Inspector, gave Kate a measure of comfort, his calm authority easing some of her anxiety.

DI Walsh responded quickly, his tone decisive. "We're going to head out and start searching. Lou, ask them to send a car," he instructed. With the authorities now involved and a search party about to be organised, Kate felt a flicker of hope. The situation was urgent, but with help arrival, they could begin the search for Elaine in earnest.

Kate walked alongside DI Walsh as they ventured into the marsh on the near-side, while the group of volunteers crossed the road to the moorland opposite. She explained about the photographs and a brief background to why they were in Ireland. He stopped to examine the Photos on her phone. He pointed in the direction of their rental cottage and explained, “These were most likely taken roughly a mile and a half away, probably from behind the old shed.”

Returning the phone to Kate, they hear a yell from across the road. One walker in the group waved a stick, trying to catch their attention. They hasten their pace, each scrambling over the wall, and move towards the group that had gathered. As they drew closer, they see something or someone slumped against a large rock formation.

Unsettled Footsteps

The wind swept relentlessly across the moor, tugging insistently at my coat as I trailed the two women at a careful distance. With each step, I lifted my phone to my eye, capturing fleeting glimpses of Kate and her friend set against the backdrop of wild, rolling hills and the stark white cottage that stood in lonely contrast to the landscape. Their laughter drifted back to me, faint and mingled with each gust, yet my attention sharpened on the subtle shadow of worry that flickered across Kate's face. She occasionally glanced over her shoulder, as though she sensed something just beyond the edge of her awareness. In those moments, I felt a surge of satisfaction. Staying unnoticed was becoming second nature; every photograph I snapped marked a quiet triumph, a testament to my growing mastery of stealth. Later, the women took their seats by the fire in the pub. They spoke in hushed tones, the room's warmth around them. I watched from outside, recalling conversation pieces—a new WhatsApp group and the excitement of their plans. I saw my chance when Kate's same friend snuck off for a smoke. With the group in the lounge and the back door unlocked, I entered. My heart hammered in my chest, the rush of pride and adrenaline almost overwhelming as I moved silently through the doorway. The house was quiet; the kitchen bathed in shifting shadows. On the table, Kate's phone lay unattended. Without hesitation, I entered her date of birth, feeling a wave of relief as I gained access to the Ireland WhatsApp group. The list of numbers appeared on the screen, and I quickly snapped a photo—an intoxicating rush of control surged through me. Now I knew exactly where to find them.

I sent the images to each of the women's mobiles, imagining the ripple of confusion my intrusion would unleash. Back in the bar, I watched as Kate stared at her phone in disbelief, her brow furrowing. She turned the screen to her friend, her voice taut and uncertain. "Who sent this?" I noted the tremor in her tone—a subtle tightening of anxiety. The companion's gaze darted to her own phone, her eyes narrowing in suspicion. The couple, bound by a sense of safety, now exchanged uneasy glances. The warmth of the room seemed to dissipate, replaced by a chill of vulnerability.

Outside, Kate's friend stood in the curling mist, her phone's glow illuminating her features as she scrolled through the unfamiliar images. She lingered there, her expression shifting from curiosity to fear as she processed what she saw. Their eyes met—my gaze cold, hers sharp with suspicion. She stiffened, the cigarette trembling in her hand. Breaking the silence, her voice rang out, edged with alarm: "Who are you? What do you want?"

I froze, suspended between the thrill of my achievement and a sudden jolt of panic. The women's reactions—confusion, fear, suspicion—were living proof of the impact I had made on their world. In their unease, I found something I craved: validation. For one brief, tense moment, I mattered.

CHAPTER FOURTEEN

1972 - Supportive Neighbours

It felt odd for her to hear her mum speak about this; she hadn't before, but in Lucy's mind's eye, she could remember vividly the occasion about which she was talking. Thugs had savagely attacked and beaten her grandad. They had waited a few moments to draw breath before finding refuge with a neighbour, where they could use their telephone to call the police. He was taken to the hospital, and her grandmother went with him in the ambulance.

Maggie – Present day

"It broke my heart to remember mums shriek when we found my father unconscious, lying in a pool of his own blood". Maggie was obviously distressed as she recalled the horrifying events of the days leading to Lucy's brother and fathers' disappearance. Lucy remembers a nice old lady who lived across the road, she took care of them. While they were only with her for one or two nights, it felt like days, and she remembered the feeling of insecurity, just wanting her mummy or her nan! She could also remember her daddy arriving and all the tears that followed! Despite the overwhelming feeling of guilt, she had every time she remembered that day, upon reflection, she realised there was nothing she could have done. She was a child!

February 1972

It was mid-afternoon, and the shop was typically quiet! Even though the attackers left through the front door, I was the sole witness to my father's assault. With its bell ringing, the ambulance leaves our street, and neighbours congregate at their gates. Mrs Gordon, a neighbour from across the street, offers to take in the children, allowing me to go to the hospital. "They will be okay with me." Mrs Gordon takes young Billy in her arms. "Your mother needs you."

Matthew Junior and Lucy's eyes are wide.

The police arrive and are waiting for me at the shop. Two plain-clothed detectives join the uniformed police officers. One of them introduces himself as DI Chaplin and hands me a card, which I place in my coat pocket. They ask me questions about who and what I see. DI Chaplin presses me about who is in the house and the whereabouts of my husband, inquiring whether Matthew joins me at any time during our visit to my parents.

Despite telling him that the children and I are the only visitors, they continue to ask questions about Matthew and Sidney.

The police eventually leave after lengthy questioning. I told them I was desperate to join my mother at the hospital, and they offered to take me to her in a police car. They informed me they would need to take a formal statement from my mum. I refused their offer of a lift as I needed to lock up the shop and check on the children. With a sense of guilt, I refrained from providing the police with any information that might incriminate my husband.

I am alone. I glance around; it's as if a hurricane has swept through. Tin, flour, broken jars, and other items from shelves litter the floor amid smeared blood, even visible against the dark wood. The police said the attack on Dad may result from a robbery but are keeping an open mind at this stage. The telephone rings, and I answer it, still feeling dazed.

"Maggie, is that you? Why are you there? I just got home, are the kids okay?" It's Matthew.

"Someone's attacked Dad." Matthew hasn't responded. "I'm leaving for the hospital now."

"Matthew. Did you hear what I just said?"

"Yes, I heard what you said. Where are the kids?"

"With Mrs Gordon," I say coldly.

"Okay, let me know how he is. Telephone me from the hospital."

I place the telephone receiver back on its cradle, lock up, and run over to Mrs Gordon to check on the children.

"I want to come," said Matthew Junior, clinging to my leg, looking up with his big blue eyes brimming. Mrs Gordon takes his hand. "Come along, my little lad. Mummy won't be long. I will get you a biscuit."

When I arrive, Dad is still not awake. His injuries are serious. He received blows to his head, back and legs. We are told he has a fractured skull, arm and collarbone. The police question Mum and me again. But we cannot add to the information I have already provided. We sit quietly; I am still trying to decipher what happened. "You had better get back to the children," we had sat in silence for so long that mum's words startle me.

"The children are fine. I am staying here!" mum doesn't reply her eyes fixed to where Dad is lying in the hospital bed.

For me, the shock is fading. People known to my husband, acting on my brother-in-law's orders, injured my father. I feel sick again. Also, Matthew's reaction on the telephone has bothered me. I told him my father was attacked, but he didn't ask any questions about how it happened, or why.

I fetch us a drink from the vending machine; "is that alright mum it looks a bit weak,"

"If it's wet and warm it will do!" she replies sipping from the plastic cup. I cannot shake this feeling; I must speak to Matthew urgently and in person!

"Mum, I am going to go home and fetch a change of clothes. Do you need anything?" My mum is watching dad for the slightest of movement, I see she is shivering.

"I will fetch you a warm jumper. You look cold."

"Yes, that will do," she replied after a long pause.

CHAPTER FIFTEEN

February 1972 – The Confrontation

I place the key in the lock and push open the front door, feeling for the light switch as I step inside. The silver glow of the television spills out from the living room, a silent sign that Matthew is watching in the dark. The sight unsettles me, and my stomach churns with apprehension, knowing that I am about to confront him and dreading what his response might be.

Matthew is stretched out on the sofa, his attention fixed on the screen. He turns his head as he senses my presence in the hallway, then reaches out and flicks on the lamp beside him, illuminating the room in a warm glow.

"I've come back for a change of clothes," I announce, my voice steady but tense.

Matthew sits up, stretches, and rubs his eyes. As he lets out a yawn, he asks, "How is he?" The casualness of his gesture, the yawn hinting at disinterest and a lack of sincerity, ignites anger within me. I grit my teeth and respond, "In a bad way, he is still unconscious!" I stay where I am, holding my ground.

The urge to scream at him, to demand answers, pulses through me. Yet, I resist the temptation and instead lock eyes with him, searching for any sign of emotion—any sign that he feels even a trace of concern or guilt. But Matthew deliberately avoids my gaze, turning his face away, unwilling to meet my eyes or offer any reassurance.

I ask pointedly, “Do you have something to tell me?”

“What are you talking about?”

“Did you know Sidney arranged for my dad to be beaten up?” I asked outright.

“What the heck!” Matthew rises to his feet.

Matthew towers above me, his intimidating presence difficult to ignore, but I stand my ground, refusing to back down. “Don’t be coming in here, throwing accusations around; I can understand you are upset...but you haven’t given me a chance to speak!” he said, the tension thick between us.

I fix my gaze at him, my voice unwavering. “If you won’t tell me what happened, then perhaps I’ll tell you what I think. Just stop me if I go wrong.” My obstinacy surprises even myself, but I press on, determined to unearth the truth.

“Is it true that you and your brother go around clubs and pubs, intimidating landlords into booking your bands?” I challenge. “No doubt you pay the musicians a pittance, and offer ‘security’ at an extra cost.”

Matthew stares at me, stunned and silent, the veins in his neck standing out as his face reddens. But I refuse to relent, letting my accusations spill forth.

“Does having access to all these people allow you to lend money, sell drugs, or even pull off the occasional robbery?” I press, determined to expose the secrets I suspect he’s hiding.

I glare at Matthew; my voice laced with disgust. "You two really have got a right little racket going on," I say. Matthew runs his hand through his hair and casts his eyes upwards, as if seeking guidance or absolution from above. But I am determined not to let him escape my questions so easily. I need answers, and I am not leaving until I have them.

"My dad threatened to go to the police," I continue, my words sharp and pointed, "so your brother arranged for him to keep his mouth shut. And all the while, you deceived me with your 'industrious husband' act, pretending to be something you're not. My dad was right all along. You and Sidney are nothing more than a pair of low-life gangsters!" The last sentence escapes my lips with venom, my frustration boiling over.

Desperate for some kind of denial, I plead, "Tell me I'm wrong!" But Matthew stays silent, refusing to offer any defence or explanation.

"What you don't know is it has become our daily routine to visit my parents, and I heard every word those bastards said; feeling the need to hide, seeing what they did to him... If I hadn't run, dragging my mother and children with me, we would have been next. We are your family!" I'm screeching now.

"Why were you there?" He said looking puzzled.

"I beg your pardon. How dare you, it's my parent's shop, why wouldn't we be there?"

"Your brother has already got away with murder; he's not getting away with this too, I'm going to the police!"

"Sidney had nothing to do with this," Matthew said, but without conviction, and I know he's lying.

"Murder? What are you talking about, you mad cow! They have got under your skin, haven't they?" Matthew scoffs.

"Why are you protecting him again? Tears stream down my face.

"I've allowed you to lie and protect that man! Don't manipulate me; it has been a long time since I realised you've been covering for Sidney. Because you couldn't have been with him on the afternoon that Mandy died because you were with me!"

"I was with Sidney all day," Matthew insists.

"It's me you are talking to now; or are you beginning to believe your own lies? On that day we met at the bottom of the Hill, and only half an hour before I saw Sidney with Rita at the church!"

Matthew's response is immediate and defensive, his eyes blazing with fury as he retorts, "That wasn't the day Mandy died; you're mistaken." The intensity in his gaze betrays both anger and a hint of desperation, as if he is desperately holding on to his version of events. The tension between us escalates, his denial clashing against my certainty and further fuelling the rift opening up between us. For a moment, the room is thick with unspoken accusations neither of us is willing to back down.

"Of course it was! It was a significant day in my life—a day I will never forget. It was the day you first asked me out," I remind him, my voice trembling slightly with the memory. "The very next day, your sister-in-law's murder happened, and because of that you stood me up. We were supposed to go to the pictures together."

Matthew looks unconvinced by my claim. His eyes narrow, reflecting his scepticism, and he hesitates before responding. The tension between us grows as I wait for him to either challenge what I have said or to admit the truth that I am desperately looking for. His uncertainty hangs in the air, adding a heavy layer to the already fraught conversation.

"If you don't want me to leave with the kids, come with me to the police and tell them everything you know," I plead.

"I can't," Matthew said.

"My father is lying in a hospital bed, and we do not know at this stage if he is going to recover."

"The attack has nothing to do with Sidney, I swear to you."

"You know who did it?" I ask. Matthew does not respond.

"Don't tell me you knew about this?" I feel a tightness in my chest, and my breathing becomes shallow. My breath escapes me in a gasp. Then I realise.

"You? God no!"

"I didn't mean for them to hurt him. I just said to give him a bit of a fright." Matthew sits down on the sofa and puts his head in his hands.

"You?" My eyes sting and I feel like I cannot breathe.

"Why?" I repeat this again, circling the room, holding my head, afraid to let go in case my brain implodes.

I run up the stairs and pull the suitcase from the top of the wardrobe.

I walk between rooms gathering belongings, shoving them into the case. Even though my thoughts are elsewhere, on autopilot, I make sure I gather everything we need.

Matthew is following me from room to room. He is ranting, but I am not listening. All I want is to escape from him.

"I am going to the hospital to be with mum and then stay at her place for a few days or perhaps longer, I need time to absorb this," I tell him.

My voice trembles as I declare, "I should go to the police!" The words spill out, though truly, they are directed at the turmoil raging inside my mind. I can no longer contain my anger; it surges to the surface, uncontrollable and raw.

"You have betrayed me! I might turn a blind eye to perfume on your clothes and lipstick on your shirts, but I will not standby as you hurt my parents and destroy our family," I am throwing items into the case.

"Maggie, you cannot go to the police!"

"I can and will!" I exclaim.

"I intend to go back to 1964 and tell them you and Sidney weren't together all day; you are both lying! In fact, your whole family is lying! Let them pick the bones out of that."

Matthew grabs my arm; he is squeezing tight. I try to shrug him off, but he is holding fast. Then he removes his grip from my arm and grabs my face, squeezing my cheeks as he puts his face close to mine.

I try to speak, but he is squeezing too hard. I am terrified as I see his furious glare. I try hard not to show it, keeping eye contact the whole time.

"I am warning you if you go to the law!" he speaks with viciousness, as I've never heard from him before.

"Matthew, let go, you are hurting me," I mutter.

Matthew let go as if coming to his senses and walked to the window to look out. I rubbed my face; it felt sore from the force of his hold. I went to the dressing-table mirror and saw red marks on both of my cheeks.

Unable to stop my tears from flowing, I reached for a smaller suitcase and continued to pack some clothes for myself, unable to speak as I felt my throat closing. Following a brief period, Matthew broke the silence, this time with calmness.

"I am sorry!" Matthew appears desperate. "I did not want your dad to get hurt. You can trust me! All I wanted was for him to be quiet!" I did not respond.

"Maggie, if you tell the police..., I could end up in prison! What will you and the kids do then?"

"Oh my! you are thinking of me, how gallant!" I say.

"Everything I do is for our family. I love you so much," Matthew spoke with sincerity.

I stopped packing and sobbed. Matthew took me in his arms. I wanted the pain I was feeling to go away. He wiped my tears and kissed them. I let him.

"Maggie, look at me, we can figure this out. I promise I will never hurt you again. Look around! Just look at what we have achieved!" I could not speak.

"Your 'Old Man' has always had it in for me. He will never be happy until he has destroyed me, destroyed us!"

I did not react to his words, but my thoughts were racing. Matthew continued to cast blame, refusing to accept accountability or admit he had done wrong.

He repeatedly said, how he had only wanted to scare Dad. Excuse for his behaviour followed an excuse. For now, I am not going to share my true feelings, but I will never accept his reasoning.

Matthew appears to me as a stranger. Or is this the real Matthew? I just had not seen it before, that age-old cliché, 'blinded by love.' For now, I allow him to hold me allowing me time to think.

"My mum needs me, and I need a few days... to clear my head," I say, in between sob breaths.

"Of course, I will manage everything, here let me help you with your bags." Matthew placed the large brown suitcase on the back seat of our green Rover, along with a few bags. I returned to the house to fetch a pack of 'Paddy Pad' disposable nappies from the under-stair cupboard. Billy needs them at night.

Matthew was talking, but I was not listening. We got into the car, and he started the ignition.

"We can make this work, Mags. I'm certain your dad will be fine."

"If we're going to make this work, cut ties with Sidney," I said. Matthew did not respond; he drove in silence.

We pulled up outside the shop, and Matthew helped me carry my belongings into the back room. He appeared not to have noticed the horrific scene. He did not even react to the sight of my dad's blood smeared across the shop floor. My blood turned cold.

I went across the street to Mrs Gordon while Matthew waited in the car.

"The kids have been little angels; I have given them their tea and settled them down for the night in the spare room. It is lovely to hear children in thc house again; it has been so quiet since now my own have left home. Anyhow, how is your father?" Mrs Gordon asks, concerned.

"He is in intensive care, unconscious. I've returned for some bits for mum," I say, referring to mum's chunky cardigan over my arm. "And to check on the children of course,"

"Oh, bless her, how is she doing? Don't you worry about the children, they are fast asleep! You go and be with your mum. Collect them in the morning," she said kindly, looking past me towards where Matthew was sitting behind the steering wheel in the car. He was smoking a cigarette, and the car engine was ticking over.

"I cannot thank-you enough," I said, handing Mrs Gordon a bag with fresh clothes for the children and some loose nappies.

"Don't be silly. Your parents have been friends of mine for years. It's the least I can do," she replied.

Taking my place beside Matthew in the car, we take the brief journey to the hospital. Matthew is surprisingly upbeat even offering to help!

“If you give me the keys to the shop, I’ll make a start in clearing up the mess once I have dropped you off.”

“My mum and dad might not be happy about that.”

“For God’s sake, Mags, just hand me the keys. Your mum cannot go back and face that!”

I hand over the bunch of keys, feeling confused. Am I wrong in my accusations or is he so in denial, having convinced himself and me of his lack of involvement in any wrongdoing. Matthew truly took offence and looked hurt at my refusal of his offer to help.

CHAPTER SIXTEEN

The Lunch Date

Lucy stepped outside the ward for a walk, the weight of emotion pressing upon her. She dialled Raymond's number, seeking comfort from the man who had always been dependable and trustworthy. Hearing his familiar voice was all she needed at that moment, but as she tried to speak, her own voice trembled, betraying her struggle to hold back tears.

Ray, at once sensing her distress, asked with concern, "What's up? Is your mum okay?"

Lucy reassured him, "She's fine, as well as can be expected. She has been talking about my dad, and it's upset me a bit."

Ray responded gently, "It's understandable. You are all still grieving. It's only early days." Lucy corrected him,

"Not George, Matthew! Maggie had a tough life with him." Lucy reflected on her involvement with the Women's Aid support committee, believing that her dedication was a way of making up for how she felt she had let her cousin down.

Ray, growing concerned, asked, "Why? What on earth has mum said?"

Lucy replied, "Oh, Ray, she is reliving events in her life. It's awful to listen to. My father, Matthew, was a villain. He organised an assault on my grandfather if what mum said is true!"

Ray's irritation was clear as he exclaimed, "This is all getting out of hand! In all these years, she has kept this knowledge to herself. Is it helpful to make these revelations now?"

Lucy recalled the many times she had attended support groups and coffee mornings at the women's refuge. She remembered sitting quietly, listening as women bravely shared their real-life stories. The experiences they described marked by a deep sense of shame about how their partners had treated them. Hearing these testimonies made Lucy realise how common these feelings were among survivors. She understood how her mother's descriptions of her own past echoed these same patterns, fitting the stereotype of someone burdened by shame and silent suffering.

"Are you on your way home?" Ray asked, his tone soft and calm.

"No, I came out for some fresh air. Mum is expecting me to return."

"Has she mentioned your brother?" asks Ray.

"No, not yet. her lucidity can change in the turn of a sixpence. Her recitals can be erratic."

"Would you like me to join you there?"

"Would you?" Lucy feels relief at her husband's offer of support.

"Of course. I'll leave work now. We can grab some food in the canteen."

"It's a date!" Lucy chuckles.

Within thirty minutes, Ray arrived at the hospital where Lucy was waiting, seated on a bench outside the main entrance. He hurried towards her, exclaiming, “The parking here gets worse!” before giving her a quick peck on the cheek.

Together, they walked down the corridor, engaging in light conversation as they made their way to the noodle bar in the hospital’s main canteen. After selecting a serving of the Vegetarian Tai Pan dish along with some Chinese dumplings, they carried their trays to a table and enjoyed their meal together.

Once they had finished eating, Ray went with Lucy to visit Maggie in her hospital ward. Maggie greeted Ray warmly, saying, “Hello Ray, you’re looking well.” Ray responded in kind, “And you’re looking better yourself, mum,” before kissing her on the cheek.

Maggie glanced at both of them and continued, “I’m pleased you’re here too because I’ve been speaking with Lucy about something important, about things that I have wanted to share for some time.”

Ray, acknowledging this, replied, “So, I hear.” Undeterred, Maggie persisted, “You may find some of this rather upsetting.”

CHAPTER SEVENTEEN

February 1972 – The Confession

Matthew parks the car in the front car park of the hospital. I gaze up at the large modern building, its windows glowing with lights on each of the six floors. He turns off the ignition, and in the gloom, I feel his eyes piercing into me.

"Are we okay?" Matthew asked.

"Yes, we're okay," I reply, defeated.

"Maggie, promise me you will not contact the police."

"No, I cannot promise! I need time to think... but rushing into anything will help no-one?"

"I'd better see how Dad is doing," I say.

What bothers me the most is his constant attempt to convince me I was mistaken about the day he first proposed a date. It weighs on my mind. "Before I go, please answer one thing. Why did you lie? about being with Sidney on the day Mandy was killed?"

"I already told you I was hanging out with Sidney and some boys all day and well into the evening.

I stay silent, sure of that Wednesday afternoon's events, with our shop's early closure. He was by himself when I met him, less than half a mile away from where it happened. It suddenly dawned on me. Matthew does not serve as Sidney's alibi, Sidney is his.

I see the expression on Matthew's face change, as if he has read my thoughts. "All water under the bridge," I say.

'It was you!' struggling to keep the words from spilling.

I realise Matthew is searching for my expression. he realises I've figured it out! although he doesn't react as one would expect if a person's wife were to think an innocent husband of murder? He doesn't vehemently assert his innocence. Instead, he is still, staring at me. His eyes dart from side to side, searching for words.

I was familiar with this case. We all were because of the local interest. I read all the newspaper clippings. I also recall an appeal for members of the public to come forward if they recognised a description of a person in his early twenties, with slicked-back dark hair and a fair complexion. There was even a television appeal on 'Shaw Taylor's Police 5' it was all our customers talked about for days. I open the car door slowly with every effort to keep a calm composure.

"Maggie... are we okay?"

I smile. but I'm shaking inside and slowly, lady- like even, I twist my body to prepare for a rapid departure from the vehicle and this monster. I feel the urge to run, but instead, keeping a calm exterior, I say,

"Yes, Matthew, we're okay. Let's talk some more later. but for now, I must go to my mum, she needs me."

"Maggie, stay here for just a minute, I have to tell you something before you go."

I freeze, my heart racing in my chest. I am pleased both feet are out of the car; I uncomfortably twist around, so I am facing Matthew.

"I can see you have doubts about me, so I should explain. It was long before us, and neither of us wanted it to happen."

"What to happen? "Despite an urge to scream I keep my composure.

"I was in love with Mandy, or I thought I was... I realise now it was an infatuation. You would have liked her..." With thoughts racing, 'is this man for real!'

"She was fun-loving, and she delighted in my blushes as she teased me. Sidney treated her like crap, I provided a listening ear, and then comfort...

"Matthew, I really must go, you don't have to say anymore, we can talk about this later." I fear what else he might tell me and the consequences that could follow.

"Mandy was expecting my baby again when she died."

This time, I cannot hide my shock, stricken by this revelation. But Matthew continued.

I'm eager to leave the car before he reveals anything else.

"What do you mean, again? Forget I asked! I don't want to hear anymore," using all my inner strength to remain calm.

"I need you to listen to this! It has driven me mad for years, I wanted to tell you, but I was afraid of what your reaction would be... Maddie is my daughter," Matthew's voice sounds close to tears.

"How can you know for sure?"

"Soon after their wedding, Sidney lost interest... but I was there!" In the dim of the lamp light, I can sense Matthew searching my face for a reaction.

"I was smitten with Mandy; I was only a kid. She was keen that we become a 'proper couple.' I was terrified. My dad would have killed me if he found out... if Sidney didn't kill me first!"

"All of this happened a long time ago, Matthew, and it really isn't relevant to what has happened to Dad, nor is it the reason I'm angry with you." I tried to sound as innocent as possible, hoping he would accept my explanation without probing further.

"At this moment, my only concern is Dad and what has been done to him. I honestly believe, deep down, that you would never intentionally hurt him, and I'm certain you would never have let things escalate to this point. But the men involved are dangerous, Matthew. For your own safety and for the sake of your family, you must distance yourself from them. Please, consider the nature of your work and think about stopping, if only for those you love."

I forced a reassuring smile. "I love you, and I know we can work all of this out. But right now, I have to go and be with Mum. We can talk about everything else later, I promise."

Matthew seemed to relax, his expression softening. He nodded, appearing satisfied with my response. "Yes, go," he said gently. "We can talk again later."

As I walk calm from the vehicle towards the hospital doors, I can feel Matthew's gaze piercing my back.

Once inside, I run to the lifts and press the button. It feels like an eternity for the lift to arrive, and I'm not even heading towards the intensive care unit where my father is.

I step out of the lift on a random floor, terrified that Matthew might have followed me.

There's a pay telephone on the wall in the lift area, and I scramble in my pocket for the card given to me earlier by the detective. The decision is mine to make.

While waiting to speak with DI Stanley Chaplin, I'm close to hanging up; when I hear his voice, even then I almost change my mind.

With urgency, I announce I have received details concerning the murder of Mandy O'Donnell and have a firm belief about the identity of her killer.

"Mrs O'Donnell, may I remind you that this is a serious matter. If you have vital information, you must tell me now."

"No, tomorrow, please. I must be with my father tonight; he is in a critical condition."

"Okay, but does this information involve your brother-in-law?" DI Chaplin said reluctantly.

"No not him, I'll come to the station tomorrow morning first thing, I promise." I am aware from the long pause that DI Chaplin is not happy. He eventually agrees that I attend the police station tomorrow morning. I searched my purse for more change. Now, it's time for the other call I must make.

CHAPTER EIGHTEEN

The Accident

Aileen continued to provide detailed information about her family, going off-piste often. Nick and Billy couldn't help but wonder how much of this related to their exploration, and she still hadn't mentioned anything more about how her brother Sidney had died.

Nick glanced down at his notes and enquired, "Are we correct in thinking you have another sister, Mary?"

"Had another sister, Mary, the eldest; she is dead now," Aileen replied. She hesitated, then continued, "Joan and I were always close, but we had a big falling out with Mary, she moved north and cut ties with all of us, including my parents."

Aileen explained that, in order to avoid upsetting her father, Jack, they made a conscious effort not to mention Mary's name again.

"What happened to Sidney?" Nick interjected, taking the opportunity as Aileen paused for reflection and took a breath.

"I'm getting to that!" Aileen snaps.

She explained that the Garda had informed them of Sidney's death. According to them, he had received a head injury at their parents' house. He reached the street but died in the ambulance on his way to the hospital.

While Aileen continued her account, Nick noticed a text message on his mobile screen. He had put his phone on silent mode before entering the house and saw that there had been eight missed calls from Kate.

"I'm sorry. I must reply to a call. It appears urgent," Nick said, seizing the chance. He left Billy listening to Aileen as she continued to talk.

Nick stepped outside using the front entrance, "Hi Kate, we are still in the meeting, we won't be...?"

Kate's voice was sharp and distressed as she interrupted, "Nick, there has been an accident!"

Immediately, Nick's concern grew. "What type of accident? Is Elaine okay?" he pressed, desperate for reassurance.

Kate quickly explained the situation over the phone. Nick listened intently, trying to absorb every word, his attention wholly focused on Kate's account of what had transpired.

Once the call ended, Nick returned to the lounge. Aileen was still talking, but the atmosphere had shifted. Billy noticed Nick's troubled expression and looked at him expectantly, sensing that something serious had happened.

Nick addressed Aileen directly, his voice apologetic but urgent. "I'm sorry, Aileen. We must go," he announced.

Billy stood up at once, prompted both by Nick's ashen complexion and the urgency in his tone. "What's happened?"

"It's Elaine, my girlfriend," Nick replied, ensuring that Aileen was aware of the gravity of the situation. "She's at the hospital."

Aileen agrees they could return if they needed to. Billy drove while Nick frantically tried to call Elaine's phone.

The call went to voicemail. Billy dropped Nick off by the accident and emergency doors before searching for a parking space. Nick spotted Kate sitting on a chair in the corridor.

"Where is she?" he asked.

"Take a seat, Nick. Elaine is in excellent hands," Kate reassured. "She has a nasty ankle break, and they're taking her to get a cast fitted,"

"Why was she out there on her own?" Nick enquired.

Kate showed him her phone and revealed some creepy photographs she had received in a text. She explained what had happened and how some people from the pub had gone looking for Elaine and found her slumped against a rock, unable to move.

As Kate finished recounting the events, Elaine arrived, being pushed in a wheelchair by a nurse. Her usually straightened red hair was now wild and curly, and her complexion was pale. A half-plaster cast was encasing her right leg up to her knee, and she was resting it on a footrest. Nick rushed forward.

"Oh my God, darling, what on earth happened to you?" he nearly tripped over the wheelchair's wheels in his haste, much to Elaine's obvious annoyance and the nurse's.

"Careful!" Elaine cautions. "This ankle bloody hurts!"

The nurse approached Nick and handed him a plastic bag containing two small boxes of medication—one with painkillers and the other with antibiotics. She also gave Elaine an appointment card, instructing her to return in three days so the temporary plaster could be changed.

Elaine sighed, expressing her desire for a cup of coffee. The nurse then provided Kate with a set of crutches for Elaine's use.

They stopped at a volunteer-run coffee shop on their way out. Billy joined them after phoning them to find out their location. Kate brought a tray to the table, setting down four takeaway cups of coffee for everyone.

"What happened? You poor thing!" Billy asked with genuine concern.

Elaine, agitated, replied, "I was standing outside the pub having a cigarette... don't look at me like that!" She shot a pointed glance at Nick, who quickly apologised. "Sorry, continue!" he said, brushing off her remark.

"Did Kate tell you about the photographs?" Elaine asked, turning to Billy.

Looking surprised, he shook his head. "No, what photos?"

Elaine hesitated. "I'll tell you later..." Nick growing impatient, pressed, "How did you injure your ankle?"

Elaine took a steady breath. "I was having a cigarette when I spotted a man about a hundred yards away, on the opposite side of the road. He was just standing there, watching me—it was really creepy!" She shuddered as she recalled the moment. "I called out to him. He started to laugh and made a sign," she explained further.

Nick frowned. "What type of sign?"

"Like a cut-throat sign," Elaine said quietly. "So, I crossed the road and asked him what he wanted, and why he was following us..."

"Why would you put yourself in danger like that?" Nick interjected, sounding exasperated.

Elaine's voice quivered as she continued, "Anger overtook fear—I wasn't thinking straight at all. The man started running backwards, all the while beckoning to me, as if he was egging me on." She paused, recalling the sense of fury that had propelled her forward. "I started walking towards him, absolutely furious. I told him I was going to call the police, but I wasn't paying attention to where I was stepping."

She explained, "My foot slipped where it was wet, and it went down between two rocks. The ground was so uneven, it just made things worse. All of a sudden, I heard my ankle snap... The pain was excruciating!"

"Ouch!" Billy exclaimed, wincing in sympathy.

"I couldn't stand, so I dragged myself toward a larger rock," Elaine continued, her voice trembling as she recounted the ordeal. "As I lay against the rock, he returned. I pleaded with him to fetch someone to help from the pub. I was terrified."

Nick's anger grew as Elaine described what happened next. "He stood just a few feet away, watching as I winced in pain. I honestly felt I was losing consciousness," she said, visibly distressed. "He seemed to enjoy watching me panic."

Elaine took a shaky breath before finishing her account. “Then, he just casually walked off. He showed no empathy at all.”

“How old was he?” asked Billy. “It was hard to say, not much older than me and certainly not older than forty,”

CHAPTER NINETEEN

Change of Plan

Earlier in the day, Lucy had spent a considerable amount of time on the phone with Nicholas, discussing the recent flurry of events. During their conversation, Nicholas explained that, due to Elaine's broken ankle, their return journey would have to be postponed. He mentioned that the temporary cast Elaine received would need to be replaced once the swelling had subsided, making immediate travel impossible.

Consequently, they decided to extend their stay at the cottage by another week. Nicholas informed Lucy that Billy would be heading home on Saturday, as work commitments required his return. However, Kate would remain with them in Ireland for the time being, providing added support during Elaine's recovery.

Lucy was still reeling from the information shared by Maggie. It was difficult to believe, and she wondered whether it was all a fantasy of an old woman with onset dementia. Did her mother suspect her father of murder? Or had his image developed over the years in her mother's imagination to be that of a monster? Was he Maddie's biological father? The guilt Lucy felt became overwhelming. If it were true, Lucy felt that her behaviour towards her cousin... sister... whoever she was, was unforgivable. She switched on the dishwasher and joined Ray in the lounge. Ray poured the last drops from the bottle of Cote de Rhône they had shared at dinner into their glasses. Lucy curled up on their high-back cushioned sofa, hugging her glass. "We must have a discussion," Ray said. "About what?" Lucy asked. "Your mother cannot keep this information to herself. She should have shared it with the police many years ago. And if what Billy and Nick say is true, there might be someone out there seeking revenge for something that happened in the past," Ray explained.

Lucy attempted to offer reassurance. "They have control of the situation. The Irish authorities are re-examining evidence from my biological father's death, and Nick is keeping in contact with the detective who helped them on the day of Elaine's accident," she explained calmly, trying to steady her nerves as she spoke.

Ray nodded in understanding. "Nicholas told me something along those lines," he said, noting silently that Lucy still struggled to say her father's name aloud.

"Did Nick mention the police have also agreed to re-investigate Matthew Junior's disappearance? It is possible they were dealing with an illegal adoption and abduction," Ray added. "They seem to be taking this situation seriously and have made arrangements to accompany Nick and Billy on a return visit to the aunt,"

CHAPTER TWENTY

February 1972 -Unveiling the Lies.

I step into the shop alongside Mum, the bell above the door giving a half-hearted chime. Matthew, true to his word, has tidied up and dropped the keys in the letterbox. As we walked through to the back room, I glanced over at Mum. She looks utterly drained—her shoulders slumped, eyes shadowed with the exhaustion of a night spent at Dad's bedside. Concern etched into every line on her face, and it's five o'clock in the morning.

Moving quietly, I fill the kettle and set it on the stove. The low hiss of gas fills the heavy silence, and I sneak another look at Mum. She sits at the kitchen table, her head buried in her hands, elbows propped up as if they're the only things keeping her upright.

"Why don't you go upstairs and get a couple of hours sleep?" I suggest softly, keeping my voice gentle. "You'll need to rest before you head back to the hospital."

She doesn't lift her head; her voice is muffled and tired. "I'm not sure I could sleep," she admits, rubbing her temples. The strain is clear in the way her hands tremble just slightly.

Trying to ease her mind, I remind her, "Mrs Gordon said she'd keep the kids until this afternoon. That'll give us a chance to catch up on sleep." I watch her closely, hoping something in my words will help lighten the weight she carries.

Mum finally looked up, her eyes clouded with worry. "Alright then but make sure I don't sleep past eight o'clock. And wake me straight away if the hospital calls." Her voice is firm, but there's a crack in it I haven't heard before. "Can you write a notice for the shop door? I suppose it's best to say 'closed until further notice'—oh, I don't know... You know what to put." She trails off, staring at nothing. I nod.

I hear her weary steps as she climbs the stairs, and for a moment I simply sit down in Dad's chair, letting the worn cushion take my weight. The room feels enormous and empty. Despite the dizziness and queasy feeling from a night without sleep, my mind won't settle—I have someone I urgently need to see this morning. The conversation with Sidney last night plays on repeat, raising more questions than answers. When I rang him about the attack on Dad, his shock had sounded genuine. He'd even offered to help, though it was clear my request to meet today had thrown him.

"As early as you like, I'll be up," he'd said when I insisted we talk.

I force myself to have a strip-wash and change into fresh clothes, then drink a quick cup of tea, the warmth settling heavy in my stomach. My mind races with everything that's happened as I step into the chilly air, the silence pressing in on me. I slip out the back door quietly, locking it behind me, and clutch my handbag and the bunch of shop keys tightly. The distorted yellow glow of the streetlamps barely lights the path as dawn breaks over the silent estate. The fog is thick, swirling in slow eddies, and the streets are empty, an eerie hush hanging over everything. I check my watch—it's ten past six. My pulse quickens, a sense of foreboding growing as I approach the gate to the O'Donnell s' house. The lights are already on.

Sidney answers the door already dressed. The acrid smell of burnt toast greets me in the hallway. He looks at me searchingly and asks, "How's your dad doing?"

I answer quietly, "As good as can be expected." I don't meet his gaze. The conversation feels like a minefield—one wrong step and everything could explode.

He gestures for me to come through. "What's this about? It sounds important."

I hesitate in the hallway, nerves fraying, uncertain if it's safe to reveal what I know here. I nearly made an excuse to leave, but something kept me rooted. Sidney tries to break the tension. "Do you want a cup of something?"

I shake my head, voice firm. "No, I'm alright." I take a breath, trying to steady my nerves. "Sit down, Sidney. What I have to say affects both of us."

He hesitates, then sits opposite me at the table. There's a flicker of surprise on his face, perhaps at his own willingness to comply. I steel myself and decide there's no gentle way to do this. Best to get Straight to the Point.

"Before Mandy died, did you ever suspect her of having an affair?" I ask, watching his face closely for any sign of emotion.

Sidney's expression doesn't change, but his steely blue eyes narrow—he's surprised, caught off guard. For all his bravado, he isn't the poker player he thinks he is.

I press on, forcing myself to meet his gaze. "How close was the relationship between Mandy and Matthew?" The words taste bitter as I speak them. I hear my voice rambling, anxiety creeping in. "Matthew's told me things, and I need to know what you know—the truth. What he's shared affects all of us." My hands knot in my lap. "What I'm about to say might upset you, but we need to stay calm. Flying off the handle won't help anyone."

Sidney interrupts, impatience flaring. "For fuck's sake, Maggie, what's he done?"

I look at him, my own fear and frustration rising. "The truth has consequences, Sidney"—so does being the keeper of secrets. I let the silence hang for a beat, then say flatly, "Matthew said he's Maddie's biological father. He claims Mandy was pregnant with his child when she died." I brace myself for an outburst, but none comes.

Instead, Sidney's mouth twists into a mocking smile. "I knew all along about their sordid little fling," he said without missing a beat. "And I've a pretty good idea Matthew's Maddie's dad as well."

I stare, stunned. Sidney's voice grows colder. "Mandy was a tease, and my little brother was at an age where he thought of nothing else. You're a woman of the world, Maggie—I shouldn't have to spell it out." I say nothing, my mind reeling.

Sidney continues, his tone matter of fact. "I thought she was amazing, beautiful, sharp, funny—at least until we got wed. And then, God help me, she was a nightmare. She craved constant attention; if I tried to leave without her, she'd kick off. She was a massive pain in the arse."

He sighs, reflectively. "I suppose she poured her heart out to Matthew, and he was naïve enough to believe every word. Mandy could act the vulnerable kitten or the tigress, depending on what she wanted."

My voice is barely above a whisper. "Did you kill her, Sidney?"

Sidney's expression softens, just for a moment. "Of course I didn't. I loved her, or at least I did once, back in the beginning."

I ask quietly, "Did Matthew know that you knew about their affair?"

He laughs, with strange pride in his voice. "Neither of them had a clue, soppy bastards. I knew not long after we married that I wasn't enough for her, but I wasn't about to let her go. Mostly pride, but also, Mum and Dad would never have stood for it if their son got divorced. So, I encouraged them. Asked Matthew to keep an eye on her. Invited him to stay. Then I'd make excuses to leave them alone. While they were together, Mandy wasn't going anywhere—and I could come and go as I pleased, at least for a while."

I press, "Wasn't that a risky game? And what about Maddie?"

Sidney shrugs, with a hint of bitterness creeping in. "Not going to lie. I was pissed off when I realised Mandy was pregnant, and it was likely Matthew was the father. It was obvious when Maddie was born—she's his double, it's in the eyes." For a moment, his expression softens, as if a flicker of compassion passes over him. His eyes glisten, but I can't tell if he's crying for Maddie or himself.

He continues, "I kept quiet, hoping motherhood would settle her. More fool me. She just got worse—goading me, dropping hints that I wasn't Maddie's dad. She even admitted she'd 'fallen in love', not thinking I'd know who she meant. A couple of times, she nearly blurted out the whole truth, but I made sure to leave the house until she'd calmed down." He grins, a spiteful edge returning. "I didn't want to hear about their affair."

"I knew Matthew would move on if someone else came along. After all, he was a kid not long out of school when it all started, and Mandy was older. After a while, I had others to occupy me, if you get my meaning. I didn't give two hoots if Mandy stayed or if she left, and she knew it," Sidney reveals.

Astounded by his revelation, I feel my jaw drop — a cycle of manipulation and emotional cruelty. Sidney continues with his account, seeming not to notice my shock.

"When I wanted her to sod off, I made sure she lost her grip on my little brother first. I even constructed the end for them. Silly cow! I encouraged Matthew to join me in the business; I was certain that he would lose interest in her. It nearly worked; except I never imagined in a million years my brother would murder the poor bitch! I did not see that coming, or wish it on her, and what's worse, I ended up being the 'prime suspect' for her murder." Sidney appears perturbed.

"Your brother murdered your wife?" I am feeling sick again.

"He got away with it! why didn't you tell the police when they were breathing down your neck?"

"Mum and Dad, I couldn't put them through it! Also, I'm not certain, but who else could it have been? And more importantly I knew I hadn't done it, but hey-ho, invaluable training for what we needed in our business later," Sidney chuckles as I swallow back bile.

"So, there you have it. it's not surprising I want little to do with the kid... or should we say your old man's kid?" Sidney's grin mutates into a sneer.

I feel heat rise from deep within, and I am about to scream and tell him that everything that has happened is of his doing, when I sense somebody standing in the doorway behind me, and I turn to see Matthew. His eyes are not the usual piercing blue but again black with rage, and he is holding a little one's hand. The next two words wipe the grin off Sidney's face.

"You Bastard!"

CHAPTER TWENTY-ONE

February 1972 – The Fatal Divide

"You bastard! Little Matthew, with wide eyes and tousled blonde curls, clutches his father's hand, looking as if he just woke up. Matthew towers above him, his expression filled with abhorrent rage, and he stares directly at Sidney.

Sidney appeared shocked by their presence, his sinister expression momentarily replaced by fear, although it is brief as the defence soon turns into attack.

"What do they say about eavesdroppers, little bruv?" Sidney said, his remark appearing to floor Matthew. I am rooted to the dining room chair.

"Go into the front room," Matthew barks, not looking at me. I do not respond.

"I said take Matthew into the other room Maggie," this time Matthew shouts, and I jump to my feet.

As I guide little Matthew by the hand, we make our way to the front room, reluctant to leave them alone. I need more answers, but I know our son should not see this escalating situation. It is the second mistake I have made that day. If I had been thinking straight, I would have left the house without delay. It may not have prevented what happened to Sidney, but it would have prevented the abominable events that followed.

I hear a muffled voice, and I can tell from the tone that it is Sidney, but he is speaking too quietly to hear what he is saying. From the room's corner, I bring over the cardboard box brimming with toys—an action man, toy cars, a doll, a couple of Ladybird books, and some Stickle Bricks. I empty its contents in front of little Matthew, and he beams at me before kneeling on the floor to play with them.

Specifically, it is Matthew's voice that I hear rising.

"Why? Why would you use me like that? I am your brother, for fuck's sake, and yet you treated me like a puppet. I was a kid!"

"You didn't have to sleep with her. No one forced you at gunpoint. And why then kill the poor bitch?"

"I had no choice. She was going to tell you, tell Mum and Dad. I didn't know what else to do!"

I leave Matthew playing and enter the room. Matthew is sitting opposite Sidney, elbows on the table and head in hand. He doesn't change his position, even when Sidney acknowledges me.

"Don't know what you thought you would achieve by raking all this up," he looks from me to Matthew, so I'm not sure which one of us he is addressing.

"You should tell them yourself," I say.

In one movement, Matthew stands and swings violently around to face me.

"What?" Does he really want me to repeat it?

"I said you should explain it to the police. Tell them what happened - an argument that escalated. explain that you didn't mean to hurt her.

It was an accident." I cannot believe what I am suggesting, but I continue.

"Tell them she was blackmailing you," I say.

"She wasn't extorting me. We didn't argue. She was happy about the pregnancy, she wanted everyone to know the truth, I didn't know what to do, I loved her, but it wasn't enough, I realised there was too much to lose should anyone find out about us or worse, found out that her kids were mine," Matthew's words sting.

"Matthew, she was pregnant! Did that mean nothing?" I ask solemnly.

Matthew stands now, as if about to address an audience, and I am not sure I want to hear any more. I have heard enough. I turn to leave but stop in my tracks when Matthew speaks.

"Maggie, stay where you are. You need to hear this. Mandy and I were not only lovers, but best friends. She knew me inside out, and I was someone she could lean on after Sidney was heavy-handed with her."

"I thought about running away with Mandy, but what could I offer? I was only a driver's mate, earning a pittance. Then you offered me cash, and lots of it—nice clothes, a status. I enjoyed it. I thought of Mum, Dad, and you! What could I do? I spent night after night fretting... she was planning to tell you everything," I thought Matthew was going to burst a gasket.

"And you sit there casually telling my wife you knew all along!" Sidney leaps out of his seat and faces Matthew, nose to nose.

"Don't you dare put this on me? You premeditated your intention. You must have planned it, waited in the shadows for Mandy to strangle the life out of her, knowing she was expecting your kid... and with another at home waiting for her tea."

'Sidney's words seem to have hit a nerve, causing Matthew to clench his fists.

"No, Matthew... so don't you dare go there. For years I've carried the realisation of what you might have done."

I feel a chill in my blood. My body is completely unresponsive, and I cannot move, speak, or even react. My body feels frozen, unable to move from the spot.

"You know what, bruv? I've got to hand it to you. Everyone thinks I am a psycho! Mandy wasn't even out of the morgue when you made a move on Maggie. And hey-ho, a brand new little domestic set up! Just to cover your tracks, and so it was Matthew taken off the radar! And that poor little cow... none the wiser!"

Sidney's voice stays steady. He swings his arm upwards, to point his finger at me or to lash out at Matthew. I'm not sure. But before I find out, Matthew grabs Sidney's arm and head-butts him, making direct contact.

Sidney holds his nose, blood dripping. He takes a swipe back at Matthew, who retaliates with a punch. There is no holding back as the brothers strike out at each other.

"Stop, stop! "I scream, and I stand between them as Sidney is about to throw another punch.

Sidney appears shocked by my action and hesitates. At that moment, he receives another punch from Matthew. He stumbles, catching his slipper in the rug, and falls hard against the corner of the table, hitting his head. As if in slow motion, Sidney slumps to the floor.

Matthew grabs me by the elbow after fetching Matthew from the front room and putting him under his arm, and ushers me out of the door.

"Sidney might be hurt badly, so I am staying here."

"Shut up!" Matthew snarled.

I can hear groaning from the back room. Matthew opened the front door. A neighbour across the street is bringing in the milk and looks up from where he is bending. He nods, and Matthew nods in response. Then he calls back as if speaking to his brother.

"Just gonna drop the 'Mrs' home. Get the fry-up going; I'll grab more bread. I will be back in a jiffy. I'm starving." Matthew's voice is jovial. If I didn't know better, I would believe he was making plans to run the errand and join his brother for breakfast.

Matthew still has hold of my elbow, and with Matthew under his other arm, we continue to the car, parked at the parking meter directly outside the house.

Matthew opens the back door of the car and instructs me to get in, which I do. He sits Matthew on my lap and casually walks around to the driver's side, gets in, and drives. Aware of the child in the car, I say nothing for the entire short journey, but I want to scream.

My husband, whom I thought I knew so well, is a stranger and a cold-blooded murderer!

We arrive down my Mum's Road, Matthew parks at the kerb outside our shop, and switches off the engine. I am struggling to get out of the vehicle as quickly as I can.

As I stand on the pavement, I expect little Matthew to reach out to hold my hand, completely taken aback by the events of the past hour and anxiously questioning what my next move should be. I glance at my watch; it is not yet nine o'clock.

Momentarily, I am confused as Matthew walks around the vehicle. While checking that the other doors are locked, Matthew opens the driver's door, gets back in, and starts the engine. I realise little Matthew is still in the car; he has his face pressed up against the glass, looking at me with sadness from his big blue eyes. This haunts me forever.

"What are you doing? Stop!" I shout. He does not look my way but pulls away from the curb slowly.

I run alongside the car, my palms stinging from slapping on the driver's window and screaming his name. I notice Matthew is smirking, as if enjoying the hysteria, and he doesn't glance in my direction once. Little Matthew is calling my name, and I recognise his cry.

No matter how hard I try, the car door handle refuses to move. Suddenly, Matthew pulls away sharply, and I fall to the ground, grazing my knees.

My mother and Mrs Gordon stand on the roadside, looking on in horror.

CHAPTER TWENTY-TWO

February 1972 – Person of Interest

Mrs Gordon explained Matthew had knocked on the door. He must have seen the house lights on. The other children were still asleep, but little Matthew was awake and playing in the hallway.

She said Matthew had told her that, given the circumstances, he had decided not to work and offered to take him to the shop, give him breakfast, and then come back for the other children when they woke up. She was unaware that he hadn't done this until she heard me screaming and saw Matthew driving away with little Matthew in the back of the car.

"He's, the boy's father. I wasn't going to refuse!" she said, sniffing into a handkerchief.

"We can't do much in these domestic situations. I'm sure your husband will be back with your boy once he has calmed down," PC Jennings said, gulping down the remnants of his tea and placing his notebook back in his pocket.

"Well, thanks for the tea. I will report this and return later to check if your husband has brought your little boy home. From my experience, he will return in a couple of hours." He said flippantly.

"Is that it?" I ask, showing frustration.

"I will radio in what you have told me, and we will keep a lookout, but believe me; I've seen this type of situation a hundred times, nothing more than a storm in a teacup; they will be back by lunchtime!"

My mum sees PC Jennings out the back door, thanking him all the while and telling him he is right.

Lucy is struggling to hold on to Billy. She is sitting in my father's chair with him on her lap, and he is wriggling, wanting to get down.

I try to get up from my seat at the dining room table, but my mum places her hand on my shoulder, an unspoken gesture for 'stay where you are... I've got this.'

"I had better get back," Mrs Gordon said, still sniffing into her hanky. "If you need anything, just knock... Oh Maggie, I'm so sorry!" This time she sobs.

"Please don't be upset. This is not your fault," I say with little conviction, not because I was casting blame, but because I feel emotionless.

Neither my mum nor Mrs Gordon is aware of the full events of this morning. I find myself uncertain as to why I have not shared the complete story with them, or why I chose not to inform PC Jennings of everything that transpired. I question whether, deep down, I am still trying to shield Matthew from blame. The answer is no; my only concern now is for the safe return of my son. I do not wish to do anything that might endanger him or make his welfare seem any less urgent to those who can help.

Time seems to pass without my noticing, as I sit quietly and watch Lucy and Billy playing with toys on the rug. Lucy is making every effort to keep her little brother entertained. She does not ask any questions—not even about where little Matthew might be. Instead, she takes on a gentle, maternal role and her flawless behaviour makes it clear to me that she understands the gravity of the situation, even if she cannot voice it.

My mother stands abruptly, determination flickering in her tired eyes. "I'm going to the hospital to be with your father," she declared, her voice weighted by both exhaustion and disappointment. She tries to sound reassuring, insisting, "I am certain PC Jennings is right! And no harm will come to Matthew when he is with his dad." Yet, her words are tinged with frustration, and she cannot keep from adding, "But that does not excuse the selfishness of the man you married... especially now." As she speaks, her tone betrays how deeply she feels the strain of the situation and her disappointment in my husband's actions.

"I should stay here with the children and wait for..."

Interrupting me, Mum insists, "Yes, you wait here until Matthew brings the little one home!" She moves with purpose, collecting her coat and hat before heading for the door.

It was approaching midday when the telephone suddenly rang. I hurried to answer, heart pounding with anticipation. On the other end of the line was Detective Stanley Chaplin.

"Mrs O'Donnell, I was expecting you to visit the police station this morning. During our telephone conversation last night, you mentioned having information for us. I understand things may be difficult for you with your father in the hospital, but I need to speak with you."

"Have you found my husband and my little boy?" I ask.

"Your husband has taken your son?" DI Chaplin sounded surprised.

"It was this morning; I reported it right after it happened. Why aren't you looking for them?"

"I didn't receive this information, but we are searching for your husband. He explains, "Mr Matthew O'Donnell is a person of interest in an incident that occurred this morning. It's necessary that I come to speak with you in person! Today!" DI Chaplin sighs before continuing.

"Mrs O'Donnell, are you still there?" he asks.

"Yes, ... I'm here," I reply.

"Sidney O'Donnell was badly injured in an incident that occurred this morning,"

"He fell, I was in the house when it happened, I went to talk with him; to see if he knew who attacked my father,"

"Why did you think that Sidney would know something?

"I don't know, I just thought..."

"Did your husband go with you to visit Sidney?

"No, he arrived after, a fight broke out between them. I saw Sidney stumble; he hit his head on the table."

"And you didn't call an ambulance?" enquired DI Chaplin, sounding surprised.

"Matthew would not let me, he led me out of the house and insisted on driving us to my parent's shop,"

"You are a key witness; but your account does not match with the severity of Sidney's injuries. Are you sure it was just a trip?"

"I don't know how badly he was injured as I said, I was ushered out of the house." My frustration with the detective's assumptions was apparent.

"Your account matches some of the information provided by a witness. Except Matthew returned to the house shortly afterwards... Sidney received severe injuries, more than would be contributed by a fall and bang to the head. He managed to stumble onto the street; Michael was seen driving off."

I say nothing.

"What you may not know is he didn't make it to the hospital; he died in the Ambulance. "I hear myself gasp.

"Do you know why they argued, was it about money?"

"I don't think so," I say.

"What was the argument about?" I swerve around the question.

"Was my son with Matthew?" I ask.

"No mention of a child, but we are using every available resource to apprehend your husband."

"I'm worried he will leave the country," I suggest.

"We have considered that possibility and have notified the ferry terminals. I will let them know he has a child with him. Is there anything you can tell us?" DI Chaplin asked.

“My husband arranged the attack on my father. There is also something else, but I’d rather not discuss it over the phone,” I revealed.

“The reason I am calling is to arrange an interview down at the station. I shall come by and pick you up, have you got someone there to watch the children?

“Yes, of course, I’ll be here,”

Contrary to what I tell DI Chaplin, as soon as we finish the call, I prepare the children and take them to Mrs Gordon’s. She is willing to take care of the children again. DI Chaplin not knowing that little Matthew was snatched by his father doesn’t inspire much confidence in the police. Their failure to communicate with each other gives Matthew several hours’ head start. So, I pack my small suitcase with items of clothing suitable for the time of year and toiletries, withdraw some cash from my post office account, and head to the train station.

CHAPTER TWENTY-THREE

February 1972 – Across Land and Sea

I hoisted my bag; I boarded the train just before dusk. The winter light cut-through the misted windows. For the first few hours, I sit alone in an empty carriage. The train rattles through the countryside. The landscape blurs past me. It's a mix of muted black and streaks of amber. With every mile, I try to organise my thoughts and map out my journey: first, this train, with its gentle swaying and rhythmic clatter, takes me towards Holyhead, the ferry port that marks the edge of Wales. From there, I plan to catch the ferry across the Irish Sea—a prospect that feels daunting with the hours still stretching ahead—then a bus journey of two hours westwards, before changing buses once more for the last, winding leg to the little seaside town on Ireland's rugged western coast.

Time blurs as the hours pass. I rehearsed my plan again, clinging to the details to stay focused. The exhaustion is bone-deep, settling into my shoulders and neck, but there's no question of sleep. I am worried about my son, and my father in the hospital. I picture Matthew's sisters on that distant shore; my in-laws and Maddie are already there too. With luck, my husband will have brought our son to them. His parents are the only ones who can talk sense into him. However, fear lurks beneath the hope. What will happen when I tell them Sidney has died?

After several hours of travel, the train pulls into Holyhead. The salty tang of the sea is sharp and bracing as I cross the windswept platform. Seeking a public phone box, I press a handful of coins into the slot, my hands trembling more from nerves than cold. The line clicks and whirrs, and then, mercifully, the Ward Sister answers and lets me speak with my mum.

Her voice when it comes through, is thin with fatigue, the words stretched taut with worry. “Maggie, the police want to know your whereabouts. DI Chaplin came to the hospital! You should have told us your plan. We could have made better arrangements for the children.”

I am overwhelmed with a sudden, intense guilt. With a constricted throat, I forced myself to swallow. “I’m sorry I didn’t stay for the police. I was left with no choice but to search for them myself. I felt so helpless. Mrs Gordon said she didn’t mind looking after the children... the kids love her!”

“Yes, she is a good friend, which is why I am not happy about taking advantage of her kindness,” I could hear the strain in Mum’s voice. “Also, the police... they believe you are in cahoots with Matthew!”

“You know I’m not! The thing is, it could be a few days before I find them. I don’t know anything about Matthew’s work or the people he knows. That part of his life was always kept separate. Yet, I know where he’d most probably go to find safety.”

Mum's voice softens with understanding, even as the tiredness lingers. "I don't want you to get into trouble, but if you think you know where he is...," I interrupt.

"I am travelling to ..." but mum doesn't want to know.

"Hush, its best you don't tell me, do whatever is necessary and bring your son home. I am so pleased you rang; your father is showing improvement they are moving him to the ward; I've got to go now; the nurse needs the phone."

Relief loosens the knot in my chest, but the ache of being so far from home doesn't fade. "With normal hospital times, I am available to care for the children, so you have my blessing. And I know your father would agree with me. So do whatever you have to, but please take care. I don't trust Matthew and you mustn't!"

Her words settle around me, bittersweet but grounding. Ending the call, I draw a shaky breath and steel myself for the next stage. The journey ahead is long—over twenty-six hours in all—and the weight of uncertainty presses down on me. Still, as the ferry's horn sounds in the distance, I set my jaw and push onwards, clinging to the hope that somehow, I will find my son and bring him home.

After the call, I continue my journey. Besides dozing on the ferry and the bus from Dublin to Galway, I haven't slept in what feels like days.

After yet another bus, I reach my destination, getting off near a picturesque fishing harbour with the ocean and mountains in the background. I walk along the main street, admiring a mix of pastel colour and whitewash buildings, and head towards a hotel sign displayed on a building across the street. The Hotel looks more like a large pub, and the interior reflects that too. As I step into The Rose Inn, a crowded, smoke-filled bar with more drinkers than I expected; Despite it being past lunchtime opening hours. There's no-one serving behind the counter, but I decide to approach it, anyway.

An older man rises from a nearby table where a group of men are playing cards. He lifts the wooden hatch to take his place behind the bar.

"Do you have any room vacancies?" I raise my voice to be heard above the chatter.

The man replied in a broad Irish accent, but I cannot understand what he is saying. After what feels like an age of me wearily smiling and nodding, he comes from behind the bar and beckons me through a side door. I follow but soon realise I entered the hotel through the wrong entrance from the street.

I stand in a stylish hotel reception area with an oak-beamed ceiling. The wall behind it holds an oak reception desk, key holder and letter rack. Oil paintings in gold-coloured frames grace the walls, painted in a deep red. A roaring fire crackles within a stone inglenook fireplace, and high-backed red leather armchairs sit on either side.

He rings a bell on the desk and yells; a woman in her late thirties or early forties appears. She smiles from the other side of the desk as the older man speaks to her using a language I do not understand before returning to the bar.

"Thank you, Father. I shall take care of our guest from here," she said. "Now, is it a single or a double room you need? Are you travelling alone?" she asks.

"A single is just fine," I reply.

"You've travelled all the way from England!" I realise this is an observation rather than a question, and I suspect she wonders why a woman would travel to these parts alone.

"Yes," I reply, contemplating my response. I don't want to cause suspicion or attract attention to my arrival, especially if Matthew's family has a well-known reputation in this town.

"It's a flying visit to catch up with family," I say, hoping this broad reply will prevent further questioning. I pay for three nights, sign the leather-bound register, and the lady fetches a key from a cubbyhole in the wall behind her. She studies the register.

"O'Donnell?" She repeats the name as if trying to associate.

"There are a few O'Donnell s in these parts," she remarks, taking a key attached to a large wooden room number from a hook, and when I do not respond, she gestures for me to follow her.

With my case in hand, we climb a narrow staircase with several twists and turns. We reach a small landing at the top of the building, with one window displaying a small vase of cut flowers on its sill. The low ceiling has black-painted beams, and there is a small door with its frame cut to the shape of the sloping roof.

"Nobody will bother you up here!" She said after catching her breath.

"And you appear fit enough to take on those stairs. Any noise from the bar won't disturb you. It can get quite noisy on weekends!"

She takes the key and places it in the lock, then steps back, allowing me to enter first. Feeling the need to duck, I enter a good-sized room with soaring ceilings. A mix of floral soft furnishings and a dusky pink quilted bedspread on a large chestnut oak bed decorates the room. A matching wardrobe stands in a corner, featuring a mirrored door.

The bed stands opposite a sizeable fireplace, though its original opening has been sealed with a sheet of painted hardboard. Resting on the hearth is a contemporary electric fire, complete with plastic logs designed to imitate the real thing. I hope it works, as a chill lingers in the air.

"This is much bigger than expected. It's lovely!" I remark, taking in the spaciousness.

"This used to be the staff quarters when the building was a private residence," the lady begins, sharing the room's story. "It belonged to a local landowner, but after he went bankrupt, the house was left vacant for many years. My husband's grandfather bought it and transformed it into an inn in the 1930s. Since then, it's remained in our family."

She walks over to the window and draws back the drapes, unveiling a large attic window. Smiling, she remarks, "I save this room for those I think will appreciate it most." She gestures outwards, noting, "From up here, you have a sea view, and if you squint hard enough to your left, you may even see America," her laughter filling the space.

I can't help but let out a small chuckle of my own. My eyes are soon drawn to the captivating scene outside: to the left, beneath a dusky, charcoal sky, fishing boats gently rock on stormy waters, their outlines softened by a lingering mist. Across the bay, the rolling countryside stretches out, eventually meeting the foot of towering mountains, whose vast shadows reach over the landscape. Along the opposite shore, a collection of brightly coloured buildings adds a vibrant contrast to the natural grandeur that surrounds them.

"It's lovely. Er... Sorry, I did not catch your name...?" I pause, awaiting the hotel manager's introduction.

"Ah, apologies for my rudeness! Call me Colleen... Mrs Colleen Blight," she answers warmly.

Smiling, I respond, "And I'm Maggie."

Peering out at the restless waters, I remark, "Wow, the sea is so choppy!" The aftereffects of the Irish Sea crossing still linger, making me feel slightly unsettled.

Colleen nods in understanding. "There's a strong wind. Most need a few days just to get accustomed to the weather in these parts."

She offers a reassuring smile as she prepares to leave. "Well, Maggie, make yourself comfortable. If there is anything you need, I am downstairs. I'll leave you to settle in," Colleen said, closing the door gently behind her.

As I unpack a few essentials and freshen up, hoping that I'll have found Matthew in less than a few days. Any concerns about the weather pale compared to the tumultuous storm raging within me. I stand here, hoping that this very place will be the backdrop for reuniting my son and the inevitable confrontation with my husband, marking concluding this harrowing ordeal.

I hang my coat on a hook behind the door and rest the emptied case on a chair next to the wardrobe. The clock on the mantel shows that it's late afternoon. I kick off my shoes, close the drapes at the window, and slump backwards onto the bed. It feels comfortable, but the room spins, and I feel nauseous. I decide to shut my eyes for just a few minutes before I embark on my search for my son.

CHAPTER TWENTY-FOUR

Rumours and Revelations

Earlier today, the hospital doctor assessed Elaine's ankle and decided that her permanent plaster cast could now be fitted, as the swelling had finally subsided to a satisfactory level. However, the medical team advised caution regarding travel, strongly recommending that Elaine refrain from flying for at least three more days due to the risk of further swelling and complications.

Consequently, the group was compelled to amend their travel plans. Billy, the only member with unavoidable work commitments, will proceed with his journey as originally scheduled. For everyone else, the flights from Dublin have been postponed until next Saturday, which is one week from tomorrow. The hope remains that Elaine's recovery continues without incident, enabling them all to travel by air as planned. If, however, further complications arise, they may need to consider alternative transportation, such as taking the ferry.

Elaine is frustrated as she can't move freely and sits with her leg up. She rarely relaxes in front of the TV, but she appreciates Kate's help. She isn't enjoying it as much as she expected.

As promised, Nick informed DI Wendy Fenimore of the situation and reported the events that involved an unknown third party. He also sought permission to share information with Garda Síochána and arrange for formal collaboration based on information he had gathered.

Nick met with Detective Garda Timothy Walsh in a professional capacity, accompanied by Billy, who provided background information. They expressed their concerns about the recent events, the one that led to Elaine's injury, and provided him with the documents Nick had gathered, including the local reports, evidence from Matthew's Green Rover, and the accidents inquest reports, dating back to the 1970s.

Timothy said he would review all the information and called last night to inform Nick that, in his view, there was enough evidence to link Matthew Junior with similar cases and requested the reopening of the missing child case too.

"The Superintendent's Office has reopened it for the Northwest Region, and I am assigned to lead the investigation." DI Walsh informed Nick in an earlier telephone conversation.

This meant that Nick had to approach his new boss again, and this time request permission to continue working on the case. She suggested sending someone else, but after evaluating the risk and considering the investigation, she agreed to let him continue. However, she insisted he keep her informed at every step.

"I'm not kidding Nick, if you discover anything that could compromise us or our national security, you must contact me day or night. If you don't, both of us will be in big trouble," she warned.

Detective Garda Timothy Walsh accompanied Nick and Billy as they settled into Aunt Aileen's cosy front room once more, the rain pattering softly against the windowpanes. Aileen sat composed yet visibly tense, her hands clasped tightly around a worn handkerchief. Nick glanced reassuringly at her before speaking.

"Thank you, Aunt Aileen, for seeing us again," Nick began, his voice gentle. "Would you mind sharing what you remember about the day Matthew and Sidney died?"

Aileen paused, searching her memory. "It's still hard, even after all these years," she admitted. "When we learned about Sidney, Mammy... oh, she was inconsolable. The doctor had to come and sedate her. I can still hear the wailing – For two days and nights she cried."

Billy nodded solemnly. "I am sure it was distressing for you all."

Timothy leaned forward, empathy in his eyes. "And your father? How did he cope?"

Aileen's voice faltered. "He tried to keep strong, but I remember him looking so pale, almost ghostly. My sister did her best to keep the younger children distracted, but Dad... he just couldn't bear it. He left, put on his coat and cap, and closed the door behind him. Later, we found out he'd walked all night through the wind and rain."

Nick exchanged a glance with Billy, then gently prompted, "What happened after that?"

Aileen dabbed her eyes. "It was only a day or two later, though the memory's blurry. We were hoping Matthew would come through the door, but instead, Patrick Reilly – the local guard and a family friend – arrived with terrible news. He told us Matthew's car had been found at the bottom of the nearby cliff."

Billy asked quietly, “Did Patrick think it was deliberate?”

Aileen shook her head. “Patrick was kind. He said the road was dangerous, especially during a storm. I believe he thought it was best for us to believe it was a tragic accident and recorded it as such. I believe he didn’t want the family to suffer any more.”

Timothy pressed gently, “But did anyone suspect otherwise?”

Aileen hesitated. “Without witnesses, there was no certainty. The London police believed Sidney died from a head injury. My father... he thought Matthew just couldn’t live with the guilt. But Paddy – Patrick – felt there was nothing to gain from assuming worse. His report reflected that.”

Nick nodded, sensing the weight of grief still present. “Thank you, Aunt Aileen. Your memories are helping us piece together what happened.”

Aileen managed to smile. “If it brings any truth to light, I’m glad to help.”

Nick saw that Aileen’s account did not impress Detective Garda Timothy Walsh, noticing the detective’s raised eyebrows of despair as she spoke.

With a trembling voice, Aileen explained, “My father passed away less than three months after my brothers. The stress was overwhelming for him; he suffered two strokes in quick succession. Joan took Mammy back to England, where they handed Maddie over to the authorities. Our own family was already large, and Maggie couldn't help, as she was barely able to care for herself and her children."

Nick and Billy both sensed a distinct change in Aileen's demeanour as she began to speak about Maggie and Maddie. Her tone became emotionally distant, almost detached.

"Mammy eventually returned to Ireland," Aileen continued, her voice laden with sorrow. "Poor Mammy—her mind was never the same after all this tragedy. She died with a troubled mind and a broken heart about a year later." The loss clearly weighed heavily on Aileen, who paused to gather herself before continuing.

Nick, attempting to probe further, asked,

"What about Matthew Junior? "Why do you think he wasn't in the car with his father?"

The question seemed to trigger another transformation in Aileen. Her manner shifted abruptly, becoming stern and authoritative, as it had been during their first encounter. "There were whispers through the grapevine that Mary took in a child in around that time, a boy! I believe that instead of driving directly from the ferry to our farm, Matthew drove the boy to Mary's place up north, to hide out. I suspect Matthew knew the police were waiting for him here and couldn't face Mam and Dad. He might have seen suicide as his only choice, but he would not have hurt his son! There was also a time lapse between the ferry's arrival and when Matthew's car went over the cliff," Aileen explained, her voice unwavering.

An investigation conducted by Timothy Walsh revealed that the eldest daughter, Mary, had moved with her husband and children to a village about forty miles north. This supported Aileen's suspicion, and further investigation revealed Matthew had travelled there first. The close community wanted to spare her already grieving mother the thought that anything other than a tragic accident caused her son and grandson's death, so records pointed towards the likelihood of an accident.

CHAPTER TWENTY-FIVE

Dinner Invitation

Billy returned to the UK on Saturday as planned, whilst the rest of the party remained in Ireland. Nick has spent much of his time over the past couple of days working with DI Walsh.

Kate and Elaine are sitting, having a coffee, when Nick bursts in through the front door. His face is red, and he looks unhappy.

"What's up?" asks Elaine.

"Gran is what's up!" Nick has returned from another meeting with DI Walsh at the local Garda station.

"Would you believe it? I am going to have to return to the UK as soon as possible to interview my grandmother! DI Walsh has retrieved ferry passenger records from February 1972. Matthew may have used another name to make the crossing, but guess whose name appeared within the foot passenger records for that week?"

Nick slams his briefcase on the table and runs his hand through his hair.

Kate and Elaine share a 'look' but do not speak.

"Mrs Margaret O'Donnell!"

"You're kidding!" said Elaine.

"Nope, she was travelling alone, a foot passenger. They must now question her in relation to Matthew's death."

"Nick, it is not possible... your grandmother lacks mental capacity!" Elaine said.

"That's what I said, but they want to apply for a medical assessment and provide support from an advocate."

"When?"

"As soon as possible. This puts a whole new light on events."

"You need to see a lawyer. This blasted ankle. If only I could travel with you, do you want me to call some of my colleagues? Elaine expresses her frustration.

"It's okay; Dad has spent most of the morning ringing around, seeking advice."

"We have spent the last two hours ringing hotels, asking for guest lists or if anyone that would remember gran... not that there were many to choose from. And guess what? After all these years, today Tim spoke with an old lady who remembers Gran clearly. We have interviewed her."

"The likelihood is we will have to travel tomorrow just for a day or two."

"You know the trouble with you, Nick... you're just too good at your job."

"Not me this time. It's DI Timothy Walsh; Tim! He's like a dog with a bone."

"He seemed very serious when I met him," Elaine remarked, her tone reflective.

Nick responded quickly, "He's actually a very nice bloke." With a playful grin, he added, "He asks me a lot of questions about you Kate."

Kate's cheeks coloured as she replied, "Despite having a similar profession, I am surprised you haven't considered it's his job to ask questions about people." Nick burst out laughing at her comment.

"Exactly, Miss Davis, which is why I know the difference between shop talk and a keen interest... and he's single!" Nick teased, giving her a pointed look.

Elaine joined in, suggesting with a mischievous smile, "You should invite him to dinner."

"Great minds think alike, but I just thought I'd run it past you girls first. Didn't want to cross the line," Nick said, glancing between them.

Kate blushed again and said, "Of course, that's fine. He seemed like a nice guy."

"Okay, dinner it is. Here tonight. I'm certain he'll accept. He kind of has already," Nick announced with a wink at Kate, before disappearing through the latch door to the first floor.

"Tonight!" Kate and Elaine say in unison, which makes them smile.

Present day-Maggie

I push away the jelly and melted ice cream that I've been playing with in the bowl for the past few minutes. Lucy has joined me for lunch, and while eating the canteen-prepared sandwiches she brought in, she explained the police may wish to interview me. How do I feel about it? The thought of being questioned by the police dampens my appetite. How could they expect me to feel anything but anxious?

Lucy has also explained that Nick is collaborating with an Irish detective, and they've uncovered some details about Matthew's accident. My stomach churns uncomfortably, and the last two mouthfuls of ice cream repeat on me.

"Mum, they have discovered you were in Ireland at the time of the car accident. I had to share with Nick what you told me." Lucy pauses, waiting for my response.

"Mum, do you understand what I'm saying?" Lucinda sounds impatient, but I do not respond.

"Also, we need to decide if the person visiting you, is Matthew Junior. We are concerned that he may have ill intentions towards our family, looking for some sort of revenge. Do you understand?"

"Of course, I understand, Lucy! You're mistaken. Matthew, the grown-up I've met, doesn't seem to intend us any harm."

"Then why doesn't he be upfront, introduce himself to us?" Lucy sounds irritated.

"I've told you before, it was a complicated situation, best that I share what happened that day as I recall it, because who knows what I'll remember from one moment to another? You need to know what led to Matthew's disappearance. I am so afraid of how differently I feel because of this dementia."

"Okay, I'm sorry," Lucy sighs.

"Sometimes I can't remember the name of the food that is in front of me," I push the bowl further away.

"But the memories of my past are so vivid, it's as if I am reliving the nightmares. I have many regrets, but motherhood is not one of them. Even though it was just a brief time with dear Matthew, my past may affect your future and the relationships you have with your siblings, so I must share the details now as I live them.

CHAPTER TWENTY-SIX

February 1972 – Ireland

Waking from a deep sleep, my head is thumping, and I feel shaky, then an overwhelming feeling of homesickness. I scramble to gather my thoughts and figure out my whereabouts, confused about the time of day. It occurs to me I am staying in a hotel hundreds of miles away from home.

I swing my legs around and sit on the side of the bed. When I go to the window and open the drapes, it is dark outside except for a few dots of light bobbing within and across the bay. I fumble around to find the light switch on a nearby standard lamp, but then I realise it is not plugged in. Once I plug it in, the room illuminates with a warm, cosy glow. Despite the ambiance, I feel my teeth chattering from the cold, so I switch on both bars of the electric fire, and the fan behind the artificial log's rattles.

Anxiety heightens as I consider what I have done—crossing the sea to Ireland, to a strange town, with no means of transportation. I don't even drive, and with a few items of clothing and the little red diary, which holds the scribbled addresses of Matthew's distant family members used for Christmas and birthdays. It's unclear whether Matthew has even brought my son to Ireland. I feel like crying, but tears don't well.

The clock on the mantel shows ten minutes to seven. I have slept for several hours. Despite my reluctance to venture outside the room, there is no time to waste. I need to use the bathroom, so I grab my washbag, a fresh change of clothes, and a towel and tiptoe to the bathroom on the floor below.

Following a shower and changing into fresh clothes, I feel better. I switch off the fire bars, but leave the lamp on, lock the door of my room, and head down to the hotel reception.

As I descend the staircase, the smell of home cooking hits me. I recognise Colleen Blight, although she has changed into slacks and a light jersey. Her dark hair is now tied in a ponytail, and she looks less formal and younger than she did upon my arrival. She exits through the door to the bar, returning a little while later carrying a tray with two plates and the remnants of a gravy-based meal. She smiles upon seeing me.

“Let me get rid of these, and I will be with you,” she said, moving across the room and exiting through another door. She reappears a few moments later.

“You look brighter. Did you have a pleasant sleep?”

“Yes, thank-you. The room is extremely comfortable, and I feel rested. Mrs Blight... I was wondering if you have a local map and a bus timetable I could borrow, as well as the contact details of a local taxi company. I don’t drive and may need to hire a driver while I’m here.”

“Colleen, please call me Colleen. Of course... now where are they?”

Colleen rummages under the desks and then places a bus timetable down on the reception desk before me.

"Buses are few and far between, so if you plan to take a bus, you will need this. My husband runs a chauffeur service from the hotel for our guests, but he is away fishing for a couple of days. Where do your relatives live?"

I hesitate, and Colleen's brow furrows. I place the little red book before her and point to the farm address where my sister-in-law and her family live, and where my in-laws and Maddie are staying.

She squints as she studies my scribbled writing. "You will need a car. The bus only goes as far as The Lamb Inn on the main road, and that farm is about two miles uphill from the stop. Access to vehicles is up a dirt track! Will they not come to fetch you?" she asks, sounding surprised.

"I... er... I hope to surprise them!" I say, but Colleen Blight looks unconvinced, her eyebrows knitting together as she studies me. When I least want it to happen, my voice cracks, my eyes well up, and hot tears blur my vision. Colleen comes to my side and places her arm around my shoulder.

"Oh, my dear, what is it? Why so many tears?" she asks. So, I reveal my husband has snatched my son, and I have travelled all this way to find them. I am a private person, but I feel drawn to this woman, and she is easy to talk to.

Colleen guides me from the reception area into a back room and an armchair.

"Now you sit there for a moment while we get rid of this mess."

Colleen addresses a young woman working in the kitchen in a language unfamiliar to Maggie. The girl nods and continues to transfer dirty plates, cups, and glasses stacked on a large central table into the adjoining scullery. Colleen helps to clear the rest of the crockery, and then, with an unspoken command not to disturb us again, she shuts the scullery door.

"Now, tell me all about it. You will feel so much better, and in strictest confidence, of course!"

I blurt out the events of the past few days, mentioning that my father had suffered an assault during a robbery and was taken to the hospital. I don't feel comfortable enough to reveal that I've also discovered my husband is the biological father of his brother's child, that he may have murdered his brother's wife, or that Matthew had also planned the attack on my dad.

"We argued after a fight with his brother, and he has taken my son. His brother has died of his injuries, and I don't even know if he is aware."

Colleen removes a boiling kettle from the stove within the inglenook fireplace and tops up the teapot. She fetches two clean cups from the dresser and pours tea for both of us, all the while listening as I continue to reveal.

"I am so sorry. You are busy," I say, dabbing my eyes with my handkerchief.

"Other than supervising Rosy, who is clearing dinner and setting the tables for breakfast, I am finished for the evening. We are not terribly busy at this time of year, so don't worry that head of yours," she assures me.

While I don't know your husband, I am well acquainted with the rest of his family and those two O'Donnell sisters... Aileen, in particular. Then there is Joan. They are close. I remember both from school, and we use their place, Aisling Farm, to buy meat and produce.

"I didn't think this through very well!" Through my tears, I say.

"Don't fret. While I wouldn't wish to interfere, I can help... if you agree. If you don't want to face the family just yet, I will drive up to Aisling Farmhouse first thing tomorrow morning, with the excuse of increasing my dairy and meat order. I intended to do this anyway now that spring is on its way. And I will let you know if the boy is there. I am familiar with the household, so I will recognise a new face among the herd."

"Um... I'm not sure what to say."

"My visit would not be out of the ordinary, and if your little boy is up there, you can plan your next move, rather than just turn up. Because believe me... you will have a battle on your hands! If those girls can cut off their own flesh and blood, they would not think twice about pulling rank against an outsider," she warns.

My expression must show bewilderment as Colleen expands on the story.

"Mary, the sister? You were told about the family feud?

I shake my head in bewilderment.

"I'm not sure what it was about, but just before your in-laws moved to England. Your husband and his brother were only little. It would have been about eighteen years ago," Colleen recollects.

"There was a massive fight between John, Mary's husband, and Aileen's husband, Tom. John worked on their farm... it is how he met Mary. The fight took place here, well, in the bar next door. It turned into a brawl that resembled something out of the Wild West. Everyone got involved, throwing chairs. My husband had to escort John out the back way, or I'm sure they would have killed him. He went into hiding. Something about stolen cash. We heard through the grapevine that Mary had to move north with their children to join him. It was all rather unpleasant... not that I'm one to gossip, of course!"

I lived with Mr and Mrs O'Donnell for years, and they never mentioned a daughter named Mary. Very odd! But then again, nothing surprises me anymore.

"My husband never mentioned her either. Are you certain?"

"Quite certain! Mary has never returned home to this town, and I believe they have not spoken since... Not much happens around here without me getting to know about it," Colleen explains. Her tone softens as she continues.

"If you take my advice, it's dark, and there is not much you can do tonight, and you are unfamiliar with the area, so I would recommend against heading out. Rest tonight, and we can sort out this sorry situation in the morning. It sounds like you need strength of mind to confront that husband of yours... and his sisters. A good night's sleep will help you deal with whatever lies ahead... Now, are you hungry?"

I accept the offer of food, and Colleen leads me to a small dining room. She brings a plate of lamb chops, potatoes and vegetables covered in a rich gravy. Once I finish my meal, I take Colleen Blight's advice and return to my room.

I wash and change into my nightie, and although I don't believe I am going to sleep, I climb between the cool, crisp sheets anyway. As my head hits the soft down pillow, thoughts race, if only for a moment or two. And then I feel myself drift, and it is not long before I am fast asleep again.

CHAPTER TWENTY-SEVEN

Search for Answers

Billy and Lucy walked down the corridor in silence. They had bickered in the car on the way to the hospital, which was a rare occurrence. Uncomfortable with confrontation, they agreed to disagree.

Entering the cubicle, they found their mother sleeping. Each of them grabbed a plastic chair and sat on either side of the bed. After about ten minutes of reading emails, texts, and scrolling through social media on their own phones, Maggie stirred.

"Hello Mum, back in the land of the living?" Billy spoke first.

"Hello Son!" Maggie replied.

"Can you help me sit up?" Billy stood up and tried to fluff her pillows and pull his mother up the bed.

"Not like that!" Lucy said, grabbing the handset to adjust the bed's position and manoeuvre it to an upright position.

Maggie seemed quite alert this evening, and the three of them engaged in trivial conversation and discussed a change in the weather.

"I've just returned from Ireland," Billy said. Maggie's expression did not change.

"Lucy mentioned that you went to Ireland once. You're full of surprises," Billy remarked, attempting a lighthearted tone to ease the tension in the room. He glanced over at Lucy, whose stern look made it clear she was not amused by his attempt to steer the conversation in this direction. With a small shrug, Billy signalled his acceptance of her disapproval, choosing to press the point further.

"Nick will be back tomorrow, and he's planning to come and see you. That will be nice, won't it?" Billy said, his voice was deliberately clear and slightly louder than usual, as though raising the volume would help Maggie understand him better. "A police officer might be with him. Also, a doctor will visit you tomorrow morning to assess whether you can speak to the police. Is that okay?"

Maggie gave him a wry smile. "Billy, I'm not deaf, well, not yet!" she replied, her tone light but edged with mild irritation at his unnccessary volume.

"Sorry, just wanted to keep you informed!" Billy responded, softening his tone as he tried to reassure her. He shifted in his chair, glancing briefly at Lucy before returning his attention to their mother.

"But we don't have to talk about this anymore, Mum!" Lucy interjected, her tone firm as she glanced warningly at Billy, making it clear she wanted to change the subject.

However, Billy pressed on, undeterred by his sister's clear disapproval. "It might be better if you told Lucy and me what happened while you were in Ireland, in the days leading up to Matthew's accident," he said, his voice calm but insistent. "If you share it with us now, before the police arrive, we'll have a better understanding of what's going on. That way, if we need to get advice or help, we'll know what we're dealing with." He ignored Lucy's sigh and the glare she shot in his direction, focusing instead on their mother and the importance of clarity before official questions began.

CHAPTER TWENTY-EIGHT

1972 – The Rosa Hotel

I rub my eyes, and it takes a while for them to adjust to the daylight. The sun is low, and its rays beam onto the hotel wall just above the headboard. I realised I hadn't pulled the drapes before going to bed. My eyelids still feel heavy, due to oversleeping. Back home, I wake up when it's dark to get the kids ready for school.

I stretch before walking towards the window. The sky is a bright pale blue; the mist lies heavy out to sea. Frost outlines the shapes of trees and hedges and covers the landscape that meets with the mist-shrouded mountains in silver. I glance at the mantel clock—it's just past nine o'clock. It's been so long since I've slept in this late.

I take my wash-bag downstairs to shower and dress. Before heading to the hotel reception area, I put on dark grey slacks, a cream baggy roll-neck jumper, and clipped up my hair.

"I was just about to come up and knock on your door," Colleen beams as she removes her scarf, gloves and wax coat.

"Come through to the parlour. I'll make you some tea. You missed a full breakfast, but I'll bring you some toast," she said.

I follow Colleen to the parlour, the same room I sat in the previous evening. She starts fussing and sets a place at the oak table with a teacup, saucer, tea-plate, a jar of orange marmalade, and small bowls of jam and butter.

"Have a seat. You'll be interested to know what I've discovered. I visited Aisling Farmhouse this morning. I used the excuse that I needed to change our dairy order. The farmhouse was lit up, but the drapes were closed. Joan came out to greet me at once. She looked as if she hadn't slept a wink. She explained there had been a death in the family and asked if I could return at a more convenient time. I offered my condolences; she said they are all in shock after hearing about the sudden death of their brother," Colleen speaks while checking the toast which is browning under the grill.

"Joan hadn't disclosed the details of what had happened, but it was clear that she was deeply upset. She did mention that they were expecting their youngest brother to arrive, although he hadn't yet appeared. I can only assume that she was referring to your husband?. In fact, Joan said if a man with a London accent was to check in at the hotel, I am to inform her straight away." Colleen watched me carefully, awaiting my reaction to this news.

The very reason I had come to Ireland was to see him, yet the thought of him actually turning up here sent a current of nervous energy through my entire body.

"I only arrived back moments before you appeared, so you can be pretty certain that your husband and son are not at Aisling Farm yet, but Joan seemed anxious" she adds.

Colleen placed two pieces of toast onto the tea-plate in front of me.

"Thank you so much and thank-you for seeing if they were at the farm," I express my gratitude.

"It's no trouble. You were so upset yesterday and forgive me for saying you appeared quite unwell. Although you're looking much better this morning, it's amazing what a good night's sleep can do," Colleen remarks.

"If Matthew hasn't gone to the farm, where else could he go? What if I'm wrong, and he didn't come to Ireland?" I doubted my intuition, which led me to leave my children behind in search of him.

Where do I go from here? This journey seems like a complete waste of time. I should have let the police search and stayed at home. But I can't give up, not yet, not until I find my son.

Sensing my despondency, Colleen attempted to reassure me.

"There are more cottages being used for short-term rentals. People have moved to the cities for work. If your husband knows this area well, he may have arranged something," she suggests.

"In fact, just yesterday, the owner of a nearby cottage mentioned to me that they had recently let their property to a family from London who were visiting for the school holidays. What made the conversation memorable was our discussion about how encouraging it is to see people travelling outside the traditional eight-week summer period. Since our community relies heavily on tourism, any shift in the usual holiday trends could be a real advantage for local businesses like ours. A broader flow of visitors throughout the year would make a significant difference to our livelihoods," Colleen explained.

"Where is it?" I asked hopefully, eager for any lead that could bring me closer to finding Matthew.

Colleen replied, "A couple of miles up the lane towards the coastal road. I would offer to run you up there, but I must get on here, I'm afraid. However, I can mark it on the map for you if you like?"

Doubt crept into my voice as I responded, "I'm not sure Matthew knows this area that well. He would have wanted us to be located nearby to his family." The uncertainty of the situation weighed heavily on me.

Colleen then asked gently, "What are you going to do now?"

I steadied myself and answered, "I am going to search the local area, look for his car." The determination to keep searching pushed me forward, even as anxiety lingered in the back of my mind.

"I could try to find someone else to drive you," Colleen offered, her concern evident.

I shook my head. "It's fine, Colleen. Thank you, but it's a lovely day, so I'll search on foot. The walk will help clear my mind and plan."

Colleen's worry deepened, and she cautioned, "Oh no, not on your own; what if you find him? Why not speak with your in-laws? Joan seemed confused by the events. Perhaps you can explain to them that your husband has lost control and what he's done. They may help you." Pouring tea and adding milk, she turned to me with a hand on her hip, her expression one of deep concern.

I tried to reassure her. "I'll be okay, and if I find him, I'll return here and call the police. I can't come all this way and do nothing. It's unlikely Matthew will just stroll into town. That's not his way." My confidence was more for her benefit than my own, but I clung to it, nonetheless.

I was certain they were staying somewhere nearby. Matthew would want to keep some sense of normality for Matthew Junior, who, by now, he would have discovered is a sensitive little soul. If he was feeling scared or unhappy, very little would console him. I knew how to manage his persistent crying, but I was unsure that Matthew could handle it on his own.

"Why not call the police now?" Colleen asks.

"The thought of the police catching up with him made him run. I'm worried that if Matthew gets spooked, he'll just take off again," I explain.

Since breakfast, I have wandered country lanes, crossed fields and marshes, and walked cliff-top paths. I have strolled along beaches and peered into isolated barns. The sun has been shining, but a biting wind has cut-through.

It is late afternoon, and I haven't eaten a thing since setting off. Now, beginning to flag, I decide to stop at a small inn on the outskirts of a tiny hamlet of whitewashed cottages overlooking the sea.

I order a bowl of stew and soda bread, and the landlady delivers the steaming bowl and bread to the booth where I am sitting out of view. The sun is going down, so I should make my way back to town once I have eaten. The walk could take a couple of hours, and I need to get back before it gets dark. I am also thinking about returning home—

to England. My other children will be missing me, and I am missing them. But how can I leave when Matthew Junior could be so nearby? I must search tomorrow. Isolated cottages speckle the landscape. If unsuccessful, I will visit my in-laws, speak with them, and if Matthew turns up, they will talk him into doing the right thing and returning my child to me. I will also suggest taking Maddie home, too. She will be overcome with grief, and all she'll want is the comfort of her family, which means me and her siblings.

I visit the lavatory, which is in an outhouse separate from the pub's main building, before setting off along the cliff path. The map on loan from Colleen shows this as the shortest route back to town, and I must get a move on if I want to get back before it gets too dark. I keep walking at a steady pace.

I have been walking for an hour and fifteen minutes. The wind has strengthened, and the sky is maroon as the sun dips. Clouds hang low around the mountain range behind me, casting shadows across the landscape. I quicken my pace, realising I may not make it back to the hotel before the sun sinks below the horizon. Although not yet dark, the pale moon is already visible.

I watch as lights go on in the seaside town in the distance, casting an orange glow along the shore of the grey Atlantic. An estuary weaves downhill behind the town towards the sea. From here, I can see I must come off the coastal path now and find the correct lane, or I risk meeting the bank of a river in the dark.

The map is becoming more difficult to read. Thankfully, Colleen had pencilled routes back into town. By following the route pencilled on the map, I can just make out the path I should take. Upon reaching a stone wall, I notice a narrow gap that is just wide enough to squeeze through. I am heading in the right direction. If I follow this route correctly, it will take me across an open field to a road that will lead down to town.

The gorse heather is thick underfoot, and in this dim light, it takes all my effort to avoid the positioned rocks. I'm wishing that I had started my journey back to the hotel sooner. As I reach the halfway mark across the open field, all-natural light from the sun has gone. Now, guided only by the moon that casts a silver glow, I see a mass of cloud being propelled inland from the sea by the strengthening wind. The change in meteorological activity had propelled the clouds that had hung around the mountains earlier inland.

I notice a bright flash of light on the horizon, and I feel a large spot of rain hit my nose, followed by another and then a low rumble of thunder.

The last thing I need is to be struck by lightning while crossing a field hundreds of miles away from home. With the map tucked in my coat pocket, I quicken my stride and head towards a distant light shining in the far corner of the field.

Fear envelops me as I rush towards it, with the narrowing gap between the lightning and thunderclaps. As I near the farthest part of the field, I see a one-story whitewashed cottage. The light is coming from a near-side window, while the far side is in complete darkness. I reach a stone boundary and a maintained wire fence. used as a cut-through, with one end hanging lower despite the obvious attempts to reinforce it. By this time, rain is dripping off my headscarf, which is tied around my chin. With the rain and strengthening wind, my face is stinging, and my chin is feeling quite sore.

I climb over the fence, and in a few steps, I am standing in front of a whitewashed cottage. A concrete hardstanding stretches from the front of it up to a small barn about ten feet away, as well as to an open gate and the lane that I should follow down to town, marked out in pencil on Colleen's map. The cottage appears on the map as well; it's identified as the property belonging to her friend—the very one she mentioned during our earlier conversation. This reassurance helps me confirm that I am indeed on the correct route, The familiar landmark offers comfort amid the worsening weather and growing darkness, grounding me to take shelter.

I think about knocking, but despite a light being on in the rear room of the building, there is no-one home. The hardstanding at the front of the cottage is empty of any vehicles. With a loud clap I run towards the open shelter of the barn.

The barn is clear and tidy but for a few bulky items stored on the back wall. It looks like furniture items, although it is too difficult to make out in this darkness. Feeling afraid, I leave the stable door ajar.

I shall wait for the worst of the storm to pass and then proceed down the lane towards town, I decide.

It has been almost thirty minutes of waiting, but it must be nearing six o'clock or later. I hear a motor coming closer, and then I see the headlights.

"Thank goodness, the occupants of this property might have a phone or may even be open to giving me a ride to town."

CHAPTER TWENTY-NINE

The Storm

DI Tim Walsh walks into the reception area of the hotel, followed closely behind by Nick. A smartly dressed young woman in her early twenties stands behind the reception desk. The area is bright, with walls painted in tones of sage green. A few fine pieces of contemporary artwork hang on the wall, featuring vibrant warm colours that complement the room's ambiance and give a modern feel to the old building. The young woman greets them with a warm smile.

"Can I help you?" she asks.

"We have an appointment with the owner," DI Walsh replies.

"I shall just give Mr Lewis, our general manager, a call. You say he is expecting you?" responds in a sing-song lilt as she picks up the telephone receiver.

Detective Jack Walsh clarifies, "Mrs. Colleen Blight is the person with whom we arranged the meeting."

The receptionist looks surprised but continues with the call.

"Your names?" She asks, cradling the receiver between her chin and neck, pen ready in hand.

Nick provides their names and ranks formally, considering they are here in a professional capacity.

"Mr Lewis, there are two detectives waiting in reception. They are here to see Mrs Blight, and they say she is expecting them," the receptionist informs Mr Lewis over the phone.

"Mr Lewis will not keep you waiting. He will be here in a moment. Please take a seat," said Katrina, as read from her name badge. She points to the two armchairs on either side of the inglenook fireplace, where a log burner gently glows. The reception has a library or doctor's surgery atmosphere, where speaking feels prohibited. Nick and DI Walsh sit in silence, glancing at each other with a sense of amusement.

Suddenly, a man appears from a side door. He is short in stature, immaculately dressed in a blue suit with a matching waistcoat and a neatly trimmed beard. He practically dances his way towards them. Nick thinks he resembles Graham Norton and even sounds like him when he speaks.

"Good afternoon, gentlemen," Mr Lewis said breezily. "Mrs Blight is expecting you. If you could please follow me, I will take you to her living quarters."

Nick and Jack follow Mr Lewis through the door from which he came, passing a staircase leading to the upper floors and walking along a corridor in a newer part of the building. They see a row of doors with RFID entry locks. From a window, they glimpse the low-level extension with its new red pitched roof, forming a U-shape around a large courtyard with a wedding pagoda at its centre.

"This hotel has been in Mrs Blight family since before the war. Of course, they have extended it over the years. Where the restaurant is now used to be a public bar back in the day," Nick thinks Mr Lewis's sales patter must be habitual as he acts as a tour guide during their walk.

Colleen's living quarters are at the farthest point away from reception, through an exit door to a private annex adjoining the main building. Mr Lewis knocks on the front door before opening it with a door card attached to a chain in his waistcoat. He calls out as they enter, "Colleen, it's only me. Your visitors have arrived. They are with me."

"Come on in!" is the reply.

The hotel manager leads Nick and Tim into a small sitting room where they see an older woman, known to be in her eighties, sitting in a high-back recliner chair. The room has a neutral decor with cream-painted walls, beige carpet and minimal furniture. There is a fold-down teak table under the window with a dining chair on either side. Mrs Blight sits next to a side table on wheels, which is strewn with clutter, including a cup and saucer, books, glasses case, pens, notepad, box of tissues, and a magazine. The sound from a regular morning TV programme Colleen is watching is blaring.

"Where's that remote?" Her movement is slow as she aims to pick up items and move them aside, bringing attention to the severe arthritis in her hands and fingers.

"Here it is! Do you want this off?" Lewis said brightly, picking up the remote and pointing it towards the TV before Colleen responds.

After introductions, Mr Lewis speaks loudly and emphasises every word.

"Colleen dear, would you like me to stay with you?"

"No, no... go about your business. Everything will be okay. I have been expecting this visit for years!

"I'm off then, buzz me when you are done," Mr Lewis hands Colleen a handset.

Colleen offers the two detectives a seat, which they accept, sitting on either side of the dining table.

"You asked me when we spoke on the phone if I knew Maggie O'Donnell and if she had ever stayed at our hotel. I said yes on both accounts... many moons ago. But I am not sure how else I can help you. We have had thousands of guests stay in this hotel over the years, and Maggie was just one of them," Colleen said.

Nick answers gently, "There is something we didn't tell you over the phone. Maggie O'Donnell is my grandmother. For many years, family members believed that her young son, my uncle, had died in a car crash along with his father when their car went over a cliff near here. But we believe the child may have survived. Can you share with us what you remember of my grandmother's stay, and do you know if she contacted her then-husband, Matthew, while she was staying here?"

Colleen looks thoughtful as she aims to recollect events. She reveals how Maggie had arrived at the hotel alone, tired, and distressed, saying her husband had snatched her son. Colleen also explains how she had visited Aisling Farm under false pretences on Maggie's behalf to see if they were there.

"One of his sisters informed me. The brother had just died, and the family was expecting Matthew's arrival from England, so he wasn't on the property when I visited. I told Maggie this on my return. Maggie felt her husband must be nearby, so she went in search. She was desperate to find her son! I can recall that evening as if it were yesterday. There was a horrendous storm, and I became frantic as night fell, and your grandmother had not returned. I was that worried. I left the hotel reception unattended to look for her, and it was the first time that I was not on hand to help serve dinners, too."

"Did you find her? Where was she?" Nick inquires.

"I drove around for a while, then I spotted her coming down the lane. I pulled over. She was extremely distressed. She said she had been searched all day and got lost while caught in the storm. I felt so sorry for the poor woman. She was soaking wet, covered in mud where she had fallen, shivering and shaken. I brought her back here. She had a hot shower. I made her some cocoa and led her to bed. She was burning up with a fever. I offered to fetch a doctor, but she wouldn't hear of it," Colleen explained.

DI Tim Walsh leaned forward, his gentle yet probing tone. "What happened next? Did you call the Garda?"

Colleen shook her head slowly. "No, I didn't call them. I let her sleep. She was utterly exhausted and delirious. She slept for most of the following day," Colleen recalled, her voice tinged with concern as she remembered Maggie's fragile state.

She continued, "I was about to fetch the doctor when I overheard some of our customers discussing an accident. They said a father and his young son had gone over a cliff in the storm. Despite rescuers at the scene, the car had been swept out to sea! I just knew it was Maggie's husband and child!" Colleen's eyes water, and she reaches for a tissue to wipe her eyes.

Colleen found herself in an impossible position, faced with the daunting task of breaking devastating news to Maggie, who had already become physically and emotionally unwell from desperately searching for her missing son. Unsure of how to deliver such tragic information, Colleen sought guidance from a trusted acquaintance—a former Garda, and friend of her father-in-law. She asked him to investigate the rumours surrounding the accident. Later that afternoon, he returned and solemnly confirmed that the rumours were, in fact, true: the accident involving Maggie's husband and son had indeed occurred, and their car had gone over the cliff.

Nick, striving to maintain his professionalism yet deeply moved by his grandmother's plight, pressed Colleen about how she responded to the situation. Colleen, aware of the gravity of her next admission, confessed that her actions might warrant arrest. The detectives exchanged uneasy glances, neither wishing to pursue such a course with this frail elderly woman.

Feeling compelled to offer Maggie some comfort and to make the prospect of receiving the heartbreaking news more bearable, Colleen decided to act. She allowed Maggie to continue sleeping, recognising her exhaustion. Meanwhile, Colleen contacted her own doctor, explaining that she was struggling with her nerves—a condition for which she had previously been prescribed Valium following her mother's death. After explaining her state, the doctor prescribed her a week's supply to help her cope.

Colleen then prepared a cup of tea for Maggie. Before bringing it to her, she crushed a Valium tablet into the tea, hoping it would help soothe Maggie's distress. She brought the medicated tea up to Maggie's room, believing this act might make the impending news less traumatic.

Nick, running his fingers through his hair and sighing, acknowledged the seriousness of administering medication covertly, especially when it was prescribed for someone else. Nevertheless, he found solace in the fact that his grandmother had survived the ordeal and silently decided to let the matter rest.

Colleen described how Maggie cried, tears streaming down her face, and it seemed clear to Colleen that a mother's intuition had allowed Maggie to sense the loss of her son even before anything was said. After preparing and delivering the cup of tea containing the Valium, Colleen waited for a short while before gently sharing the news her father-in-law had confirmed: the devastating truth about the accident. She watched Maggie's reaction, expecting an outpouring of grief, but realised the sedative had taken effect when Maggie did not respond as Colleen had anticipated.

Reflecting on the moment, Colleen said, "I believe Maggie had already begun to accept the reality that her child was gone." Taking a sip of water, Colleen finished recounting the sequence of events.

"The following day, Maggie told me she needed to leave as soon as possible so she could return home to be with her other children and prepare for official confirmation about the accident from the authorities. She asked me not to mention her stay to anyone, explaining that it could further complicate an already difficult situation." Colleen explained that she readily agreed and honoured Maggie's request.

Before Maggie left, Colleen explained that she had given her Valium and offered her the remaining tablets to help her cope in the difficult days ahead. Maggie gratefully accepted the medication and thanked Colleen for her kindness. Colleen's husband then drove Maggie to the ferry, and that was the last time Colleen saw or heard from her—"Except for a single Christmas card that arrived a year later. The card, presumed to be from Maggie, simply read: Thanks for everything, Maggie."

CHAPTER THIRTY

Sense of Relief

"Hi Mum, we have just landed," Nick announced as he rang home. A car was meeting them at the airport and would take them straight to the police station. "Please can you leave a key out for me?"

His mother, sounding weary, replied, "Of course! Do you know what time you will be here? Nick hesitated for a moment. He wasn't sure. They had a meeting with DI Fenimore at half past five. During the meeting, they would be discussing whether he could continue working on this case. Realistically, it was unlikely, so he mentioned the possibility of his grandmother being questioned by DI Walsh. "I'm being stood down, Tim may have to question gran, possibly with my boss DI Fenimore since we are working alongside the Irish team on this case,"

"Oh gosh, my stomach is in knots," his mother revealed. "What do you think will happen?"

Nick paused before adding, "To be honest, I don't know, but I am eager to get back to Elaine and Kate. They are on their own in that isolated cottage," Nick did stock up on provisions, and Tim –DI Walsh—had arranged for one of men to drive past occasionally. Still, both women were adamant that he was fussing over nothing.

Nick then shifted the conversation, asking, "How is Gran?"

"She isn't good, Nick. All of this questioning and remembering the past will end up being the death of her... or me!" Lucy admitted, her voice trembling with worry. The strain of recent events was clearly taking its toll on both of them.

Trying to provide some context, Lucy continued, “Billy and I spent the evening with Mum last night, and she told us she went to Ireland. But from what I gather, she did not get to see Matthew.” It was clear Lucy had pressed their mother for details, hoping to clarify the situation. Nick asked, “are you sure?” Lucy replied earnestly, “As sure as I can be.” Nick offered some reassurance. “That fits with what we have been told, although I am unable to go into detail. Anyway, see you soon,” he concluded, drawing the conversation to a close.

Billy had left work mid-morning upon receiving a call from his sister requesting to join her to meet with authorities at the hospital. An unfamiliar doctor led Billy and Lucy to the family room, and they met Detective Inspector Fenimore and DI Walsh there. The doctor explained that, following an assessment conducted by him and a female colleague, they had decided that Maggie was unfit to be questioned that day.

Detective Inspector Fenimore told Lucy and Billy that, given Maggie’s recent medical update, it was important to inform them in person about new findings.

DI Walsh revealed that a man in Canada claims to be their brother, and authorities are verifying his claim. Nick had been informed but is currently off the case while the investigation continues. Evidence suggests the man may indeed be their brother, having been illegally adopted and taken to the USA in 1972 with a false birth certificate He is cooperating with American authorities and has agreed to a DNA test, leaving Lucy and Billy stunned by the news.

Detective Inspector Fenimore addressed their concerns with sensitivity, acknowledging the difficulty of the situation. She stressed "The recent visitor received by your mother, is not your brother; this clarification is crucial to prevent any further confusion or distress in her vulnerable state."

Driven by curiosity, Billy sought clarification about a possible link between these revelations and the recent events in Ireland that resulted in Elaine's injury. Detective Inspector Walsh responded by reassuring them that, based on their current information,

"It is highly unlikely that there is any connection." He explained.

"The man believed to be your brother has not travelled to the UK or Ireland since March of this year, making it improbable that he engaged in the incident concerning Elaine.

DI Fenimore stated that, after reviewing all evidence and interviewing witnesses, there was no need to question their mother about her trip to Ireland during the week of her first husband's death. They determined that Matthew, facing legal trouble and unable to confront his parents, took his son to his sister's and likely died by suicide.

"We know that Maggie travelled to Ireland in an attempt to locate her son. However, based on the evidence we have gathered, it seems she left Ireland without contacting her husband, or any other family members."

Despite the initial shock of discovering that their brother was still alive, both Lucy and Billy experienced a sense of relief following Detective Inspector Fenimore's detailed explanation. The uncertainty was, at least in part, lifted by her clarity and compassion.

Detective Inspector Fenimore assured them that the police were committed to supporting any efforts to reunite their family. She acknowledged that, given the many years that had passed, there were no guarantees. Nevertheless, the UK police would continue working closely with their Irish counterparts to ensure a thorough investigation. Their focus was not only on verifying the authenticity of their brother's identity but also on holding accountable those responsible for orchestrating the illegal adoption that had separated him from his family.

Ireland – Elaine & Kate

In Ireland, Elaine and Kate sat on the sofa, drinking glasses of red wine from lunch and discussing the evening prior to Nick's departure to the UK, attended by DI Tim Walsh.

"He was smitten with you," Elaine said, but Kate dismissed her remark by shaking her head.

"I believe he is just really intense person, I have noticed he observes everyone closely and really listens to what is said" Kate replied.

"I'm sorry, but he wasn't looking deep into Nick's eyes or mine over dinner, not like he did with yours," Elaine laughed.

"Could the attraction be mutual by any chance?" Elaine beamed.

"Will you stop it!" Kate laughed.

"Ah, saved by the bell, or should I say WhatsApp?" she said, reaching for Elaine's mobile and passing it to her.

"I'll leave you to chat. I'm going to take a bath," said Kate before going upstairs.

Elaine waved in acknowledgment as she answered Nick's call.

"Hello, you. How are things?"

Nick provided Elaine with an update of recent events and explained that DI Walsh and his boss were visiting the hospital to speak with his family as they spoke. "This is massive news for your poor family. What a shock for them," Elaine said. "We catch the flight back this evening." "Good, I miss you! And has your Irish companion mention our Kate anymore? Do you think he might be interested?" Elaine asked. "Will you stop playing matchmaker and leave these matters to Cupid, please," Nick laughed. "Just asking! I believe Kate may be keen on him too," Elaine said.

"Talking of Kate, I have to break some news to her when I get back. I am not looking forward to it, but I offer to relieve some stress from my mum following the shock of finding out her brother is most likely alive."

Elaine's tone shifts, growing more serious as she asks, "Is it about the stalker?"

"No, that continues to be a mystery for now. I can't tell you yet, however much I want to. I have to speak with Kate first, but she may not like what I have to tell her."

Elaine probes further, "More revelations?"

"Something like that."

"We are leaving for Heathrow Airport as soon as Tim returns from the hospital. Our flight back to Ireland is scheduled for late this afternoon, and I have some good news – they extend my leave until next week. So, I can concentrate on time spent with you, without drama! We can return to London next week and get on with the rest of our lives."

"Ditto! can't wait to see you,"

Upstairs, Kate dresses in a lounge suit, applies moisturiser to her face and arms, and tosses the damp towel wrapped around her hair into the laundry basket. She started the hairdryer and began blow-drying her hair. After a minute, she turned the hairdryer off, thinking she heard a thud from downstairs. She listened for a moment, but there was silence, so she switched the hairdryer back on. Once her hair was dry, she tidied up the pretty guest room where she was staying during their visit. She straightened the hotel-style white duvet cover and picked up the clothes she had discarded on the floor before showering. She descended the staircase and opened the latch to the lounge door. Elaine was still seated on the sofa with her foot in a plaster cast, propped up on the pouffe in front of her. Everything seemed fine, just as it was when Kate left Elaine alone to speak with Nick. However, she now noticed that Elaine's expression was one of fear. It's as if she was trying to communicate without words, her wide eyes conveying a message. "Are you okay?" Kate asked, concerned about Elaine's expression. Then she spotted him inside the room. He held something in his hand, and Kate's horror grew as she realised that the stranger present was holding a shotgun.

CHAPTER THIRTY-ONE

The Betrayal

Ray sat hunched over paperwork in his study when the front doorbell rang, its sound abrupt in the hush of their house. Lucy was sleeping upstairs—a fragile peace he hoped would last. Since their return from the hospital, he'd often heard her muffled sobs drifting from behind their bedroom door. No matter how he tried, his comfort could not quiet the grief that had washed over her upon learning her brother was alive. Ray sensed she shed more tears than she ever let him see, as though she now mourned the years lost as much as the reunion itself. He wiped a hand over his tired face and tiptoed down the hallway, opening the door to find a woman in her mid-sixties standing on the step, silver hair pulled back in a neat twist. A faint musk-smelling perfume wafted up as she shifted her handbag and looked at him with searching eyes.

"I'm looking for Mrs Langford," she began, her Welsh accent drawing out the words, reminding Ray of Catherine Jenkins's gentle lilt.

"My wife's resting now. I'm Ray. Can I help?" He kept his voice low, wary of disturbing Lucy. The woman hesitated, her hands worrying the strap of her bag, fingers trembling.

"It is important. I was hoping your wife might be able to help, but you may be able to... I'm searching for my nephew Julian, I believe Kathryn Davis, his sister works for you?

Ray blinked, the names tumbling together. For a moment, the web of relations twisted in his mind. Then recognition flickered "You mean My mother-in-law's nurse, Kate?"

"I fear my nephew may have travelled to London to make contact." She paused, scanning Ray's face for a reaction. He sensed the weight behind her words; the concern pressed into the lines around her eyes. He stepped back, gesturing for her to come inside. "Come in. Let's not talk on the doorstep."

In the kitchen, Ray filled the kettle, his movements deliberate. "Milk and sugar?"

"Just milk, thank-you." She wrapped delicate hands around the mug when he set it before her, gratitude flickering in her eyes before a deep unease claimed her features again. Ray took the chair opposite, the kitchen feeling too large and silent. The woman introduced herself as Charlotte Lewis.

"You said your nephew is Kate's brother?" he prompted, his curiosity piqued. The woman nodded, "Well half-brother, my sister Jane is... or I should say was, Julian's mother. She died of breast cancer when Julian was a baby." Charlotte's gaze drifted to the steam curling from her mug. "After Jane passed, my brother-in-law James remarried—This caused a great deal of pain; she was Julian's nanny; this drove a wedge through the family. They had a child together, Kathryn!"

Ray watched her. She looked as though she were recalling each memory in vivid detail: the bitterness, the confusion. "So, Kate and Julian are half-siblings—same father, different mothers."

"That's right. James's decision to marry Madeline, led to a family rift that lasted years. My parents, estranged from their grandson, suffered deeply, they became frail, and I moved home to care for them.

Ray sensed her regret.

"Then one day, quite out of the blue, James contacted my parents and revealed that Madeline had left him taking their daughter with her. He explained he realised Madeline had married him for his money, and the marriage was a disaster. He said she left him for her lover, abandoning Julian and separating him from his sister.

Ray reflected on how differently Charlotte Lewis told the story compared to what Maddie had shared with his wife. Charlotte depicted James Davis as a saint.

"James was sorry for his mistakes and asked we care for Julian; just for a few weeks while he dealt with some matters and consulted his solicitor about dissolving their marriage. I took responsibility, being single, and because of my parents' frailty. Ray noted Charlotte seemed almost apologetic for her single status.

"I saw firsthand how distraught Julian was. It was cruel, Madeline insisted he call her 'Mummy,' erasing my beloved sister's memory. She forbade mention of Jane's name, and there were no photographs of Jane in their home. Julian was a baby when Jane died, so Madeline robbed him of his memories; he was distraught when he first came to stay. then we were visited by the police who brought us the horrific news!"

Charlotte Lewis hesitated, her hands trembling as she set her cup down. "Poor James—Julian's father—lost his mind after everything Madeline put him through. They said Madeline went to their home, to torment the poor man, and James just... snapped. He shot her, then himself. Tragic!"

Ray let out a slow breath, shaken by the bluntness of her words. "What happened to Julian after that?"

"I became his legal guardian and Julian lived with us until—until recently when he found out his sister Kathryn was alive."

Ray's brows drew together. "Why would he have thought otherwise?"

Charlotte pressed her lips together, glancing away.

"Because that is what we told him... we thought it was for the best, we were not in a position to take in the child, so, we made him think Kathryn died with his parents,"

Ray considered, reflecting on Charlotte's words and the underlying sentiment. He wondered whether her reluctance stemmed not only from her single status and her parents' frailty but also from a deep-seated hesitation to take in the child of the 'scarlet woman'. The implication lingered that Charlotte, despite her compassion for Julian, struggled with the idea of caring for the daughter of a woman whose actions had brought so much pain and scandal upon the family.

"He lost both parents so young, he was too young to understand; but all hell broke loose when he discovered we lied to him about his sister..."

Ray nodded, sensing the weight of her words. “How did he find out the truth?”

“James ‘solicitors! besides the trust fund set up for him, there is an inheritance from the estate to be shared equally between siblings when the younger of the two reached an age. When they were unable to trace Kathryn at her last known address, they contacted Julian to ask if he knew her whereabouts.”

“How did you manage to hide her existence from him for so many years?” Ray asked. Charlotte became defensive.

“Mr Langford; you must understand I was a mother figure to Julian; he trusted me with his financial affairs; the trust fund set up for him after his father’s death paid for his schooling and university fees and anything else he needed. I paid him an allowance; and he was happy with the arrangement!

Ray shifted in his seat, rubbing his hands together as he absorbed Charlotte’s defensive tone. He leaned forward slightly, voice gentle but firm, striving to reassure her. “Charlotte, I’m not blaming you—I just want to understand what happened. We need to make sure Kate... Kathryn is safe, that’s all.”

“He was furious with me.” Charlotte twisted her fingers together. “He started smashing things, shouting, so out of character! he became obsessed. calling the solicitor daily for news. It wasn’t about the money,” she added.

Ray frowned, searching her face. “He was desperate to find his sister?”

Charlotte nodded.

She drew a shaky breath. “When Julian disappeared, I searched his room and found a notepad with hospital numbers, council contacts and your street address. That’s how I found you.”

“Someone has been following Kate, frightening her!” Ray said, watching her reaction. “Do you believe this could be Julian?”

Charlotte bristled, her voice rising with indignation. “Mr Langford, I have known Julian since he was a boy. He is a gentle soul!”

Ray’s tone softened as he recognised the strain in Charlotte’s voice. “But Julian—he’s endured so much,” Ray said gently. “He’s lost his parents and grandparents, and he’s been separated from his sister. It’s only natural that he’s finding things difficult. But the situation has become very serious now. Kathryn’s friend has been hurt. I really think you should talk to my son. He’s a detective and can help you, help Julian, and ensure everyone’s safety.”

Charlotte hesitated, her worry clear. She wrung her hands, torn between loyalty and fear, her voice trembling as she finally spoke. “Mr Langford, please contact your son. I will speak with him. I was not going to say in case I got him into trouble, but one of our vehicles and a shotgun is missing—I am frightened that Julian might hurt himself, just as his father did.”

Ray clenched his fists at his sides, struggling to keep himself steady.

Ray nodded, fully understanding the depth of her concern for Julian.

CHAPTER THIRTY-TWO

Unveiling Julian's Past

Travelling with hand luggage only, Nick and Tim swiftly make it through the airport. Tim searched his pocket for the car park ticket he had prepared earlier, and the barrier rose, allowing them to exit.

Nick's phone bleeps again, letting him know of missed calls. "This is becoming a recurrence," he thinks. He sees his dad has tried to call him multiple times during the return flight to Dublin.

"It's my dad. I better call him back," Nick said apologetically. DI Walsh smiles and nods in acknowledgment.

"Hi, Dad. What's up?" Nick listens intently as Ray explains Charlotte Lewis' visit.

"So, it sounds plausible that Kate's brother is the one who has been following her. What's his name?" Nick scrambles for a pen and a scrap of paper.

Timothy Walsh realised Nick is being told something significant. "There's a pad in the glove compartment," he said.

Nick takes the notepad from the glove compartment and starts scribbling down the information he is receiving from his father.

"Shit, shit, shit," he said.

"We're a good couple of hours away, but I'll call the Gardai and ask someone to make sure the women are okay." he finished his call and relays the information to Tim. He reacts by putting his foot down, increasing their speed.

"I'll call Solly. He'll go to the house to check everything is okay," Tim uses the Bluetooth on the steering column, scrolling through names on the Sat nav screen and calling his colleague based at the nearest Garda Station to the rental cottage. He explains the urgency of the situation.

Nick feels sick at the thought of the danger the two women may be in. Based on what his father said, Kate's brother sounds like he may have a weapon! He tries what-sapping Elaine's phone, then Kate's, but both calls ring out.

At the cottage, Elaine and Kate sit motionless on the sofa while the stranger's mood shifts from hatred and anger to sorrow and despair, and back again. He has been repeating himself for hours. The women only engage when he targets his rants at them, afraid of saying the wrong thing, as he hasn't released the gun during that entire time.

This time, the man is directing the rant towards Kate.

I've struggled with guilt all my life, believing my dad shot you. Left behind, I was haunted by questions—why did he spare me, not you? Did he want to be with you and Mum instead of me? Was my suffering intentional?

"I don't know. Today is the first time I've heard any of this. I cannot remember anyone you're speaking about," Kate said with trepidation. "From what you've said, your father was very unwell. He probably wasn't thinking any of those things." Her eyes glisten, and a single tear falls.

"You really don't remember me? I used to read you stories and comfort you when our parents fought. Dad would lock the door before work, so I'd crawl through the bathroom window to get the key mum hid in the shed, then return it without him knowing. It happened most often during school breaks. Do you recall the day you left?"

"No, if what you say is true, I wasn't even two years old. How could I?"

"I'll never forget that day. At seven, I waited for Mum as usual, but she didn't come. Teachers kept me busy and gave me biscuits until Dad picked me up. He spent days blaming Madeline, saying she left becausc I wasn't hers and she didn't love me." The man claiming to be Kate's brother is crying again.

Elaine believes he doesn't mean them harm, but with so much pent-up emotion and anger, who knows how he will react in a highly emotional moment? She wishes he would drop the weapon, and the more he reveals, the more concerned she becomes for his safety. If he doesn't drop the gun, this won't end well.

"You went through an awful ordeal. It must have been difficult for you as a child to accept what happened," Elaine said, her heart thumping and her hands trembling during this moment.

"It was. And then my dad left me with people he said were my grandparents. I didn't know them! The parents of the mother who meant nothing to me, the mother who died not long after I was born. Their house was a shrine to her existence. She was someone I didn't even know. And instead, they made me grieve for a stranger and the two people...” tears stream down his face as he tries to compose himself.

“The two people that I loved more than anything in the world were dead—my mum and my sister. I even missed my father, the man who kept me awake night after night, taunting Mummy. Yet, these strangers insisted that the only woman I knew as Mum, the one person I knew loved me, was evil, so I couldn’t even grieve for her.

Kate speaks with conviction, and Elaine hears anger in her voice. “Why are you angry with me? When I was two years old, they put me into care. The people I knew as parents died when I was young, and I was alone.” Kate paused. Elaine believes she’s trying to control her own emotions before adding, “Why would you terrorise me for months, and why the gun? I didn’t even know you existed.”

Holding the shotgun, he looks at it with surprise, not directing it at the women but pointing it towards the wall.

“You didn’t exist either until about eighteen months ago. The solicitor of my father informed me you are alive and entitled to half of my inheritance, starting from your thirty fifth birthday.

“Is this about money? Because if it is, I don’t want your money,” Kate said, which at once antagonises him.

“It’s not about money. I don’t care about money. I’ve had access to plenty of money throughout my life: an allowance, an inheritance from my grandparents, and I will undoubtedly inherit from my spinster aunt. My father was a multimillionaire, so I will have more money than one person needs in a lifetime,” he shouts angrily.

"This is about years of unhappiness, guilt, betrayal, and lies."

"I haven't lied or betrayed you," said Kate meekly.

Suddenly there is a knock on the door, and another, which startles him, and he points the gun directly at the two women.

"Who's that? "He asks in a whisper.

"You and Kate can work this out, can't you, Kate?" whispers Elaine.

"Yes, yes, of course!" agreed Kate.

"But you must get rid of the gun! Because of my fall, my fiancé has asked some people he knows to come and check on us. It's them. If we don't answer, they may call the police..." Elaine does not reveal that the probability is the Gardai are knocking right now.

"Quiet and get down!" he said, crouching. The women obediently follow his command. Positioned behind them on the sofa, the small windows in this room of the cottage ensure they stay out of sight, not visible to anyone who might peer in. The light from the TV boxes illuminated the darkness only, and the dimmed down-lights fitted within the bookcases on either side of the fireplace.

Elaine holds her breath, afraid that if he becomes spooked, he will use the gun. They watch as a torch bobs past the windows, briefly illuminating the walls of the lounge opposite them. Then darkness descends again, accompanied by silence.

"Please put the gun down," said Elaine.

"Shut up, please shut up!" The intruder sounds less aggressive and more afraid.

Elaine's phone screen lights up green, and Nick's profile picture shows on the screen accompanied by its continuous, distinctive ringing tone.

"It is my fiancé again. He is aware I can't get far with my foot injury. Please, let me answer, and I will tell him we are okay; otherwise, he may call the Police."

"I know that bloke of yours he is a police officer!" With him whispering, a Welsh accent is detected.

"Not here in Ireland! We are on holiday," he doesn't reply.

Elaine's phone keeps ringing, and this time, Kate responds in a whisper.

"I don't get it, you say you feel betrayed for not knowing I did not die at the hand of our natural Father, yet you want to ruin any chance of making up for lost time," the intruder looks puzzled, fatigue has set in and Kate is reacting to having sat on the sofa for hours whilst the man claiming to be a brother she did not know existed until a few hours ago is waving a gun around.

"What is it you want from me? Do you want to shoot me? Or why not give us a chance to get to know each other, build a relationship to make up for years where we could have found strength in each other? We are still young people with the rest of our lives ahead of us,"

"I don't believe you want to use the gun, so put it down because you are putting yourself and us in danger. Elaine adds,

"If the police suspect you are armed, we all face danger."

"Shut up, both of you, shut up!"

CHAPTER THIRTY-THREE

The Quiet Watch

The response is for Elaine's phone to ring out. Nick repeats the action by pressing the dial icon. During the journey, DI Garda, Tim Walsh and Nick discussed the information Ray had relayed.

"The women aren't answering their phones—he must be inside. It's too late to warn them now. I told them both to always keep the doors locked," Nick said, frustrated.

DI Walsh tried to present a rational alternative. "You do not know any of this for certain. Could they have called a taxi and gone to the pub?" he suggested, trying to find a reasonable explanation for the silence.

Nick shook his head, worry still etched across his face. "No, Elaine is struggling to get about with her ankle. She's in too much pain," he replied. "She mentioned they were planning to finish a TV series they've been watching while waiting for my return. The mobile signal within the cottage is dire, so we're communicating with each other through social media apps. Unless the internet has gone down again too, but then it wouldn't ring at all, would it?" Nick's words grew more hurried as he tried to reassure himself yet doubt lingered in his tone.

His thumb hovered above the phone screen, knuckles white as he fought the urge to panic. He pressed the dial icon once more, heart pounding in his chest. The only response was silence; Elaine's phone rang out, still unanswered. The echo of the unanswered call gnawed at his nerves, heightening the tension in the car.

Tim Walsh remained silent. The air grew heavy, thick with unease. Tim drummed his fingers on the steering wheel, glancing at Tim, awaiting any sign of reassurance. The tension lingered until the Sat nav on the dashboard interrupted with an incoming call. It was Solly, the reliable, middle-aged guard whom Tim had contacted earlier for help.

Tim answered promptly, his voice was steady. "Hi Solly, what's going on?"

Solly's response came clearly through the speakerphone. "I have taken the patrol car up to the cottage. I have young Simon with me. All is quiet. We have knocked on the door, but the house is in darkness except for a security lamp or something of that sort in the lounge. I don't think anyone is at home, Tim," he reported, keeping a tone that balanced caution with professionalism.

Tim pressed for more details. "Are you sure? Are there any outbuildings?" He glanced at Nick, who shook his head, showing that he was unaware of any other structures nearby.

Solly responded swiftly, his voice was steady but cautious. "There's a small potting shed. We have looked in there, but it's all quiet."

Nick's anxiety was palpable as he interjected, "Solly, they must be there. He may have them held inside."

Recognising the urgency, Solly suggested, "Tim, should I alert the ERU?" He considered attempting entry, despite the clear calm.

Tim responded with clear instructions. "We know little about the guy who has been stalking Kate. Organise a check on his name and alert ERU. We are about thirty-five minutes away. We will come straight there."

Staying focused, DI Tim Walsh provided Sergeant Solly Maguire with all the necessary details to begin checks on Kate's brother. Tim, determined to keep Nick's anxieties under control, cautioned, "Proceed with caution, Sergeant Maguire. I have a gut feeling about this situation, and We have reason to believe this man has a weapon."

After calling in for backup, Sergeant Maguire sat quietly in the driver's seat of the patrol car. The vehicle was parked down the lane, close enough to see the cottage but far enough to remain hidden. He whispered to the young Garda sitting beside him, careful not to draw attention.

"Something doesn't feel right. After years of doing this job, you just get that feeling. We may not see through the twelve-inch walls of that cottage, but you can be sure they're in there."

Garda Simon Ross, anxious but hopeful, asked, "How can you be certain?"

Sergeant Maguire replied, "I can smell them!"

Garda Ross laughed, thinking it was a joke, but Sergeant Maguire insisted, "No, I'm not joking. You smell that air. Go on, you can expect the pending disorder, especially when you've been doing the job as long as I have."

The laughter faded as the gravity of the situation sank in. Sergeant Maguire added, “Just hope we’re not too late and the worst hasn’t happened.”

Garda Ross, growing increasingly uneasy, asked, “Shouldn’t we try to get in somehow? What about the back door?”

Sergeant Solly Maguire shook his head and replied, “We should wait until backup arrives.”

“Aren’t they coming from Galway? It’s going to take a while,” Garda Ross pointed out, concern clear in his voice.

Sergeant Maguire took a moment to assess the situation. He knew backup would not arrive quickly; the sirens were distant, and resources were limited. Unlike in the movies, there would be no helicopters or task forces swooping in on a gut feeling—there simply was not the budget for that sort of operation.

Turning to Ross, Sergeant Maguire said quietly, “Come on, let’s creep around to the rear of the cottage. We may be able to hear something if they think we’ve left.”

With a measured sense of urgency, Solly opened the car door and signalled for Ross to follow. They moved cautiously, ducking as they made their way up the drive, taking care to stay out of sight. When they reached behind the property, they edged towards the kitchen window. Sergeant Maguire tried to peer inside, holding onto the windowsill and balancing on tiptoe, but his view was blocked by overgrown plants and an array of cleaning bottles cluttering the kitchen shelf.

Undeterred, he gestured for Ross to follow as they continued to move silently towards the rear door. Positioning themselves on either side of the door, Sergeant Maguire slowly reached for the doorknob. He twisted it gently, it unlatched. In the tense silence, the sudden sound of a mobile phone ringing from within the cottage made him pause. The phone stopped, then started ringing again, amplifying the sense of anticipation and uncertainty.

He can now hear what he thinks are hushed voices coming from within the cottage. In this moment, he must consider whether to call out and make themselves known or follow the procedure as if the women are being held against their will without clear evidence.

Garda Ross has also heard the whispers and mouths without verbalising, “They’re in there! What should we do?”

The realisation hits them that the only tools they’re carrying to protect themselves are batons and pepper spray. As if reading his mind, Garda Simon Ross takes his baton from its holder and holds it expect entering the property.

Sergeant Maguire raises his hand to prevent Simon from reacting too soon. After all, the first process of gathering intelligence is incomplete, and he knows they should wait for the ERU to arrive and secure the perimeter. However, he is keen to know if this is an actual hostage situation and if the women are unharmed. So, he signals to Garda Ross that he’s about to speak without entering.

"Hello, is anyone home? This is the Gardai. Miss Kate Davis, Miss Elaine Robson, are you home? Please answer... I am informing you we are coming in."

Sergeant Maguire strained to listen, certain that he could hear hushed voices drifting from within the cottage.

Garda Ross, having also caught the sound of whispers, silently mouthed to Maguire, "They're in there! What should we do?" The realisation dawned upon both officers that their only defensive equipment consisted of their batons and pepper spray. Sensing Maguire's concern, Garda Simon Ross instinctively unclipped his baton and gripped it, ready for what might await them should they enter the property.

Sergeant Maguire reacted swiftly, raising his hand to caution Simon against acting prematurely. He knew that gathering proper intelligence was crucial and that, according to procedure, they ought to wait for the Emergency Response Unit to arrive and secure the area. Yet Maguire's concern for the safety of the women inside made him anxious to confirm whether this was truly a hostage situation and whether Elaine and Kate were unharmed.

A sudden gunshot echoes from inside the cottage, directed towards the rear entrance where the officers had positioned themselves. Instinctively, both officers leap for cover, retreating swiftly to the safety of the lane and their patrol vehicle. Without hesitation, they radio headquarters, urgently reporting that a shot has been fired from within the property and requesting immediate reinforcements.

Both Elaine and Kate jump and cover their ears as the intruder aims and fires the gun towards the back door, where someone claiming to be a Garda was standing. Kate's tears fall as she realises he has crossed a boundary with no return. He had taken aim to shoot a police officer, putting the officer's life in jeopardy.

Elaine is the first to speak. "Please put the gun down. This won't end well. If they believe you intend to harm Kate, myself, or anyone who approaches the cottage, they will shoot you."

"Kate and I can vouch for you. We can tell the police that the voice of the Garda startled you, and the gun went off. You must allow us to speak to someone, anyone who can relay that you don't mean any harm," Elaine said, displaying her negotiation skills honed from her job and the courtroom.

In the dimly lit room, it's difficult to read the man's expression. Surprisingly, he responds, "Call your boyfriend!"

Elaine doesn't hesitate and calls Nick's phone, which he answers.

"Are you okay? What's going on? there was a gunshot!" Nick said.

"We are unhurt," Elaine replies, keeping her voice calm and brief to avoid alarming the man standing in front of her. She looks to him for guidance.

"Tell them I won't hurt anyone if the police leave the immediate area and don't enter."

Tim gestures to Nick, urging him to put the call on loudspeaker so that he, too, can follow the conversation unfolding with the intruder. As Nick complies, both men listen intently, able now to hear every word spoken by the man inside the cottage. The tension is palpable, each exchange carrying weight as they navigate the delicate situation. Assessing their position, Tim estimates that they are approximately eight minutes away from reaching the town. He calculates that by taking a shortcut, they should be able to arrive at the cottage in about fifteen, allowing them to intervene swiftly and lend their support to the ongoing negotiations.

Elaine reiterates the demand with calm authority, looking to reassure Julian and diffuse the tension. Nick then addresses Julian directly, confirming his identity. "Julian, it is Julian, isn't it? This is Nick speaking; The Gardai cannot leave the immediate area while this situation is ongoing. They need assurance that Elaine and Kate are safe and that you don't mean them or yourself any harm." Nick's tone is measured, aiming to set up trust and keep control of the situation.

Tim, seeing the interaction, nods and gives Nick a thumbs-up, signalling for him to continue the dialogue and support the ongoing negotiations.

Nick attempts to reach Julian on a personal level, appealing to his character and the unusual circumstances. "So, what's all this about, Julian? From what I hear, you're an honest, hard-working, and successful guy who hasn't even a parking ticket. Why is this happening?"

Julian responds with agitation, questioning Nick's source of information. "What do you mean, from what you hear? Who told you?" Nick and Tim exchange worried glances before Nick replies,

“Your Aunt Charlotte. She is worried about you. She travelled to London to find you; she has explained everything.”

Nick continues, gently addressing the emotional turmoil Julian must have experienced. “You must have felt confused when you found out that your sister is alive and well, especially as people you trusted told you she was dead. You must be feeling upset and hurt. You can see that it’s a good thing? The person you have grieved for is alive and well and sitting nearby.” Nick’s words are intended to provide comfort and perspective, inviting Julian to recognise the positive aspect of the situation.

Nick checks in, ensuring Julian is still engaged. “Julian, can you hear me?” Julian responds, confirming his attention. “Yes, yes, I hear you.”

“So why frighten the person you loved and missed so much, thinking you had lost her? Nick said this, trying to convince Julian with reasoning:

Nick tries to reach Julian with empathy, emphasising the unique opportunity he has. “You are the fortunate one among all the grieving people out there because you can reunite with a sister you thought was dead.” Despite Nick’s attempts to connect, the conversation stays tense during their journey. Each time Nick senses progress, Julian puts up resistance.

Julian, his voice strained, insists, “I don’t want to hurt anyone.”

Nick responds reassuringly, “Julian, I am a police officer. You can trust me. I am working on your behalf too, and I want to make sure that this situation ends safely.”

Julian, however, cuts through Nick’s words. “Don’t bullshit me.”

Nick presses on, “Julian, your feelings are justified. They’re making you act irrationally, but a medical professional can help you to understand them.”

Julian interrupts sharply, “I’m not mad.”

Nick quickly clarifies, “No, I’m not saying you’re mad.” He tries again to build trust. But Julian stays silent, offering no response.

The mood grows heavier than Julian’s resolve falters. “There is no point in me going on. I’m finished now anyhow,” he said, his voice wavering, a mix of hurt and suspicion clear. Nick and Tim exchange troubled glances, recognising the depth of Julian’s pain.

Nick speaks gently, offering reassurance. “Your Aunt Charlotte. She’s been worried sick about you. She even travelled to London, desperate to speak with you,. She wanted to help you understand everything.”

Julian looks away, fists clenched. “I can’t make sense of any of this. I was told for years that Kate was gone. I spent so long grieving – she’s here, alive, after all this time?” His voice cracks, and the tension in the room intensifies as the reality of the situation settles over them.

Nick softens his tone, his words measured and sincere. “Julian, I can’t imagine what you’re going through right now. Although, my own family has faced something similar, and I know how shocking it is to discover that what you believed to be true is, in fact, a lie." He pauses, allowing the gravity of the moment to settle. "Just like you, I needed answers before anything could make sense."

"But think about it: the person you missed, the person you mourned, is here. She is alive and safe, and she is not going anywhere.

Julian's eyes flicker, uncertain. "But why didn't anyone tell me?"

Before Nick can answer, the phone connection crackles with static and abruptly cuts out. The sudden silence rings with tension, Elaine, and Kate holding their breath as the weight of Julian's turmoil presses down.

Kate, steadying herself, steps forward. Her voice is quiet but unwavering. "Julian, I know this is overwhelming. I can't imagine the pain you've carried. I would never want you to hurt." She hesitates, searching his face. "But I'm here now. I want to be your sister again if you'll let me."

"How can I trust you?" Julian points the gun in Kate's direction.

Elaine intervened

"No Julian Kate is your sister, the mobile rings again, she lets it ring out.

Julian's frustration boils over, his voice shaking with emotion. "Too many people are talking and telling me how I should feel," he insists, his anger palpable. "The truth is none of you could imagine what I have been through. How scared I was, going to live with strangers." He paces the small space restlessly, unable to hold his agitation.

He continues, revealing the depth of his hurt. “I found out recently I wasn’t even listed as a living relative should Kate wish to find her birth family. I am nobody as far as they are concerned—not even worthy of a mention in a file!” Julian’s fury is clear not only in his words but also in his tense posture, the pain, and indignity of his experiences clear for all to see.

Elaine spoke gently, addressing Julian directly. “It must have been a tremendous shock to discover that Kate is alive, and not only that, but working as a nurse—a job that many people would shy away from. It involves dealing with blood, with the messiness of life, and facing demanding situations every single day. It takes a truly special kind of person to do that work. I honestly doubt anyone who cared only about money would choose such a path.” She paused, allowing Julian time to process her words.

Elaine continued, her voice steady but compassionate. “While Kate has been with the family, she has always shown kindness and care. In my view, she would never deceive anyone. You were told by people you trusted that your father killed your sister, and now, finding out she is alive must be unimaginably traumatic.”

Just then, the phone rang again, slicing through the heavy silence in the room.

“Answer it!” Julian urged. It was Nick, determined to continue the conversation despite the mounting tension that both Elaine and Kate could feel in the air.

Amidst the mounting tension, Kate's calm presence proved invaluable. While the situation teetered on a knife-edge, Kate quietly gathered her courage and assessed the room. Noticing Julian's attention waver as Nick spoke, Kate made a subtle, deliberate move—placing herself between Julian and Elaine, ready to shield her injured companion if things escalated.

Kate stepped forward, her voice steady yet firm. "Get back. Don't come any closer." She stood her ground, unwavering in her resolve.

Turning her attention directly to Julian, Kate's determination was unmistakable. "No, I'm sorry, Julian. I've had enough of this."

With raw emotion, Kate continued, "So after all these years, you feel wronged because you thought I was dead. Now what? Are you going to kill me? Ironic, don't you think?" She gestured around the room, her frustration clear. "We have been held here for hours. You're my brother, but I am also a victim of all of this. The difference is, I choose not to be defined by it. I was abandoned and left with complete strangers. I could have wallowed in self-pity, but instead, I chose to move on with my life."

Kate's gaze never wavered from Julian. "From where I'm standing, it seems like you've had a pretty privileged life, raised by family members who, at the end of the day, were only trying to protect your feelings—rightly or wrongly."

Julian appeared stunned, struggling to process Kate's words.

Kate's voice broke through the tense atmosphere, her words cutting to the heart of their predicament. "You have put us all at risk. It isn't like in films. Hostage situations rarely end well when someone is holding a gun." Her statement hung in the air, a solemn reminder of the danger they all faced.

The room fell silent. Everyone presents, drawing on their training and experience, understood just how quickly the situation could take a turn for the worse. The tension was palpable; each person held their breath, acutely aware that any sudden movement or misspoken word could escalate things beyond control.

Sensing the urgency within, Nick spoke softly to reassure Kate.

"Kate, I've got this," Nick said gently, his voice carrying a calm authority even though he was only present as a voice on the phone. Although he felt at a disadvantage by not being physically present, he took it upon himself to assume control of the situation. His words were intended to steady the nerves of everyone involved, providing a sense of reassurance and leadership amidst the heightened tension.

Despite Nick's attempt to calm her, Kate pressed on, unwilling to back down.

She faced Julian, her frustration clear. "What did you hope to achieve by frightening me... us?" she demanded, her arms gesturing to include everyone in the room.

Elaine, watching the exchange, felt her heart race with anxiety. Meanwhile, those listening on the other end of the phone grew increasingly concerned as the situation unfolded. Recognising the danger, Tim began waving commands to the officers nearby, signalling them to get into position and prepare for any escalation.

Julian, overcome with emotion, began to cry. “I don’t know! At first I just wanted to be sure it was you!” he admitted, tears streaming down his face.

Seeing his distress, Kate’s tone softened. She spoke gently, trying to reach him. “Well, it is me, and I am a real person with real feelings who would love to have a real family too. I have that now, and it could all be taken away by what you choose to do next,” she said, her own eyes filling with tears.

Julian’s voice trembled as he tried to explain himself. “I never meant for this, not in the beginning. I went to the social services office to see if I could find you, but then I saw his mother there, asking about you,” he said, nodding toward the phone in the room.

Kate looked at him, confused. “Whose mother?” she asked, trying to make sense of the situation.

Julian clarified, “His, the policeman’s mother. She was asking about you. They had her listed as family, but couldn’t tell me anything, and I am your real family!”

Elaine and Kate exchanged bewildered glances, unable to piece together what Julian was saying.

Julian continued, his words coming in between sobs. “I started to follow the family members to find out more. Then I watched you for weeks; I wanted to make memories as you are now,”

“Why didn’t you approach me tell me who you were? Kate asked exasperated.

Julian hesitated, his voice faltering as he tried to explain the depth of his actions. “I nearly approached you a few times,” he admitted, “but instead, I befriended the old lady just so I could be close by; hear her stories.” He explained that there was much more happening within the family than anyone seemed to realise.

He continued, “Maggie, the old lady, welcomed me into her home on many occasions. She let me stay in one of the rooms—the one she said was waiting for me. She even recognised me as her son.” Julian’s words revealed the emotional bond he had formed with Maggie, who often shared stories from their mother’s childhood, deepening his sense of belonging.

However, the situation changed when Maggie was hospitalised. Julian confessed, “So, I stole your keys. I just couldn’t let go.” He recounted how Maggie had revealed a painful truth: she had left her own son in Ireland to survive alone. This revelation stirred anger in Julian, as he felt both her son and him had been abandoned.

Everyone in the room was stunned by Julian’s admission that Maggie had unknowingly sheltered a stranger in her home. The weight of this revelation hung heavily, leaving each person visibly drained. Even Julian, who had carried the burden of his secret for so long, appeared exhausted—his shoulders slumped in defeat.

Recognising the shift in the atmosphere, Kate seized the opportunity to act. She approached Julian, her voice steady yet gentle. “Here, give me the gun...” she urged, hoping to persuade him to relinquish the weapon. Julian remained unresponsive at first, but his demeanour had changed; tears streamed down his face, signalling that he was overwhelmed by emotion and surrender.

Kate tried once more, her plea filled with compassion and urgency. "Julian, please give me the gun."

Kate hid her surprise. Julian handed her the shotgun. "Nick, I have the gun!" Julian slumped in a chair. He put his head in his hands and sobbed. "Elaine, can you walk?" he asked. "Yes, my crutches are nearby," she replied. "Kate, put the gun down carefully. Put it somewhere safe. Julian, is the gun loaded?" "I saw him put bullets in it," Kate said. "Cartridges, it has cartridges," Elaine corrected urgently. "It's a shotgun!" Nick told them what to expect when they left. "Okay, Julian, I will pass you to my friend Tim. He is a police officer."

From here on, Tim takes over. The armed unit has arrived, and everyone has positioned themselves in case Julian changed his mind. "Julian, is that the only weapon? Kate, Elaine, are you aware of any other weapons?" Tim asks. Julian answers, "There are no other weapons."

"It's the only one that we are aware of," Elaine confirms.

"Julian, please put your hands up and on your head. Keep still," Tim instructs. Kate opens the door wide and follows the instructions.

An armed officer signals he has a view of the assailant and confirms that Julian appears to have followed the instructions and is unarmed.

"Kate, please raise your hands and place them on your head. Move to your left," Tim instructs. Kate experiences a surge of bile and squints as she walks out onto the floodlit gravel drive. Two armed Gardai on her left body search her and guide her to safety. Elaine follows similar instructions, trying to hop on her good leg.

"Now, Julian, leave the property, keeping your hands where they are."

Julian follows instructions, tears flowing. He lies down on his stomach on the gravel. Several Gardai approach Julian. They search him for the possibility of more weapons or explosives on his person. Once they have made sure that he is restrained, Nick and Jack make their way towards the women. Nick takes Elaine in his arms, while. Tim lingers, "Are you okay?" Kate nods.

CHAPTER THIRTY-FOUR

The Joining of Kin

In anticipation of the call, Maggie, recently discharged from hospital, sat at the kitchen table alongside Billy and Lucy. Billy had already set up his laptop, ensuring it was ready to receive the video call. He pointed out to Maggie exactly where she should look on the screen, making a few final adjustments to the settings as they waited for the call to connect.

After a short dialling tone, the screen flickered to life, and a figure appeared—Billy's brother. Prior to this, Billy had taken the opportunity to speak to his brother privately over the phone, explaining their mother's current condition and updating him on recent events. During that conversation, Billy found his brother to be gentle and understanding, responding with genuine empathy and concern for their mother. There was no trace of resentment, frustration or anger; instead, his brother accepted the situation calmly and with compassion.

Lucy positioned herself to the side of the screen, making sure she stayed out of the camera's view. She watched quietly, her anxiety preventing her from eating all morning. With her stomach in knots, she waited for the late afternoon, when the time differences across the Atlantic would finally align so the video call could take place at a reasonable hour for every family member.

Lucy was surprised at how instantly she recognised her younger brother. Though he no longer sported a mop of curly blonde hair—instead, it was grey, cropped short, and neat—his eyes remained wide and blue. Overcome with emotion, Lucy felt tears prick behind her eyes and her chest tighten, but she held herself together, determined to stay composed for her mother's sake. Maggie, who was about to meet the son she had believed dead for more than forty years, appeared unexpectedly calm and collected.

Matthew was the first to speak, his clear American accent filling the room. "Hi, Mom, I can't tell you how excited I am to see you," he said, his voice brimming with emotion. Billy, ever thoughtful, leaned in to help Maggie navigate the technology, pointing out exactly where she should speak so Matthew could both see and hear her clearly.

"Hi, Matthew. Mum has been just as excited, haven't you, Mum?" Billy prompted gently. "Just talk here normally—he'll be able to see and hear you as if you're in the same room." Taking a deep breath, Maggie followed Billy's guidance.

"Hello, dear. I am so happy to see you after all these years," Maggie said, her voice warm and steady despite the enormity of the moment. After their heartfelt greetings, the conversation turned to lighter topics, beginning with a brief exchange about the weather on each side of the Atlantic. As the call continued, the families introduced themselves to one another. Matthew proudly brought his own family and children into view, making sure everyone had a chance to say hello. Although Maggie was clearly overwhelmed by the experience, she kept her composure, even managing a lighthearted chuckle.

“How lovely you all are!” she exclaimed. “You’ll have to write everyone’s name down, Billy, so I don’t forget.”

As the conversation paused, Maggie took a deep breath and looked directly at the screen. “Matthew, I am so sorry...” she began, her voice trembling with the weight of decades lost. Sensing the significance of the moment, everyone else quietly stepped back from the camera’s view, giving mother and son the privacy they needed to share this intensely personal exchange.

Lucy, overwhelmed by the tension, felt her heart skip a beat as she awaited her estranged brother’s response. Unable to bear the suspense, she moved to the sink, busying herself with imaginary chores to steady her nerves.

Matthew answered slowly, his words filled with emotion and reassurance. “Hey Mom. It’s all water under the bridge. Let’s concentrate on what’s to come. We’re now thinking of coming to London for Christmas, as we have a good reason to bring forward something we’ve been talking about for years.”

CHAPTER THIRTY-FIVE

Autumn Leaves

It's been a month since they returned from Ireland, and Nick is driving Elaine home from a hospital appointment to remove the plaster cast from her ankle. They discuss recent events.

"Kate has returned to Ireland to visit Julian twice since last month, and she said that each time he seems improved. Let's hope he gets the help he needs," said Elaine.

Following the hostage situation, they hospitalised Julian, and he is being held in a secure unit. They adjourned his court hearing pending medical reports and ongoing assessments.

"What sentence do you reckon he will get?" Nick enquired.

"I am not sure! it depends on the jurisdiction and particular circumstances."

They sit in rush hour traffic, both reflecting on happenings in Ireland. Nick considers how lucky he is to have Elaine sitting beside him. He realises that things might have gone differently.

Nick's Irish counterparts commended him for negotiating the conclusion of the siege without harm to the public or the assailant. He also received a formal thank-you from his own superiors. Elaine breaks the silence.

"Guess who's visiting London this weekend?" Elaine asks, with a hint of excitement in her voice.

"Timothy Walsh," replied Nick at once.

Elaine laughed. "Aha, you know!"

Nick explained, "He called for a list of decent hotels, so I suggested a few. But it turns out Kate has offered to show him around Windsor at some point over the weekend."

"Correct, Mr Detective. Kate and I had a long chat last night. She's still really concerned for Julian, so I don't think romance is at the forefront of her mind right now," Elaine remarked.

"Much to your annoyance!" Nick smiles at how quickly Elaine responds.

Elaine shook her head. "No, not at all. After being stalked for months, held hostage, and then discovering your mother orchestrated her employment with the family after recognising Kate's name that day on the hill—under these circumstances she's coped exceptionally well. Many would have run for the hills." Elaine paused, thinking for a moment before continuing. "Remind me not to get on the wrong side of your mother,"

Nick replies, understanding the implication of Elaine's comment but also feeling the need to defend his mother. "To be fair, Mum was affected deeply by events of her childhood, she learnt to mask well!"

Elaine added thoughtfully, "Speaking of which, how is your grandmother settling in at home?"

Nick nodded. "Good. Her mobility has improved, and she still has Kate living with her and providing nursing care. Although other avenues for Gran's care are now being explored since discovering Kate is family, it's considered inappropriate for her to continue—

even though Kate is quite happy to do so for now." Nick's brow furrowed with concern, unsure if this was truly best for Gran, despite the circumstances of the decision.

Elaine noticed Nick's uncertainty and offered reassurance. "I know it feels strange, but maybe having someone else step in might even give Kate a bit of a break. She's done so much already." Her words conveyed empathy for Kate's situation, acknowledging recent events. Elaine then turned the conversation in a lighter direction, smiling as she added, "She's not the only one!" This remark recognised that many people had been involved and contributed throughout the recent difficulties, hinting at the collective effort behind Gran's care and well-being.

With a cheerful grin, Elaine concluded, "And not forgetting her pending fortune!" Her comment alluded to changes ahead for Kate, suggesting that brighter times and new opportunities were on the horizon.

Nick smiled. "I am pleased life is looking up for Kate. She deserves it; she's one of life's optimists who sees the brightness in everything and everyone. She even understands my mum's actions, although that doesn't help Mum's embarrassment about the entire situation."

Hampstead

Billy watches Lucy fussing about their mother. Although Maggie appears healthy enough. Kate is away for the weekend, so Maggie needs someone to stay at home with her. Billy offered, but Lucy insisted, saying it's no trouble since they were less likely to visit their Oxfordshire house on weekends during the autumn.

"Do you need to go outside in this weather?" Lucy enquired, glancing toward the garden with concern from her position behind Maggie's favourite chair.

Whilst the sun is shining, they watch autumn leaves being whipped up by a strengthening wind. Maggie is wrapped in a scarf and garden jacket in anticipation.

"The doctors said I should walk the garden daily, that is until I can venture out onto the heath again, and I want to be alone," insists Maggie. Billy and Lucy share a knowing look and laugh.

"She'll be fine." Billy said. Lucy opens the French door for her mother and helps her down the step.

"Okay, go ahead, but be careful, no more hospital visits, please!" Lucy called out, her tone a blend of gentle caution and affection. She watched as her mother stepped through the French doors, making her way towards the garden path that bordered the wide, immaculately kept lawn—the flattest and safest part of the garden. Despite the suggestion from others, Maggie steadfastly refused to use a walking frame, insisting instead on relying on her stick for support.

The past few weeks had felt almost unreal to Lucy and Billy, as they slowly adjusted to the astonishing news of having a brother living in Canada. Since their first online introduction, they had spoken to Matthew a handful of times over Skype, each call helping to bridge the years and distance between them. Now, Matthew was planning to visit at Christmas, and he would not be coming alone—his wife, teenage daughter, and two sons would be joining him, promising a festive season like no other for the family.

The family has grown almost overnight, and both Lucy and Billy are keenly aware that this has brought Maggie a renewed sense of purpose and energy. Recognising this, they have decided to convert the snug into a comfortable bedroom with an adjoining shower room, ensuring that Maggie's needs are met as she continues to embrace life with newfound vigour. Plans for the renovation will begin without delay, reflecting their eagerness to provide a supportive environment. In addition, they have warmly invited Kate to move in with them for as long as she wishes. Lucy and Billy understand that she has much to think about, and they want her to know she is welcome and supported during this period of change and reflection.

Kate

When Kate reflects on the events that took place in Ireland, she finds it difficult to recognise herself as the person who played such a pivotal part in bringing the siege to its conclusion. The emotional strain of visiting Ireland several times in the past month has weighed heavily on her, prompting her decision to take time out for herself this weekend. Too weary to travel any great distance, she chose Windsor as an ideal retreat, a place where she could reconnect with her foster parents and indulge a deep yearning for a time in her life before she knew her true origins.

Windsor holds a special place in Kate's heart. During her school holidays, her foster parents would bring her here for day trips. She remembers with fondness feeding the swans while waiting for the ferry, embarking on boat trips along the river, and ending the day with a leisurely walk through the Great Park, stopping to enjoy a picnic together.

Since her brother's arrest, Tim Walsh has kept her informed with regular updates about the progress of the case. Kate, meanwhile, has taken charge of arranging solicitors to work on behalf of her brother, determined to ensure he receives the best possible support. Although Kate senses a connection between herself and Tim, she realises that she is not currently in the right frame of mind to embark on a new relationship. Nevertheless, when Tim mentioned he would be coming to London for the weekend, Kate found herself inviting him to join her for a guided tour of Windsor, despite her first desire for solitude and respite from the recent turmoil. The future of their relationship is still uncertain, but perhaps, in time, something more may develop.

Maggie

The wind feels cool against my face, and I can sense the silk scarf I wear over my hair flapping as I stroll through my garden. I love being outside at this time of year. It's not too cold, and it helps blow away the cobwebs. I used to enjoy sweeping and clearing leaves, but I'll leave that for next year. Since discovering that my lost boy, Matthew, is alive and living in the United States, I've decided not to let my dementia diagnosis stop me from living. I've also learned that I have three more grandchildren, and if I include Kate, four. I have so much to live for.

My family informed me that the man who visited me in my garden and in the hospital was Kate's half-brother. From what I've heard, he put Kate and Nicholas's fiancé... I keep forgetting her name. Anyway, he put them through quite an ordeal whilst they were holidaying in Ireland. But from what I am told, it's because he is unwell.

There are still days when my memory grows misty, and I find myself searching for the right word or needing gentle reminders, especially with the names of everyday objects. Yet, the laughter and warmth of my family and the vivid tapestry of our shared memories are still wonderfully clear. Lately, with my legs feeling steadier beneath me, I've relished wandering along the garden path, pausing to touch the rough bark of the willow tree planted years ago in memory of lost family members, or listen to the crisp crunch of leaves beneath my boots. Sometimes, I even manage the steps up to the house in one confident go, grinning at my own progress. Each morning, I set myself a tiny goal—whether it's making a pot of tea by myself or jotting down a memory in my notebook—and I celebrate these little victories with a smile or a quiet cuppa by the window. As autumn's golden leaves swirl past outside and the scent of damp earth drifts in on the breeze, I feel a quiet determination growing within me. This season, once a gentle reminder of endings, now signals fresh beginnings. I'm embracing each new day with hope and curiosity, dreaming of the adventures still to come—perhaps even a visit to

America. Whatever the future holds, I move forward with the intention of keeping my family's worries at bay and filling our days with as much joy as the changing seasons outside my door.

I realise that the main reason I have chosen not to reveal the truth about that day is because of the uncertainty surrounding my memory. I am deeply concerned that, should my memory deteriorate further, I might inadvertently confess everything to one of my family members. If such a moment ever arrives, I can only hope that I am spared the knowledge of how my revelation might affect those I love, and of the consequences it may have on their feelings of me.

Throughout this year, I have found myself teetering on the edge of confession, wrestling with the thought of sharing everything. Yet, for now, I am convinced it is wiser to remain the keeper of this secret, to protect my family from truths that could reshape their understanding of our lives.

EPILOGUE

Ireland - February 1972

I've been waiting for half an hour, but the storm shows no sign of clearing. It's too dark to read my watch, but it must be nearing six o'clock or later. I hear a car engine approaching, and a few moments later, I see the headlights of a vehicle pulling into the driveway.

"Thank goodness. The people in this house might have a telephone or be willing to give me a lift to town."

I decide to wait and see who is driving before approaching them, hoping it's a family returning home from a trip out. I peer through a gap to get a better view. As the driver turns off the lights from the vehicle, I hear voices. I recognise them! My first instinct is to rush towards the security of familiarity, but I stop myself on recognising their tone.

"This is going to kill your mother. I blame myself. I should have stopped it, stopped her from creating this arracht!" My father-in-law's Irish accent bellows, even above the noise of the storm.

I hear the car door slam and watch as Jack strides towards the entrance of the cottage, his arms flailing. Matthew follows like a sullen boy, searching his pockets.

"Let's get in out of this weather... where are the keys?" Jack barks.

"I've got them here!"

Jack snatches the keys that Matthew is holding up and unlocks the front door. A light comes on. My heart races in my chest as I watch the men enter the property, but they do not close the door behind them. Stuck fast, consumed by my own thoughts,

Where is Matthew Junior? Is this where they are staying? Have some maternal supernatural being or force guided me here? What do I do now? Stepping out of the barn, I walk towards the cottage. I'm not sure if I feel prepared enough to confront Matthew just yet, but I must find out where my darling little boy is.

I stand with my back against the outer wall, straining to listen against the sound of the pounding rain to hear what the men are saying. If only it would ease... just for a moment. I need not worry; my father-in-law's voice is amplified within what I imagine being a sparsely furnished rental.

"Tell me what happened?"

"I have no idea; he was fine! I did not touch him. "I love Sidney... I am as devastated as you," Matthew's voice cracked.

"So why do the police say you hurt your brother?"

"Beats me!"

"Were you with him?"

"Yes!"

Jack's voice distorts and croaks, asking, "When he died?" Matthew does not answer my father-in-law's question with a straight answer.

"Dad, I swear to you, I arrived with Matthew Junior at the house. I thought we could have breakfast together as a special treat. Maggie was with Sidney; they had been arguing about something. His head was bleeding, and he was already unsteady and disoriented.

"Maggie?" Jack sounds shocked.

"Yes, Maggie! I... I didn't know what to do. Despite appearing hurt, Sidney insisted he was fine. Maggie was accusing him of hurting her father. She was hysterical. I thought she might attack him again. It was necessary for me to take her away from the house. I led her out and drove her to her parents' shop. I thought her mother could talk some sense into her... It was when we were in the car that I realised I could not leave Matthew Junior with her. She was acting crazy, like a wild banshee." I paused for Jack's reply, but when he didn't say anything, Matthew stepped in to continue the conversation.

"I told Maggie to get out of the car because I had to go back and check if my brother was okay. She went bonkers. Obviously, I couldn't leave the child with her, so I took Matthew Junior to a good friend of mine. They stayed with my lad while I went to check on Sidney. He was fine! Although he said Maggie had attacked him and struck him with something on the head."

"Maggie?" my father-in-law repeats.

I feel my wet face burn with rage. Fury rises from the pit of my stomach. It takes every bit of resistance to stop myself from running into the room right now and confronting this lying bastard. But I need to know where Matthew Junior is, and Matthew may reveal his whereabouts to his father. There is also a part of me that is terrified of this man. I know what he is capable of.

"Yes, Dad, Maggie! I know... it's hard to believe, but I swear she has not been right in the head for some time. She fantasies about stuff, becomes jealous, fixated on trivial crap. I've kept it quiet for the sake of the kids and for her sake, but it has been a living nightmare... being married to her has become a living hell."

Matthew takes a long pause, as if waiting for sympathy from his father, but I do not hear Jack respond.

"I worry she will do something stupid. Our children are a constant source of worry for me."

"Why did Maggie think Sidney hurt Bill?" Jack's tone has changed, and he sounds calm.

Matthew hesitates, struggling to find the right words. "I don't know! I think it's something to do with a mental disorder. She gets paranoid and starts to believe strange things. There was a robbery at her father's shop. Bill was badly hurt in the incident; the poor sod received a severe beating and now he's in intensive care. I didn't know what to do... I was completely torn between looking after my wife and checking on Sidney."

Despite the cold and wetness, my skin burns with frustration. I can hardly believe what I am hearing — 'Oh, my goodness, is this man for real?'

"After returning to your house to check on Sidney, I found him seemingly unharmed. He assured me he was fine, other than the cut to his head from earlier, there were no visible signs of injury. Relieved, I then went to collect little Matthew and drove directly here. Dad, I was at a complete loss as to how to deal with the situation involving Maggie. The turmoil in our marriage left me confused and anxious, and I desperately needed advice from you and Mum. I wanted to know how I might begin to repair our relationship and, more importantly, what I could do to support Maggie during this difficult time."

Overwhelmed by anxiety, I edged myself closer to the front door, trying to steady my nerves. Suddenly, a flash of lightning lit up the sky, immediately followed by a deafening clap of thunder. The sudden noise startled me, causing me to knock over a garden spade that had been propped against the outside wall. The spade crashed onto the hard ground, echoing in the night. I held my breath, tightly closing my eyes, convinced that both men would emerge to investigate the commotion. To my relief, no-one appeared at the doorway.

Matthew, anxious and seeking reassurance, asks Jack, "What did you tell Mum and the sisters? Do they know I'm here?"

Jack shakes his head and replies, "No, I didn't tell them anything. When I saw you parked up in the lane, I told them I was going for a walk. Your mother is grief-stricken, and your sisters are taking good care of her. And after the Garda visited and said you were on the run and a suspect for murdering your brother... well, I didn't believe it. Not my son! And you and your brothers being as thick as thieves! So, I thought I'd meet you with nobody knowing about it, to hear your account of events and see what we're dealing with."

"Thanks, Dad!"

"I don't know why you're thanking me, son... because I don't believe a single word that has come out of your mouth. I think you... you are a lying little fucker!"

"What!" Matthew sounds surprised.

"You believe your own bullshit; there are too many holes in your little story. For one, if you believed Sidney was fine, why not come straight to the farm when you arrived in Ireland? Why park up out of sight and then call to me like a fugitive when I pass? If you were so worried about your boy, why is he not here with you? You're aware that we have nothing to do with our Mary, not since she married that thieving bastard, especially after what he did... so why take your son there? And where is your luggage? If I think you have laid one hand on my son's head and caused his death, I will hand you over to the Gardai myself, you little shit," Jack spat out this last part with venom.

"I knew you wouldn't believe me! Sidney was always your favourite, and then the girls. I have always been the outcast. You have always hated me!"

Matthew's whine resembles that of a schoolboy. Is this the same man I fell in love with?

Jack, his patience worn thin, explodes with pent-up frustration. "Shut up! You boys... and I mean both of you... have been a thorn in my side for years. If it weren't for your mother, who you both had twisted around your little finger, I would have disowned both of you years ago."

He continues, his words heavy with accusation and disappointment. "I know all about Maddie. It's been obvious what's been going on. I saw the state of that poor girl Rita when Sidney brought her to us to clean up, and Amanda... well, where do I start? You couldn't make it up."

Jack's anger intensifies as he recalls more recent events, his voice growing sharper. "The last straw for me was when, a couple of weeks ago, Maggie's father asked to meet me."

Matthew, clearly desperate for answers, interrupts with urgency, "Why, tell me, what did he want?" I listen closely as well, eager to hear Jack's reply and to finally understand what prompted this confrontation.

"He showed me letters and documents provided by Rita. She said she had to escape in the dead of night because our Sidney had beaten her black and blue. Bill worried about his daughter... and what would happen to Maggie if you went to prison. He also expressed concern about whether his grandchildren, as well as ours, might follow your example. He sought my thoughts on this matter, asking– as one parent to another how I would feel if one of my daughters were to marry someone of your character, and recommended that I discuss this with you directly. Then I thought of our Mary and how I felt when she received the beatings, and when that slimy bastard swindled the money from the farm, and I realised then... that both my sons are no better than him."

Matthew's voice trembles with indignation as he protests, "He was lying! I told you Maggie was paranoid. She must have told him all sorts of rubbish!" His attempt to deflect blame is met with no sympathy.

Jack, not tolerating any more excuses, cuts him off sternly. "I said shut up! I wanted to bring your mother to Ireland to make sure she was out of the way because, once I weighed up all the information that Bill laid out in front of me, I agreed to go with him to the police!" Jack's admission is heavy; his decision clearly made after careful consideration of the evidence presented by Bill.

The revelation strikes Matthew like a blow. His anger erupts. "You did what? You are a stupid, stupid old man. Why would you do that? This is all because of you. Everything that's happened over the past couple of days is because of you and Bill... you pair of—" His words are laced with fury and accusation, barely containing his rage.

Jack, sensing the aggression, interrupts sharply. "Don't you dare! Is that a threat?" The tension between them crackles, each word charged with years of resentment and suspicion.

I hear a crash and then a thud. I grab the spade from the ground before entering the front door, where Matthew is on top of his father, with hands around his throat. The old man's face is changing colour, turning a deep purple. Oh my god! He is going to kill him!

I swing the spade with all my might and hit Matthew on the shoulder. He yells in agony. I find it difficult to control the spade but dare not let it go. Matthew turns to see where the strike came from. He looks shocked to see me standing there, holding the spade in position, ready to swing again should the need arise.

"Leave him alone, Matthew... move away from your father.... Jack, are you okay?"

All that Jack can muster is a groan. My instinct is to go to him, but I decide to stay put in case I need to protect us again.

"What are you doing here?" He doesn't wait for a response and winces as he holds his shoulder. "Maggie, put the spade down!"

"Move away from your dad, and I will put the spade down... Jack, answer me! Are you okay?" Jack does not respond, but groans. He is holding his chest and appears to be struggling to breathe.

"Matthew, your dad is badly hurt. Move away from him!" This time I shout the instruction. Matthew laughs.

"Why are you laughing? Move away from your dad. Give him some space; he needs air to breathe."

Matthew springs to his feet and lunges towards me. The spade drops from my hand, and I turn on my heel and run for my life. Because Matthew trips over the spade, it gives me a head start. I reach the threshold of the barn in an instant and slip inside the stable door I had left ajar.

Despite my observation of him searching the yard, I'm not sure if Matthew saw me run the few strides towards the barn. He looks along and behind the boundary wall, behind a bin, and inside and around his car. He heads towards the lane. I head towards the back of the barn, where furniture is stored under dust sheets and blankets. I crouch against the back wall, between an old wardrobe and table.

My heart is pounding in my chest, and I can hear the throb of my pulse in my neck. My breathing is rapid, and I try to hold it, which makes me feel light-headed. I'm trembling, too. I try to stop my teeth from chattering, but the coldness of my clothes and fear make it impossible. I hear Matthew's footsteps outside the barn, and then they come to a halt. The barn door is being pushed open, and it catches on the ground.

Footsteps echo ominously around the barn, each one sending a jolt of fear through me. Matthew's silhouette, warped and larger than life, is cast across the wall as he moves about, searching for me. His presence is impossible to ignore, looming in the dim light.

Footsteps reverberate around the barn, creating an eerie sense of anticipation. Matthew's silhouette looms large and distorted on the wall as he moves about, his presence impossible to ignore. I hear Matthew's footsteps coming nearer to where I am hiding.

"Maggie... it's me. C'mon, what are you playing at? I will not hurt you."

"If you come out now, I will... or we... can fetch little Matthew so you can take him home. This has all got out of hand now, but we can sort it. The trolley boy, your trolley boy, can sort anything. I love you. Now stop being silly."

Something snaps within me.

"Silly? Silly? How dare you call me silly!" I am standing in the shadow of furniture and other household items, holding a large poker above my head that I took from an abandoned scuttle nearby. I feel ready to strike if necessary.

"Where is my son?" I shriek.

"Stop being a prat and put that down. You're going to hurt yourself," scoffs Matthew.

"Yes, that's right, you laugh... stupid, naïve Maggie!"

In the darkness, I cannot read Matthew's expression, but from his silence, I believe my outburst has startled him. I hear him creeping towards me.

"Don't move another step forward!"

"And what are you going to do?" he said mockingly.

"Where is our son? What have you done with him? He's just a baby."

"Enough! He's my son too. If you'd paid more attention to me instead of only the kids, maybe things would be different."

"Do you really think I care what you think of me? You're insane... you murdering bastard."

"Thank goodness your father can see through your lies. How could you murder a defenceless woman in cold blood, attack your own brother, and arrange the near death of an old man? let me correct that, two old men if we count how, you just attacked your own father. You are evil, an evil coward."

"Shut your mouth!" snarls Matthew. By his reaction, I have touched a nerve. His silhouette is approaching.

"Don't come any nearer, I mean it!" I raise the poker higher, hoping it acts as a deterrent. There is only a curb stool stacked on top of another, acting as the barrier between me and my husband. Matthew continues to move towards me.

"Give that to me!" Matthew demands, his hand outstretched and visible now that my eyes have adjusted to the gloom. He stands firm, blocking my way, tension crackling in the air between us.

I meet his gaze, keeping my grip tight on the poker. "Let me pass by so I can check that your dad is okay," I insist, my voice steady despite the panic rising inside me. "You've hurt him!"

"He's fine!"

"Yes, Maggie, it's okay. I'm fine, no thanks to him!" Jack's voice startles Matthew, and he swings around to see his dad standing in the doorway.

"It's over, son! Why don't you come with me to the farm? Say goodbye to your mother, and then you must give yourself up to the Gardai!" Jack's lilt is a little croaky. He is hanging onto the barn door, for if it weren't there, his legs would give way beneath him.

Jack, his voice strained and slightly trembling, clings to the barn door for support. The weight of the moment is clear in both his words and his posture. Through a croaky lilt, he addresses Matthew with a finality that cannot be mistaken.

"Mind Your Own Business, Dad... this is between me and Maggie!"

"It is my business. You are not well. We can get you help."

“There is nothing wrong with me... it’s you... you and Bill, stitching me up, grassing on me to the Old Bill. What kind of father would do that? Matthew spoke in a wavering tone.

“And as for you!” Matthew directs this venom towards me.

“Leave her be!” Jack speaks in a patriarchal tone.

“I’ve had it with you, Dad... Shut your mouth!”

Matthew moves and within a few strides, he is towering above his father, screaming obscenities into his face. He raises his fist, and in this moment, I believe my father-in-law to be in danger, under attack at the hands of his own son. And as if another being has taken over, and before I can consider the consequences, I am standing behind the father of my children, the man I have lived with and adored for all these years, and always ready to defend. With all my force, I crash the poker down onto Matthew’s back. He yells out in pain but turns. I strike again with a similar force, but this time I catch him on the front of his head.

The shock on Matthew’s face and the hurt clear in his eyes as he realises, he is hurt will stay with me forever. I am rigid, frozen to the spot, and as if in slow motion, I watch as Matthew falls to his knees before slumping sideways onto the barn floor.

I can’t describe my horror at the fact that I may have inflicted irreversible damage. The doorway framing the inclement weather outside mirrors the emotional turbulence I am feeling.

Jack kneels besides Matthew, feeling for a pulse. I am overcome with an electric current that zips through me, watching for the expression on the old man's face, and here it is... his face crumples as Jack lets out a whimpering sob. And in that moment, I realise that our lives as we knew them have changed forever.

Within the wilderness of this wild country, I hear the scream of a banshee. The sound pierces my eardrums, and I feel them pop. It is me! I am screaming. I feel a sharp sting of a slap to my face, and with the strike, the noise stops.

"Maggie, Maggie!" Contrary to his actions, his words are gentle.

"Maggie, you must take control. Now breathe, in through your nose... and out." I try to follow Jack's instructions, but I feel myself hyperventilating.

Jack is clutching his chest, he is crying and stifling sobs as he goes down to kneel besides his son. Watching him double in pain is too much for Maggie to bare.

"I didn't mean to hurt him; I thought he was going to kill you or me! ... Jack wipes his nose and face on his cuff he sniffs and gasps trying to catch his breath before standing and facing Maggie.

"Maggie, this was not your fault, do you hear me? We were both under attack. Matthew was out of control."

"We should call an ambulance!" I sob.

"He's dead, my girl. Matthew is dead." Jack is holding me by my shoulders. His eyes well, and another tear slips free.

"This was his life, not yours, not mine, or his mother's. Violence was at the core of his being, and his brothers too. And because of their own actions, both my sons have lost their lives at the hands of... not strangers, gang members, or sworn enemies, but by the people who loved them the most." Jack's expression changes to one of anger. He lets go of my shoulders and runs his fingers through his grey thinning hair; an action I have seen his son do many times before when he felt stressed. He next speaks with determination.

"Maggie, you must go, leave Ireland, and return to your children. They need you. But first, you must help me move him."

"No, Jack! We must call the police!"

Jack clutched his chest again and shakes his arm as if trying to shake out the pain etched on his face.

"Maggie, listen to me. We cannot bring Matthew back, and we should not risk calling the Gardai. A lengthy trial in these parts, the likely outcome is unfavourable for a wife murdering her husband."

I feel the panic rising, and I hyperventilate again.

"But you said it was an accident... Jack, it was an accident!"

"Maggie, you acted in self-defence. I know that you know that! But it would be the police and then a jury that you need to convince. And if Matthew has been telling the lies to others that he tried to spin to me this evening... it will cast doubt."

"Who knows you are in Ireland?"

"No, no, I didn't tell anyone!" I sob. I am shaking, unable to control my limbs.

"Okay, you must leave Ireland as soon as possible. But first... you must help me. We must dispose of Matthew's body. Maggie, do you understand? You must help me!"

Before I realise what, I am doing, I am helping Jack drag Matthew across the hard standing, the short distance to the car. Between the two of us, we struggle to bundle Matthew's body into the back seat. Jack locks up the cottage, holding the spade, and stands the spade against the exterior wall.

"Where was this? Here?"

I nod.

"Margaret, is this where it was? Have I placed it where you found it?"

"Yes, yes!" I shriek.

I stand in the rain, shivering, while Jack enters the barn. He comes out only moments later, holding the poker with its twisted decorative metal handle—the end I had struck Matthew covered in blood. He hands it to me, and I hesitate before taking it.

"Hold on to this! We will have to get rid of it. Come on, into the car."

Jack is in the driving seat, and I sit next to him in the passenger seat, holding my breath, not daring to look over my shoulder at the body of my husband slumped in the back seat.

Rain drenches us, rivulets streaming from our hair and noses. Jack drives the car in silence, headlights off, the darkness pressing in on all sides. My nerves jangle with every turn, the constant patter of rain echoing the frantic beat of my heart. He turns right onto the lane, then, after a few tense minutes, veers left, guiding us uphill until we reach a plateau of land. My breath catches as he parks, the car shuddering to a stop. Jack opens the door and leans out, peering down to check that the car is firmly on the gravel, careful not to let it slip onto the grass verge. I sit frozen in my seat, anxiety prickling beneath my skin, every sense on high alert as the night swallows us whole.

"Wait here!" Jack walks a short distance towards what I can see, even in this darkness, a cliff edge. He is holding a poker. He peers over the edge, throws the poker, and then returns to the car.

"Come on, help me!"

I follow Jack's instructions, and with extreme difficulty, we battle for what feels like ages to drag Matthew's body from the Green Rover. Between the two of us, we roll his body to the cliff edge. He is becoming heavier with each roll as he picks up sodden mud. My hands and knees have mud caked on them, and the cold tightens the skin on my hands.

I feel giddy, even though I lie on my front on the ground, peering over the edge at the crashing waves down below. Jack sets out further instructions for me to help turn Matthew. He positions his body sideways, remarkably close. to the edge. In fact, too close for comfort because if we are not careful, we could fall over the cliff edge with him. Where my actions have been robotic up to this moment, I now feel hysteria in anticipation of rolling my dead husband and the father of my children off the edge of a cliff.

"I can't do it. Please Jack, let's call someone. I can explain what happened. Please, please don't make me do this!" I am shouting against the strength of the wind. My hair is sticking to my face where it has come loose from the pins holding it in place.

Jack ignores my pleas as he struggles alone to push his son towards the edge. With one last shove, I hear myself scream out as Matthew's body disappears. Jack struggles to his feet and edges closer to peer over. He backs up towards me and reaches for my hand. I am sobbing. Instead of speaking, he guides me back to the car. He opens the boot and rummages for items of clothing. He hands me a towel that feels rough.

"Here, use this to get off the worst."

He uses one of Matthew's shirts to wipe mud from the knees of his own trousers and puts his face and hands towards the heavens, using the rain to shower away any remnants of mud. With the gesture, he directs me to do the same. Once back in the car, Jack switches on the engine and fiddles with the heating dial on the dashboard.

"It will take a while, but it should heat soon enough to warm you a bit." Jack reverses the car down the track before turning into a lay-by and manoeuvring the vehicle in the direction we came from. The engine continues to tick over. I notice the pain written on Jack's face. He speaks.

"I am sorry... I am sorry that I needed to ask for your help, but I'm afraid it had to be done. Now you must head back to the hotel on foot. We must avoid being seen together, and Maggie, you must never divulge what happened. Do you hear me?"

My tears continue to flow.

"It is necessary for me to get my son. I must pick him up from your daughter. Oh my god, what have I done? What about my poor baby?"

"Hey, hey, don't you fret. I will dispose of the car. You need not know any more. You go back to the hotel, return to London. Everyone will consider it a terrible accident. Mary will come forward to reveal Matthew visited her first, and that she has been caring for her nephew. And I promise you, I will bring little Matthew home to you, whatever her husband is like. Mary is a good girl, and she will take good care of him. And once she hears Matthew has died, she will bring him home to me!"

"What if she doesn't?"

"She will. I will make sure of it."

Of course, he didn't, because Jack became quite unwell within days of my return to London. I received a letter from him, apologising for not fulfilling his promise of returning my lost boy, which I only read upon my discharge from the hospital, and later heard he had died. I remember little about my arrival back in England because I collapsed and spent the next three months in a hospital. They said I had suffered a nervous breakdown and, therefore, I avoided having to face questions from DI Stanley Chaplin. They believed that Sidney's death and Matthew's presumed death had broken the criminal ring and caused their case to fall apart.

Another regret was not spending the last days and hours with my dad because he never recovered from his injuries, and he died too while I was being treated in the hospital. In the same hospital where I met George, he became my protector, my saviour. He also provided security, and with two of my children, we moved into this house, away from anything or anyone that would remind me of Matthew and his family.

After Dad died, Mum decided to sell the shop. She lived for another ten years, spending her final years with us. In the latter days of her life, her mind began to slip away. I often felt like a stranger to her, just another nameless face in the room. Yet, there were fleeting moments when a certain pain would cross her face—those were the rare times I knew that she remembered who I was.

The possibility of George ever discovering my secret filled me with dread. Each passing year, I found myself rationalising my decision not to search for my little boy. I always told myself that keeping a stable environment for my other two children was the most important thing. That justification became my shield, allowing me to delay facing the truth and seeking out my lost son.

Matthew Jr. is of the opinion that I am not to blame. This makes me want to jump for joy. Yet, I feel a little envious, robbed of seeing my child grow into the man he has become. I cannot wait for his planned visit at Christmas, where we will meet for the first time in fifty years. I hope I recognise him; from discussions I have had with Matthew online, he is the sensitive soul I remember, kind and forgiving.

In recent weeks, I have learned to live-at the moment and use an app on my tablet; daily I record audio of how I feel. When listening back, I cannot always remember why I said what I have. I begin with gratitude, and this is consistent, grateful for a loving family and finding my lost son. I also include a lesson for the day. The lesson that appears most days is this: life doesn't come with a manual. Even now, with muddled thoughts, I continue to learn from past mistakes. We have one go on this planet, and it's never too late, so I must try to forgive myself.

The end.

ABOUT THE AUTHOR

Angela O'Malley was born in Middlesex in 1966 and spent her early years in Harrow. Thirteen years ago, she moved to Thame, Oxfordshire, with her husband. Angela's family includes three daughters and a granddaughter and grandson. Her blended family also embraces her husband's three children and six grandsons.

Angela has managed volunteers, community and housing projects that empower older adults to live alone. She later specialised in developing professional training for those working with people with learning disabilities. In Thame, Oxfordshire, Angela is employed in Learning and Development, where she develops training programmes for health and social care professionals.

Angela has always loved listening to and sharing stories, which eventually led her to pursue writing. Inspired by her passion for social care and her experiences working in the care sector, she wrote her debut novel, Veiled Memories, to bring imagination and meaningful stories to a wider audience.

www.ingramcontent.com/pod-product-compliance
Lightning Source LLC
Chambersburg PA
CBHW030629310726
48979CB00003B/933

* 9 7 8 1 9 1 9 4 6 9 2 1 8 *